Ghost Geographies
Fictions

Also by Tamas Dobozy:

When X Equals Marylou (Arsenal Pulp, 2003)
Last Notes and Other Stories (HarperCollins / Arcade, 2005)
Siege 13 (Thomas Allen / Milkweed, 2012)
5 Mishaps (School Gallery, 2021)

TAMAS DOBOZY

GHOST GEOGRAPHIES

FICTIO S

VANCOUVER ▪ NEW STAR BOOKS ▪ 20 21

NEW STAR BOOKS LTD

No. 107–3477 Commercial St., Vancouver, BC V5N 4E8 CANADA
1574 Gulf Road, No. 1517 Point Roberts, WA 98281 USA
newstarbooks.com · info@newstarbooks.com

The publisher acknowledges the financial support of the Canada Council for
the Arts, the British Columbia Arts Council, and the Government of Canada.

Cataloguing information for this book is available from Library
and Archives Canada, www.collectionscanada.gc.ca.

Cover design by Oliver McPartlin
Typeset by New Star Books
Printed and bound in Canada by Imprimerie Gauvin, Gatineau, QC

First printing September 2021

To Marcy, for everything.

Das Individuum macht sich oft seine Vorstellungen von sich selbst
von hohen Absichten, herrlichen Taten, die es ausführen wolle, von
der Wichtigkeit, die es selbst habe, die es berechtigt sei in Anspruch
zu nehmen, die zum Heile der Welt diene. Was solche Vorstellungen
betrifft, so müssen sie an ihren Ort gestellt bleiben.

Often an individual imagines himself, his high ideals, the
glorious deeds he means to carry out, his own importance
which he is surely right to take as justification, as serving t e
betterment of the world. These ideas must be left behind.

— G.W.F. Hege

Content s

The Hobo and the Archivist

In 1976 Adelbert Wuyts received a personal letter from General Secretary János Kádár inviting him to come to Budapest. The letter was so enthusiastic, so overflowing with praise, that Wuyts read it four times and decided communism in Eastern Europe had finally become a good thing. "At least people there can eat!" he said to a friend.

"Yes they can eat — shit!" his friend replied, and Wuyts got so mad he didn't even say good-bye when, a week later, he defected with the third-class train ticket Kádár had sent with the letter (though he did leave a note asking the friend to look after his place).

Wuyts never thought for a second to ask how anyone behind the Iron Curtain, never mind *főtitkár* Kádár, had heard of his work, falling completely for what the letter said about him being "universally admired almost everywhere in Hungary." By the time he pulled out of Brussels the Western world had receded so far from Wuyts' thinking that the train seemed to be passing through a mirage, and if you touched any of the buildings — the banks, the offices, the villas — they'd have disintegrated in a flurry of bank notes.

He had only one regret, and it burned hotter as the train clacked toward Hungary: he'd left behind his card catalog. It was the only thing of value Wuyts owned — an enormous piece of furniture that stored everything ever known about the cities

3

of the world, right back to the earliest human settlements. It was made of a wood called arbutus, incredibly brittle, that had been imported from British Columbia in the late nineteenth century, polished to a high gloss, and when fully assembled took up an entire wall, right up to the sixteen-foot ceilings in the apartment in Brussels where he lived.

Its size kept it from being stolen, that plus the fact that it was filled to bursting with the bits of paper on which he'd written and rewritten, drawn and redrawn his ideas, always compressing them further so they'd all continue to fit. Wuyts thought the cards beautiful, works of art, not only for the exactness of the cataloging system he'd devised, but because of what they promised when his project was finally complete: a city free of the mistakes that had ruined every city in the past. He was like so many of those other utopianists born into fin-de-siècle Europe, so woefully ordinary, camouflaged in middle management suits and overcoats, indistinguishable from the other file clerks along the sidewalk, even as their brains clacked and whirred with the gears of intricate dreams.

When Wuyts wasn't sorting files in the ministry where he worked he was sorting files in his cabinet, and when he wasn't sorting files in the cabinet he was publishing articles: pamphlets, broadsides, chapbooks printed on out-of-date hardware, old presses in attics and basements run by the usual eccentrics — tubercular anarchists, outlawed theorists, poets too far ahead of their times — everything printed in watery ink on paper already moldering by the time it went through the machines, to be hated, later, by every archivist charged with preserving them, including the longest article Wuyts had written, "Design for a Classless City Conducive to the Function of a Communist Society" (1963), which had been quoted in Kádár's invitation, and was being furled and unfurled by Dezső Ernyő when he met Wuyts at the Nyugati *pályaudvar* upon his arrival from Brussels.

Wuyts got off the train with his little suitcase. It was the dirtiest train station he'd ever seen. It looked like someone had been blasting the walls with soot every day for fifty years. When Ernyő came to shake his hand Wuyts kept looking over the man's shoulder and all around for Secretary Kádár and the rest of the delegation. But there was no one other than this slightly fat, nervously smiling man.

"The guards took away my passport at the border," Wuyts said, gazing down the platform at the enormous glass wall of the train station, designed at the turn of the century by Gustave Eiffel, and beyond that at the tramcars striking sparks off overhead wires, people streaming past in black and gray. "He said there was a problem with my visa." Wuyts looked at Ernyő accusingly.

"We've prepared a . . . reception for you," Ernyő replied, in horrifically bad French, and Wuyts meditated on it a minute before nodding.

They walked up the *körút*, Wuyts wondering why there wasn't a limo waiting, or a taxi, or, at worst, a tram ticket. The suitcase banged against his leg, the January rain fell with bits of ice in it, and the two of them finally turned off into the truly grimy alleys of the Eighth District. The smell of piss was overwhelming in the stairwell of Ernyő's building, spiraling up around the iron grillwork of a secessionist-style elevator now out of order. Budapest had been a grand city once, long ago, Wuyts could see that.

Ernyő opened the door to his apartment with a skeleton key, turning it back and forth as if there were tumblers inside and you needed to know the sequence. He found five people waiting for him, though only four of them — three men and one woman — rose up and rushed over to greet Wuyts, helping ease off his overcoat, take his suitcase, ask if he was hungry. The kitchen table held salami, pickled beets, yellow peppers, slabs of smoked bacon, and even a bowl of what at first looked like genuine beluga caviar.

"Where's Kádár?" said Wuyts after he'd tasted the caviar, like a spoonful of salt soaked in cod-liver oil, and taken a mouth-puckering sip of what they said was "Hungary's best champagne." He took another sip to show them he'd actually tasted it, so someone better explain what was going on, but no one said a word, and it

a perfect world. Everyone, that is, except Szép, who was only occasionally there anyhow, sitting in a corner in his filthy clothes, leaves stuck in his hair, crinkling every time he moved with the plastic bags he wore under his clothes to keep himself warm and dry.

Gyüri's diagrams looked like something out of streamlined science fiction — all silent elevators, towers climbing into the sky, rectilinear elegance. As he went through the pictures he pointed out the social improvements with an old cane, as if he were some professor making arguments in nimble, logical steps.

"In my utopia," he said, "men would be free to use their abilities. They would be permitted to rise from the lowest orders on the merit of their talents, intelligence, ingenuity, and pluck."

Gábor, Ernyő, and Katalin all — all except Szép — nodded along. Wuyts couldn't believe it; they were taking this idiot seriously.

"The key," continued Gyüri, "would be to minimize the role of government in interfering with individual freedom. The government would run the military to safeguard the nation and make sure everyone was forced by law to observe Christian morality, but otherwise stay out of people's business."

"What the hell are you talking about?" shouted Wuyts. "This is not . . . not utopia. This is," he stuttered for a full minute, his tongue flip-flopping, out of control, then took a deep breath, calmed himself, and continued, "this is capitalism." He gestured in the general direction of the Western world. "What happens with poverty?"

"In my world, poverty would only afflict the lazy," Gyüri said, "or the amoral. The market would take care of those willing to work, as long as it was left free to do so."

Wuyts bent over, trying to hold together the fragments of his head. "No, no, no, no," he groaned, "this can't be right. You can't really be thinking this."

"I agree with Wuyts," said Katalin. "Your world would never end up looking like that," she said, thrusting her chin at Gyüri's pictures.

"And your world would?" Gyüri said.

"My world," said Gábor, cutting in, "would be ruled by a perfect king, one anointed by God through generations of a single unadulterated royal bloodline." Wuyts stared at him in horror. Where had he ended up? Who were these people?

"He would rule because God had seen his bloodline fit to rule," continued Gábor, staring around the room fiercely. "All of society would be dedicated to achieving the order laid down by Christ as represented in his holy majesty the king."

Wuyts gulped back the four fingers of *pálinka* they'd poured for him.

"In my perfect world," shouted Ernyő, "there would be not one single Jew."

"Shut up!" shouted Wuyts, getting up and smashing the *pálinka* bottle to the ground. "How can you all be so stupid?" He grabbed his coat and stumbled out the rickety front door into the glow of the streetlights ringing Gyüri's apartment, so bright they were like bare fluorescent bulbs, the light cutting into Wuyts like some x-ray, painting him white. He shuffled along the open walkway around the courtyard to the darkened stairwell, finally in shadow. Behind him he thought he heard whooping laughter, or shouts of outrage, it was hard to tell, and somewhere between the walk home and his drunken head hitting the pillow Katalin caught up to him and said it was cruel, they were just joking around, having fun at Wuyts' expense, they didn't mean any of it, and their beautiful pictures and diagrams and charts really were about a better world and tomorrow or the next day when Wuyts woke up and the hangover was gone they'd go back to Gyüri's apartment and he'd see what they truly thought, such beautiful visions. But Wuyts shook off her hand in front of his door and told her, Go away, and went inside, crying quietly for his cabinet, until she crept in through the open door and lay beside him.

"Tell me about that cabinet," she whispered, smoothing his hair.

"There's this one drawing I made," he mumbled drunkenly. "A rainy November afternoon. I was trying to create a picture for Van Woyden's anti-Babylon. You know the one, the treatise . . ." Katalin nodded quietly. "It took me forever to get the right color of blue. It was incredible. There was my home . . ." he paused, choking up, "there was my home, filled with supplies, a million paints and pastel crayons and bottles of ink, and nowhere the blue I needed. So I went to the Jubelpark and found a peacock."

"A peacock?"

Wuyts nodded, nearly asleep. "Their feathers were the exact color. I glued them in." Katalin lifted up on an elbow, staring at him like he was some marvelous beast. "Katalin," Wuyts asked, his voice dreamy, "why am I here? Who are you? Do you have any interest in . . . ?"

She put her finger on his lips. "We need you to help the revolution."

"What revolution? This place already had one."

"No." She shook her head. "That was no revolution. That was only a takeover."

"Well . . . whatever, same thing." Wuyts was slurring. "You have the chance for real communism now. You might even see it in your own lifetime." He was asleep.

■

The next morning, Katalin was sitting in the kitchen with a coffee when he crawled out of bed, still holding his head together, and remembered that she'd spent the night, though little else. She watched him stumble into the bathroom in his underwear and close the door and retch and retch again. Water ran in the sink. Then he came into the kitchen and dropped into a chair, sweating along his hairline, blank-eyed, muttering to himself.

She leaned across, whispering, "If you could have your cabinet you'd be happy here?" She didn't wait for him to respond. "I know someone who could help!"

Wuyts looked at her. It was true, every day, every night, he felt happy enough but never as happy as he *could have been*; there was always the cabinet, the question of what had become of it, the vault of all possible cities, of his attempts to classify and thereby alter reality, to take a stand against it, to assert his powers, as if there would always be more life in that work than in any of the days and years he was actually living, no matter how blissful. The happier he was in Budapest, the sadder he became in the place that *wasn't* Budapest or for that matter anywhere else, the cabinet where he was always *also* alive, the cabinet that he couldn't leave if he wanted to, never mind that it was still in Brussels. "Who?" he asked. "Who could possibly help me?"

"Szép," she said, looking around the kitchen as if someone might be eavesdropping. "He's able to get out." She nodded eagerly when Wuyts raised his eyebrows. "He gets out and gets back in again."

Wuyts looked like he wanted to retch a third time, and wiped his lips with the back of a hand. Then it was his turn to lean across the table. "How in God's name," he hissed back at her, "someone like that — never mind," he waved his hand across the tablecloth, "never mind if he can get back in — going to carry that cabinet across the border? That," he said, finally releasing all his pent-up frustration, "is the stupidest idea I've ever heard."

"You don't know Szép," she said, leaning back, displeased. "He is the hobo of the Eastern Bloc! His ability to slip across borders is legendary."

"Wow, a hobo," said Wuyts, and he was so frustrated he kicked the table leg and sent her coffee cup flying.

"You don't understand," Katalin said after a while, dabbing the front of her shirt with a tea towel. "We talk about utopia. We envision it. But Szép — he *is* utopia."

■

Wuyts had no idea what she was talking about, and he didn't care, all he wanted was for Katalin to leave, thinking back to the night

"Things are changing around here, too," she said.

Wuyts was confused. Changing? Why, because Elvis had died? The place seemed exactly the same to him. Red stars on buildings. Signs posted every time you came near a radar installation, a power station, the high cables bringing electricity into and out of the city — a picture of a camera in a red circle with a line through it, instructions in several languages, sometimes even Flemish, spelling out the penalty for snapping pictures in any of these places. The level of paranoia and threat was as high as it had ever been.

"You know," she said, "I've never told you about my perfect world."

Wuyts looked at her, amazed. It was true. How had he missed it, all those evenings at Ernyő's place? Not once had he heard Katalin mention any ideas of her own, though she'd argued often enough about the ideas of others, and he wondered at himself that he hadn't noticed, that it had never occurred to him, though not for a second could he figure out why. Was it because she was a woman? Of course — that was it! Wuyts felt ashamed, and he wondered whether it was too late, six years too late, to apologize to her.

"In my perfect world," she said, "there would be no sexes."

"Yes!" he said. "We'd all be equal, men and women. I've often thought of it, too. It just kind of slipped in all the . . . the excitement, you know . . . I'm sorry about that."

She smiled at him as if he'd accidentally recited the seven-times table when he'd really been asked to recite the six. "That's sweet of you." She patted his hand. "But it's not what I meant. In a perfect world everyone would be a man. I mean we'd get rid of all the women — except for me. I'd have my pick of any guy I wanted whenever I wanted him."

Wuyts stared at her. "God, not you too," he muttered.

"And today," she said, "I would choose you." And she reached over and grabbed his shirt and pulled him over the table for a kiss.

Later that night he showed Katalin the fragments of the cabinet on the floor, squatting naked in front of her and describing its outline, his fingers scratching lines and curves across the parquet. Then he reached down and slipped the elastic band off his cards and thumbed through them until he came to the one he was looking for, and brought her over to the window so she could look at it in the glare of a streetlight. "In the seventh-century poetry of Ibn al-Sharif," he whispered, "the Whore of Babylon was a new kind of mother, not a beast at all. I made a million variations of her out of every queen of hearts I could find, adding colors, extra drawings. She is all the variations: freedom from norms, sexual laws, regulations of the perverse. I joined them all together into one index card foot feet long, like a snake, an accordion of paper covered with every female form imaginable. It's stored in the tenth drawer, for over, top tier." He stared at the card in his hand. "Once I have my cabinet, I'll show you." He waited for her to respond, and then finally, putting the card back into the stack and replacing the rubber band, he said, "Her city lasts only as long as nightfall, every day, then it fades."

"I know what that's like," she sighed, bending down and kissing him, Budapest honking and blaring and roaring below them along Mártírok útja.

■

Nineteen eighty-three became 1984 became 1985 became 1986. More and more Wuyts felt at home. He even thought he had learned to speak the language, forming grammatically perfect sentences in his head, almost without thinking, that no one else could understand because of the thickness of his accent, though when he finally wrote down what he was saying the grocers in the market would nod and say "Igen," meaning he had mastered the intricacies of Hungarian grammar in an almost perfectly useless way. Once in a while he'd come home and find another bit of cabinet, or even several, wrapped in newspaper and hanging from his door-knob on a knotted length of string like some weird wind chime. He'd managed to reassemble a number of full drawers, and there were even enough cards now to fill them. But the problem was they all smelled like Szép, and the thought that the hobo had smuggled everything across the border under his clothes was too much for Wuyts to bear. Still, Wuyts was happy, and he was making new cards by the dozen, spending time in the Turkish collection of the Hungarian National Archives, looking at old government directives, poems, drawings that described Ottoman plans for Europe, an empire perfected through plunder, slavery, mass slaughter. The dreams were golden, and Wuyts gained fifteen pounds going to the Gerbeaud Cukrászda and eating their *sajtkrém torta* just to get the bits of gold foil he used in making the illustrations on the file cards.

The rest of the utopianists, by contrast, were getting sad. Their visions were increasingly dim, as if light was the enemy of happiness. Ernyő was borrowing heavily from secessionist painters, describing a world faintly illuminated by gas lamps, the peace of long shadows and dim silver. Gábor spoke of worlds envisioned by the blind, such as those of the American thinker Jasper Horst Fredericks, who in the 1830s claimed that sight was the enemy of human progress, and the world where everyone put out his eyes would be one ruled by the harmonies of human touch. Even Katalin, when she came to visit, insisted on keeping the blinds drawn right into the afternoon, saying it was like heaven in his apartment, all that terrible light blocked out. There was no excitement to their voices, they were drinking more, and their passion had been replaced by the drone of each person going on and on, cataloging ever more pedantic bits of research.

"Why are those guys so depressed these days?" asked Wuyts one night, opening his door just as Szép was about to knock on it.

Szép shrugged. "End of the gravy train? Misspent youth? Resistance to change?" Wuyts was instantly depressed by this,

and for a second he wondered why. The collapse of communism?
"Things seem the same as ever to me," he said.

"I'm sure they do," said Szép. He waited, then handed over a rancid old plastic bag filled with bits of cabinet. "Your friend in Brussels says good-bye . . . for the hundredth time. He also says he'd like to get this cabinet business over with. It's going to take forever this way." Szép gazed at him, waiting.

But Wuyts was working with different questions. "Why do you do it?" he asked.

"No reason," Szép replied. He stared at Wuyts. "Nothing's urgent. I go when it's easy to where it's easy. Nobody yells, nobody fires a shot. I don't know why. I get to Brussels and your friend's there with another bag full of cabinet, opens the door a crack, hands it over, tells me to get lost, Stinky. I don't care." Szép stared off into the distance, then asked, "Do you ever wonder if there are others?"

"Others?"

"Utopianists. Many others. All from elsewhere. All brought here by someone . . . or maybe a group of people."

"No," said Wuyts, wondering why he felt so inconsequential all of a sudden. It should have been a good thing — more utopianists — but it put him right back on that sidewalk in Brussels walking to and from his file clerk job with all the other file clerks, like a string of sausages being pumped out the back door of every bank and office.

Szép waved his hand at the city. "They're all over," he said. "Everywhere. I do odd jobs for them, too. But you've never met any of them."

Wuyts willed himself not to believe it. "Why are you telling me this?"

"The cabinet," said Szép. "You're the only one with a cabinet. It's like a big balloon. Until you grab it. Then it turns into an anchor."

"Whatever," said Wuyts. "It's the only thing saving me." And thinking of the cabinet, the work he'd put into it, the oppressive feeling of anonymity lifted.

"So who is the person, or people, who brought us here?" said Wuyts. "And why are they paying so much money to make sure we don't leave?"

"I think you know," said Szép, shrugging.

■

By 1987 it was all Gorbachev, *glasnost*, *perestroika*, the meetings were fewer than ever, Gyüri showing up with some matchboxes they passed around in the candlelight of Wuyts' kitchen — they were meeting more than ever at Wuyts' place — sliding them open to find tiny photographs of dogs fucking women. "What's utopian about these?" Wuyts asked, looking around the room, but he was unable to resist looking at the next one.

"These are from the good old days, when pornography could get you jail, interrogation, even deportation," Ernyő replied.

"But for a little while, these matchboxes made us happy," said Gábor, as if this in any way answered Wuyts' question.

■

By 1988 Wuyts was alone, watching TV, trying to understand what was going on. The uprising of 1956 was no longer being called a fascist counterrevolution but a war of liberation. Imre Nagy was being lionized. Most importantly, Szép was showing up more and more often with bits of cabinet, which was standing now, almost complete except for a few drawers and little less than a thousand cards. "Have you seen Ernyő or the others lately?" He noticed Szép was wearing a tuxedo, still filthy, but it was a tuxedo. "Are you celebrating something?" he asked. Szép looked at Wuyts like he couldn't believe it.

■

In 1989 they met for the last time. It was by invitation. The ghost of Kádár was inviting Wuyts to a party, RSVP, 36 54 39 42 28 8, 14 Mártírok útja. Wuyts didn't get it. Kádár was still alive. What kind of ghost was dead before it was dead? But even more

perplexing was the fact that the phone number was his own,
well as the address, so to whom was he supposed to respor
himself? He checked the envelope — both the "to" and "retu
addresses were the same. He picked up the phone, dialed t
number, and heard a clicking sound, and when he put the pho
down it started ringing, but there was no one on the other er
"I'm coming to the party," he whispered to his empty apartme
which made no sound in return.

On October seventeenth they showed up at his door. Wuy
was waiting. There'd been a delivery of champagne earlier
the day. He'd stepped out on his balcony to sign for it, noti
the big smile on the face of the deliveryman, the sound of hor
blaring in celebration all over the city, the depressing sense
Wuyts had to admit it — that communism was over, multipar
democracy arrived, all the old truths turned around.

Ernyő was the first through the door, bounding in. Ne
came Katalin, kissing Wuyts on the mouth with what seem
a desperate joy. Then Gyüri, then Gábor, then Szép, still in th
tuxedo, probably the same tuxedo Wuyts had seen on him a ye
ago. "Oh, champagne," said Ernyő, looking at the bucket. "Tha
a great idea, buying champagne." He lifted one of the bottl
out immediately, fired off the cork, and made some laborio
toast to "the forces of the free market." But Wuyts wasn't rea
listening because all he could think was: If Ernyő hadn't paid f
the champagne then who had?

Wuyts' weekly checks had stopped arriving three mont
earlier, he was living on savings, and he'd hoped one of the gues
would admit to ordering the champagne so he could figure o
who'd been paying him all along. He lifted his glass mechanica
failing to clink, bringing it to his mouth and drinking witho
tasting a thing.

For an hour he sat there, more or less silent, once in a wh
nodding, saying yes to another glass, each word they sa
punching another hole in his stomach — Kádár stepping dov
the rehabilitation of Imre Nagy, the dismantling of the bord

between Hungary and Austria allowing thousands of Polish and East German refugees to go streaming to the West — until finally to stop the pain Wuyts jumped up, the movement almost involuntary, and yelled, "We've got to figure out who was helping us! Who was . . ." he waved his arms around the apartment, "paying for all this! Who brought us all together. There's still time; if we had enough money we could go underground, that's what subversives would do, we could keep fighting for utopia . . ." He heard Ernyő snicker, and stopped, as if he were seeing everyone in the room for the first time that night.

Gábor had his hand over his mouth. He was giggling, trying to hide it.

"I don't know," said Katalin. "I don't know. Pornography's going to be legal now. That's just an example. And things are a lot looser here in terms of . . . regulations," she said. "If you got a jump on the business, you could make quite a lot of money."

"It's true," said Gyüri. "The post office is finally letting through stuff from my brother who left in '56. Lives in Philadelphia." He pulled a magazine out of his coat, and showed them the cover: *The Strategic Investor*. "You wouldn't believe the stuff they have out there. There's this thing called 'penny stocks.' They can make you rich!"

"The thing to do," said Ernyő, "is when the Western companies come in here and start buying up all the Hungarian industries, you get in on that business . . ."

"I've always had this dream," interrupted Gábor. "I could rent out one of those big parking lots east of Pest. I could go around and buy cheap all the cars people didn't want, and I could park them, you know, in this nice pattern, and fix them up — I have a little knowledge, enough to get them running for a while — then raise the prices a little so there'd be some profit. Those nice purple suits are on sale at the Vásárcsarnok. I could get one of those, maybe some sunglasses."

"No!" Wutys said, getting up, speaking less to them than himself, wandering back and forth by the window as if trying to escape a thought. "This is wrong. You're not . . . This isn't wh t it's supposed to be. None of you are really . . ."

"Oh, that reminds me, I've got something for you," Ernyő sa d, pulling an envelope from his jacket. "This came to my place la t week." He handed it to Wuyts, who stared at the official se l. There was a long letter inside on official letterhead, in bac y translated Flemish, as well as the passport, long expired, th t he'd last seen at the Austrian-Hungarian border. Wuyts read t, his mind two words ahead, predicting every twist and turn f a bureaucratic language covering its ass, apologizing one st o short of admitting fault: yes, mistakes had been made, an ov r- zealous border guard, misfiled reports, absence of due proce s, but they were as much the fault of the Belgian embassy, not o mention lack of "diligence" by Wuyts, even going so far as o say he'd given up too early and too easily on the whole thir g. Anyhow, he was now free to go, and he better go soon, son e- time in the next month, or face "prosecution for being in t e country illegally."

Wuyts looked up and everyone, everyone but Szép, w s smiling at him. Their mouths looked strained, as if they we e holding back tears. "I think I just want to be alone," Wuyts wh s- pered. They nodded, still smiling, and fled out into the nig t, the streetlamps everywhere aglow, the lit windows of hom s up Rózsadomb, the sound of celebrations, fireworks. As Wu s closed the door he could hear laughter down the corridor, but e was too tired and disheartened to think it through.

He turned, walked back down the corridor to the living roo i, and over the remains of champagne and bad caviar and cracke s, he watched Szép slowly unwrap the last fragment of the cabir t and reach around to slip it into place.

"It's done," the hobo said, facing the cabinet. "Fully arrive ." Even from behind Szép looked proud — proud in his stain d and worn and once upon a time very expensive suit, stinki g with doing whatever he wanted, going wherever he pleased, li e Howard Hughes in his exquisite and entitled indifference o what anyone might think — and Wuyts imagined the look on his face, lit up by the long joke finally arriving at its punch line. He grabbed a champagne bottle, raising it up.

"It could have walked by itself," said Szép, lifting his hands like a conjurer, as if at a word the cabinet would have risen, heavy on its feet, and waddled forward two or three steps, creaking with the weight of itself. "But like you, it prefers to be carried," he continued, and there was something bad in his voice, a clacking like drawers slamming in and out, as if the cabinet were speaking for Szép and it had grown a terrible set of teeth. "It likes being looked after, and regularly greased, and left to dream."

"I should just leave it here," said Wuyts. "Sell it."

"Getting rid of it just to get it back," said Szép. "I suppose that would make you happy again. We build you people, you know. Drawer by drawer, file card by file card, every next thing, we build you. Countries, cities, cabinets, these are what we turn you into." Szép laughed, and in it Wuyts could hear every laugh he'd ever heard since leaving Brussels. "In my perfect world everyone will know they're going to get what they want — and they'll be stuck in that moment, before it actually arrives, forever." He laughed again, short and dry. "Now *that* would be utopia."

And Wuyts had to admit, holding the bottle over Szép's head, that he knew exactly what the dirty old hobo meant.

Ray Electric

Before he became the late great Ray Electric, he was Károly Bánko, training every day at the Wrestling Academy on Lakosdi utca. That's where Ray Electric was born, Bánko would always say, on an April day in the year of the Rome Olympics, which was supposed to have been his big moment, his shot at gold.

What happened then was the fault of Maxim Zabrovsky, a diehard Kunist from 1919 whose real name had been Ervin Aczél before he'd changed it, like so many Bolsheviks before him, to something cryptic. Behind Zabrovsky's back, the wrestlers called him "The Pseudo-Russian," but only if they knew the wrestler they were talking to was safe. Most of them, as Bánko would learn, were safe. It was a macho thing, not being political, in a world where politics was everywhere characterized by bullying, hypocrisy, and cringing.

When Kun's chrysanthemum revolution fell in late 19__, Zabrovsky followed the great leader to the Crimea, assisting in the happy task of murdering the 50,000 Whites who'd surrendered to the Reds on the false promise of amnesty. Then they were assigned to Germany, where the two of them finally had a falling out, with Zabrovsky denouncing Kun's plans for the workers' uprising in a letter sent direct to Lenin. It was because of this that the words "idiot" and "Kun" would become interchangeable in Soviet cant. In return, Zabrovsky was rewarded with work in the NKVD until 1945, when he was promptly sent back to Hungary "to facilitate the effective deployment of those techniques he'd honed to such refinement in the USSR for the benefit of the proletariat." During his time with ÁVO, from the late-1940s to the early '50s, Zabrovsky was the go-to guy for "disciplinary efficacy," a term that covered an excruciatingly wide range of activities. But with Stalin's death, and the revolution of 1956, and the subsequent attempt by Kádár to put a friendlier face on iron-fisted totalitarianism, he fell from grace and was demoted and demoted and demoted until he landed here: director of the Hungarian wrestling team, a sport he knew exactly zero about.

It was the early days of the East German doping trials, and Zabrovsky was convinced it was just the edge the wrestlers needed. What could he say? He was a visionary. They had them shipped in from labs in East Berlin — Dianabol, Pervitin, Turinabol — and started the athletes young — fourteen, thirteen, twelve — on a daily regimen of "vitamins." Zabrovsky's terminology fooled no one. There were already whispers running through the athletic community about what that shit did to you. Liver disease. Bloating and headaches. Acne up and down the body. Women whose pubic hair grew like shag up their torsos. Cuts that wouldn't stop bleeding. Ovaries blossoming with cysts the size of apples. As far as Bánko could tell those vitamins had turned the East German women's shot-put team into the East German men's shot-put team.

Zabrovsky held a meeting of medical personnel, coaches and assistants, the other wrestlers, and called out Bánko. So, you want the bourgeoisie to win? He shouted in his face. You want the capitalists to collect all the gold like always? Bánko was stammering, trying to respond. He'd always been a good communist. When he thought of himself he thought of constructivist posters from the 1920s, workers solid and blocky, faces turned toward utopia, reflecting its glow. He'd spent his life in service to the state, training himself to win glory, unlike this Zabrovsky character, who wasn't a communist at all, but just another sadist. Maybe you're thinking of defecting and going to wrestle for them, Zabrovsky shouted, leering at Bánko as if he was already strapped to a chair, someone in the background adjusting a blowtorch to an impossibly fine and scorching point. It was the first time Bánko had ever seen Zabrovsky show the least bit of interest in the wrestling program. Mainly, he arrived late, stinking of vodka and someone else's wife, stayed in the office all day, and left team management to the subordinates. But here, now, he was electric, as if his one talent, that old flare for terror, was once again being allowed to shine. Maybe you wanted to lose all along. Maybe you insinuated yourself into our program. Maybe you've been a counterrevolutionary since your whore of a mother shit you out of her ass.

No one had ever spoken to Bánko like that in the regular world. He'd heard plenty on the mats, whispers from pinned opponents, but those were tactical, meant to rattle his game, and in that situation he knew to block them out, to resist the emotion, to stay scientific.

But this was something else. His body responded before his mind, stepping up to Zabrovsky, who thrust out his arms as if to push him away. Bánko twisted slightly, but only to move more easily into the embrace, shouldering the hands aside, leaping up light as any ballerina and flipping over the director's shoulder to grab him around the waist and bring him over hard onto his head. The move would come to be known as "the flying squirrel," introduced by a very different wrestler, but at the time it was an experimental technique Bánko was working on, one he hoped would get him to the top of the podium. He'd practiced it so long it was like getting up from bed.

He could almost smell the granite of chipped teeth in Zabrovsky's head. The director's body convulsed beneath him, not like an opponent trying to escape, but arbitrarily, this way and that, like a snake with a crushed head. There was a low gurgle. It had happened so quickly, so without him really willing it, that Bánko felt as if he was a bystander to himself. He recognized the feeling, even in that very moment, as surprise over his capacity for violence. It made him feel sleepy, nostalgic. He remembered library books — fantastic stories of galleons and beasts and golden armour — brought home from school and taken from him by his father when he was eight, telling him he should read only enough to scrape through school and not a word more. Books were for sissies, dreamers. Best to devote himself to sport. He remembered a collection of stamps given to him by a distant uncle one Christmas — pictures of the Soviet rocket program; great thinkers such as Marx, Engels, Lenin; monuments of communist architecture such as the Shukhov Tower, the Volkhov Hydroelectric Station, the Rusakov House of Culture, the Tsentrosoyuz Building, the Melnikov House — worlds beyond anything he'd imagined, until the day he turned his room upside down looking for it and his mother said he must have lost it, even though he knew he hadn't, that the collection was too important to him to have been so careless, always putting it back in the same sacred place on the shelf. His mother could see that the boy knew exactly who'd lost the stamps for him. He remembered girls — Éva, Mariska, Flori, and now Írén — the friendships, infatuation, crushes, lust he'd kept secret from everyone, because at first the company of girls was regarded as suspect, then a distraction, and finally as a trap by his father. "Do what you need to," his father said. "But do it quickly, and don't get involved. There'll be time for that later." For Zabrovsky and the team sex was a squandering of vital energy. The wrestlers were expected to live like monks, out of their heads with abstinence, and to channel it into a fury of throws and holds.

From as early as he could recall, everyone — parents, grandparents, teachers — had never allowed him any possibility other than athletics. That's who he was. Whenever he voiced an alternative they laughed and patted him on the head and said there was no denying what God, and later the State, had made him for. And now, with Zabrovsky seizing beneath him,

Bánko realized there was only Irén, that in her was contain d whatever he might have been if not a wrestler. But it was too la e. He was dead.

There were four wrestlers between Bánko and the door. All fo r were teammates. The coaches and assistants were howling, st)-ping in, stepping out, too scared to actually lay hands on hi 1. The other wrestlers looked at each other as if they'd just met, ju t this second, and found themselves in the gym, clothes myste i-ously replaced by singlets. Then they were moving. Bánko wou d never see it again, not anywhere, not in Austria after the esca e, not on any of the wrestling circuits, no matter how theatric l, in Canada. They were as good as acrobats, tripping over ea h other and the coaches and assistants in an attempt to get to hi 1, a tangle of arms and legs loose enough for him to fight his w y through. At the door, he took one look back at the four of the 1, piled on top of László Erő, the vice-director, who was screami g at them to get off. Every time one of them made a move o e way, the next one would compensate with a different move th t locked them in place again. It was so quick and subtle — t e whole thing lasting fifteen seconds — that Bánko felt a wave f gratitude and then regret, thinking how good the team cou d have been, how close they might have come to winning it all. I e wanted to say thank you, but he knew the four of them wou d have trouble enough without his words implicating them. o he said "Idiots" instead, trying to help them as much as they d helped him, and then he turned toward the stairs.

In a second he was down two flights and into the stre t, running straight for Irén's. Five blocks later, when the par c subsided, he realized he couldn't go there. If they found hi 1 she'd be arrested as well. Irén was his best secret, and Bán realized, standing on the pavement that April day, she mig t have to stay that way forever. Unless maybe he could come with a plan to get her out too. He hated the idea of giving 1 wrestling, but the thought of giving up Irén? That wasn't ev 1 hate. It was something else, a pit opening in his stomach or a

broke free of them and stepped in front of a streetcar. His mother's heart lasted for a few months after that. It was impossible for her to stop seeing it — the moment of impact. Huba found her body in the vestibule of her apartment one morning, fallen under an open umbrella.

His father's incarceration was the end of Huba's job at Ferihegy airport. You couldn't employ the offspring of a reactionary. All things considered he'd been lucky. They could have jailed him for life, brought in the torturer, made him disappear. Had Huba been a member of the party that's probably what would have happened, and when he laughed during that time, which wasn't often, it was at that — how he'd been saved from the regime by his reluctance to join it. Instead, all they did was deny Huba an income, leaving him to starve to death. Now he was unofficially unemployed, which, apart from the word "official," was the same as being officially unemployed. But some of the residents of his building came together and paid him piecework for fixing vents and pipes, stoves and fridges, hinges, parquet floors, cracked cement. The suitcase in his closet, first conceived when his father vanished, was less a plan than a shrine to the idea of escape, and every night he'd take it out and check to make sure everything was in place in the event that magic indeed existed and he suddenly found himself airlifted to the corner of Philharmoniker Straße and Kärtner Straße, hankering for a nice espresso. The truth is, Huba was terrified of escape, and that tiny suitcase, and the hope it signified, might have been enough of the west for the rest of his life. He could have subsisted on that, up late, unpacking and repacking the suitcase in the light of the red star rising above the ministry building across the street.

But on that April afternoon Bánko burst in, rivulets of sweat running down his shirt. He let loose a torrent of gibberish: *wrestling, Zabrovsky, murder, Írén, escape*. It took Huba an hour to calm him down with brimming shots of *pálinka*, until the morning's events came out in logical sequence and attention turned to the suitcase. You can't be serious, Huba told him, but Bánko just

got up nervously and paced from window to window. They
going to be coming for me. Huba went and peered out, unsu
of what he should be looking for except maybe uniformed poli
Seeing none, he went back to his seat by the table and slumped
it, resting his chin on his fore-arms. You can't be serious.
Bánko kept up his nervous pacing, but it didn't surprise Hu
Bánko was always like this, supercharged, whether he thoug
he'd just killed someone or not. He was the only guy Huba kne
who'd come out for a walk with you and end up crossing t
street to look at something, then cross back to walk beside y
for ten or fifteen paces, then enter some building for fifte
minutes, come out the back way, and meet up with you tw
blocks later, then disappear once more into a public garden or
to intercept you at the door of the bar you'd agreed upon. He h
the motion, the energy, of ten men, and sometimes Írén teas
him with the nickname, "Csapat." That was Bánko since as lo
as Huba could remember — stronger, braver, always with t
best girl — and Huba would have felt jealous except there was
way any of Bánko's attributes could ever have belonged to hi
It was outside the realm of possibility. He might as well have f
jealous of Buddha or Jesus or Elvis.

The American embassy, said Huba, sitting up. I'm sure they
love to see you defect. You could join their Olympic team. E
Bánko just shook his head, saying it was the first place they
look for him. The two of them sat for so long in the silence th
eventually Huba had to get up and turn on the lights. We ha
only one option, Bánko said. We have to build that ballo
Balloon? Bánko nodded. The one in your suitcase.

Oh, that balloon. Huba had looked over the design so ma
times he could recall the bar napkin stain by stain. Sheets
taffeta stitched together into an inflatable sphere, a gas burr
kerosene, what could go wrong? We wouldn't have to fly
Bánko said, if we take off from the southwest, say Nemesmedv
or thereabouts. At night, up in the sky like that? Too high
searchlights? They wouldn't even know we were there. W

only have to travel ten miles at the most and then we'd be in Austria.

We'd be over Austria, Huba said. Two hundred feet over it. During the next day, he put everything he had into dissuading Bánko, managing to keep up an argument against him for a whole hour before the wrestler's energy burned him out. It was only on day two that Huba thought he'd come up with a surefire objection: Okay, let's say we go through with it. Let's say we find a ride down there. We'll find a ride down there, answered Bánko. Right, continued Huba, so we have a ride. Let's say we find that gas burner, kerosene. Huba nodded after each word, authoritative as a teacher putting check marks along an assignment. Huba had expected all of his certainty, there was nothing but confidence with Bánko, but for the first time ever he felt as if he had the upper hand, that he was the one setting the trap. All this is fine, said Huba, albeit insane. But the big question is: Who's going to sew the sheets together for the balloon? You? Because I can certainly tell you it isn't going to be me. To prove his point he indicated the jagged and crooked curtains over the window — which looked as if they'd been hacked with a machete from a roll of fabric while it was still rolled up — held in place over the rod with a mixture of adhesive tape and bent paper clips jabbed through the fabric. Shit, said Bánko, you're right, his hand making stitching motions in the air, as if miming it like that was practice enough, as if it might give him the ability to master sewing right then and there. He stopped suddenly, thoughtful.

So that's that, said Huba. We can't do it. We'll have to figure out something else. Bánko screwed up an eye. It almost sounded as if he hadn't prepared what he was going to say next. Írén can sew, he whispered, and at those words Huba realized he'd been the one standing on the trapdoor the whole time, Bánko fingering the lever even as Huba believed he'd won the argument. Írén? I thought you wanted her left out of this. Bánko shrugged and said there was no other option, and Huba wondered at his

friend. It was unlike Bánko to risk the lives of those he loved,
matter what the cost to himself. He would have died first. If t
Soviet authority found out that Bánko had escaped, and Hu
and Írén had helped him, they would be arrested, imprison ,
and worse. Had the incident with Zabrovsky frightened hi
that badly?

3

Huba would get the answer to this later, after they contacted Ír .
He wasn't certain the police were watching him — his friendsh
with Bánko was strong but infrequent — but for sure they'd
watching her. Their relationship was secret only in Bánko's mi
Huba knew she took her afternoon coffee break every day in t
corner booth at the Magyar Képzőművészeti Egyetem, arou
the corner from where she worked as a low-level clerk — al
having refused to join the party — at the OTP. He met her the
the first and last Wednesday of every month, when they usua
talked about Bánko, though for Huba the meeting was rea
just a chance to sit in her presence and remember, once aga
how much brighter Bánko's world was. Írén had lost her motl
fifteen years ago, rounded up with thousands of other dissidei
after the war, and her father had spent those years with a stri
of mistresses that frequently took him from home, and so s
loved routine, reliability, days predetermined to the minu
She had finally put a stop to her father's infrequent visits
moving out of their place in Szeged, off to Budapest, leavi
no forwarding address. Once in a while the old man someh(v
made contact, finding out where she lived through mutt l
acquaintances or relatives not so good at keeping her secr t,
and demanded she observe her filial obligations, he was h r
father after all, and send money. But she almost never did. Ea 1
time, she reminded him of the paternal obligations he in tu 1
had failed to live up to. Then she'd be forced to move again. In l
things she demanded consistency, fairness. It's what made h r

and Bánko so perfect, a synthesis of opposites, to use a Marxist figure Huba detested but which for reasons of twelve years of education he couldn't get away from. The problem was Írén didn't see it that way; she thought Bánko and she were the same.

Huba slipped into the café early, wrote her a note between the designs of a coaster he left upside down on the table where Írén always sat, knowing that her rage for order would force her to turn it right side up. It read: B. is safe for now, at my place. Would you be willing to sew something for him? It's rather large. I'll be in the Flemish Baroque room of the Szépművészeti Múzeum between 5:00 and 5:15.

She came straight over after work, not a minute earlier. At the same time, she was breathless. Huba had never before met anyone whose impulses so obviously and inescapably pulled her in two directions. He told her about what had happened with Zabrovsky. I know, she replied. I read the newspaper. Paralyzed from the waist down. They're not sure if he'll recover. But they're hopeful. He's been such a good and loyal comrade. Huba nodded, though he preferred to stay away from the newspapers. If you read them regularly it became too easy to believe what they said. Their rhythms got inside your brain. He told her Bánko's idea about the balloon. Írén shook her head. You have to stop him, she said, then paused when she saw the look of disbelief — did you really just say that, me stop Bánko? — on Huba's face. Right, she nodded. Sure, I can sew. Better me than Bánko. She shook her head. He actually would try to do it himself — she just knew it. With zero experience or knowledge he would imagine what sewing was and then put it into practice. Maybe he'd manage to get thirty feet off the ground, just high enough to injure or kill himself. I'll send word, said Huba as he left the grand hall of the museum, but it'll need to be ready as soon as possible, and he handed over the illustration copied from *Neues Deutschland*, plus additional information he'd dug up on the shape of the balloon, how its seams were to be sewn and sealed, the shape and size of the deflation port, the type of brass rings needed to secure the

ropes to the basket. It doesn't have to get him around the wor
Huba finished. Just across the border.
Arranging transport to Nemesmedves was easier. Huba kn
a guy. He was unofficially unemployed like himself, but mad
decent living as a re-seller of goods purchased in the capital a
then toured through the tiny villages along the southern pe
of the country, from east to west. A proto-capitalist. That's he
he saw his calling, giving it a romantic air of petty larceny. I
charged three times the price of a standard rail ticket to smug
Bánko and the equipment down there, in the back of his goo
truck at night. And no, he didn't want to know who the guy w
or why he couldn't take state transport like everyone else, or wh
that contraption stinking of kerosene was. Huba and Írén to
the train down, meeting at the edge of the meadow they'd pick
just west of town.

It was early spring, the air sharp on exposed skin. Towe
blinked red and green in the distance, the X's of their girde
visible against a sky deepening from blue to black, spotligl
flitting around like bats looking for holes in the ceiling. T
bedsheets billowed above them in a quilted sphere. The basl
was four garbage cans roped together, the middle one filled wi
the burner Huba had built in the furnace room on Víllányi
Bánko put his satchel into one of them, then pulled from i
bottle of the best Törley champagne. Before I go, a toast, he sa
Huba and Írén looked at each other. This was a bit much, even
Bánko's standards. He was staring at Írén, because he knew s
was the stronger of the two, though both of them were fear
preferring the certainty of a bad situation — where the da
insults and deprivations could be counted on — to risking t
unknown for maybe a shot at something better (which, as Hu
would have said, was also a shot at something worse). Here's
phony elections, said Bánko, raising his glass. Here's to rande
arrests. Here's to having your daily ear- and eyeful of hypocri
Here's to watching those in power press their noses to the car
tions in their lapels while your noses are pressed into their ass

41

Here's to both of you going home to root through the husks of your dreams, until all that's left of them is the loss of something you no longer remember. Here's to growing old in this fucking place with nothing to look forward to but some filthy room at the Szent Antal Szanatórium with twelve other wheezing catatonics whose brains were turned off for survival purposes decades ago! Here's, he said, when neither of them drank, to your loyalty to the regime that killed both your parents.

Okay, Bánko. Okay. Írén stared at the ground, shaking. I knew I would have to come with you. Bánko looked as if he too had known it all along. You could have saved yourself the speech, she said. I didn't write it, he muttered. I copied it. Well, except for that last line, but that part was easy. Írén looked at Huba, who shrugged and said, I didn't write it either. That's not why I'm looking at you, Írén replied. You know Bánko hasn't got a hope of piloting this thing. But you could. Huba looked up at the balloon, still billowing but fuller now, and realized they'd left it almost too long. Untie the ropes!

Írén and Bánko looked at him. The balloon listed to one side, then the other. The three of them ran around, pulling up stakes, then each quickly climbed into his or her garbage can and up they rose, Huba feeding the burner. The chill of the air increased with altitude. They watched searchlights play out along the tops of trees, bushes, nearby roads, and they seemed grey to Huba, not white at all, and he imagined himself pinned in place by one of them the way he'd felt pinned to his suit every day on the way to Ferihegy, stuck inside the same suit every day, the same obsequious, cautious-eyed, mincing routine. And he knew Bánko was right. There was no other choice. He looked at Írén, hunkered beneath the rim of her garbage can, eyes closed, and agreed with her — it was much better directing air traffic while you were still on the ground.

We're running out of fuel, Huba yelled at Bánko. You didn't plan for enough fuel! What happened to your math? Why couldn't you remember to add properly? Bánko yelled back, Figuring out

the fuel was your job! Shit, thought Huba, he was right. I did
think there'd be three of us, he screamed back. How could y
not have thought that? returned Bánko. You should have kno\
I'd force you to come! How could you not have known that? Hu
stared at him and nodded. Bánko was right again.
They were losing altitude quickly, but not quickly enough.
this point they'd still be a good forty or fifty feet off the grou
when the fuel suddenly gave out. Huba looked back at Bán
and for a second it looked as if he, absurdly, were blowing h
air out of his mouth in the direction of the balloon, as if he h
the power to do even that. At least the searchlights were behi
them. They'd drifted far enough to be in Austria.

Over there! Írén yelled, having opened her eyes and stood
the sound of the two men arguing. She pointed at a glinti
rectangle of light a quarter of a kilometer off. Surrounded
a chain link fence, overarching lights, a large pump-house
one side — it was an outdoor swimming pool. Bánko shouted
Írén that he loved her. He really loved her! He had one leg alrea
over the side. Huba and Írén exchanged glances. Let him go fi
Huba yelled at her. But Bánko yelled back: You won't get a seco
chance. By the time I land, the balloon will have drifted pa
You're right, yelled Huba, but we're going to wait anyhow. Th
watched as Bánko hopped into the air and fell, arms and le
flailing, straight into the deep end. By that point they'd drift
past the edge of the pool, falling fast. Huba looked at Írén a
she looked at him. He was right, Huba said. We should ha
jumped when he did. The words went streaming past his fa
as they descended, gripping the edges of the garbage cans. A
then the balloon caught on one of the hooked lamps and t
ropes gave a great jerk and their spines jolted sending pain alo
every nerve ending and they were saved too.

When the authorities arrived, twenty minutes later, th
found the three of them in the pool, laughing and splashii
They'd made it.

4

Still distrusting the Americans, West Germans, French, British, and suspecting the Hungarians would have agents stationed around these embassies for him, Bánko went to the Canadians, mainly because it was a country not known for its wrestling. He sat for a while in a waiting room. They'd been in Vienna a week. The government had put them up in a hostel. Otherwise, Bánko found the city unlivable. Írén and he wandered up and down the streets trying to escape the impenetrable cheerfulness, the monotony of *Grüß Gott* from smiling mouths, the undifferentiated plenitude of markets, stores, street vendors. She put her arm around his waist whenever he flinched at a smile or wave or someone asking if he could help. There was too much on offer here. Bánko was anxious without a certain tension, the awkward eye of challengers, a coach or trainer or director yelling at him, the possibility of conflict, someone to defeat. But here, at the Canadian embassy, he found a happier mix of helpfulness and discouragement. The man behind the desk was Hank Graner, a first-generation Hungarian, born in Powell River, British Columbia, a town whose pulp and paper mill, he said, was one of the largest, if not *the* largest, in the world. Why this was important was beyond Bánko. Hank looked as if he was nineteen, his grasp of Hungarian efficient, workmanlike. When Bánko walked into the room he jumped from his seat and rushed around to extend his hand, saying, Wow, Charles Bánko, the real Charles Bánko, I can't believe it. Bánko shook the hand and nodded, not sure how to react. I saw the reels of your takedown of Abukamov in the Moscow finals last year. Magnificent. I even managed to catch your Northwestern regionals championship in Esztergom in person back in February. That move you pulled, grabbing the guy by the waist and flipping him backwards. I didn't know the human spine could work that way. Yours must be a steel spring. Oh, please, have a seat.

Bánko sat, still not sure what to say. Finally, while Graner sto
there staring, a ludicrous smile on his face, Bánko gestured a
said, My papers? Oh yes, replied Graner. When I heard you
applied for refugee status, well, I begged them to let me hanc
the file, because you see I'm such a fan. I train a bit in my spa
time, and I wonder if maybe, if you have a moment you coulc
mean if you have time . . . well, there are rumours that you
going to debut, well that you were going to . . . debut a new mo
at the Olympics. Graner stopped, out of breath. Bánko rubb
his hands back and forth along his thighs and looked arour
Right, said Graner. Your file. It looks good, really good. Yo
friends, the air traffic controller, Mr. Huba? Yes? And Ms. Agnc
Let's see, yes, bank clerk. Everything seems great, really gre
It's a process of course, but I don't see any red flags. Well, ac
ally, there's the matter of your alleged assault on . . . He shuffl
some papers. Maxim Zabrovsky? Graner's mouth curled intc
grin. What charges won't those Commies invent to retain the
top talent? We've looked into this Zabrovsky character. Do y
know he didn't even exist before 1919 or so?

Bánko tapped his fingers on his thighs. Fine, he said, I w
train with you.

Wow, that would be just amazing, Mr. Bánko.

Afterwards, Bánko stood outside the embassy watchi
Vienna churn out another cheery day, and he thought to hims
so this is my first lesson on capitalism: you need luck to g
anywhere. Well, he'd take it.

During the twenty weeks they waited for their papers, Bán
went to the gym with Graner every other day. The workout roor
were cleaner than any he'd seen. So were the bodies of the m
muscles so defined they looked as if they'd been traced witl
needlepoint. Every night someone came around and wip
down the weights, Bánko had no idea why. Even the lifti
they did, it didn't seem to him like work, ten, fifteen, twer
seconds at the most, then rest, as if there was something wro
something dirty, in sweat. He flicked Graner around like

flyswatter, and even then he was holding back, being nice, not wanting to jeopardize their emigration. Wow, great move, great move, said Graner, rising from the mat like a wall of bricks with the mortar missing. But I'm ready for you now. Bánko tried not to feel ashamed for lending himself to this, for not breaking Graner's neck immediately.

It was at the end of their second session that he finally asked, So who do I need to see about getting onto the Canadian Olympic team? Graner stopped, looked at him. The Olympic team? Bánko nodded. When I get to Canada I'll be the best wrestler in the country. Graner shifted on his feet, though Bánko could tell the real shifting was going on inside, where the advantage belonged entirely to the younger man. Well, Graner said, I think it's a bit late, you know? The Olympics are only a few months away. I'm ready, said Bánko, as if the problem might be a question of training rather than a universe of politics. Graner was thinking hard. There are other . . . wrestling things you might do, he said. Other things? Yes, nodded Graner, there are many, many other things!

Bánko had no idea what he was talking about. I actually wanted to speak with you about this, said Graner. I brought you something. Maybe we should go have a coffee?

The file was half a foot thick with photographs and articles. Most of the pictures were of men wearing multicolored masks. They looked like devils. Instead of the singlets of Greco-Roman wrestling they wore multicolored briefs that matched their masks. More disorienting was the fact that they were in a ring rather than on a mat, and in some of the pictures they were flying off the ropes, fists raised. They were kicking each other. They were punching. Their moves were not part of any repertoire Bánko had encountered. The best he could say was that they seemed competent acrobats. The worst was that they reminded him of clowns.

But Graner was not finished. There was a deeper layer to the file. Here, the wrestlers, if you could call them that, didn't wear

costumes. In fact, they reminded Bánko of a prison detail h
once seen on the outskirts of Szeged. They had the same look
their eyes as they glared at him driving past, men for whom t
faintest hope was kept alive only through an intensity of hatr
either for the system that had done this to them, or the peo]
who'd put them there, or some moment in the past that h
turned them into who they were. Or for no reason at all, becau
hatred was what had kept them in their skin for as long as th
could remember, because it had existed first, before anythi
else, and they'd found or invented reasons for it later, in t
confessional or courtroom, long after it had already done
work. As long as they could hate they had something to lo
forward to, plans to make, a reason to live another thirty yea
And when they turned away, when their eyes left him, Bán
felt erased.

In Graner's pictures there was sometimes a ring, but mo
often than not there was a paddock, or the floor of a barn,
what looked like a cellar. There was even one where the men we
inside a cage, and in another what looked like a large square]
Some of the men had cuts on their faces, blood up their fo
arms, spattered on their chests, mugging at the camera as if th
wanted you to count their missing teeth.

There are all kinds of places you could go with a talent li
yours, Graner said. This time Bánko knew exactly what to s
but he didn't say it, worried it might jeopardize their appli
tion. Graner pressed the file on him. I made it for you, he sa
There are contacts in there. People who could help you find wo
Bánko stood there holding the file, helpless for the first time
his life.

That night, Írén went through the file. She paused at certa
pictures, horrified. What kind of country are we going
Bánko? I'm not sure this has anything to do with a speci
country, he replied. She lay back in bed. You are an Olym]
champion. Promise me you won't do it. I'm not an Olym]
champion, Bánko muttered. I never will be. Írén rolled over a

kissed him. But her lips were hard, crushed into his, bitter rather than consoling, the quickest way to hurt him. You would have left me behind, she said. This was what they were truly talking about, Bánko realized now. What they'd been talking about ever since he'd returned with Graner's file under his arm. You went to Huba, not me, she said. Bánko waited as a tram screeched past on the road below. He thought of the acrid *villamos* he rode to Lakosdi utca every morning, smelling of ashtrays, the corrosive breath of proles drunk on *pálinka* before they even showed up for work, the tang of old urine in a corner by the door. I thought, Bánko finally said, that it would be better to know you were alive, even if I could never see you again, than to risk you dying. He waited, wondering what Írén would reply. So, you would have risked Huba's life but not mine? Yes, Bánko replied. But you gave him the choice? Shit, thought Bánko, she's got me. He could already see her next move. Why wouldn't you extend to me the same choice? He thought for a minute. Because you would have said yes. You would have come with me. I *did* come with you, she answered. But that's only when I already knew for sure we could make it! You decided for me, before and after, Írén continued. So you're saying that if things had been reversed you would have given me the choice? Bánko asked. Even knowing that I might die? Yes, she nodded. Of course. Well then, it's clear, he said, you don't love me as much as I love you. Bullshit, she replied. That's not true. Okay, Bánko nodded his head. Just wait. You'll see I'm right.

Could you both please shut up? yelled Huba from the bed on the other side of the room. I'm trying to sleep.

5

The first years in Canada were impossible. Huba went from airport to airport, starting at Pearson International, its airspace thick with transatlantic traffic, then Toronto Island, then one regional airport after another, until he finally got hired loading

and unloading bags from tiny twin engines at the Region
Waterloo Airport, called "international" only because of the o
flight that left every morning for Chicago, and which otherwi
serviced tiny northern towns with engineers, teachers, logge
medical personnel. They said he might work his way up to i
traffic controller. He replied that it was the best job he'd had
a while, not adding that it was the only one. Írén found wo
in a bank, doing exactly what she'd done back in Budapest,
irony she made sure was not lost on any of them. Bánko look
up his contacts in wrestling, but it was as Graner had said, t
Olympics were too close, he was too late, and judging from I
age it was unlikely he'd be competitive for the next one. He tri
very hard not to cry, crawling into bed at night beside Írén
the tiny house Huba found for them in Kitchener, a brick a
mortar shoebox that had been the reward given to Canadi
soldiers returned from the war, to make up for all those missi
arms and legs. So Írén cried for Bánko instead, cradling I
face between her hands. It wasn't long before he found hims
dipping into Graner's file, chasing down contacts, one refer
leading to another until he was given two shifts, Friday a
Saturday night, from eleven until three, as a bouncer at t
Ripsaw in Uptown. He hated it — busting heads. Within thi
months he was fired for being too rough with a customer. Bán
was lucky, the manager said, that he hadn't paralyzed the g
He had a knife, Bánko replied, which was his way of saying it v
the guy who'd been lucky for not getting paralyzed.

Not long after, he received a call from John Stockton, who
read the police notice in the newspaper and said he'd hea
Bánko was looking for work and would he be interested
some exhibition matches, what Stockton called semi-prof
sional bouts? You'll need a stage name, Stockton said, a kind
brand. Bánko found it on his way to their first meeting, drivi
the used Volvo Huba had bought for them by combining I
and Írén's earnings. It was a huge sign painted on a brick w
in Galt: "Ray Electric Limited, southern Ontario's large

provider of Heating, Cooling, and Refrigeration Systems." Ray Electric, Bánko thought. It was fast, powerful, shocking. He liked it very much. Stockton provided him steady work for a while. Some of it was even real. Once in a while they worked some of his Olympic techniques — already fading, loose and disconnected from any competitive strategy — into the matches. After being away, traveling through the little towns of southern Ontario and New England, he'd return home to find Huba and Írén on the back porch. Once in a while a large insect would explode against the heat lamp Huba had installed. The two of them grew quiet as Bánko told them about the crowds, the other wrestlers, the dirt roads of towns, until he realized his own voice had grown quiet in the telling. Sometimes he returned home with a trophy or ribbon — The No-Holds Barred Trout Creek Trophy, 1963; The Lindemaar Big Man's Cup, 1966; The Brakhage Powerhouse Pennant, 1967 — putting them on the ground at Írén's feet, though they already seemed ephemera, gathering the kind of dust that covered other such trophies — little-league baseball, seniors' curling, pub dart competitions — on the shelves of pawnshops and Salvation Army stores, twenty-five cents apiece.

Huba and Írén listened. Bánko didn't seem to get it. When he realized his voice was growing quiet, he'd get up, take a deep breath and turn up the volume again. But behind it they could see what was happening, as each opponent, each venue, each set of rules became less theatrical and more stripped down, elemental. Soon there would be no rules at all. But Bánko was hopeful. The early matches had received some media attention, even some television coverage on local stations. They'd interviewed him, asked about his past on the Hungarian team, the rigor of his training, whether he felt that coming to Canada had been a good career move. This was his glorious blip in sports history. Some of the promoters even told him there was talk of creating a Canadian pro circuit, similar to what was devel-

oping in the States and Mexico. But Írén could see it evaporati
the moment he told her about it. She could only imagine wh
they said, the people Bánko talked to on the phone, the way
brought up the subject more and more forcefully each time
called, as if sensing their growing reluctance to grant him tl
reality. The problem was, Bánko could never stand the sho
business side of things, sooner or later insisting that somethi
in the matches be real, as if with enough effort he could will l
way back into the ranks of true athletes. Sooner or later ho
break with the script, the choreography, and injure someo
or get injured himself. He was demoted, suspended, fired, ev
arrested a few times, in a free-fall down the ladder of oppor
nities until he really was fighting — in cellars and back roor
barns, fenced-in lots, cages, that square pit dug into the earth
Graner's old photograph.

Írén tried to make him stay. She could see him looking at Hu
or around the house, saying he couldn't, they needed the mon
It was the first thing he always handed her, coming home. F
her part, Írén was always at the door, waiting on his return. T
minute there were footsteps on the porch she'd flinch, hati
herself for it, but then she'd drop everything and run, yanki
open the handle on a vacuum cleaner salesman, or some g
hawking encyclopedias, or a life insurance representative,
a shamefaced ex-drunk requesting funds for the MacAlist;
Halfway House, or a Jehovah's Witness, Mormon, even a Moor
or two. She was always so eager, so rushed, she didn't have tir
to back down from the emotion, and ended up inviting the
in, more to allay her disappointment than anything, and mc
often than not buying whatever was on offer — a policy, a do
tion, a pile of religious tracts. All she could ever say was yes. Hu
saw it when he came home and she told him how much of th
money she'd spent. It was all about Bánko, and later, after t
accident, Huba would look back on Írén's life and see in it bo
her problem and its solution.

6

She didn't know how to make Bánko stop except by saying her and Huba's earnings would be enough for all three of them until he found better work. This only made him make more phone calls, chase down every offer no matter how sketchy. Huba kept his distance. Once in a while Bánko asked how his job was going, but then cut him off when Huba shrugged, trying to downplay his promotion to parking lot manager. Huba's role was not to speak, but to listen, since Bánko told him everything he couldn't tell Írén. The details would remain with Huba like the whisper of the torturer long after a captive's been released, back into what everyone believes is normal life. Stories about the greasy promoters who set up the matches. The white trash who came to watch. The liquor and pills they gave Bánko to bring it all violently alive — every inhibition gone — and also to sweep it away, so many instants forgotten in the mix, lost to blackout and hangover, like a prescription of amnesia for the disease of memory. Bánko watched his friend's face carefully as he went through the details, the injuries that kept him away after the matches ended, waiting to heal before he returned to Írén. Torn ligaments. Fractured orbital bones. Herniated disks. But every bit of harm he'd received was compensated for by something he'd done to his opponents, and, Huba suspected, by the harm and injury Bánko was doing in telling him all this. They too were engaged in battle, he thought, trying very hard not to zero in on what they were both after, or, when he couldn't manage that, at least trying not to think of Írén as a trophy.

After Bánko left he sat at the table with Írén, or on the couch, even sometimes with his arm around her, saying the real problem was Bánko's refusal to acknowledge that it was the two of them he was punishing. It wasn't Bánko down in those pits getting beat on but Huba and Írén. He brought us out here, Huba said, against our will, and he feels bad about it. Írén laughed. It's not a joke, he continued. Bánko was a big deal back in Hungary. In

certain circles. We should be more grateful to him for what
gave up for us, even if we couldn't understand it at the time.
She leaned over and kissed him. It was meant as a gestu
of friendship, but she missed and ended up on his lips. Lat
both of them would wonder why they hadn't pulled back, ma
a correction. They would wonder for days, weeks, months, yea
sitting in bed trying to sort it. How had they ended up togeth
Was it because Bánko was always away? No, it had been li
that before, too, back in Hungary. He was always flying off
competitions, or disappearing to some retreat in the country i
intensive training. Sometimes they'd go without sex for mont
Írén said. It wasn't that.

From the start, Huba suspected he knew the reason. With
half a year he was positive. But he didn't want to say it. Ír
was with him because he was the shadow, the placeholder, t
only man she could be with and at the same time still be wi
Bánko. He was the one she could have kids with, who'd rai
them, who'd be there every day at 5:30 home from work, and s
open his doors when Bánko came back to town. The worst thi
was knowing he would accept it, live with it, even if it ate in
him over time, as if he was stronger than any need for the pri
honour and self-respect he'd been taught, over and over, by I
father and mother, by the books he read, his school, the wh
national mythology of warriors and freedom fighters and sai
on which he'd been raised. Every year it would bother him a lit
more, make him a little weaker, until he was like one of the
houses riddled with termites, holes everywhere, but someh
still standing. Huba looked into the mirror every night at 3 a.
and told himself the whole thing was wrong — cheating on l
friend, coveting Írén — then he'd leave and stand over the bed
the dark and climb back in beside her.

If Bánko noticed, he never said a thing. He came back wh
he came back, sometimes after a week, sometimes two, a
he seemed to look around the house with approval. The m
noticeable change in Bánko's behavior was how he took whatev

job was offered. The phone would ring. He'd get on, nod, say a word or two, then head upstairs to pack. He didn't bargain or plead or turn down offers anymore. They called, he went, and when he came back he was worse — spine stiffer, knees aching, scars along his head where the hair refused to grow back, an imprint on one shoulder as if he'd been pressed into red hot chainlink, a bruise on his sternum in the shape of a cricket bat, skin shredded along the back of his thighs as if he'd fallen into a bin of cheese graters. That, Huba felt, was really his statement on him and Írén, the marks left by the pain he used to blot out his despair, and the sight of which he used to inspire the same feeling in them, making sure to walk through the house with his shirt off as much as possible. The only problem with Bánko's strategy was that the only way for Huba to deal with the guilt was to fuck it all away. How the sex functioned for Írén he wasn't sure, but she sought it out the minute Bánko was out the door, and so he thought it was the same.

By September she was visibly pregnant. By now, Huba was managing the loading and unloading of luggage at the airport, largely a desk job, gone the usual eight hours a day of work for a salaried position that required him to stay at the office past dinnertime in a swivel chair, going over schedules and manifests and customs regulations until his spine felt like a corkscrew. It didn't stop him from taking a break every fifteen minutes, wondering how Bánko would react to the promotion. Every time Huba asked Írén whose child it was she glared and told him not to ask stupid questions. This was not, he felt, a satisfying answer. I'm the luckiest woman in the world, she added. That felt even less satisfying. A child, any child, she said, is a gift. Now Huba was really crazy, part of him wishing Bánko would come home and sort out this mess. A child is the purpose of life!

It was an early autumn day when Bánko finally arrived, hobbling up the front steps, face covered in Band-Aids. There was a strip of gauze wound vertically around his head, as if he

needed something to keep his jaw attached. Írén was standi
in the back door, probably on purpose, where the late afterno
sun showed her in full silhouette underneath a gauzy dress, h
stomach finally showing, like a small half-moon.

Bánko stopped in the kitchen and smiled. He put down l
suitcase and forgot his injuries, moving toward her as if he w
still sixteen, lifting her off her feet. Írén smiled at him and h
his face between her hands. Now will you stay? she said. V
you stay?

And Huba finally understood what they'd been doing eve
night, sneaking between bedrooms, or sharing a bed wh
Bánko's absence allowed them to. They, or rather Írén, had be
trying to save Bánko's life. This had been her plan all along, a
if it didn't work with Bánko himself, if he couldn't get her pr
nant, then she'd decided to give Huba a try. It turned out tl
both of them had been desperate for Bánko to leave, but or
one of them hoped for his return. For Írén, it was about getti
Bánko back on the road only so that she could one day keep h
at home forever.

Will you stay? she asked again.

Bánko smiled at her with every assurance she'd ever need.

So it's up to me, then, thought Huba. His own answer to Íré
betrayal arrived late at night, during another 3:00 a.m. wake
call, risen again into the insomnia that always divided his nigl
between the sleep that came over him instantly, from a day
overwork, the moment his head hit the pillow, and the sleep tl
came slow, after he was startled awake, three or four hours la
by his fixation on Írén, tossing and turning and begging God
let him slip back into dreams.

They were piling wood in the back yard when he told Bán
Actually, it was Bánko piling the wood, ignoring the pain in l
hips and shoulders, stacking the wheelbarrow five feet hi
with a special technique he'd devised, then carefully balanci
it across the lawn to the back door. Once in a while Huba wou
lift a piece of wood, but his back seemed frozen into the postu

of a man sitting at a desk, as if he still carried the swivel chair glued invisible to his ass. There was a point, Huba discovered that morning, waking in a black fury that darkened further whenever he looked at Írén, where anger could carry you across the threshold of fear, where what made you panic, hesitate, run off, was left behind, and your whole world, your only thought, was this thing you needed to defeat. It was a narrowing of vision so extreme it cancelled everything else, and Huba wondered if this was where Bánko had always been, in the midst of a rage so intense it left him no choice but to act. We've been sleeping together, Huba said. We've been sleeping together a long time. Whenever you go away, and sometimes when you're still here. The child is mine.

Bánko dropped the overloaded wheelbarrow, the wedges and rounds spilling out. His moment of bravery gone, Huba picked up one of them and held it over his head, facing his friend. This is new, smiled Bánko. I've been hit with chairs, two by fours, but never that. He shook his head and feinted in the direction of Huba, who brought the piece of wood down just as Bánko moved to one side. The momentum carried Huba forward onto his knees. Bánko stomped on him hard, on the ass, and he fell face forward into the wet lawn, feeling the wrestler sit hard on top of his thighs, trapping his arms next to his body with his knees, then reach forward with both hands, grab Huba's chin, and pull his head up and back until it reached some absolute limit for the curvature of spine. Do you think because I'm a wrestler I don't know how to add? Bánko hissed. I know exactly where I was when Írén got pregnant. He continued to hold Huba there. Camel clutch, he whispered. I learned it four or five years back, on the road. Illegal at the Olympics, of course, but not illegal — nothing's illegal — in the places I've been. And where I'll be going back to. Huba closed his eyes, feeling every one of his vertebrae shift and re-align. Going back? Each letter of the question popped off his teeth. It's all I can do now, replied Bánko.

He held Huba for what felt like half an hour, though it mu
have been shorter than that, and when he finally let go and stro
off through the grass, Huba rose, his back pain-free for the fii
time in years. Bánko had pulled the corkscrew straight again

7

He was gone that evening. Huba knew Írén would never forgi
him. Everything that happened after that seemed like a puni
ment she'd devised for him. Within three and a half years s
was pregnant twice more. They had three boys — György, Krísu
Tamás — just like that, three years apart. Huba was so busy
could barely breathe, up all night with babies, off to work ea
in the morning, back home again to help with dinners, laund
tidying the house, then collapsing into bed to wake up and
it all over again. Marriage was not what he'd been led to belie
watching his father come home from work to pour himsel
beer and sit in front of the newspaper while his mother d
everything, so meek and submissive that her exertions we
all but invisible, and his father could easily believe he was t
only one who had a real job. Írén was not like that at all. It v
Canada's fault. Canada had turned her into a boss, a taskmasu
an angel of vengeance. Every day before leaving work he'd bo
his head and utter an anti-prayer of damnation. Bánko wou
never have allowed himself to be put into this situation.

Still, he had sex with Írén as often as possible. She seem
to have these moments of tenderness, even lust, as if she kno
this was what Huba required to get through the next round
household chores. She modulated things. Every three mont
the stress would build to a huge fight, in which Huba wou
accuse her of seeking revenge on him for having spoiled h
plans with Bánko, and Írén would shake her head and tell hi
no, he had it all wrong, she was sorry for how she'd played the
and Huba knew, he just knew, that this too, this phony empat
and remorse, masked the most terrifying of aggression. It w

all part of her strategy — to isolate and then destroy him with affirmation. This is what you do, he yelled, whenever there's a problem. You just say yes to everyone. I see it every time some salesman or charity case or religious nut comes to the door. He lifted a handful of *Watchtower* magazines sitting on the desk. You need to learn how to say no. Not to mention, Forget It, Get Lost, and Fuck Off. How many encyclopedias have you bought? Life insurance policies? Do we really need two vacuum cleaners? Do you realize what it's like for me at work, wearing a chair on my butt? And you spend the money on this? Huba stopped. What the hell was he talking about? Not this, he realized, staring at the bunched-up magazines in his fist, that was for sure. It was Írén's yes he was mad at. Her constant yes.

In his best moments Huba admitted it — he'd betrayed her and Bánko both, he didn't deserve forgiveness — and she told him he was wrong, she'd used him, and if anyone needed forgiving it was her, and he'd go crazy, telling Írén sure, he was just a weakling, led by the nose. What else can I do to make you believe me? Írén cried. How about telling me the truth? I am telling you the truth! No, he replied, you're leaving me all alone with it. I'm all alone here! No you're not! We're in this together. Oh God, he said, holding his head. You're really good at this. And I thought Bánko was a world champion.

Then there were Bánko's visits home, which were not nearly as frequent as they'd once been, but which always coincided with some terrible fight they'd had, to the point where Huba suspected she was calling him, or sending telegrams, or maybe smoke signals, saying, Now, this is the moment, Huba's at his lowest, come home! There was an awkwardness between the two men, walking around each other in the kitchen or living room as if they were on stilts, always balancing, afraid of tipping over, getting in each other's way. Bánko's energy, if anything, was more manic than ever. Even before he'd recovered from his broken ankle — he refused to tell them how he'd gotten it — and the fifteen stitches down the middle of his scalp, he was

doing dishes, vacuuming floors, carrying garbage in and o
making lunches and dinners, changing beds, all the little jo
that lightened Írén's load during the day, and Huba's at night.
course, he stayed away from the bigger jobs — fixing a saggi
door, installing new rain gutters, repairing the plumbing
the upstairs sink — that he claimed were beyond him, that h
never been taught how to do, having missed this crucial p
of a boy's education during the years he was being trained
dismantle opponents on the mat. Huba didn't believe it fo
second. What Bánko was really doing was helping Írén, happ
doing all the jobs Huba constantly complained about, no dou
to confirm the enormity of her mistake.

At the airport, Huba was promoted to assistant air traf
controller. He was one step away from the job of his drear
This, despite the fact that not a week went by without h
checking the pocket calendar he'd started keeping of Bánk
visits home, trying to figure out how they did or did n
coincide with the dates of Írén's pregnancies, always faili
to find a formula that proved without a doubt that Bán
was or was not the father of their three children. In the end
was only the first one, George — who as it turned out was Hub
favourite — that he couldn't be totally sure about, though th
didn't stop him from trying not to be sure about the other t
It didn't help that back at home Bánko seemed to be very care
about not favouring George over the other two, always givi
them equal time. It only made Huba that much more suspicio
driving him deeper into his pocket calendar and equations.

Whenever Bánko left again, Írén would beg him not to.
Huba could think was, What were you two doing with ea
other while I was at work? Of course, he'd provide his own bitt
answer: Exactly what they should have been doing all along.
overheard Bánko on the phone during those nights when he w
arguing with promoters. They want me to do what? Against h
many? Using what? Oh, just for show? You know what happen
to me the last time I heard that . . . ? How long can I hold r

breath? Why is that important? Wait a minute . . . As he walked
out the door Bánko kissed Írén passionately on either cheek, but
it seemed to Huba as if she was tilting her face this way and that
not to help him but because she was trying to zero in on his lips,
and Bánko was trying to zero in on hers, only their movements
were out of synch, so they kept missing. My god, thought Huba
to himself, I've gone completely insane.

I won't be back for a long time, said Bánko, holding out a
hand for his old friend to shake. It seemed like a promise. Huba
wanted to cry. If he stayed away, Huba would lose. If Bánko came
back, he'd lose too. There was no way to win. And wasn't that just
like Bánko? You don't need to go, Írén said. You can stay here. We
have enough money. Maybe Huba can get you a job at the airport.
Huba looked at Bánko, bowed and scarred, his body showing
the years that had gone by and the damage he'd taken on, and
yet for all that he seemed stronger than ever, as if he required
more and more injuries only because they'd become less and less
effective as a disguise, wearing thinner with each visit, to hide
a spiritual vitality growing in leaps and bounds. Make sure you
get good and hurt for us for next time around, Huba said, angry
and frightened at the same time, smiling as the words came out,
as if it were a joke. Bánko looked at him and nodded, and nodded
again, then turned and left without another look at Írén, who
closed the door and exploded. What is wrong with you!?

8

That fight lasted three days. Írén was relentless. Repeat after
me, she yelled. *I'm not using you to get back at Bánko.* Huba refused
to repeat it. Get it through your head, she said, trying again.
You and I are in the same place, in perfect agreement! Huba
disagreed. If they were anywhere together it was in this, the
fight that engaged them. She snorted. You think I didn't have
a choice? You think I just went with whatever man was easiest?
You think I was too soft for what was out there? She pointed at

the door through which Bánko had left. I chose not to follow hi
I chose not to live that life. To stay here. Me.
That's right, Huba finally agreed. That is exactly what y(
chose: Not Bánko. But it wasn't me. He rose from the table. Y(
chose a place. I just happened to be standing in it. She rolled h
eyes. It would have been so easy for her to ask what the dif
ence was, to say that place is nothing more than the people
it, but she never did, and Huba refused to give her the chan
looking at his watch, saying it was time, he was going to be la
for work, he needed to go. But what he was really saying w
Ha! Beat that!

It was the last thing he'd ever say to her. Later that morni
Írén was hit by a forklift transporting engine parts to t
airport hangars. It was, in keeping with her string of victories
perfectly timed death, one last word like no other, though Hu
didn't put it to himself exactly like that. In fact, he didn't pu
to himself at all. The defeat was more like a feeling he kept ali
undescribed, as if words might diminish or alter it, subjec
to a sense under which it might not survive. This was, he kn
still a form of spite, made hotter, more scarring, when combin
with the guilt and loss he mixed into the emotional cocktail
made for himself every morning getting out of bed, sipping
it all day.

She was bringing him the lunch he'd forgotten at home wh
he broke off their argument. I'm going to be late for work, h
said. But it wasn't true. There was still time. She watched fro
the doorway as he walked to the bus stop, preferring to stand
the cold, the wind picking up, blistering his face with snowflak
It was only after he'd gotten on the bus that Írén saw the lun
running out with it to the car, still in her housecoat, which w
a uniform, Huba would later think, for the martyr housew
killed on a winter's day delivering the sandwich she'd made t
a husband who had so little respect for her he couldn't even
bothered to remember it. She followed behind the bus as it tr
elled down Weber, turned left on Victoria, en route to the airp(

Whenever Huba peeked at her she was holding up his lunch bag behind the windshield. Then a cloud of snow swirled off the roof of the bus or a nearby truck and obscured her car. It was a full-fledged blizzard now. Huba settled into his seat. Once in a while she honked. The bus driver was getting agitated, peering into the rearview mirror. Craning his head Huba saw her at the stop lights. He was worried she'd get out, in the midst of traffic, and come over and pound on the door of the bus and force him to take his goddamned lunch bag so she could get back to the kids, who for all she knew might not even be sleeping anymore. He would later wonder about that: Írén wanted so much to give him what she thought he needed she'd abandoned her own kids. There was something seriously wrong in that. It confirmed a flaw in her he'd always suspected, nevermind if that flaw was the reason she loved him.

When they got to the airport he bolted from the bus, straight for the hangars. He was actually ashamed now. At any point he could have gotten off that bus for his lunch. But, no, he had to punish her. Out of the corner of his eye he could see her running after him, housecoat flapping. By God she was going to get him that lunch, she didn't care how. She was going to win this. The storm hurled itself at them in gusts of stinging snowflakes, aimed straight for their eyes. That's what the forklift driver would say to the police. She was rounding the corner of the hangar. The convex mirrors placed there were covered in snow. But he'd been driving too fast. Everyone agreed. He was trying to get the job done quick so he could get back inside to the heaters and hot coffee.

Írén seemed like some dreamer, lying there on the pavement. One of her arms was outstretched, and her face was resting on it, gazing in the direction the finger pointed. The rest of her followed casually in line, with only one of her legs bent up at the knee, the foot listing to one side, to mar the design. She might as well have been lying on a bed one Sunday afternoon, the horizon lost in soft focus, her mind slipping between daydreams. But there was a pool of blood, growing larger. didn't seem to belong to her, it was too thick, too heavy lookii like the raspberry syrup Huba's mother made when he wa: kid, boiling down the fruit until it was sugar and crimson a: whatever essence there was that gave it that flavour. He founc hard to believe something that clotted could flow through a bo wondering exactly that when they pulled him out of it, kneeli there, his pants warm with her blood, then frozen stiff.

At home, there were three boys to explain it to. For on Huba was faced with a job, unlike loving Írén, he could avoid. Or, rather, he avoided it by telling them the truth, dire Your mother has died. She was hit by a forklift. She won't coming back. He didn't add that she was in Heaven. Írén h not believed in that. Later, watching the three of them tangl in the sheets of his bed, Huba realized how lazy he'd been. On again he'd refused to do the work of coming up with a bett language to put around it. The unadorned sentences had cor easiest, leaving the boys with the work of managing the pa they delivered. Afterwards, they'd gone to sleep quietly, unco prehending, arms around each other in a way Huba had nev before seen, twined in the bed as if they were a raft floating aw from him. Most of the tears would come years later. That, pl fighting. Plus slipping grades. Plus reports from teachers a: vice-principals. And finally trips to therapy. Only Thomas can through unscathed, two years old at the time, no memory of t mother to whose loss he could have pinned all his difficulti There was, for Huba, no way to redeem any of it.

9

The only thing that calmed the boys was Bánko, who came soon as he heard. They sat in the living room at three in t morning, and Huba went through all seven of the life insuran policies Írén had taken out. I'll never have to work again, he sa looking up. I mean never. The way we live, he looked around t small house, the money will last forever. He didn't want to add what he was feeling, but which he suspected Bánko knew—that Írén was already becoming a memory of the best thing God had given him, which was, of course, only what Bánko himself had felt, ten years back, when Huba stole her. Once again, Bánko had gotten there first.

She never knew how to say no, said Bánko, feeling no need to add the one qualifier: except to me. She always said yes to everything.

Huba looked at him with suspicion. What, exactly, had she said yes to? Were there yesses he didn't know about? Was there another world, maybe many worlds, she'd affirmed beyond the one they'd made together?

Bánko's gaze moved around the house. Huba followed it. He had to admit the place seemed different now, partly because of Írén's death, but also because of what the insurance money from that death added up to: the mortgage paid off, seven hundred thousand dollars in the bank, an educational fund for the boys. There was also the other legacy of her passing: he'd given notice at the airport. He'd never be an air traffic controller, either in Hungary or in Canada. From this point forward he committed himself to getting kids to school, making lunches, helping with homework, making sure the laundry got done, the house was cleaned. Was it atonement? Probably not, that would have required too definitive an inventory of sins and their remediation. Was it shock? Depression? A rage that left him incapable of anything but holding a vacuum? Was that what he wanted, as if loss could be an object, as if you could pick it up, pull it toward you, and maybe for a second realize what Írén had been in herself, purged of everything that might refer her to someone or something else, as if you could grasp her life outside the part she'd played in yours? Huba had no idea. But he admitted it was less stressful, all that housework he'd hated before, without having to do it on top of his eight-hour shift at the airport. In the afternoons there was often an hour or two in which to read,

watch TV, walk around the block, not that he could imagine Ír
having done these things. He realized he had no idea what Ír
had done with her time, beyond chores. Sometimes, on one
those walks, Huba would stare up at the trees and listen to the
branches clacking in the wind. One thing was for sure: he got
of the salesmen and zealots who showed up like clockwork f
a while, before they realized Írén would never again meet the
at the door with coffee and baking, pen ready to sign whatev
they put in front of her. Now there was just this nasty guy w
looked like he'd put paint stripper on his face.

10

As for Bánko, he was back to visit more often now, appearing
the doorstep wired, shaking and loquacious with the four wee
of non-stop liquor and the STDs he'd picked up from the lad
in Vancouver, Calgary, Regina, Winnipeg, Toronto, Montreal
whatever city he'd been left at after touring hundreds of ba
water towns with this or that fighting outfit. This was a no
development, his scattered comments about the ladies, and
shocked Huba, because he thought there'd never been anyo
for Bánko but Írén.

There was no question he'd been fired again, no question
was now regularly losing rather than winning bouts. His fa
was ridged with scars old and new, tanned with bruises. Son
times he forgot very simple things, for instance that he'd eat
breakfast already, that he'd said the same thing he was sayi
now ten minutes ago, that Huba and he were not twenty-fo
years old and at the height of their powers. But he never forg
that Írén was dead, or the story he had to tell the boys over a
over every time he visited, of how he'd single-handedly beat
the Hungarian men's wrestling team in the spring of 1960.
was it the winter?

He never called beforehand. When had he ever? There'd be
honk outside. Looking out the window Huba and the boys saw

taxi pull into the driveway, its door swing open, and Bánko's face appear out of the murk in the back seat. It looked as if someone had wrapped his head in barbed wire then torn it off, spinning him like a top. Before Bánko managed to get his feet under him on the driveway, Huba was already there, racing out the back door, catching his friend as he tried to take a step.

This time, thought Huba, this time he's finally broken, and all his hate for me is going to come pouring out. Hopefully. With the help of the boys they managed to get Bánko inside, then Huba paid the cabbie, slipping him an extra twenty when he complained about the mess Bánko had left on the backseat, which you could smell through the open window ten feet from the car. I should have taken him straight to emergency, the cabbie said, but he told me if I didn't get him to your place he was going to die right here in my car, but before that he was going to kill me first. Huba nodded.

Inside, the boys had gotten Bánko into a bath, and put all his clothes into the garbage, touching them only with the tips of their fingers. When he got out he looked bewildered, a straggler arrived at the end of the parade — footsore, confetti on his lapels, not sure where the floats and beauty queens had gotten to. Huba made the usual concoction of tomato juice, Unicum, powdered Aspirin, and caplets of vitamin B12, mixing all three together as Bánko settled into a chair in the living room and the children gathered around their hero — the circumstances of Bánko's arrival already forgotten — who took a sip of his drink and prepared to tell it, the story everyone in the room knew, word for word.

Weren't you scared? asked George afterwards. Yes I was, said Bánko, and Huba rolled his eyes. How could he lie like that? To children? Especially when Huba and the rest of them knew very well that Bánko had never been afraid of anything — not men, not politicians, not fighting, not hard moral choices, not the demands of decency, not the expectations of selflessness, nothing. Not even when it cost him the thing he'd wanted most.

Well, you must have been at least, I don't know, you must ha
been . . . uncertain? George moved his hands in the air wh
he talked, just like his mother, and Huba always watched hi
amazed at the miracle of genes. The old wrestler took a sip of l
hangover concoction and said it had happened too fast for hi
to be afraid, not because he was immune to fear.

When Christopher asked what he was afraid of, and Thom
nodded along eagerly with the question, Bánko glanced at Hu
who shifted in his chair, hoping that maybe, just this once, l
friend could avoid bullshitting a bunch of kids.

There was this big house on Andrássy út, Bánko said, aski
the boys to picture it, which they did, with the eagerness y
bring to the worst scenes in horror films, a curiosity ma
stronger by not wanting to see it, not wanting to listen, the s
in your fingers growing wider with each scream and spatter.
was a street that had been built for midnight carriages and t
hats, ladies lifting a hand to footmen, a time when politics w
all upper-class, refined and underhanded, when oppressi
seemed less engineered than part of the natural order. The bc
looked at each other. They had no idea what Bánko was talki
about. Huba glowered.

The house that scared Bánko stood alongside the pride
Austro-Hungarian mansions, three- and four-storeyed, paint
with the secessionist motifs of empire, gold and scarlet. Insi
the house, in the basement, they had cells so narrow men cou
only fit into them standing up, and they left them there, like th
for weeks, bringing them out only for beatings. Bánko asked t
boys to imagine being kept awake for days, bathtubs filled wi
acid, electrical wires taped to testicles, the sharpened plie
iron baton, china cup filled with broken teeth. The childre
eyes were wide, imagining more than Bánko could fit into t
story, as if he were lighting fuses that exploded into priva
visions, nightmares beyond any of his words. That's where th
took you, said Bánko, if you'd done something like what I'd do
   Okay, that's enough, said Huba. This stuff—the acid batht

the electrocuted testicles — this was new, part of the steady addition of detail Bánko always brought to his children's story. Not appropriate! Besides, Huba interrupted him, the Terror Háza was no longer in operation in 1960, when you fell out with Zabrovsky. Or are you forgetting that important detail? Bánko looked sadly at the boys, more pained than they were by how their father always wrecked it, as if he loved the three of them so much he'd sacrifice anything, even history, for their happiness. It didn't exist *physically* maybe, he said, but it was there in my mind. He tapped his temple and the boys nodded, irritated by their father's intrusion.

Huba didn't give a shit about who was happy and who wasn't. This is not, he said, an adventure story. It was a real thing that happened to real people. George looked at him, at his brothers, at Bánko. I thought that was the point, he muttered. Huba sighed, and while the boys turned back to Bánko he got up and went to the kitchen and made his old friend another hangover cure. When he brought it back he watched Bánko reach for it, fingers trembling on the glass as if they had only partial feeling, or were too weak to grip it right, and he wondered at the tangle of nerves that must be inside, under the skin.

They were the four toughest guys on the team, said Bánko. Next to me, of course. Sure shots for the Olympics. And there they were, between me and the door. Huba shook his head. He couldn't take it. He interrupted the story again, to say something about checking on dinner, and Bánko paused to watch him go, then hung his head a minute, trying to remember how the story went, the lies he needed to remember so that it would stay consistent.

He described the moves that got him from Zabrovsky's body to the door — double-leg takedown, gut wrench, snap-down, back suplex — and left out the fear driving him, like nothing he'd ever experienced. There was such energy in it. He left out the disappointment he felt that it had all happened without him really willing it, a bystander to his greatest victory. After that, I

ran straight to your mother's place, he said. Wait a minute. Th
wasn't right. Bánko felt like a ventriloquist's dummy, someo
putting words in his mouth. I thought you went to my fathe
place? said George. Oh, yes, silly me, said Bánko, shaking l
head. He reached up to massage his temples.

Írén's picture turned her smile on him from its place (
the wall.

The next morning Huba awoke to the smell of burni
things. Bacon. Pancakes. Hot chocolate. For Bánko, there we
only two temperatures on the stove: Off and High. He walk
down and found him flipping pancakes toward the ceiling,
the delight of the boys, though Huba could tell it pained hi
like an electric shock running from his wrist to his elbow
his neck to the small of his back to his hips, knees, ankles,
the points in his personal constellation of pain. But good (
Bánko fought through it, smiling. He handed the pan to t
boys in turn, telling them to try. They had to get it as close
the plaster as possible, points deducted for actually hitting
He demonstrated the technique to them. It was all wrist, a
an unconscious feel for distance. The four of them craned th
heads to watch each pancake fly.

Írén would never have stood for such behaviour, thoug
Huba. But Írén was dead, and here were the boys, for the fi
time in months, smiling and laughing for more than seconds
a time. Huba got himself a coffee, hoping they wouldn't noti
him, and sat in the living room, where he could watch throu
the doorway. It was always the same, every time Banko h
visited since Iren's funeral. Was this what it was like in tho
roadshows, or whatever they were, where Bánko worked?
occurred to Huba he'd never actually gone to see a single mat
his friend had participated in since they'd come to Canada. N
had Írén, as far as he knew. He wondered if this had hurt
bothered Bánko or if he preferred it that way. He wonder
now at the loneliness of that work, seeing the vision in a haze
soft focus, black and white, the crowd howling in slow-moti

wanting only to see another feat of pain, of damage, indifferent to whatever it was the men in the ring might have actually felt, or the economic necessities driving them, or the way they sometimes peered at the audience looking for a single friend. Then Huba opened his eyes wider, shook his head. He didn't have a clue.

For the next few weeks, he knew how it would be. Every day Bánko picked up the boys from school, leading them home across rail yards forbidden by law to pedestrians, over chain-link fences around loading docks, trucking lanes behind factories and mini-malls with their strewn garbage and bulging graffiti and occasional junkie snarling in a corner. These were places Huba would never go, not with the kids, not alone, and which he kept the boys out of, or at least tried to, with stories of train amputations, trespassing laws, the fines and jail-time they led to, what a sick man with a bloody syringe could do to your organs and immune system. But of course with Bánko it was adventure, the boys helping the old wrestler over fences when his knees and back failed, or witnessing the tussles he got into with the various teenagers and security guards and train engineers they met up with. Huba shook his head. He couldn't put a stop to it.

Four, maybe five weeks, until Bánko healed. There were wrestling demonstrations in the back yard. There were stories of the various circuits Bánko went out on, the list of trophies and pennants he'd won and which had all disappeared, left behind in busses or trains or taxis, hawked for a few dollars, given away, though to the boys they sounded as glorious and magical as any Olympic gold. There were feasts Bánko cooked every night, lunches he made, laundry he washed and folded and put away. It freed Huba to take care of chores neglected for months — taxes, registration for the boys' summer and winter sports, groceries, home repair, replacing last year's outgrown clothes and gear. Sometimes Huba could even just stop, just stand there staring at the trees, wander off for a day, returning to find everything in order except for the boisterous yelling and laughter and horse-

play and Bánko in Írén's old apron. He looked even stronger in
somehow. His barrel chest, the span of his shoulders, the thi
and hairy forearms stood in stark contrast to the lace edgi
He was the only guy Huba knew who could get away with it. A
every time he saw this, Huba's relief soured into a hatred he h
to get rid of, swallowing it like balled wire, before he inadv
tently voiced some gratitude in front of Bánko.

Every morning the old wrestler would ask for money a
Huba would grumble about "carrying him." But he reached in
his pocket anyhow and pulled out a pile of crumpled bills Bán
accepted with a solemn nod. From the window Huba watch
his friend hobble down the sidewalk with the hand-cart he us
at Kitchener market, and wondered how long he'd stick it (
this time, how long before this part of the cycle of self-destr
tion ended — injuries healed, a few months' sobriety, depressi
giving way to the manic — and Huba would come home one c
to find him packing a suitcase. Because the truth was, Bán
was better off depressed, sick, injured. He would always wa
him against leaving. It would fail. Bánko thought too little
him to accept any more help than he was already getting.
was too tough for that. The plan was to be the better man ri
to the end.

Later that night, the two men sat in a silence broken only
the scratch, pop, and skip of a needle traveling around the ba
of an old Sebő Miklós LP. There was nothing to say, but it seem
sufficient, a silence they could break at any time, and whi
was anyway filled with a lifetime of conversation. Finally, Bán
opened things up by apologizing for bringing up the Terr
Háza. Huba didn't buy it. Bánko always brought up the Terr
Háza whenever he told that story, and he always would.

Bánko also knew the story of Huba's father. It was all connect
now in Huba's mind — 60 Andrássy út with his father's leap in
traffic with Írén's eerily similar death — as if what the wrestl
was really after with his repetitious story and anachronisi
was reminding Huba how he'd been born into bad luck a

71

infected everyone around him. This — when Huba really thought about it — was the real reason Bánko kept coming back. This was his revenge, delicate and subtle and all the more satisfying for the fact that Bánko never once needed to mention her or give any sign of anger or do anything other than spurn even Huba's charity by going away to slowly kill himself with fighting.

Huba wanted to say it, to tell him he knew. But Bánko was always out in front of him, and tonight would prove no exception. Huba, Bánko said, they want me to fight a bear. Huba turned, shot glass of Unicum lifted partway to his lips. What? Bánko nodded. Huba shifted in his seat. He had the odd feeling that the paper in his pocket — a receipt, a grocery list, two fives and a ten — was suddenly rustling there by itself, responding to some frequency silent to the two of them. They can't be serious. Well, it's old and sick. Barely any teeth. Shits itself. They think it'll make a good show.

Bánko rose from his chair to peer at the picture on the wall, the three of them dressed in the Red Cross clothes they'd been given after climbing from the Austrian swimming pool, standing under the yellow glare of the lamps. Bánko had his arm around Írén while Huba stood to one side, fingering the lapel of his new jacket as if unsure of the quality of the material. He watched his old friend touch the picture, and thought it must be killing him not to be able to ask for a photograph, for any memento of Írén, but of course Bánko would never give Huba the satisfaction of handing over something of hers as if it was his to give, as if he was in any way responsible for her gifts.

You can't fight a bear, Bánko. I don't care how old and sick it is. Bánko turned from the photo, the scars on his face catching the light. From certain angles it looked as if he'd borrowed someone else's skin, ill-fitting and outworn and long ago discarded after one too many repairs. Then he'd settle squarely in front of you and the light would shift and most of the scars would sink back into his face. I haven't got any money left, Huba. I've run through every outfit out there. No one wants to hire me anymore. I'm too

72

old. Huba rose from his chair, sat back down. His entire bo
was itchy, from the inside out. That's because you never listen
anybody. You always have to do it your way. And now look whe
you are.

Bánko flinched and almost turned away. It was the first tir
Huba had ever seen a response like that, lasting less than hal
second, and he didn't know how to read it. True, Bánko fina
said. I never listen to anybody. Very true.

You can't fight a bear. Bánko shook his head. Probably not.]
poured the last shot of Unicum into his mouth and slid it side
side, holding it in his cheek before swallowing. You can't figh
bear, Huba repeated, aware that it was like asking Bánko to st
forever. I don't believe you're going to fight it. Huba was tryi
to laugh now, a dry ticking sound, like water disappearing in
gravel. Bánko stared at him a minute, then dropped his han
Okay, I'm not fighting a bear, he said quietly. And then, fina
as if uncorking a howl, Huba replied, You're making it all up
get to me, anyway, there's no truth to it, and anyhow tell me h(
many years has it been since Írén made her choice?

There it was. Huba looked up to find Bánko shaking his he:
But it was neither disagreement nor pity. More like Bán
had fallen down and risen quickly in surprise, embarrass(
wondering what had tripped him. You were always like th
Huba continued, coming and going. The words were an c
argument, replayed many times in his head, but they sound
different as actual sound, like nothing he cared to say. She sa
I disappeared, Huba. She said I always disappeared. But n(
she's the one who's gone. Though sometimes . . . Bánko look
around the house as if Írén's ghost had just blown past betwe
them, as if it was her passing that had left the clean floors a
tidy beds, stacked dishes and spotless counters, dust swept fr(
every corner deposited in the trash, three children sleepi
happily in anticipation of another day. But if Bánko's wc
was an attempt to summon Írén back to this world it was l(
on Huba, who saw in it only that, an attempt to realize a de

woman in the fact that she wasn't there, to reach his friend's guilt through the loss they shared.

You're right, Huba, Bánko said. You've been right about it all along. He got up and put a hand on Huba's shoulder, moving past him up the stairs. But Huba was not ready to leave it, not now. Instead of making up this bear story, why not just admit that you hate me? he said. For the sake of our friendship, you could at least admit that. But there was no answer and for a second he was tempted to chase after Bánko and beg him to stay a little longer. But it was a waste of time. Bánko would never have agreed. He was battered and sick. He'd come here to sleep.

An hour later, when Huba finally rose to go to bed he heard the creaking of floorboards overhead, the opening and closing of drawers. It was the sound of Bánko packing. Huba tried not to race up the stairs. He tried to measure his steps, to focus on the details around him. The cracks in the old plaster ceiling above the staircase seemed to have lengthened and branched off into newer cracks since the last time he'd looked at them, each with some private directive. All but one of the four lights in the chandelier had died. He stood in front of Bánko's room like a passing breeze, fist held in the air, wanting to move on instead of knock, not at all happy with the place where all this feeling was coming from. It was always like this, he angrily thought. Bánko arrived injured, tottering on the threshold like a pile of wreckage, exploited Huba's hospitality and bank account, turned the place into a madhouse, then vanished with the abruptness of someone checking out of a hotel — no warning, no farewells — the boys running home from school to find the house empty, their father's silence in place of Bánko's horseplay and laughter and stories. He was tired of being the focus of their disappointment. Bánko couldn't be allowed to leave, Huba knew it, even as he dropped his hand and turned and went to bed.

But he didn't sleep that night. He stared at the ceiling until the movement in the next room stopped, but still he listened, not for Bánko packing, but that other sound, one he'd woken

to during one of his friend's visits home many years ago, aft
Írén's death. It wasn't a sob, exactly, but a strangulation, o
that came not from a wire or pair of hands around the thro
but some pressure inside, as if Bánko was choking on his ov
stomach. There it was again. Huba got up and crept to the do
hoping to catch him doing it. That's all he wanted, to catch hi
at it, just once. But every time he opened the door, as he d
tonight, the sound died. There was only Bánko snoring and t
sheets rising and falling.

11

Bánko was gone the next morning before anyone awoke. Hu
jerked up in bed, an hour after he should have had the bo
ready for school, and raced around flicking on bedroom ligh
and tearing blankets off three sleepy bodies that shambl
into the bathroom to stand in line by the toilet to pee. Whe
is Bánko? they asked, looking around. He'd been getting the
out of bed and ready for school for weeks. He's gone, Huba sa
wanting to find Bánko and kill him for the disappointment
saw in their eyes, for the way George cried, old enough if n
consciously to know, then unconsciously to suspect that Bán
might soon be dead. Do you think he'll come back? Of cour
said Huba, though he was no more sure of it than his son.

Once the boys had eaten and been delivered to school he we
through Bánko's room, tearing sheets off the bed, emptyi
the laundry hamper of stray socks and underwear and T-shi
left behind either because they were soiled or because they h
holes. He found a few cheque stubs, matchbooks picked up
hotel lobbies, a tourist brochure, unbelievably enough, fro
some place called Coal Lake, Ontario. He added these, as
always did, to the pile of stuff Bánko left behind last time, a
which, as far as Huba could tell, he hadn't touched or looked
since. Later that afternoon, during a visit to the Kitchener Pub
Library, Huba went through this stuff, noting down releva

phone numbers and using the library's resources to find the rest. In between visits to directories and phone books and business registries, especially when a phone number or address proved elusive, he was drawn into a certain section of the stacks. It was like some nightmare corridor, at the end of which is the door you don't want to open, and seems to be approaching you rather than the other way around, the knob reaching for your hand in slow motion, as if it was you being twisted and opened. He was looking up articles on bear attacks. He couldn't help himself. Each picture, each news article he found there was worse than the last. He kept superimposing Bánko's face on the victims. Men with their heads crushed between jaws. Arms broken, dislocated. Crawling a half mile on shredded legs before the bear returned to finish them off. It didn't help that most of the animals in the reports were old and sick and injured themselves, which was the reason they'd come so close to civilization in the first place. Once in a while somebody fought one off, thumbs gouged into the animal's eyes, knife between the ribs or across a major artery, their dogs driving it into the forest or up a tree or over a cliff. There was also the flip side of the story, equally terrifying and sad, of years of abuse, starvation, indignity, the bears finally lashing out under the big top, in a sideshow, the back of a cage at the zoo, taking a performer or trainer or keeper with them. Who fought a bear if he didn't have to? wondered Huba.

In the evenings, he called the numbers. The people on the other end had no time for him or his questions. Their conversations were measured in seconds. Is Ray Electric there? Never heard of him. He might go by the name of Károly Bánko. Nope. Charles Banks? What are you, the FBI? Big guy, scars on his face, wrestler? Sounds like my mother-in-law. Look, if you hear anything can you call me, please? No. The conversations went on that way, if they even got past the first two sentences. Still, Huba went through with it, getting nowhere, crossing each number off his list.

12

The phone finally rings two days later, at night, after the bc
have long been in bed. Huba? The voice on the other end arriv
from a distant star. Huba, what's going on? Is everything oka
They've never spoken before when Bánko was on the road. Hu
you've been calling everybody. What's going on?
Huba stares at the phone. All those days and weeks of fail
attempts to track Bánko down and here he is. Where are yc
Huba asks. Bánko says he's at the Motel Six in Thunder Bay, b
only for another two nights. Then he has to travel to Deer La
By canoe. No roads, you see. Huba's mind reels. You can't fig
the bear, he says. I know I've said it before, but I mean it. Y
need to come home. Home? asks Bánko, and it seems to Hu
as if Bánko were in shock, as if he'd been waiting many years i
Huba to say that one word—home. Maybe, he whispers. May
I should. Is this real, Huba wonders, or a feint?

If you're broke I could send money, Huba replies. I have lc
of money. This last bit is too much, Huba realizes. A cheap sh
It doesn't cost much for a bus ticket, replies Bánko, showi
such restraint with the answer he might have given it feels
Huba as if he's been knocked to the floor. He sits there a minu
uncertain of what to say next. Or, rather, how to say it, sin
he knows the what, only he's never been able to put the kind
words around it that didn't imply total surrender, acknowled,
ment of all he's done wrong. Come home, Bánko, he says aga
Come home. There's a long pause, then a sound, somethi
indrawn, a breath or a thought. I'll need money, Huba.

He wires it that afternoon, asking the bank clerk to se
confirmation to the front desk of the Motel Six. He watches t
clerk struggling on the phone with someone he keeps ref
ring to as "the concierge" on the other end. Concierge, he sa
You know what that is? That's your job. There's shouting frc
the receiver. The clerk has to pull the phone from his he;

Okay, he says. Okay, Frank. We are wiring money to one of your guests, Frank. Is that okay with you? Another long pause, more yelling from the receiver. How about I just give you the details, Frank? After that, Huba checks the train and bus schedules every day. He sits in the living room staring at the clock, trying to predict how long it will take Bánko to get from either of the terminals to his place. He watches the minute hand. After a while he gets up and goes to the kitchen, trying not to go back to the schedules to see when the next train and bus are coming in. He tries not to think of the pit with the bear in it, Bánko lowered down on ropes, the sand on the floor, the jagged grins along the faces encircling him. As one day turns into another, Huba finds himself detouring on his way home from the library, and then on his way to the library, until he isn't going to the library at all. He's sitting on a bench in the train station, under the roof when it rains, outside when it's hot, watching commuters line up along the platform, alight from carriages, heat billowing from under the wheels. The train conductors, the ticket takers, they know him on sight now, nodding a curt hello. Or he's in the bus station, glancing at the expectant faces of those lined up, already tired from the journey ahead. He's there so often he recognizes some of them. They are all regulars now. Whenever a bus pulls in he gets to his feet, craning his head. He's already seeing Bánko get off the bus, eyes down, ashamed at having made him wait for so many weeks and months and years, in what amounts to the first real cheap shot of his career. But then Bánko opens up his arms to wrap them around his old friend, and Huba, finally sensing an opening, gives him a good one, right in the face.

Four by Kline Car

They are premiering Kline Caro's *Corroded* (2003) at the Gra
Théâtre Lumière in Cannes. The light of the screen h
Caro's face like a blue wash over a renaissance Madonna. He h
a ring of coke around one nostril.

The film's setting is a dinner party in a villa in the Rózsadon
District of Budapest — cornices dripping with motifs of poppi
gardens filled with towering lilacs; grounds encircled by an c
stone wall. The guests are in their mid-thirties, alighting fro
expensive cars in the breezeway. By the time hors d'oeuvr
are served they are middle-aged. When soup arrives they a
sixty. At the main course they are seventy-five or more. Eati
dessert, they look half dead, wrinkled bags of bones and faili
organs, gibbering nonsensically, most of the food ending up
a cheekbone or chin. And just before the mercy of the end cred
aperitifs are served to a party of corpses rotting in their chair
    Their dinner conversation starts with a woman saying th
didn't know. Nobody knew. How could they have? The peop
were put on trains, and why, she'd like to know, should anyo
have thought there was anything wrong with that? She tr
elled by train herself during the war. Okay, first class, b
still. Even Horthy, the great Regent, thought Hitler was on
shipping them out for slave labor. Strictly slave labor! Not o
mention of murder anywhere. You should also remember th
are a people condemned to suffer until the end of time. Tha

their lot in history — nothing to be done about it. It even says so in the Bible, and they should know because they wrote it! At least Horthy managed to save most of them in the capital, until he was deposed and a puppet government installed — so that's something. Sure, the ones in the countryside all died, but that's only five hundred and fifty thousand, give or take. A drop in the bucket compared to what happened in places like Poland. And let's face it, that number's probably exaggerated. It's probably closer to five hundred thousand, even four. Who knows how many exploited the situation to disappear, get out of debt, escape a failing marriage, emigrate to Israel, put some distance between themselves and the kids? And now, when they're ruining the country all over again, everyone expects us to applaud them like a bunch of monkeys just because of what happened back then, which wasn't even our fault to begin with.

Frame by frame, with a subliminal grace, the villa ages with them, its bricks and mortar turning slowly into flesh — first pink, then gray — the veins and arteries ever more visible — green, then blue, then black. Once in a while, a guest pulls back a curtain and peers out and recoils from a figure glimpsed in the failing light. The figures have the bodies and heads of humans, but tails like rats — a shirtless man covered in blue tattoos holding a young girl on a leash; a leering geriatric counting keys, forelocks swinging; two barrel-chested thugs blowing each other. Each time the guests peer out, the figures have multiplied and the villa has decayed further into a mound of waste.

After the premiere, Caro is interviewed in *Le Figaro*. The dateline of the article is Cannes, May 19, 2003. In the accompanying photograph he is standing by the beach, under a palm tree, with a young woman, Donna Giacobbo, whose uncertain relationship with the director has all the mystery and erotics of a fashion spread. She films the entire interview with a digital recorder. The day is overcast, pre-storm, dark clouds massing on the horizon. Caro seems present enough in the photograph, but his answers to the interviewer are so vague it's like the ink

they're written in is about to evaporate from the page. Ask
about his family, he responds: "There are people so stupid th
are impervious to reality. The best you can hope for is to offe
them so deeply you become a permanent part of their men
landscape. Like a specter. Whenever they begin to feel happy,
have a moment of joy, they remember you and the things you
said and it spoils everything." Caro smiles as if he intends
wrap his lips around his head. His teeth are crooked and yell(
the ends of his fingers brown with nicotine. "I used to go hor
whenever I felt that my presence had worn off. That they need
a reminder. But you see," he smiles until it seems his mouth
too full of teeth, more teeth than any one person should have
was too successful." He closes his eyes. "I can still feel their ra
across half a continent. It comes to me like radio waves." T
interviewer presses for more detail but Caro looks at the s
and reminds him that Kline Caro is not his real name. "Yor
never track down those people," he says. "All you'll get of them
what you see in the films — an impotent wrath." These are t
last words of the interview. Caro refuses to answer any mc
questions. Giacobbo remains silent as well. Her camera e
follows Caro to the beach, his smile faded, his eyes lost in t
rain-spattered haze.

■

At the same time, in Berlin, another woman, Sela Petschau
also in her mid-twenties, imagines Caro's next film. She h
seen *Corroded* twenty times and each time laughed longer th.
before. She writes Caro a letter and includes with it a pictu
her face in the low light of the theater. She says he's the fi
filmmaker she's seen — the first writer, first musician, fi
artist, first anything — in whose work every cell of the bo
seems either a cog or a wheel. Only he hasn't fully realized tl
in *Corroded*. But next time he will.

   It's not clear what happens next, what the nature of th(
correspondence, if any, is, since the only surviving letter is th

first one, lovingly captured by Giacobbo's digital recorder. But she is there, along with Giacobbo, at the premiere of *Unsalvageable* (2006) at the Toronto International Film Festival. The two women are always standing apart, though Giacobbo is more on the periphery than Petschauer. There is a photograph from the opening gala showing Caro next to David Cronenberg and Kathryn Bigelow. Only half of Giacobbo's face can be seen, in profile. Petschauer is on the other side of the group, also in profile. It's as if the two women are guarding Caro from some unseen guest, but Petschauer is holding a pen and notebook, its pages covered in scribble. At the CIBC/Fontana Reception, traditionally held on the third night, both women linger at the edge of Caro's circle, while Caro, teeth bared, holds his hands high in the air in imitation of some monster from the silent era. In paparazzi photos taken during the festival, Giacobbo and Petschauer are always to either side of Caro, never closer than arm's length, often several or more bodies away. Petschauer is never without her notebook, Giacobbo never without the digital recorder. Other celebrities avoid them, and when they can't there are sharp words, and Petschauer has to tear out a page and give it to one of them, and Giacobbo must prove that she has in fact deleted the scene.

Unsalvageable is the story of rats. Many at TIFF thought it would be a children's movie, maybe animation, but it is neither. These are not cartoon rats, nor CGI rats, but actual rats in an actual medical-grade dumpster filled with what looks like actual biological waste. Here, the rats make their home, sucking on the ends of syringes, nosing between vials filled with secretions, nibbling biological matter dropped into trays, bags, and buckets during operations. The characters all speak in rat, their words transcribed in subtitles at the bottom of the screen. But ultimately *Unsalvageable* is a melodrama about the naming of a child. Rat A (1), who has named his son, Rat A (2), after himself, would like his grandchild, Rat A (3), similarly named, in keeping with tradition.

"This is the way it is done in the dumpster—the eldest s‹ takes the father's name," he says, towering over Rat A (2) wi his broader shoulders, longer rear legs, sharper claws, outsiz teeth, and wellsprings of mindless rage. "I've given you my nar and you must do the same for your son."

"Your name — *our* name —" Rat A (2) replies, "is a bullsl name: Rat A. Who the fuck ever heard of a name like that? W not Benjamin? Or Henry? Or Sam?"

"Sam," snorts Rat A (1). He pronounces it "Shah-muh." "Tha no goddamn kind of name. It sounds like one of *them*."

There is a subplot involving the hospital's medical staff. Wh they bring out garbage or step outside to have a smoke or ev drive past the dumpster in a car, the rats grow paranoid. "We surrounded," they say. "Everyone would like to see us go extin‹ It gives their appetites a merciless edge. They are always on t lookout for traps, exterminators, poison, always safeguardi what is theirs with extreme prejudice, taking the moral hi‹ ground when other creatures — mice, crows, dogs — cor begging. They say they need to preserve themselves, the culture, first, before helping anybody else, even if it means ne‹ helping anybody else. It's the correct thing to do.

"So, your first impulse is to preserve a people whose fii impulse is to think only of themselves?" one of the crows fina asks, desperate with the onset of winter. "What's the point saving yourselves? Wouldn't it be better if you all disappeared

"Oh, you'd love that wouldn't you?" they reply.

In the culminating scene Rats A (1), (2), and (3) are on the ed of what looks like a large piece of raw liver, clearly diseas‹ surrounded by a pool of viscous liquid, green-tinged, in whi they are planning to christen Rat A (3).

"Name him after me," says Rat A (1). His tone is final, viole beyond reason.

Rat A (2) is holding the baby protectively, shaking his he‹ "His name is Sam."

"It's that mate of yours — the one this time around — isn't

That's the problem. I should never have let you marry her. Tell me," Rat A (1) continues. "She's not from the dumpster, is she? Snuck in from somewhere else, right?"

"Her family has been here three generations," says Rat A (2).

"Three! That's all?" Rat A (1)'s teeth make a snicking sound, like knife points coming together. "Is she a believer at least?"

At first Rat A (2) says nothing, staring blankly at a puddle in which the audience sees his father's reflection towering over his. Then, without lifting his head, he says softly, "She's got nothing to do with you."

"She's got *everything* to do with me," Rat A (1) growls. "You — all of you — are part of me — *my* family, *my* lineage — including that cunt wife of yours. You got that?" This time Rat A (2) stays silent, and Rat A (1) grins at him as if he's less than shit. "You know as well as I do that it's the mother's job to put those children's hands together to pray before they go to bed." Rat A (1) does not wait for Rat A (2) to respond to the criticism. "Does she believe in anything at all?" he continues, bringing his lips, black and sinuous, close to Rat A (2)'s ears. "Is she one of those people who thinks you can be *spiritual*," he spits the word, "without being *religious*?" He grabs Rat A (2) by the shoulders and spins him around. "Or does she," he smirks, "believe in 'a spirit that moves all things?'" He laughs derisively now, bending down to leer into his son's face. "Or is she—" and here Rat A (1) pauses for effect — "one of the *tribe*?"

Rat A (2) is looking at the ground, making a soft mewling sound to quiet Rat A (3), who has begun squirming in his arms.

"I knew it!" says Rat A (1). "Nothing against them, you know. Don't think I'm a racist or anything. Well," he sighs, "our family's never been good with money, so maybe Rat A (3) will inherit that at least."

Rat A (2) finally breaks his silence. "That's not his name! That will never be his name! You can fucking well forget it."

Rat A (1) scuttles closer to him, cranes his neck, peers into his eyes. "Is that so?"

Rat A (2) tries to take a step back, but stops, since he's alrea
at the edge of the liver, his talons swiping at the liquid behi
him, looking for a foothold. "Yes, that's so." When Rat A (1) tak
a step closer, Rat A (2) makes a last attempt to save himself. "W
would you even want him named after you, anyway, if he's g
her blood in him?"

It is the final provocation. "My grandson will never have a dr
of her blood in him." Rat A (1)'s voice is terrifying, pure ha
as if a trap had snapped on his tail. The older rat is on his s
then, with a fury that envelops them in a blur of spinning bodi
and rapid-fire clicking of teeth. Rat A (2) tries to fight back, b
he's hampered by trying to protect Rat A (3), and is smaller a
weaker in any case, and soon he's a bloody mess, missing a p;
half a leg, huddled on the floor breathing in and out of a hole
his throat as if each breath were the breaking of a rib cage. F
A (1) rises above him but then does something strange. Inste
of finishing off Rat A (2) he steps over him and presses his no
to the baby, still blind, eyes sealed, squirming on the grou
where he's fallen.

Then Rat A (1) eats his grandchild alive.

He starts at the feet and moves up from there, tearing into t
baby. In a frenzy of squeals Rat A (2) tries to rise, but his bo
spasms whenever it leaves the ground, blood pumping from l
wounds, and he grows weaker and weaker until all he can do
lie there, staring in horror. The grandfather's jaws crunch dov
on the baby's head.

Credits.

The audience sits in a silence broken only by shuffling feet, t
creak of chairs. They are whispering — "That bit, eating the ba
was that real?" — and the longer they wonder, the more th
refusal to acknowledge it feels like cowardice. Rat A (2)'s attack
Rat A (1) seemed fake, computer enhanced, while the devouri
of the baby had the rushed and jittery feel of a documenta
reminiscent of war zones and tsunamis and riots spilling in
the street — the sort of shot for which you only get one take.

Halfway into the credits someone in the theater begins to laugh. It's Caro, head thrown back, one hand across his gut, laughing and laughing as if he's about to lose control of his bladder. At this point, ninety-nine percent of the audience flees. It's almost a stampede. Tomorrow the critics will be horrified, scathing. They'll say Caro went too far, from the careful black comedy of *Corroded* into a tasteless American sensationalism.

But those who stay for the end credits see something else: the camera moves like an X-ray into the belly of Rat A (1), who has tunneled into a pile of wet garbage to sleep off his meal. The camera travels through fur, skin, ribs, the stomach wall, chewed up bits of grandchild, down to the level of cells, which are gold. Each one is a cog or a wheel. One after another, they click into place, until there's a hundred, a thousand, a million, turning on themselves. When the camera pans out again we see the baby rat, alive inside his grandfather's belly, opening his eyes, then mouth, his sharp little teeth easily capable of chewing their way out. But instead of doing that, he turns, and there in the background is a golden city. Then the screen goes black. The five people left in the Lightbox, including Caro and Giacobbo and Petschauer, stand and clap.

Unsalvageable goes on to a limited first run. None of the critics mention the post-credits scene. But the following year it starts to rise in cult status, moving from art-house to art-house cinema as a deeper layer of critical insight — driven by scholars rather than reviewers — begins to reappraise it. The film's notoriety is helped along by animal-rights protesters, who add it to their lists of westerns and war movies and biblical epics that profit from the violation of animal life. There are scattered protests in Berlin, Rome, Paris, Los Angeles, with pickets and chanting and Caro wanting to have his photograph taken alongside them. One time, in London, he is knocked to the ground after asking a tired picketer if he can hold her placard for her. Three protestors jump him and Caro rolls around on the ground, absolutely stoned, elated with the pain. In defense of *Unsalvage-*

able, cinephiles cite the work of Dorothea Leimann, the fi
scholar to publish an article on the importance of the film
twenty-first-century European cinema. "Here are all the old r
of Hungary —" she writes, "fascism, patriarchy, xenophobia
except they are not old at all. They have kept themselves you
through cannibalism." The essay ends with a direct messa
to Caro himself: "The next logical step is through the gates
the yellow city glimpsed in the post-credits scene. Here, Car
filmmaking comes to an end."

It is unclear whether Caro contacts Leimann as a result of t
article, or if she contacts him. But she is present, along wi
Giacobbo and Petschauer, in Budapest during Caro's term
head jurist at the Új Európa Film Verseny in 2009. In pho
graphs the three of them are constantly watching Caro ma
a fool of himself. He closes down the gala evening in a stup
He is the last to leave the barge party during the tradition
mid-festival "second gala," falling from the gangplank in
the Danube, bobbing and swallowing water until he is rescu
near the Erzsébet híd. He remains on the Halászbástya fo
full day and night after the closing festivities, refusing to lea
when pressed by security, finally bribing them to be allowed
stay and sending a guard to buy more champagne. He invit
passersby to join in and pays the orchestra overtime until t
lead violinist falls over from exhaustion. There are pictures
Caro in casinos, at private parties, in the homes of sponso
goofing on the red carpet with celebrities, riding a bicycle do
the *rakpart,* teeth rattling in his gums. In every photograph t
women seem less companions of Caro than witnesses to hi
Leimann stands closest, though always beyond reach. Past k
stands Petschauer, and then, further out, Giacobbo, her face (
in half by the frame, as if she were already spinning out of or
detached from whatever pull Caro first exerted. By this poi
no one from the press is allowed to speak with Caro, unle
they're asking what he'd like to drink. Pointed questions end
drawing in one of the women, who quietly takes the journal

aside while Caro laughs and turns away as if he never heard anything at all. The women's answers are so exact, so distilled, they seem like code. When asked what his next film will look like, Leimann answers, "Like lemons." When asked what the subject matter will be, Petschauer replies, "Traffic." When asked who the principal actors will be, Giacobbo responds, "The missing." *Decrepit* (2009) is preceded by rumors. The critics are now talking about Caro's final three films as a trilogy. None of them mention that they ever thought of *Unsalvageable* as anything but a masterpiece. By then, Caro and the three women are living in a restored villa in the Rózsadomb District. At night they wander drunk down terraced steps. They stop to smoke cigarettes between stone walls overflowing with roses. Streetlights rise into the night air on cinderblock pylons. The silence and scents of the old gardens are overpowering, broken only by an occasional car slowly following the curves up the hill. It could be a scene from Caro's films, rather than what it is — a documentary.

Decrepit opens with a man standing in thick, wet smog. It is not a romantic image. It looks, in fact, as if the sky were swimming in piss. The suitcase in his hand, the long trench coat, the trilby hat suggest the man has just arrived in the city. He looks closely at a wall, reaches out, peels off a chip of paint. Beneath it there is more paint, an earlier coat exactly the same color, cracked like eggshell, and he digs a fingernail into that, peeling off a flake, only to find more of the same. The camera pans back and the audience sees that the whole city, every wall, is covered in the same paint, to the exclusion of any other, except for the windows, which reflect the smog. With a hand on his heart, the man takes a deep breath and moves along, searching for an address written in an official letter.

This is pretty much the movie: a camera follows the man — who seems to be a detective — from address to address in the yellow city, each office more bureaucratic and run-down and unclear in its function than the last. In each of them he pulls out

a photograph of Rat A (3) from *Unsalvageable* and asks if they
seen or heard or received paperwork about this missing ch
Nobody reacts to the fact that it is a photograph of a rat. Th
responses are abusive non sequiturs.

DETECTIVE: Have you by any chance come across this b
  [Shows the picture.] Last name A (3), first name Rat? I've go
  reason to believe he came to this city.
CLERK: I believe the Roma of Zámoly have no place amo
  human beings.
DETECTIVE: Please, anything at all would help. He's just a kid.
CLERK: North African and Arab animals — nothing but hyena
DETECTIVE: No, no identifying features to speak of, apart fr
  being a rat. I suppose he'd get by on scavenging, which cou
  mean multiple addresses. Or none at all.
CLERK: There is only one reason for the endless manufactur
  migrant crises in Europe: the extermination of the white ra
DETECTIVE: All I know is that he was headed toward a golden c
  Kids, you know?
CLERK: It's high time to assess how many MPs and governme
  members are of Jewish origin and present a national secur
  risk.
DETECTIVE: It was several days' journey. This is the only pla
  around that fits the description. I figured he might have fou
  his way to you or another of these offices. Maybe he got pick
  up by the police?
CLERK: Why would any man want to stick his dingdong in
  another man's shitty asshole?
DETECTIVE: Well, okay, thanks anyhow.

The detective winds his way deeper into the city. The numl
of street kids increases, but none of them are rats. In fact,
does not find a rat anywhere, despite rooting through rott
garbage bags in back alleys, descending into sewers, openi
stall door after stall door in filthy underground latrines. In t

last scene, he calls the client who hired him, Rat A (3)'s grandmother, whom he simply refers to as Mrs. A (1). The detective painstakingly lists the places he's searched, people he's spoken to, expenses he's incurred, in trying to find her grandchild. He says he's sorry, he's done all he can, there are no leads, no offices left to visit, no nooks and crannies in the city he hasn't checked.

The voice at the other end grows more and more shrill until the audience can hear it whistling from the receiver: "I believe in something called normalcy. I have also learned that what is outside the scope of normalcy is not normal. We are living in the context of a two-thousand-year-old culture, or on the ruins of this culture. It is not a woman's task to earn the same amount of money as a man. Her job is to fulfill the female principle — namely to belong to someone and to give birth to children for someone."

The detective waits patiently for her to finish. "Yes, I understand. I am sorry for your loss. Please accept my condolences." He presses the button to hang up.

When he turns, there is a large rat waiting for him. It leaps at his throat.

The end.

The credit sequence unfurls against a background of yellow flakes falling through darkness. The post-credits scene is nothing more than this deepening pile of paint chips burying the screen.

Many in the audience fidget during the premiere. Many more leave. There are reports of people standing during the show and yelling at the characters. The film is banned in Russia, Poland, Hungary, everywhere in the Middle East. There is talk of banning it in the US. Somehow it manages to offend both the right and the left.

The critics are unanimous in their praise. Caro has brought political agency back to the movies. He is drunk continuously at the Cannes Film Festival. He trips and stumbles and lies on his

back, refusing to rise from the red carpet during the premie
In the end, the three women go in without him. Petschauer
visibly pregnant in her Dior gown. On day three of the festi
Caro is photographed snorting heroin in the ladies' room
the Gotha Nightclub. On day five he is asked to leave the fam
Ocho Water Park, where he is caught going down the childre
waterslide in a tuxedo he claims he hasn't taken off—much le
cleaned—the entire time he's been at the festival. On day
he is asked to leave. The scandal, and the banning of the fil
in so many countries, ensures *Decrepit*'s success. It is the mc
profitable of Caro's films.

■

From here, the story descends into domesticity. Caro returns
the villa in Rózsadomb. There are no interviews. Reports surfa
that he has signed away his freedom for a stint at the Paracels
Recovery Facility in Switzerland, but the few photos shot
paparazzi show an indistinct man who might or might not
Caro sitting on a park bench in the facility's garden. Once ir
while he plucks a flower and tries feeding it to a squirrel.

One year becomes two, two turn into three, by year fo
Criterion has remastered Caro's films into Blu-ray and bundl
them into a trilogy, *Three by Kline Caro*, including a fourth DVD
outtakes, interviews, and commentary and a booklet featuri
essays by prominent scholars. It is the sort of release th
suggests the summation of a life's work.

His reputation improves with obscurity. Caro become:
visionary, part of a radical seam in European intellectualism
madman who nonetheless predicted the rising tide of anti-Se
itism, Muslim-hatred, economic xenophobia, the ever-
creasing incidence of men and women in the retro uniforms
extremism. There is no compromise in his films, no mercy,
dissolve into sentiment. Once in a while a centrist or left-wi
politician will quote him or publicly wonder what Caro wor
say about it all.

Rat Cinema appears six years after *Decrepit*. The director of photography is Donna Giacobbo, the film editor Sela Petschauer, and the executive producer Dorothea Leimann. It has the feel of old newsreels, the melancholy of images once thought vitally important now faded. Images of Caro moving around a film set, talking to actors. Images of Caro discussing scripts. Images of Caro in Berlin, New York, Los Angeles, London, Paris, Shanghai, Sydney, São Paulo — drunk and belligerent all over the world. The three women hold exactly one interview for the documentary, at its premiere in Venice. Giacobbo says it was Caro's idea from the start, that he hired them to record the most important years of his career. She is not crying as she says it. In fact, she is not even frowning. "This is his last film," adds Leimann, "the completion of his tetralogy." In the audience, a representative from Criterion sputters, but Leimann shrugs. Giacobbo picks up where she left off. "Caro paid us very well," she says. "He needed to, given the shit we had to put up with." Petschauer watches the women talk, but says nothing.

In *Rat Cinema* Kline Caro finally goes home. The scenes feel like outtakes. A camera, shaky and handheld, walks itself through an iron gate set into an old stone wall, through a garden filled with towering lilacs, to the back door of a villa dripping with motifs of poppies. The camera enters without knocking, establishing an intimacy with the place, moving first to a study lined with immaculate books on Loos, Gropius, Le Corbusier, Niemeyer, van der Rohe. The high desk is covered in blueprints. The camera moves through rooms filled with original oils, secessionist furniture, Herend porcelain, and finds an old man, gray hair sticking in every direction, sitting on a wooden bench in the courtyard, reading a book on Ödön Lechner. He seems old only in the face and is otherwise a big man, a good half foot taller than Caro, broad-shouldered, stout, filled with purposeful energy. He looks up and brightens, as if the camera is his long-estranged son.

The view swivels now onto Caro, whose face has collapsed, decades of self-harm suddenly removed without filling in what

has grown old and worn. He looks like a freakishly aged chi
"Tamás," Caro says to his father. He extends a hand, but t
gesture is preceded by a slight forward motion, as if he wa1
something more, to throw himself into the old man's arms. F
father brushes aside the handshake and clasps his son in a h
so tight it makes Caro bare his teeth. "Tamás yourself," he sa
It's clear now they're speaking in Hungarian, golden subtit]
scurrying across the bottom of the screen. The old man hol
Caro at arm's length, worried by what he sees. "Kline Caro i:
skeleton," he says unhappily. "Come." The camera shoulders
way after the old man, passing into a kitchen tiled in color1
ceramic, with a wooden sideboard covered in Székely carvin
photographs of Caro's dead mother in frames of Murano glas
    Caro watches the old man critically, suddenly recovered fro
his timidity. The camera buzzes around the room like an agitat
fly. At times, the hanging chandelier throws the shadows of t
three women on the walls or floor. "You're supposed to menti
my films," Caro says. "You're supposed to tell me you have
watched a film in twenty-five years. You're supposed to say y
find movies boring." The old man turns, back bent, in the mid(
of slicing red onion, tomatoes, peppers, kolbász. "Don't y
remember? 'I'm an old man.' That's what you always say. Tha
your best excuse."
    "Sorry," the old man mutters. He looks like a soldier who's be
ambushed, searching for some means to defend himself.
    "It's okay," sneers Caro. "When you get a chance."
    The old man turns back to preparing food, but his back
straighter now, on guard, his hands' movements less delibera
as if he can't recall what they're doing.
    "Listen," says Caro. "Even if you haven't seen the movies you
read about them. Animal cruelty. Attacking Hungary. Painti
the Flóriáns in the blackest of colors." The old man adds a
removes cold cuts from plates, like someone digging holes a
then filling them in. "I know what you're thinking, even if y
won't come out and say it." Caro apes his father's delivery: "

won't work — changing your name, disowning your family, ingratiating yourself with those people. They're all Jews in the movie business, you're not one of them, they will never make you famous.'"

The old man looks angrily at the movie camera, counting the heads of the three women behind it, though it looks, eerily, as if he's asking for help from the audience. "There is no replacement for family, *Caro*," he finally whispers. The last word of the sentence is spoken not with derision but with care, so quiet it seems to have drifted in from elsewhere, as if the old man were trying everything to acknowledge his son's wishes, to appease him, to be patient.

Caro looks at the floor, one hand across his chest, grasping the opposite shoulder. The camera travels the track marks on his arms like a fragment of some hellish itinerary. Birdsong blows in through the window.

"Do you remember the summers?" the old man says. "We used to go hiking, fishing, bicycling. I'd take you to the Balaton, to the *üdülő*. Do you remember sailing across the waves? The color of the water?" Tamás Flórián looks at the ceiling. "It was like emerald." He shakes his head. "It isn't that color anymore."

"I loved that," says Caro, looking at the camera. Don't miss this part, he seems to be saying. Or else he's telling them to turn it off. But the camera keeps running.

"God," says Caro, turning back to his father. "Can't you say any of it with feeling?" The old man, exasperated, throws up his hands. Caro continues: "Remember, during those same summers you're so nostalgic for, you used to tell me how you fought in 1956 to free Hungary from the *idegenek*. You quizzed me, over and over during those sailing trips, about the original Jewish names of General Secretary Rákosi and his 'inner circle of murderers.' I fought for 'true Hungarians.' That's what you said."

The film buzzes with static, as if the camera has shorted. When the scene resumes Caro is seated at the kitchen table. His

father is on the other side of the room, staring out the Fren
doors, wide open, lace curtains streaming into the room.]
is in the middle of a speech, as if the scene had started sor
time before.

". . . never disowned you, not even with the hate mail, the dea
threats. Not even when the neo-Nazis praised us for 'being t
sacrificial victims of liberalism.'"

Caro interrupts: "Just for the record: you agree with t
neo-Nazis, maybe not on some of the finer points, but on t
broad strokes."

"But that's not the point," the old man replies.

"Right. But it's still there, underneath it all."

"The main thing is privacy," says the old man. "Taking care
family."

"'The family name,'" quotes Caro, "'is a man's reason f
existing.'" He laughs. "Carrying those seven letters, freight
with the dead, from one generation to the next."

The old man frowns.

The frame is filled again with static.

Now Caro is standing in the garden holding an open bot
of *pálinka*. His father is seated on a bench, face in hands. Ca
has drawn himself up in imitation of the old man — puffi
out his chest, squaring his shoulders, rising on his toes. H
talking about an architectural project he's working on, a n
shopping center on the outskirts of Budapest, commissioned
"Chinks." Caro delivers the word with an edge of harshness, a
challenging his father to contradict him. The old man mumb
something, but it barely registers under the chirping songbir
in the garden. Caro laughs. "It's what they are: Chinks. Y
know, one of the partners, Mr. Wong, he was sick the other d
I asked him if he had the Hong Kong Flu." The old man looks
at Caro. He is close to tears. "You know what?" Caro says, leeri
down. "Mr. Wong didn't even smile." Caro apes being genuin
perplexed. "No sense of humor, I guess." The old man opens I
mouth, wanting to say something, but there is only a dry sou

possibly nothing more than an error in the audio. He seems resigned, diminished, his shoulders riding up his neck. "Will you let me try to be your father?" He breaks down. "Can't I at least be allowed to try?" He straightens up. "How many second chances did *you* get?"

Caro brings his hand to his mouth in shock. But then he starts to laugh, manically, bent over at the waist, the bottle falling from his hand.

Static.

Now the two men are dressed in different clothes, sitting at a small table draped with a white tablecloth in the middle of the garden. Tamás Flórián keeps adjusting his belt as if his suit is a size too small. There is wine on the table, *paprikás csirke, uborkasaláta*, an ashtray in front of Caro filled with cigarettes butted out and burning. Dinner proceeds in a muted way, as if they are having trouble finding things to talk about. Once in a while one of the women edges into the scene, then flashes out. The old man is trying to bring up Caro's successes at Cannes — "What was it like, when the juries selected your first film? I was so proud!" — but Caro, clearly drunk, and probably stoned, just sits there shaking his head, staring at him.

"Okay, listen, we're talking about a household where . . ." Caro closes his eyes to stop the world from spinning, "where there were no stories." He keeps his eyes closed.

His father adjusts his belt again. "In architecture, we have our own version of fame," he says. "Of course. But I couldn't help imagining the parties you must have . . ."

"No funny anecdotes," interrupts Caro. "No talk of what happened that day. Only what was truth and how the politicians did or didn't abide by it."

"The actresses, for example. Did you ever meet . . ."

"Endless moralizing. Outrage. Self-righteous indignation. Every progressive policy imagined in its worst-case outcome. An obsessive return, over and over again, to a need for dogmatic security." Caro opens his eyes now, looks at his father, who has

also leaned back in his chair, arms crossed in equal exasperati(
Caro leans toward him, his thumb and middle and index fing(
pressed to a point that he stabs into the air between them. "T
world outside, in all its beautiful chaos, is cancelled out, or y
wish you could cancel it out." He stares at his father, waiting 1
him to get it. "Listen, I say something, anything, personal, a1
you respond with a cliché, okay? Okay?" The old man gets up a1
walks out of the frame. Caro yells after him: " 'In every bad thi1
there's always something good.' " He laughs. "Wow, I was alwa
a fan of that one." He is performing for the camera now. "Or h(
about: 'Men do all the work, women just sign the check.' " 1
gazes off across the garden in the direction of his father. " 'Do
go out with wet hair or you'll become bald!' " He walks over to t
camera, grabs the lens on either side as if it were a face, lifts
over his head, and smashes it to the ground.

Now they are eating schnitzel off TV trays, sitting at oppos
sides of a room. Caro's father is pointedly ignoring the thr
women doing the filming. "C'mon," yells Caro. "Look at the1
When the old man gazes at the camera in bewilderment, Ca
walks over and pulls him from his seat. The old man yells
protest, but falls to the floor, wincing, cradling his wrist. Ca
ignores him and again changes his body language to reseml
the old man's, turning back to the camera. "What did you s
your name was?" His voice is a raspy falsetto. "Petschauer?" Ca
says. "What kind of name is that?"

The old man rises from the floor holding his wrist. "Cra
You're totally crazy."

Caro ignores him. His face narrows. His eyes turn mean. 1
begins to wave a hand at the camera. "Is this who you want
marry?" he asks, looking at his father. "Is this why you're t
ashamed to come visit your family?" The old man's eyes are wi
dancing in their sockets. "Don't you know," Caro yells, half bl1
bering, "that it's the mother's beliefs that become all the child
inside? Have you any idea how hard I've worked, how hard 1
father worked, how hard his father worked, for the benefit of o

country, to keep the interests of our people first?" he flutters a hand at the lens as if dismissing a fly, but really to call Petschauer over. "One of the beautiful things . . ." he says, lifting her shirt to adjust the foam pregnancy belly around her waist, then lowering the shirt again and presenting her to the old man. "One of the beautiful things in the world is all the different races in it. And it's our job to keep it that way!"

Caro steps back. "You see, that's how it's done. If you had any responsibility to your talent, to your craft, you'd have known all this shit already. You'd have been professional enough to *prepare*."

"Fuck you, you psychopath, I quit," says the old man. "Shove it up your ass!"

The screen goes black.

Caro is standing in front of the door, arms splayed, preventing the departure of the old man, who looks at the three women for help. "Why can't you just go and visit your real parents?" he says finally. Caro doesn't move. "Seriously," the old man continues. "This is supposed to be a documentary." He walks over to Caro. "Go see your real father. He'll be able to act the part properly." Caro backs up against the door. The old man steps closer, puts his hands on Caro's arms. Then it is as if Caro expects the old man to hold him up, because he begins sliding down the door, and when the old man tries to stop him the filmmaker falls into his arms, gripping him first around the chest, then waist, then knees, the old man straining against the weight. "I did do my homework," the old man says, looking for an appropriate gesture, finally settling for patting Caro's hair. He looks to the women for help. "I watched all his movies. You know what they reminded me of? Some kid crying for attention. For the love he never got." The old man lifts one leg out of Caro's embrace, then the other, watching as the director crumples. "Your father loves you, and he's a fucking monster. It's an impossible act."

The camera rests not on Caro but on the old man. It follows him down the stairs as he leans heavily on the handrail and glances back every few steps in irritation. There, on the margin

of pavement between camera and man, fall the shadows of t
three women. But you can hear Caro whispering over top
it. "They died years ago," he says, "my images weighing do\
their eyelids." The old actor disappears around a corner, but t
camera continues on straight. It moves past dilapidated sto\
and homes, and one of the shadows peels off the sidewalk
front of it and also disappears. "My dialogue stopping up th\
ears." It moves past factories and the waterfront, and by t
time it reaches the edge of a highway the other two shado\
have likewise gone their way. "They could have broken into t
world whenever they wanted but they wanted the coffins I pri
open with each film." Somehow the camera keeps going, ridi
its own shadow along a meridian, over an embankment, hi\
enough to catch the last of dusk, then down the other side o\
a fence into a junkyard stacked with flattened cars. "And this l\
one is mine," he says. "This one, too." There are no credits.

Lester's Ex

Lester Jones was active for such a short time you'd be forgiv
for not having heard of him. Official records consist mair
of photographs in newspapers between 2007 and 2013: Lester
the Northumberland conservative rally, January 4, 1995, stari
at the photographer teeth bared as if he wants to chew throu
the page; Lester under the low light of Laff'n Gaffs, howling
black and white; Lester at the G20 summit in Toronto, arr
raised against a police baton at such an impossible angle tł
he seems like the poster of a man blown into the frame. No
of the photos or articles identifies Lester by name, and anyo
who didn't know him would think he was there by accident
bystander to some other, larger story.

But then his preference was always anonymity. Myles Lyn
owner of the Laff'n Gaffs chain of comedy clubs, still ca
describe what Lester looked like. "That's probably," he gri
"because he came around in disguise so often, especially ne
the end." Lynch shrugs, troubled by memory. "By then I w
telling the bouncers to watch for him, you know? Don't let hi
in. Can you blame me? The comics were terrified — even thou
he made a lot of their careers." The windows of Lynch's offi
are smeared red and orange and blue by neon refracted in t
raindrops. "Well, Lester had a demon inside. He'd go after y
and wouldn't stop. It didn't matter what the comics threw ba
or if the audience turned against him, Lester didn't back dov

The only thing you could do was beat him up. I told him people were starting to come around to see him more than the guys on stage. You should have seen his reaction."

∎

Lester Jones was born to Nathan and Marion Jones on September 23, 1969, in Fort Erie, the second of two children. His older sister, Erika, had been killed in an automobile accident three months before he arrived. Her police file, available through the Canadian Freedom of Information Act, is filled with details of the accident, along with a snapshot given to the officers by her parents: a blonde girl in the late afternoon sun, four years old, sitting like a cowboy on the back of a black Labrador. "The family was destroyed by the accident," says Lieutenant Karl Jeffries, the investigating officer. "That part was normal anyhow." He turns the cover of the dossier back and forth. "But the guy, the father, he kept coming back to it, you know? Couldn't shake it. Had the whole file copied for himself, looked at it all the time, even added a few things of his own, like the case was some kind of conspiracy. Kept calling me for years. Said he had 'new questions.' But they were nothing. 'Was she smiling when they found her? Was she still on the dog when she got hit? Was there any hair between her fingers, like she was clinging to it when the car rounded the alley?' Crazy stuff. Stuff that made no difference one way or the other."

He closes the folder and puts a hand on it. "I'd think of Nathan Jones when I heard, later, about Lester. Of course, I was never involved in his arrests. For some reason, his cases never came to me." The light glances every which way off the surface of the photograph. "They were minor infractions." He waves his hands in the air as if clearing smoke. "At least the stuff they actually brought him in for. Misdemeanors, public intoxication, disturbing the peace — assignments they give to the junior guys. But whenever I heard about Lester I'd think of this picture, what it must have been like in that house. I mean his old man, he

called me two nights before he died. Can you believe it? Eigh
years old, stuck in a hospital bed, tubes everywhere, and
wants to know if there was any alcohol, not in her system, but
the dog's. I told him we didn't do an autopsy on the freaking do   "

∎

The last address for Lester Jones was 4B-74 Jarvis Street, ov   -
looking Saint James Park. There are half a dozen prostitut
sitting curbside. "Hey, sweetheart, if you're going in there, ta
me with you." But they go quiet at mention of his name. Lest
always treated them well, they say, though when asked abo
what that "treatment" consisted of, they go quiet again, th
disperse, muttering insults. One of them lingers a mome   ,
introduces herself as "Susie," and says she'll reveal everything s
knows about Lester "for three hundred dollars." Then, witho
waiting for a reply, she lifts her middle finger while backi
away. "You want the real story on the Heckler, you come find n   "
She turns, her body stringy in the arms and legs but flabby in t
belly and hips. The polyester skirt rides high on her backside, t
zipper only half done up. There are buttons missing from t
front of her shirt, runs in her nylons. One of the other girls ye
from across the street: "Don't listen to her. I'll tell you everythi
about Lester. Cheaper. Two hundred bucks!"
    The current tenant of Lester's apartment is Alfredo Espino   ,
a streetcar driver. "I own this place now. He was just a rent   "
sniffs Espinoza. "He left everything behind, believe it or n   .
Everything." He gestures at the closet, says it was full of cloth   ,
bags and bags of vintage three-piece suits, tuxedos, sequ
dresses, wigs — enough disguises for an army of spies. T
shelves were filled with books. Posters, paintings, newspap
clippings, personal photographs on the walls. There was still h   .
a bottle of Johnny Walker Blue in the top drawer of the dress   ,
beneath the underwear. "Who the fuck leaves behind half or ev
a half inch of Johnny Walker Blue?" asks Espinoza. "Never mi
his underwear," he mutters, pulling an old suitcase from und

his bed filled with all the memorabilia of Lester he thought worth keeping. Here are the clippings of Lester at various demonstrations, political rallies, theater events, public exhibitions, in each one of them his face circled violently in red and crossed out as if he hated the sight of himself. There's a photograph of Marion and Nathan and young Lester, who is maybe seven years old, severe in its contrasts, his mother and father in the foreground wearing black and white clothes, young Lester a step or three back, near the edge of the frame, like someone arrived uninvited. None of them are touching. None of them are smiling. The surface of the image is buried under the oil of fingerprints.

There are also five or six books checked out from the Toronto Public Library, long overdue. Paging through them, Espinoza stops at passages underlined by Lester:

> The heckler has scant interest in sole creation, the thing beautiful unto itself, being neither actor nor artist but an agent of interruption, dedicated, as we have chanced to hear, to the pause, the digression, or what our brethren to the east call the non sequitur. (Bartholomeus Wrocklage, "Fragments of a Cutting," trans. and ed. Harold Feinstein [1682]).

> Marcel Delisle — terror of dancehalls, theatres, and salons from Boston to Savannah and back again — claimed "an exclusive devotion to the accidental," stepping "naked of resources, every night, into [his] customary seat at the back of the room, taking up only the tools and opportunities made available by chance, which were in turn left behind when [he was] forcibly ejected into the street." (Madrigal de Flor [pseud.] *Pecadillos de Amor*, trans. and ed. Elise Floria Sánchez [1891]).

> Christ's announcement, at the Last Supper, that He was dining with His betrayer may have baffled the other disci-

ples, but Judas only heckled Him: "Surely, you don't mean me, Lord?" Judas knew perfectly well who the Lord meant! In this regard, the kiss in the garden was the ultimate catcall. Like all hecklers, Judas made his target rise to the occasion, to realize His full potential — the redemption of humanity itself. Then, afterwards, in an act of violent renunciation, Judas committed suicide, noose around neck having refused even that most basic of thank-yous — the thirty pieces of silver. "Better not to have been born" was the final verdict, his entire life distilled to one point in someone else's destiny, given over to realizing someone else's glory without any reward or recognition other than everlasting infamy. This, it seems to me, is the distillation of heckling to its purest, most ethical form. (Horatio Thomas, *The Cheap Seats* [1946]).

These are only a small sampling of the materials Lester collect on heckling (if his user history at the Toronto Library is to believed), though nowhere is there a notebook, or letters, or a other kind of evidence to suggest he might have been gatheri information for a study. The bits of underlining in Espinoz books seem more like an inventory of consolations, stray wor and sentences to remind Lester he wasn't alone in history.

This isolation is visible in the few videos of him. An appe - ance at Centre Stage's improv night shows him leaning ove table like a dog looking for scraps, except he's barking at B Farney, an up-and-coming comic back then, long before t international tours and movies and best sellers. The sound the footage is scratchy, fading in and out as if the micropho were a fly zooming across the room. The visuals are equally fr - mented, handheld, panning violently from Farney to Lester a back again.

"Lester Jones," Farney yells from the stage. "Still looking f acts to ruin?"

"Why, Farney, you got one?" Lester yells back.

Farney scowls, mutters something under his breath, then leaps to the edge of the stage, leaning out over the audience. "You think you're doing us a service? Like you're on a crusade? Don't you ever get sick of pretending you're not a motherfucker?" "Come on, Farney. I've given your mother a lot of satisfaction over the years."

The crowd's laughter drowns out the next exchange, at the end of which Lester again receives a roar of approval. Leaning out further, Farney lifts his middle finger. "If you want my comeback, you'll have to squeeze your ass cheeks together," he shouts.

"Oh, was that you back there? I didn't know cunts could fuck assholes."

"Well, you're an asshole who fucks cunts, so it makes sense that . . ." The remainder of the sentence disappears in the general howl.

"True. I heard the ex-wife fucked you pretty hard on that divorce settlement."

"Well, she's your sister, so you should know how hard she fucks." Lester smiles. "Nice one, Farney."

"Wish I could say the same, dickhead."

Then Lester is put into a headlock by a bouncer and dragged out the door.

■

The other videos are even more fragmented: security footage of Lester being bounced off walls; an iPhone clip of Lester mooing at a fat comic; a newsclip of Lester spitting insults at a rally. This last one, according to documentary filmmaker Hailey Nelson, is part of a CBC news report from April 23, 2013, at a campaign stop for conservative MLA Kenneth Williams in Etobicoke. Lester is standing near the podium. He keeps wiping his eyes as if the wind's blowing sand in his face. There are protestors shouting through bullhorns, waving signs, being shoved back by police whose hands are already on their canisters of pepper spray before Williams has even begun to speak. Here and there you see

groups of young men who'd later be disowned by official prot(
groups, misnamed "anarchists" in the press, milling with t
crowd, indifferent to all politics, already delirious with the id
of violence, looking for any excuse to jump in, strike out, sma
windows, set cars on fire. When the noise of the crowd subsid
Lester's lips move, almost imperceptibly, though judging fro
Williams' reaction, whatever Lester is saying doesn't need
be said loudly to take effect. Within minutes, the politicia)
handlers are pushing aside the crowd from one side, and t
police, taking note, are moving in from the other. Lester duc
into the mass of bodies.

Then the crowd loses control.

"I was working on the riot," Nelson says, running the foota
backward and stopping at a close-up of Lester's face. "It was ju
an accident that I ran across this at the CBC archives. I had
even heard about Lester before that."

She zooms in on Lester's mouth, then runs the film forwa
frame by frame to make out the shape of his lips around eve
word spoken. "From what I can see, he's saying, '*Honcho* ma;
zine, gay porn, nineteen-seventies.' He's accusing Williar
Look there! He's saying a name. David Punctual? Donald Mutu
Dunstan Mundy? I can't quite make it out. But here, look . . ." S
skips ahead a few seconds. "Look at that. If he isn't saying 'Gera
Knox,' I'll give up filmmaking forever."

It was Knox's office that shut down Nelson's documenta
long after Lester disappeared. Until the Etobicoke riot, Williar
had been Knox's main opponent in the elections and had be
up five points in the polls, a lead obliterated after he came o
and admitted to a series of risqué photo shoots in "two or thr
gay magazines" in the 1970s under the pseudonym David Mutu
Nelson received a cease-and-desist order shortly after maki
contact with Knox's senior advisor, Margot Ramsay, requesti
an interview with Knox on the connection between his office a)
that of Lester Jones. "This was the early days of my documenta
I was still putting together the proposal," she says. "They nev

even returned my call." Her grant applications were rejected. "Most of the financing comes from provincial and federal governments. Knox's office spiked them." She pulls a file and opens it. Inside is *Honcho*, issue twenty-three, December 1975, dog-eared, staples loose and rusted along the spine. One of the layouts features two men, one of them dressed as a construction worker, the other in housewife drag, fairly tame by today's standards, though revealing enough to ruin a political career. Nelson bends over the photos, adjusts the lamp, and points at the construction worker, whose face is obscured by the hard hat. "For a while I had this theory that the other guy was Gerald Knox, under the name . . ." She runs her finger along a lurid caption underneath. "Here it is. Vincent Barbaria." She laughs. "But the pictures are so shaded, especially on the face. I can't be sure. But that," she says, pointing to the housewife, "there's no question who David Mutual is." She smiles. "A good-looking guy, even in a dress."

She finds a photo of Williams from thirty-five years later. The likeness is unmistakable. "A left-wing candidate might have been able to get away with the scandal, maybe even turn it to advantage. But Williams was running on the social conservative ticket — pro-family, anti-abortion, welfare is for lazy people, the environment doesn't exist — the whole bit. It killed him. And, of course, Knox's office had the most to gain. But it would have been death, given the sympathies of their base, to reveal Williams' past directly or to risk blackmail, or if anyone found out that someone in Knox's office had contracted Lester to do it." Nelson leans over the table spread with photographs and newsclippings. "In fact, they went out of their way to express sympathy for Williams, congratulating him on his courage to come forward." She picks up one of the pictures of Lester. "He probably hated himself for doing what he did, but he must have hated Williams' politics more. There are very few appearances by Lester after that date, two or three at the most. By the end of the year, he'd disappeared."

Nelson's documentary remains no more than that: a fr,
ment of Lester whispering secrets at a rally in Etobicoke. "Th
— Knox's office — they killed my project before I even go
chance to get it going." Nelson shrugs now, though it's evide
that abandoning the project has not lessened her fascinatic
with Lester. "It wasn't even the politics that brought me to   "
she says. "It was his loneliness, you know? Here was a guy w'
went around heckling people, but I always got the sense th
there was something fiercely moral behind it. A desire to ma
the world rise to the occasion, without anyone ever finding c
that he'd done it, much less being able to thank him. In fact
sometimes wonder if it was really Knox's office that killed r
film, or Lester."

■

Margot Ramsay lives in the Annex neighborhood of Toronto. S
no longer works for Gerald Knox or his party. Officially, sh
a "political consultant," linked to a number of lobbying effo
around Indigenous issues — land claims, drinking water, edu   -
tional initiatives, dry reserves — as if she'd picked the faste   ,
hottest humanitarian cause to regain her political capital. H
rise and fall within Knox's office was swift. She guided him
the legislature and then, shortly after Lester's own disappe   -
ance, resigned for "personal reasons" never made clear. B
long ago — before the Masters in Political Science from McG
before the PhD in Governance and Management from Princetc
before involvement in community advocacy around Toron   ,
canvassing for civic politicians on the left; before the work
an aide in City Hall and then the provincial legislature — s
worked for a year in the office of Nathan Jones, MD.

Even now, two years after Etobicoke, Ramsay is wary. S
refuses to open the door until it's clear there will be no questio
about Knox or Williams. "Did I know a boy called Lester Jon
once? Sure." Margot waits, suspicious, looking for the hidd
agenda, the trick question that will lead her into talking abc

Etobicoke before she even realizes she's doing it. She fingers the lace doily on her armchair as if weighing how much she really owes Knox. Maybe, in the end, her debt is actually to Lester, to reveal at least the truth of his story. Or maybe revealing his story is actually a form of revenge, a way to get back at him for what his actions cost her.

"I've never seen such a lonely kid. He was shaking with it, you know? Like it was building up inside. There were always problems — always." She pulls out a photo album and opens it. Inside are pictures of the Jones family and Margot's own. "My parents were great friends with Marion and Nathan before Erika died. Afterwards, I don't think the Joneses were friends with anybody." She leafs through a few pages and then hands the album over. The dominant theme is backyards, barbecues, cocktails — the high summers of white-collar affluence. Nathan and Ralph Ramsay lift martinis above flowerbeds. Erika is pushed on a swing while everyone stands around, wineglasses in hand. Marion and Louise Ramsay laugh in front of a picnic table filled with salads, cold cuts, cheeses, and bottles of champagne on the day of Erika's christening. Marion, three or four months pregnant, smokes a cigarette and lifts a cocktail shaker over her head like a movie star at the Copacabana, the lights of the parlor reflecting off the darkened windows.

"I was eight years older than Erika. I remember her. Angelic and adventurous. The kind of kid, two, three years old, you have to watch all the time, or else she'll slip out the door and run off across the highway to the park. Everyone loved her, especially Nathan. He was so proud of her. Always horsing around, doing crazy things, like putting her on that dog . . ." She frowns, pauses. "Kids weren't looked after so carefully in those days. I'm not saying it was anyone's fault." Margot sits up on the couch, puts her knees together, and rests her elbows on them. "Well, once she was gone, it was different."

It was as if Erika had never existed. Her toys and clothes and even pictures were dumped on the front sidewalk the day

after her death. Nathan and Marion broke off all relations wi
neighbors and friends. They never mentioned Erika again, not
anyone. And if one of those acquaintances happened to menti
her, both Nathan and Marion would go quiet with an awkwa
ness so excruciating that sooner or later everyone else stopp
speaking of her as well, conditioned by the Jones' hostile silen
The funeral held shortly after her death was so private it mig
as well have been done at night. Not a single person was invit
"They'd been best friends — my parents and the Joneses — b
they stopped coming over, stopped inviting us. We'd see Nath
leave every morning, off to work at the clinic, and come hor
Spent just enough time outside to get in and out of the car. I
was still a good doctor, but he was distant, professional. Lest
on the other hand, we'd see around a lot. He was a lonely kid, b
not a quiet one. We didn't hear it from the Joneses, but everyo
knew the reports. I talked to him once in a while, early on, wh
he was still able to hold a conversation, before it all became sni
remarks and insults."

Margot stops, makes a silent decision, and then describ
what it must have been like in Lester's home, filled with wh
could not be spoken of, like dust on every word, a silent moth
and father brooding between meals and chores. Once in a wh
an eruption of temper or a depression so deep the boy spe
afternoons pulling at the locked doorknob of his father's stu
his mother's bedroom. Days spent at the window watching oth
kids come and go — to baseball, to piano lessons, to afternoo
in the park, to trick-or-treat. It was a life as barren as the mo
and after awhile it must have come to feel normal — bei
weightless, ignored, invisible — until it became a kind of pr
ciple or craving.

"His first name wasn't even a first name," Margot says, laughi
without actually finding it funny. "It was his mother's maid
name, Leicester, though he always spelled it L-E-S-T-E-R. It w
like Nathan and Marion couldn't handle bringing another ext
sion of themselves into the world, so they refused to give him l

own identity. Not that we were invited to the christening. They'd closed the door to everyone by then."

She remembers how it played, Lester's childhood, acting up in whatever way he could — dropping glasses, breaking windows, climbing roofs. Later, it was drugs and alcohol and as much sex as possible. Petty thefts from his mother's purse, his father's wallet, then shoplifting, breaking into vending machines, swiping the charity bank in front of the cashier, behavior so corrosive to his teachers' authority that multiple suspensions finally led to expulsion — each act planned for maximum outrage.

"He was sixteen when his father kicked him out." The whole neighborhood heard about it — shouting, slamming doors, Lester's good-bye delivered in the form of a rock hurled through the window — and also about the final transgression that proved more than his parents could stand. He went down to city hall, got up on a railing on the upper mezzanine. It looked down over the main concourse. As the city councilors walked back and forth, Lester began hurling abuse. "Alderman Grove, aka Mr. Moron, planning the Estatesway Parking Lot on the Indigenous burial ground. You knew damn well what it was. Nobody buys that shit. What? You want a piece of me? Come up here and get it, pussy." "Councilor Eberly, yeah you, jackass, what made you think getting rid of the walking mall on Main at 16th would make this a better city? Got tired of seeing your daughter down there turning tricks?" "Hey, look everyone, it's our fuckwit mayor. Coming back from your six-beer lunch in the private parking stall on P2? What, you trying to say something? I can't hear you. You're slurring your words. Drunk mayor, drunk mayor, drunk mayor." It took five policemen to get Lester down, and he spent a night in jail before being released, briefly, into his parents' custody.

"He disappeared after that. But a long time later, back in . . . Well, years ago, I ran into him — quite by accident, really — on the street in Toronto. He already had some notoriety, in the clubs, among certain political circles. I was expecting the old,

surly Lester, but he was very quiet, almost humble. He seemec
don't know . . . He seemed holy." Margot smiles, shakes her he ,
looks at the floor. "I know that sounds ridiculous: Saint Lest :
But it turned out he'd kept track of me. I was flattered. He ask :
if there was anything he could do to help. . ."

■

But as far as help is concerned, only one comic, Adele Jones (
relation), is willing to credit Lester. She snorts at some of t
remarks made about Lester by other comics over the years.
think he was careful, almost prescient, about whom he heckl(.
Name one single target of his heckling who didn't go places. Jt
look at the list: me, Jim Dement, Sally Hay, George Hayter, Jε
Billings, even Ben Farney. You ask them what their big night w ,
when they finally realized they'd come into their own. If they t
you any story that doesn't include Lester, they're lying." Adε
is calling from Chicago, where she's headlining six sold-c
months at the Fun Factory. The call is interrupted by regu]
requests from stage managers and room service and her age ,
all of whom she whispers away, hand cupped over the receiv .
"Why not ask them this: Of all the comics Lester could ha
heckled — and believe me he didn't heckle that many, not if yι
look at how many he might have heckled over those years — w
you? Why us? Night after night, he'd turn up, bringing the au -
ence with him, staying on until we'd kicked his ass decisivε .
Then he was gone. We never saw him again."

She whistles loudly to get someone's attention, whispers in: -
dibly, then returns to the phone with a story of their last meeti
in the early winter of 2013. Lester was sitting in a greasy spoon -
one of those East End places where you can buy bacon and eg
for $2.99. He was with a twitchy young woman, her face a mε
of scabs. Adele saw him through the window past a painted-
advertisement for all-day breakfasts. When she went in aι
approached him, Lester looked as if he wanted to sink throu;
the floor or, barring that, pretend they'd never met. Adele sto(

there. She'd just wanted to say thank you. Lester looked worn to the bone, his hair hanging in gray strands, his beard also gray, fallen into the deep hollows of his cheeks, and his clothes stained with what looked like months spent in restaurants like this. Adele persisted, telling him that before his arrival at Linklater's Improv Night she'd just been trying it on, half-hearted, showing up at the same place every week because it was easy and allowed her to keep a day job. Lester sighed and muttered: "Rise to the occasion or die." Then, as she continued to stand there, he scowled. "I don't even want to be a footnote." He rose from the table, and she saw how shrunken he'd become, eaten away, amazed that this same person had once been so relentless, glaring from the back row at Linklater's night after night with a ready torrent of abuse. But his tone was soft. "Glad you made it, Adele. But there are enough stories about me already." After that, there was nothing more for her to say. It seemed he'd accepted her thanks. Lester was still standing there, facing the spot where she'd thanked him, when Adele passed through the door and along the windows and off into the life Lester had prepared her for.

■

Adele wasn't the last person to see Lester alive. That was Susie Johnston, twenty-four years old, on a night in March, an exact date she no longer remembers. It was snowing then, at the long end of one of those Toronto winters, minus thirty degrees Celsius, stretching far into the spring. She was coming down from a week of bad tricks, bruised and torn, days on meth, and Lester had taken her in, given her his bed while he eased his own wrecked body under a sheet on the couch.

He was drinking a lot, she says, but it was all good stuff — Bushmills Twenty-One Year Old, Blanton's, Johnny Walker Blue, Aberlour 18 — and he was never drunk, just keeping it going glass after glass, steady from noon until night. It was as if the drinking didn't matter as much as disposing of the roll of money

in the dresser, enough fifties and hundreds to clog a doz
toilets. He'd pull out another handful of bills and head to t
nearest liquor store, leaving the dresser drawer open, not cari
if it tempted her, if she stole, telling her to take what she want
though Susie swears she never did. She loved Lester too mu
for that. Now, against the ball of her thumb, she riffles the thr
hundred dollars she's received to tell his story.

"He'd come back with groceries, more booze. That was the or
time he ever went out. We were there for weeks like that, a
the whole time I couldn't figure out if he was hiding becau
someone was after him or because he needed to burrow away f
a while to figure things out. He was making up his mind abc
something."

They never slept together. Lester insisted he was too old f
Susie. The only time he came near her was to hold her dov
when she shook from withdrawal, to bar the door when she we
insane for more, when she wanted to get down to the street,
hustle, to take another loan from her dealer. He pulled cott
balls and iodine from behind the bathroom mirror and swabb
the abscesses along her arms, above her heel, down the side
her neck. He held her fingers when she started picking at sca
her nails traveling from one sore to the next like some torturo
connect-the-dots. He would rock her gently, humming. Wh
she screamed on the toilet from taking a piss, Lester put ice
a bag for her to hold between her legs. And all night he sat w
her, smiling as she spewed rage and hate, every curse she cou
think of, until days and nights later she was too exhausted f
anything but sleep. When Susie awoke, she was always tucked

And in the quiet moments between symptoms, she listen
He was setting out the problem, always in shorthand, like
thousand-piece jigsaw of sea and sky, each one too difficult
fit with the rest. He mentioned a name, "Knox," several tim
and described him as a "protégé," someone he'd helped rise
local and provincial politics. "Lester said Knox had failed hi
Susie says. "He only used his power to keep himself in offi

Lester said Knox was like a rat trapped in the plumbing." She wasn't sure if he hated Knox or was afraid of him. "I should never have gotten involved in politics," he said. Whenever Williams' resignation came up, or, worse, the Etobicoke riot, on television, in a newspaper, including the three people who'd died in the stampede, crushed up against cars and fences, Lester turned the page or turned the program off.

At other times, Lester talked about his childhood, his parents, and then his sister. He knew very little about Erika, next to nothing. But discovering her had been the most important moment of his life. "I wasn't a good person, not a very good person at all, before I found out about Erika." He said it as if the discovery had come too late to save him. "She made me think about what others had lost," he mumbled. "She lost everything. And I think, my father and mother, they lost everything with her as well."

"I told Lester no," Susie says, shaking her head. "They didn't lose everything. They still had him. You know what he said to that? 'I did the same in return. I thought only of myself.'"

Susie fingers the wad of bills as if she wants to separate them in half and give part of the money back. In another second she comes out and says she thinks Knox killed Lester. It's the only theory that makes sense, she says, that explains the weeks of locked doors, furtive exits and entrances, the gazes at the street through the crinkled Venetian blinds, the steady sips of whiskey.

But then Susie's eyes refocus, and she says no, she remembers Lester calling afterward. Or does she? He sounded a long way off. There were noises in the background. Zooming cars. Seagulls. The ding-ding of cars and trucks running tires across driveway bells. It was a gas station, she thinks, somewhere way out, beyond Toronto. But en route to where?

"I don't know," she says. "I was so high by then." She takes the wad of money and pushes it back across the table. "Lester was gone three, four days, and I was already high." She looks away.

On the phone, Lester asked if she was okay. Susie said she w
fine; it sounded like a stray sentence spoken by someone else a
picked up at random by the receiver. There was a long silen
"Better not to have been born," he whispered. She could still he
the gulls and traffic and driveway bell and the receiver knocki
against the phone booth where he'd left it dangling as he walk
away. Was that the last time they spoke?

Susie waits, shaking her head. "No, there was one mo
call." She reaches for the money again, draws it across t
table, over the edge and into her lap. Lester's voice was like
rasp. The seagulls and zooming cars were gone from the ba
ground. Susie thought she heard the sea, or maybe a lake, wav
crashing on shore. Lester told her that when his father died t
doctors had contacted him. His mother, Marion, had pass
years before that, rotting in a hospital bed waiting for one l:
visit from Lester, who never even attended the funeral. He we
through the house, though he hadn't wanted to, having left
he'd hoped, forever. In his father's study he found heaped boo
medical journals, bottles, letters, as if the old doctor had spe
the last years trying to bury his life. Under one of the piles w
a box for a model airplane, a Messerschmitt Bf 109 G-2, th
Lester remembered building when he was a kid one afterno
with his father. It was the one thing they'd done together, t
only one he could remember, and he tore off the cover to see
this tiny memento of their time, as if it acknowledged son
thing between them, as if maybe the safekeeping of the moc
meant his father had remembered those few hours too, may
even treasured them. Instead, Lester found police and foren:
reports, covered with Post-its and handwritten notes, so ma
of them that in places they'd been erased and new notes writt
over top. He found newspaper clippings, photographs of t
bodies of a girl and dog outlined in orange on the sidewa
Finally, there was the picture of Erika herself, the sister th
until that moment he'd never known he had, whose name
one in that house had ever mentioned out loud, though the)

been speaking and screaming and crying it across the absolute silence of those years. She was sitting on a dog, a black lab that looked as if it could have lifted three or four of her. It had probably been some grown-up's idea of a joke, Lester had thought while looking at it. His father must have placed her on its back, something silly to do between tending to the barbecue and the next scotch and soda. In the picture, the dog was already bolting out the garden gate, and Erika's face, the look on it, seemed to be jeering at Lester: "You think you had it bad? You think you lost your childhood? You think it was a joke?"

Susie still has the photograph. It is the only thing she took from Lester. She thinks he left it on purpose, as a gift, not to keep Susie straight or to reform her, but just to help her think sometimes about what she was, what she still might be, before she too disappeared. Susie pulls it out now, smiles at the girl in the picture, and reluctantly turns it over as if afraid that another pair of eyes might steal its magic, as if afterward there will be nothing but a black square. But the girl in the photo is not so easily extinguished. She seems to grow brighter and brighter with every second she's looked at, as if her image were lit from within, too generous for the eyes. She's holding onto the dog with one hand, fingers wrapped in its fur for dear life. The other is tossed high, waving hello and farewell, as if inviting you to step forth into her vanishing. In a trick of the light, her skin looks silver.

The Glory Days of
Donkey Kon

Emil Tóth had been a judge in Budapest during the 1950s the bad years — but he was still pretty sure, maybe nine ninety-five percent, that every person he'd sentenced to dea had deserved it. Odds are they'd definitely done what they we charged with — kidnapping, rape, murder — but every once a while, maybe, who knows with the way politics worked in t country then, the random arrests and confessions tortured c of prisoners by the ÁVO, some of the accused might have be charged with crimes they didn't commit. After all, not everyo who was falsely arrested, tried, and sentenced was made a b deal of. Only a tiny minority got starring roles in show tri with all the attendant furor in newspapers and on radio. Some them — the no-names, the non-entities, the unpersons — we gotten rid of quick and clean, no need for public confessions histrionics or extra propaganda for the regime, any trump up charge would do. Still, the old man would always swear himself, even after coming to Canada, that he'd never knowin sentenced people for political sins — not for being reactionari or counterrevolutionaries, or traitors — much less for crim he didn't believe were actually theirs. But the truth is — and would have loved to talk about this, had anyone asked — t lawyers of that time had been as good at being lawyers as was at being a judge, which meant it was possible that some them had been clever enough with the facts and evidence a storytelling needed to string them together to make him believe someone was guilty when they were in fact innocent. In the end, Tóth just couldn't be totally certain, but if he had to put money on it, or someone held a gun to his head and said "choose," he'd have gone with guilty every time.

So, did he still believe in the death penalty? It was the sort of question he'd ask himself while shuffling around Kitchener on a cane, as if the trials were still going on, he was weighing the evidence, and there was plenty of time to render a verdict. Ten years ago Tóth had been let out of Csillag Prison and emigrated West into the non-life he now lived — jobless and friendless and prematurely aged, dressed in clothes that had once been quite fine, even tailor made, but were now held together with staples and tape. The question always came to him in the voices of his relatives, though they'd never asked it, since they already believed he was indifferent to any life but his own. They might have been surprised to discover that he'd never really believed in the death penalty, had no opinion on it one way or the other. Back then, it had been the sentence prescribed by law for certain crimes. Kidnapping? Rape? Murder? Death by hanging. Period. No further consideration necessary. Of course Tóth had meditated on it in private, and even now, had anyone been curious about his opinion, he would have recalled the usual arguments — that capital punishment was a deterrent; that it had a spiritual value in turning the criminal toward repentance and thus salvation; that it saved the state a lot of money otherwise spent on keeping people alive while they served out life sentences — but beyond these, each flawed in its way, there was a better argument, one that trumped all the rest, and he'd have loved to debate it had there been anyone to debate it with.

The last time he'd had a real conversation was 1970. This was days before his release from Csillag Prison. Comrade Maxim Zabrovsky had manoeuvred his wheelchair into the place for visitors on the other side of the glass, informing Tóth of the conditions the party had set for his release. It wasn't the first

time Zabrovsky had visited, they were friends of a sort, havi
met over the years at Party functions, dinners, galas, two eml
tered cripples who for some reason always ended up seat
next to each other instead of anyone else. Zabrovsky was t
only person Tóth had felt safe confiding in during his time
prison (being a judge was not the best thing to have been pri
to becoming a convict), though friendship meant nothing ba
then, when neighbors and family spied on each other for t
state. In fact, Tóth knew it was a mistake, every single conv
sation he'd had with Zabrovsky, before, during, and after l
internment, all of it undoubtedly reported immediately to t
communist authority—getting information was probably t
reason Zabrovsky was visiting him in the first place—but Tó
was desperate and lonely, beyond caring, and he knew that on
he got out he'd have to leave the country, and if he manag
to do that, which was a pretty big if, then his family, alrea
emigrated to Canada, were not going to be in a listening mo
either. It was his last chance to have someone sit patiently a
hear his side of what had happened on October 30, 1956.

The revolution had been going on for a week by then, ev
since the shootings at the radio station, the processions
Bem Square, people in the thousands waving Hungarian fla
with ragged holes where they'd burned the hammer and sicl
out of the cloth. Since then, the streets had been filled wi
demonstrations; the hurling of Molotov cocktails; men, wom
and children formed into militias with rifles and handgu
to fight against a mechanized Soviet army; students rushi
angrily through the streets with their sixteen-point manifes
reports and rumors (they were the same thing in those da
of suspected ÁVO agents seized by mobs, strung up on ma
shift gallows, sometimes by the neck, sometimes by the fe
beaten, set on fire, a pile of money left beneath their corpses
let everyone know who they were, the work they'd done, h
they'd profited from it, and the numberless men and wom
they'd treated to similar torture and death.

Tóth had followed it closely, trying to decide whether to escape to the countryside, or if the Red Army would soon restore order. He was paralyzed by the same indecision that had overtaken the government, and going to the party headquarters at Köztársaság tér to gauge the situation had been a big mistake, arriving there to find a mob already assembled, whispering among themselves of catacombs under the building, secret tunnels, political criminals locked into tiny cells, someone with his ear to the asphalt saying he could hear them crying for help. Tóth nodded in agreement, though he couldn't hear a thing; he chanted the same demands, though he knew they wouldn't be fulfilled; he joined the rush into the building, though there was nothing inside but party hacks and secret police. The first people entering the building were arrested. The guards opened fire. Tanks arrived. The revolutionaries fired back. Within a short time the tanks were smoking ruins, or had retreated, and the crowd re-entered the building, carrying along Tóth, to hunt for secret policemen hiding in offices and storerooms and closets, dragging them from under desks, tearing off their clothes, smashing their ribs and arms and skulls, people jumping up and down on the bodies, then stringing them up from trees and lampposts. It was Álbert Berec who gave him away, staring at Tóth past his broken nose, blood pooling in the sockets of his eyes, squirming on the sticky parquet floor. "Emil, please," he'd whispered, "stop please . . ." and Tóth had for one second thought of kicking him in the mouth, breaking his teeth, before he spoke his name again, which under the circumstances would have been the best thing to do. But they were friends, so Tóth did the worst possible thing — he turned and ran.

They were after him in a second, leaving Berec lying there (he'd later thank Tóth for saving his life, but would not show up offering support at the trial, and would even make a public comment on how Tóth's long delay in sentencing "the boys," which is what he called the revolutionaries, was "a sign of ideological vacillation"). There were maybe twelve of them, young

men, each one as fast as Tóth had been in those days, thou
he knew the building better than they did, mounting the sta
to the second floor, straight into Imre Mező's office, thinki
with that frantic logic of escape, that he'd be safe there, Me
was known to move in progressive circles, was even a suppor
of Imre Nagy, the reformer much beloved by the revolutionari
But they came for him anyway. He thought, still crazily, tha
he stood in the doorway he could maybe take them one by o
he'd been good at boxing once, during those mandatory yea
in the military, excelling not only in the ring but in those me
exercises where they'd shown him how to move when there we
two, three, four opponents.

But there were far more than that now. He hit the first o
in the face as hard as he could, right on the bridge of the no
then shoved him back into the rest, but already two of the
were ducking beneath the weight of the body, coming for hi
Tóth turned to the window, deliberated a moment, then lea
the one shattering story down, straight onto his right anl
whose throbbing he'd ignore for the next ten hours, until t
damage was permanent, fleeing across the square, cutting ba
and forth, the boys hurling various bombs from above, roc
bouncing off his skull, bricks smashing into his shoulders a
back, fragments of glass lancing his skin.

He ran for hours through the city. Every time he turnec
corner he seemed to see one of the boys, who in turn caug
sight of him. Then he was running again, trying to blend
The revolution was unlike any battle he'd ever seen or hea
about, and he'd seen the worst ten years ago — the Easte
Front, the deportations, the siege — as if the fighting had be
fragmented into scenes, discrete eruptions of violence, wh
elsewhere everyday life continued. One minute he was trying
hide behind a line of people waiting for bread outside a groce
pigeons cooing around their ankles, the next he was dodgi
behind cars as people fought with paving stones and Molot
cocktails and rifles against Russian soldiers. One minute

was staring at a nicely kept building with women on balconies watering plants, the next he was running past a smoldering ruin filled with policemen identifying bodies. One minute there was a man cleaning the fender of his car with a rag, the next there was another salvaging firearms from a gutted tank. One minute his flight was impeded by a group spilling from a church, greeting each other, shaking hands, the next he was stopped by bodies lining the gutters, as if they'd died looking for something — a dropped letter, loose change, a cigarette with a few drags still left in it.

He ran, learning their faces as they came, all students of one kind or another, from ELTE or the Technical University, the mass of them triangulating against his escape. Whenever he stopped to walk, it was his haste that gave him away, the harried look in his eyes, and he realized too late that in this moment, under these conditions, the most normal and unnoticeable way to proceed through Budapest was to run. "You're ÁVO aren't you?" an old woman would say. "Get him," someone else yelled. Two men jumped on Tóth, pinned his arms. Someone ran into an apartment building for a stepladder and some rope.

He wept the sincerest of tears. "No, I'm not ÁVO. I'm just a judge."

The man with the rope couldn't figure out how to tie a noose. An exasperated woman grabbed it out of his hands — "I'm surprised you can tie your own shoes," she snarled — and in six or seven flicks of the wrist had it done, the rope coiled around itself, fitted over Tóth's head. "I know I wasn't a great judge. I could have paid more attention. But I'm not a political person, I just..."

In the middle of his pleading there were shots, someone was hit, the rest of them scattered, and Tóth turned to see an armored car approaching, the hammer and sickle barely visible in what light there was, an hour after curfew, and he ran as well, the noose still around his neck, snaking in the air behind him like a whip.

It was late at night by the time he made it to his brothe
house, collapsing on the threshold from which they — Mikl
wife and sons — dragged him inside. He was raving about h(
he didn't deserve such notoriety, he'd always done his job quie
weighing evidence not ideology, focusing on the crime its(
the faces of the accused, seeing in them a guilt or innocen
untainted by extralegal considerations.

One of his nephews suggested they send him back in
the street.

■

Fifteen years later the street was exactly where they put hi
Tóth would shuttle from the room he rented at his sister's hou
— Tundë had emigrated many years earlier — to Kitchene
bridge tournaments, bocce courts, and bingo palaces, sitti
there month after month, year after year, wishing for somethi
other than these old people playing old people's games. Fro
there, until the start of the 1980s, he worked his way throu
the city's pool halls, bowling alleys, and outdoor skating rin
before finally arriving at Toop's Arcade, drawn by the you
flashing lights, the bleeps and chirps of a place where it seem
to him the future was being made. In 1981 he was fifty-five yea
old, and Toop's was in the middle of a golden age, the era
Galaga, Frogger, Turbo, and Tóth's favorite, Donkey Kong. I
loved the virtuosic Mario — jumping flaming barrels, climbi
crooked ladders, bringing down the hammer — but even mo
than that the ape who always got away, carrying Lady off in t
last second, as if no matter what Mario did, how quick and ag
he was, it was all the same. Tóth laughed when Donkey Ko
escaped — gutting himself each time — and the kids looked
him like he was crazy.

At first, he didn't try to play. He just stood there watchii
sometimes handing out quarters, which was the only tir
the kids were willing to speak with him. Unable to pronoun
his name, they called him "Mister Tote," as did Joe Toop, t

proprietor, who made no secret of the fact that he tolerated Tóth because he helped kids play when they were otherwise broke and headed home. But Tóth knew they also felt bad for him because he was a cripple. It didn't matter that he had a certain bearing — a military posture he'd adopted young, even a certain athleticism — it was always the bad leg they saw, as if it was leading him on, the rest of his body jerking against it, to places like the arcade, where he didn't belong and wasn't wanted.

As fall became winter Tóth went from watching Donkey Kong to playing it, tentatively at first, losing his three lives in less than a minute, jerking the joystick around as if he wanted to tear it from the console. But slowly, as September became October became November, December, January, February, his initials climbed to the top of the high-score list and he became the unacknowledged king, working the controls with the delicacy of a queen sipping tea. Sometimes he'd even show off by getting Mario to the top of the screen only to turn around, go back to the start, and climb all the way back up again, just to prove that he could do it before the clock ran out.

But mastering the game, the jumping and running and climbing the best players could predict ahead of the beat, also meant that the kids' opinion of him slowly turned from derision to envy to hate — which Tóth knew from experience was the most dangerous form of respect — as day by day his time at Donkey Kong approached the kill screen, where the score maxed out and the game glitched, giving him seven impossible seconds to complete the level. "Here, take these quarters, I don't need them," Tóth would say to whoever was watching, pleased to give not because he felt he owed it to them, or because he required something in return, but because he could, it was in his power, and it had been a long time since he'd felt like that. They took it reluctantly, unable to resist their own greed, feeling even more pathetic for the fact that it was late in the day, Toop's was closing, they'd have no chance to spend it before tomorrow, and by then Tóth would be back hogging Donkey Kong again. They hated

him even more for his charity, the way he looked at them as th
stood there hands outstretched, as if he could see not only t
bad things they'd done, but all the bad things they would ev
do. The verdict was in.

By the time March rolled around it was Illio who decided
tell the old man to take a break, get lost, him and Cramp an
bunch of other kids wouldn't mind some time playing Donk
Kong once in a while. It was the second Tuesday of the mon
when it happened. Toop was lowering the grate when he hea
the boys' voices from around the corner, down the alley, whe
they were blocking Tóth from going home.

"I don't care about your quarters," yelled Illio.

Tóth carefully put the quarters back into his pocket, and plac
both his hands on his cane. "Your name is Illio?" he said, th
turned to the other one. "Cramp?" The boys looked at each oth
and laughed, as if this was some strategy on the old man's par
distraction, delay, a last-ditch attempt at becoming friends. B
then Tóth said, "These are not your real names. These are nam
you have made for yourselves."

"Listen to Mr. Tote," Illio sneered.

"As you say," replied Tóth. "I am familiar with this idea,"
continued. "I knew a man once — very powerful! — who call
himself Maxim Zabrovsky. But his real name was Ervin Acz
Tóth looked at the boys, knowing it was all lost on them, eve
single thing that had happened in Eastern Europe over the l
hundred and fifty years, including men like Zabrovsky — Mus
vites who escaped from the fascists between the wars by living
the Soviet Union, then returned when Hitler was defeated a
the Politburo needed puppets to rule the Eastern Bloc, rea
to do exactly as they were told. Many of them were so fanati
they continued believing in Stalin even as they were being tri
for crimes they didn't commit and the noose tightened arou
their necks.

Tóth tried speaking to the boys again. "Zabrovsky told r
that no one would fear anyone named Ervin. Stalin hims

suggested he change it. But more interesting than that was his attitude toward capital punishment . . ."

"Take a vacation from Toop's, freak," said Illio, and Cramp stepped forward and glared at the older man with a hardness in the eyes he'd taken from his favorite punk album cover and perfected in the mirror every morning.

Tóth wanted to tell them it was Zabrovsky who'd demanded, in the early days of 1957, that he prosecute the boys, not only those who'd tried to kill him but others as well, not "revolutionaries" anymore, but "reactionaries," "fascists," "counterrevolutionaries," who'd tried to destroy the people's republic with their pistols and explosives. By that point all the boys were the same to Tóth — those who'd attacked him, those who hadn't — but he still didn't want to put them to death for political reasons, and it was in the midst of this discussion that Zabrovsky told him about how he'd changed his name, leaving Tóth to wonder if it hadn't been a sign from one old comrade to another, a warning on the consequences of refusing the case, or its opposite, that in taking it on he was being set up by their bosses. Maybe Zabrovsky was hinting that Tóth too should change his name, disappear, before going through with what they were asking.

"Long ago I promised myself I would never again run from boys like you," Tóth said, staring past Illio and Cramp to where Toop stood on the sidewalk.

"Why don't you guys head home, leave him alone," Toop snarled, still out on the sidewalk, not too happy at the thought of entering the alley.

Tóth turned and began to walk away, Illio letting out a wolf whistle. "We're not finished with you yet, Mrs. Tote!"

■

It took him an hour to get from Toop's to Tundë's, arriving there feet aching, a lancing chill running from behind his right knee through the hamstring and low into his spine.

Tundë always came to the door when he entered, but it w
just something she did, saying hello, as much a formality as t
offer to introduce him to the guests who'd come to sip cockta
with her and Tony Norman, Tundë's husband of twenty yea
and one of the biggest real estate agents Kitchener had ev
seen, with his white-tie galas and Mercedes and twenty-fi
year old scotch, though he adjusted the image every few yea
by buying an old property and rezoning it for low-incor
housing. This philanthropy was the first thing Tundë wou
tell you about when you were introduced to Tony, and not a wo
about her brother living in exile in the back room.

Tóth said no, he didn't want to meet the guests, as Tun
knew he would, which is what made it safe for her to ask h
in the first place. Then, as always, he limped quietly into t
kitchen to forage through the fridge for leftovers of the me
Tundë's maid had just served, and to which he was alwa
invited with the same non-invitation he'd just received to me
the evening's guests.

From there he shuffled into his tiny bedroom, once t
sleeping quarters for a butler, and looked at the trunk wedg
into the corner below the window. Every once in a while, he
open the lock and take out something — a ring, a bracelet
rolled up print — and present it to Tundë in return for his roo
and board. While at first she'd hesitated to touch these thin
— as if her aversion to his "filthy loot stolen from countless far
lies," as one family member had once put it, was greater th
her love for rich and beautiful things — Tundë eventually to
them, her eyes glittering at the sight of her brother standi
there in his threadbare clothes, nowhere else to go, his pri
long fallen away. After that awkward first time Tóth decid
just to leave them on the secretaire she kept by the telepho
instead of handing them to Tundë in person. She didn't enj
taking money from him any more than the boys at Toop's d
— she was just as ashamed of her greed — but Tundë was afi

all his sister and so Tóth spared her the added shame of having him witness it. Still, this was as much of a concession as he was willing to make, and when she first handed him an envelope full of money, he took four tens out of it, one for each week of the month, and left the rest, saying it was room and board, he wouldn't take another penny, and besides he was an old washed up ex-convict who didn't need anything, neither new clothes nor a fancy car nor twenty-five year old scotch, even as Tóth knew that what he was really doing was refusing to be bought off, to assuage her guilt at taking his treasures. He wanted Tundë to feel that she was as tainted by their transactions as he was. But underestimating people was a habit with Tóth, and within the first year Tundë started leaving out only those tens, not even speaking to him about it, as if she could have it both ways — take the money despite her conscience, and at the same time deprive Tóth of any satisfaction in confronting her with the fact that she was as bad as he was. The best he got was once in a while finding Tundë in his room staring at the trunk as if she'd just closed the lid on hearing him come in, nervously tucking a strand of hair behind her ear as she shouldered past him wordlessly back into the kitchen.

At night when he was alone in his room, Tóth would lecture an absent Tundë on the fact that Tony's wealth was as dirty as his own — her husband was in the business of swindling people too — and if they were so righteous they would have tried to find the owners of the valuables he handed over instead of just keeping them. It was better this way, dialoguing with phantoms, than risk Tundë coming back at him with one of her perfect counter-arguments, for instance, that Tóth was the only one in a position to make amends, or that she and Tony, unlike him, had worked hard for what they had, and done it honestly, saving up and denying themselves in order to get ahead.

He didn't want to hear it, the convenient story Tundë told herself and anyone who'd listen, ignoring the fact that Tony was

already rich when they met at the Helikon Ball back in Toron
in 1961, and that the only claim she could make to helping hi
get even richer was how cheap she was — never tipping mo
than five percent; haggling with workmen and contractors dov
to the penny; tapping her society friends for free places to st
in the Muskokas or Hawaii or Saint-Tropez during vacatio1
assembling the liquor for her parties from the gifts provided
Tony's grateful clients — as if the richer Tundë became the mc
she was determined not to pay.

"It's how rich people are," sighed Tóth to himself, sitting 1
on his mattress in the coat and shoes he sometimes fell asle
in, as if he needed to be ready to run at any moment. He we
over to the trunk and opened the lid in another of the fran
gestures that marked his life at Tundë's. What would his sist
do when he ran out of necklaces and pendants and etchin ؟
Where would he go when he couldn't pay to stay here? But as
ran his fingers over the loot, Tóth actually found himself hopi
the level in the trunk had fallen, that his stash was running o
and would soon be exhausted, because the truth was it nev
seemed to diminish, and he realized that worse than his fear
being kicked out of Tundë's was the fear that the trunk wou
never be emptied, it would always be there, filled with the sar
mass of glittering stuff, as if by spending it he saved it, as if
paying his debts he incurred them, and his punishment w
to lug the trunk right to the very end. "How can I still have
this? How can it still be here?" Tóth asked himself, crawli
horrified back into his bed. It was hard to believe there'd be
a time when he'd been interested in collecting the lost treasu1
of the Austro-Hungarian Empire, buying it cheap from sho
where people who'd once owned the world — the petit bo
geois, the aristocracy, the nobles — had sold it to make en
meet, or had it confiscated and redistributed. Tóth bought th
heirlooms at bargain prices, yes, but he'd never stolen anythi1
always going to an official jeweler's or *antikvárium*, avoidi
questions of provenance and paying for it with money h

earned. He'd seen himself as a collector not of valuables but beauty, never dreaming he'd ever have to sell them to pay his way, or that in the end they'd come to own him rather than the other way around.

He'd closed his eyes, and was consoling himself with the lights and colors of Donkey Kong, when Tundë came into his room. The minute she opened her mouth the barrels ran straight into Mario and Tóth could hear the screwy music that always announced his death. "Are your guests gone?" he asked, not opening his eyes.

"Miklós and Hajna are coming over with the kids and grandkids tomorrow," she said. "Of course we'd love it if you were present as well." There was a tiredness to Tundë's voice, a resignation, as if she was as sick of these formalities as Tóth.

No, he shook his head without opening his eyes. "No thank you. I have plans."

"Plans?" She sighed. "I've told you a thousand times you're always welcome." It was a sham, her invitation, he could hear it in her voice.

"I'm sure," Tóth replied, his voice crackling like an old LP.

∎

Several times a year, the relatives would gather at Tundë's, and Tóth would disappear, walking out the door a half hour before anyone walked in, heading off to Toop's or, when it was closed, the park (if it was summer) or some café (if it was winter) to sit there until after midnight when everyone had gone home, not wanting to run into them even accidentally. He'd close his eyes and imagine the family in there drinking beer and *pálinka*. *Málna szörp* for the kids. Feasting on the food they'd ordered from some Hungarian restaurant. Going on about who'd fought in 1956 against the communists (or at least made the symbolic gesture by leaving the country); who'd resisted joining the Party even though they knew they'd suffer for it; who'd continued to go to church every Sunday under the watchful eyes of the ÁVO;

who'd never, not once, taken part in the sham elections whe
there was only one name on the ballot; on and on, the litany
acts magnified into heroism either by the addition of tiny li
or a slight warping of storylines, or simply by force of repe
tion and agreement, everyone in the room getting their sha
of admiration as long as they provided admiration in turn, t
conspiratorial game of this great family, all of whom — exce
for one — had been so principled in the face of terror.

But Tóth didn't stay away because he was afraid of the
disdain. He stayed away because if he didn't they'd be remind
of the number of times they'd come to him, the man in t
Party, when there was trouble — someone's child wanted
get into university and needed his *protekció*; someone tryi
to get a better apartment required his connections; someo
was short ten thousand forints and he was the only one wi
money; someone needed a visa and if his name was there a;
guarantor for sure they'd get it — all the things he'd done f
them back in Hungary, staying dirty so they could stay cle.
That's what really bothered them, why they preferred he not
there, his presence like black mold across their stories. Eve
time they looked at him their voices lost a little power, the wor
came out with less conviction, they had to stare at the car
while repeating the lines. It was also why they hated him n
more than they'd hated him then, since at least in those da
he'd been useful, always invited to family events — weddin
anniversaries, holidays — to keep up good relations, whereas
Canada he was a reminder of a history they'd not been able
leave as easily as the country itself, or of the fact that there we
two countries, one that was a physical place — rivers and fore;
and mountains you could escape — and another whose borde
followed you forever, expanding in advance of your flight, a
in the middle of it stood Tóth like some crooked king who ne\
said a word, enforcing a citizenship that could neither be revis
nor revoked.

■

It was freezing on Friday night, spring still a long way off. Tóth was out of quarters, having given away the last of them the day before, so he took up his cane at four in the afternoon and headed out with nowhere to go. He walked for a long time up Duke Street, circled down Frederick, turned right along Charles, and finally without thinking turned up Water onto King, cursing himself for not being able to resist Toop's. He was addicted, his evil leg drawing him on against his will. But he did manage to cross over to the other side of the street before getting to the front door, wondering if Illio and Cramp were inside waiting for him. It took every bit of Tóth's willpower not to go in there and try explaining things, to promise that from now on he'd share the game, wouldn't play for so long, take a few days off every week to give others a chance. It occurred to him for the first time that he might not be able to go back to Toop's until this was sorted out, that maybe Joe was happy to have let Illio and Cramp settle the problem of Tóth's presence. The thought made him stop for a second. The arcade was all he had left.

Tóth limped four blocks to Hibner Park, sitting down on a bench and staring down the long hill to where he could see the arcade's neon signaling to him through the dark, as certain of its power over him as Zabrovsky had been, though unlike the sign Zabrovsky's certainty had waned as day after day, month after month, year after year, the trials for those young men dragged on. This was after thousands of other revolutionaries had been arrested, imprisoned, sent to gulags, executed. The twelve trials Tóth presided over seemed neverending. The boys they'd initially brought before him slowly became young men, their faces lined from time in jail, malnourishment, nights of interrogation, but worst of all the uncertainty of the proceedings. The old judge seemed to enjoy squeezing their time out of them, hour after hour, not even allowing them the minor glory of admitting that

they had indeed participated in the revolution, never mind t
high honor of martyrdom on the Soviet scaffolds. Meanwh
Zabrovsky and the party lawyers were just as outraged, thou
their complaint was Tóth's refusal to accept ideological treas
as a crime, his insistence on proof of actual wrongdoing
break-ins, theft, destruction of property, beatings, murder
constantly sending the prosecution back out for more, the tri
in perpetual recess, until they lost their patience and start
manufacturing evidence, not only material but photograp
and eye-witnesses, so much of it that crimes against the Sov
the Party, Marxist doctrine, even the state didn't need to
mentioned, that in any society at any time these boys would ha
been guilty of the most universal of crimes. But it was not wl
Zabrovsky wanted them sentenced for. It deprived the proce
ings of every drop of worthwhile propaganda. And it took un
1962 for Tóth to feel there was enough evidence to send them
to die. By then the regime was just waiting for him to get t
trial over with so they could arrest him in turn, and this tir
the presiding judge had no problem with sentencing someo
for failing the tenets of Bolshevism, or for lack of evidence. Tó
spent the next seven years in Csillag Prison, and when he g
out he didn't have a single friend anywhere — in the state
outside of it.

Tóth put his arms around himself and rubbed up and dov
gazing at a crowd of what — kids? young people? — smoki
something under the monkey bars. They looked away as
stared at them, laughing among themselves, and then o
of them came over to the park bench with a joint between l
thumb and fingernail, staring into Tóth's face.

The old man stood up, and spoke before the boy had a chan
"You know Illio and Cramp?" When he said nothing, Tóth thoug
he recognized him as one of Toop's friendlier customers. "Ha
I seen you at the arcade?"

"Who wants to know?"

"Emil Tóth, *tanácsvezető bíró.*"

"What the fuck is that?"

"Someone who sentenced people to death. Do you know what that is?"

"Of course I know what that is," said the boy, making a grab for Tóth's cane and missing when Tóth pulled it back. "I'm not sure you do, though."

"Oh, yes," said Tóth. He took a step back, glancing at the other boys, who were coming closer now, crowding around. He wondered how to phrase it in English, so that they would understand. "It's a very interesting thing," he said. "There are many arguments. Perhaps you have even thought of some of them."

"What the fuck is he talking about?" laughed the boy to his friends, making a gesture at the side of his head to mock Tóth's craziness.

Tóth looked around; he was surrounded. Their faces were peering in, not so much out of curiosity as further intrusion into his space. He wanted so much to explain it, if only to make them — and not just them, but Illio and Cramp, all the kids at Toop's — understand that they were all on the same level, all equal. "The death penalty has been around as long as murder," he said, trying again. "It has never taught anybody anything. It has never stopped the next murder from happening." He smiled, hoping they'd appreciate the argument, but the boy only laughed and made a grab for his cane again, and Tóth had to be careful not to back into those behind him. Tóth struggled for better English. "And no one who is . . . so happy to see a body swinging from a tree, or maybe being electrocuted in a chair, not one of these people is thinking about how much money is saved by not sending these people to jail."

"Listen to this old fuck," laughed the boy, who'd managed now to get ahold of Tóth's cane. "You guys have any idea what he's talking about?"

Tóth made one last attempt to make him understand. "Some say it helps with . . . repentance, salvation . . ." He stopped. The

only words that came to him now were Hungarian, a whisp
running inside his head, saying that repentance in the midst
physical pain or psychological duress was neither rational n
heartfelt, not really. It was just fear, not love. As the boy jerked
the cane, Tóth held on with both hands, his mind going on au
matically, forming the arguments he'd been making for yea
"No," Tóth shook his head like a dog with a spine between
teeth, "the only reason for the death penalty is revenge." It w
hot, what he was feeling now, as quick and intoxicating as t
drugs the boys were taking. "Revenge, revenge," he mumbl
holding onto the cane. It had been almost twenty years sin
he'd felt this way, the only thing he had left in common wi
his sister and brother and humanity itself, for while Tun
and Miklós had rejoiced in 1956, and continued to rejoice, at
those ÁVOsok finally getting their own, they'd not lost with
the ability to love one another, their spouses, their children,
if contrary to that old cliché the lust for revenge did not can
out your ability to feel other emotions — love, affection, pea
— that Tóth still craved, and craving kept alive inside hims
They'd been allowed to have it all — to want payback, to get
and then have that rage and ecstasy fade and be replaced
more refined pleasures — so why not him? Why was this all
had left?

Someone pushed him from behind, and Tóth glanced arou
for half a second before turning back to the boy, who'd let go
the cane and stepped in to hit him. It was a clumsy maneuv
the sort of thing they trained you not to do when boxing, a
Tóth feinted to one side, then swung the silver head of his ca
into the boy's face with all his strength. The boy stood the
shocked, a sudden gash appearing, deep and red, seconds af
the old man pulled back his weapon. Tóth sighed despite hims
It had never been about Donkey Kong, he knew that, only th
the reason he'd come to Toop's in the first place. He hit him aga
and now the boy spun and sat heavily on the bench facing aw
from him, as though gazing in the direction of the arcade, blo

pouring from his face. Tóth hit him once more, the silver handle of the cane sticking for a second in the boy's skull, pulling up his head with it, before jerking loose to let him fall face-first onto the bench.

Tóth stopped then, turning to deal with the other children.

The Rise and Rise an
Rise of Thomas Sargi

On Friday afternoon the conference banners came down a
the delegates went back to Paris, London, New York, a
other points west, so impressed by what they'd seen of Sov
culture they couldn't stop talking about it, which had been t
whole point of hosting the conference in Budapest to begin wi
It was also the day — February 4, 1950 — that Lujza Galamb
led Professor Thomas Sargis away from his life. He'd met her fi
days previous, at the opening banquet, and then, as now, h
face, her body, her voice were animated with such energy —
innocent as freedom — it made the weightiest decision see
unimportant. "Put off your flight another week," she said,
want you to stay with me a little longer." Sure, why not, Sarg
thought, another week is nothing, though he knew that any tir
limit — a week, a month, a year — was there only to appea
his conscience, to let him *pretend* he was returning home —
spoiled students and endless marking and department me
ings over whether to use one or two adjectives to describe t
program, to diapers and arguments and a sexless marriage a
that aimless wandering he did every Saturday in his own hor
He was *never* going back.

The first three years in Budapest would remain freshest
memory — one reception, symposium, keynote address to t
next — with Russian caviar and vodka and the best Törley cha
pagne. He was a celebrity, featured in newspapers on both sid

of the Iron Curtain, because after all who ever defected to the East? And at night there was best of all Lujza beside him in bed, then with him in the day, knotting on the black tie delivered fresh as roses every afternoon, the limousine outside, carrying on their conversation as the driver navigated the maze of the old capital, because Lujza had read all his books and articles praising Stalin's "advances" in the 1930s, the man of steel's superhuman efforts at modernization, the revolutionary politics he'd initiated on behalf of the proletariat. She had a way of repeating his arguments, the lines she'd memorized, in a particularly breathless way, with just the right amount of Hungarian exoticism to her otherwise perfect English. Here, suddenly, was everything Sargis had written off as beyond reach back in Toronto: influence, fame, passion. It did not seem like a bad trade, not at the time, not with the speed at which things were progressing.

Lujza abolished boredom. They had their pick of a thousand things to do every day — afternoons with the communist literati at the New York Kávéház; dinner at Gundel; a stroll through the Városliget; research at the National Archives for Sargis' latest book on the phony charges of rape against the Red Army at the end of the war, or the unfortunate but necessary duty of the *gulag* guards in bringing about utopia, or how the Soviet secret police really were morally better than any other such organization at any other time in history. Lujza was as thrilled by the discoveries as he was. But best of all — in what was for Sargis the biggest surprise — was doing nothing at all. For three years it was like that, the two of them driving down — in the Škoda now, no chauffeur, just like any other couple — to the state-owned villa at Lake Velence, preferably in the fall or winter after the tourists had gone, picking up groceries and wine along the way, then letting the days pass unnumbered, making dinners, doing laundry, working on whatever manuscript or lecture the state needed from him. There was Lujza dusting bookshelves, sneezing in a cloud of motes glittering around her in the September sunlight; or shouting hysterically

as the two of them chased a runaway garbage can blown do\
the hill by a storm, Sargis trying to catch shreds of butche
wrap out of the air like he was still sixteen on the baseball fie
or flushing apple cores and potato peels and orange rinds li
she had no idea what a toilet was for, until it plugged up o
day and they had to evacuate; or shaking so badly with laughı
she couldn't handle the iodine, gauze, and tape the day Sarç
tried drilling through a board balanced on his knee and pu
tured his thigh. These were the things he'd think of later — du
garbage, sewage, slapstick — when he thought of Lujza as
impostor, his state-appointed escort, as if there was no w
she could have faked those moments. They were too ordina
she *must* have found in them the same delight, that perfect
of what *was* with what *should be*, that he'd never for an insta
experienced back in Toronto, where every second with Rebec
and the girls felt stolen from him forever, sitting with them
breakfast already crushed by the thought of another dull hour
the playground. That had been Lujza's greatest talent — Sarç
refused to believe it was training — making him feel as if t
moment contained everything.

Nor did that feeling change when he was awakened by Lujz
nightmares, always louder, more extreme, in the winter mont
the Danube creaking with slabs of ice, stars glinting in a sky cle
and pitiless, Lujza tossing in her sleep, and Sargis beside her
the sheets, knees drawn up, listening. Most nights he was awa
anyway, trying to escape his own past — the country and w
and kids he'd betrayed, and whose memory irritated his hap
ness — alert to Lujza mumbling and screaming along some tra
of nightmare that often went silent for minutes, or segued ir
something less intense, and occasionally even became one
those blessed dreams, her body jerking with laughter, thou
inevitably she came back to the worst of it, howling out t
words, throttled by a memory that lived as much in her spine
her brain. Every night it was the same. He wondered how Luj
ever let herself fall asleep knowing what was awaiting her, a

the few times he moved to her side hoping his touch would draw her like a hook from what she was drowning in, she would leap out of bed, from unconsciousness to the wall opposite, staring at Sargis as if she'd revealed something unpardonable, something she'd been told to keep secret on pain of death. "What did I say?" she hissed.

"Something about the war, or siege. *Ostrom*. Is that it?" he asked, draping a sheet around her. "The Siege of Budapest?" Lujza always seemed relieved to hear this, happy to elaborate on his bad guess. "It was so cold then," she said. "We were so hungry." She slid to the floor. "Then the soldiers came, as cold and hungry as we were." Lujza paused. "No — colder, hungrier."

After a while, he didn't know why, maybe bored or hopeful, Sargis began writing down Lujza's nightmare monologues. If he could edit out the gibberish and put the fragments in order there was a chance he could get the story and help her. Looking back, he realized it was a lover's ploy: deluding yourself into thinking you're trying to help when all you really want is possession of what your lover is withholding, the bits and pieces of Lujza he needed to claim in order to claim her entirely.

But he ran out of nights, never got past a few scattered notes, and in the years to come Sargis would wonder what might have happened if he'd had more time, if instead of dying on March 5, 1953, Stalin had gone on living another ten, twenty years. Would Lujza have come to see him as more than an assignment, as someone she could have trusted?

They stayed up that March night huddled by the radio. There was the usual propaganda in the form of nostalgia, but behind it everyone was waiting to see where power would shift, who'd outmaneuver whom for the top spot, none of them yet daring to mention the last two decades of atrocity. Sargis was listening not so much to the meaning of the words as their *sound*, to detect in any of it a tone of quiet jubilation, an exhalation of breath held in painfully long. What he should have been doing, he later realized, was watching Lujza, because it would all have regis-

tered there — that fake fervor suddenly switched off in her voi
a hatred-filled satisfaction curling into a smile, the arrival
relief as she slumped her shoulders and tilted back her head a
closed her eyes.

By the time morning came, Lujza was packed, though Sar
was so enthralled by the radio, by what Stalin's passing mea
for him personally — he owed that great man everything — th
she was standing by the door before he noticed. She was ready
go, pulling on white gloves, overcoat already belted, sunglass
lipstick, hair tucked in under a kerchief, as if she was sor
starlet running to catch a flight to Venice or Cannes rather th
a grimy elevator down to the equally grimy streets of an Easte
Bloc capital, from there to continue on foot, stripped of t
chauffeur and limousine and flowers with which their nigh
usually began, and which she'd known all along were never rea
theirs, not even the nights themselves, only props to be retriev
by the set designers when the last scene ended (for *him* as mu
as her, Sargis realized). Even this get-up, the one in which s
was now walking out on him, was just a final reminder of whe
given the best performance, who was the *real* star of the show
"What? Where are you . . . ?" Sargis stopped in the midst of h
question when he realized Lujza was sneering at him. But it w
the dullness of her eyes that shocked him the most, somethi
he'd for sure seen over the last year as rumors of Stalin's heal
circulated, mistaking it not for a loss of love but a reflecti
of his own fading glow, either projected onto her or there
sympathy, since what he'd provided the communists — notorio
sensationalism, controversy — was what by its very nature h
to diminish, get replaced, die like an ember. But he'd thoug
his loss of celebrity meant nothing to her, was immaterial, ju
another thing for their relationship to survive.

"You idiot," she said. "All the things you squandered." It w
he'd later reflect, maybe the only honest thing she'd ever said
him, the one moment when Lujza had told him to look aroun
really look around, and think about what he'd so easily gotten

a man like him — and thus so easily lost. She would have killed for his life in Canada.

It was then he said it, less a response to her accusation than something he'd only in that moment realized, spoken in a halting murmur: "All the things I've said and written" — things trotted out to podiums East and West, talking about the glory of the Soviet — "they were just . . . my fascination, my passion." Lujza nodded, still sneering. She knew what he meant — it had all been coded declarations of his love for her.

"They knew love would always bring you back from Vienna, Paris, Stockholm — and not love of communism." She shook her head, picked up her suitcase, and left. Sargis followed the descent of the elevator, running down the spiral stairs that encircled it, then out into the street, a torrent of words, pleading and delusional, pouring from his throat. *Her* words, though, would remain absolutely clear, like some perfect recording in his brain, and Sargis would later play it on infinite loop, sifting each tone for nuance, and decide she'd answered him so viciously not out of obedience to directives but rather the fear that they'd grown too close, that she couldn't leave him except by saying or doing something irreparable. "You think that prying into my sleep teaches you anything?" she yelled. "You don't think that maybe they trained me for that, too — talking in my sleep, what to say — that it's all made up?" He stopped trying to speak then, and Lujza stopped too, gazing up at their balcony with a smile on her face, lips twitching. He thought she was going to laugh. "Maybe it's an idiotic idea," she said, "but how do you know?" She waited, as if he might have an answer. "Or what if the only reason I'm here, with you, is because of what's in my head, what I refuse to remember? And what happens to us — to you and me — if you manage to make me actually forget?" Lujza took a few steps back toward him. "Would you still want to help me, knowing that?" She looked at Sargis sadly and shook her head. "Or are you so capable of love that you'd still go ahead, deny yourself, in order to make my life better?"

Sargis had no response to that, would not have one for decad
though he did raise his hand as if he wanted to say somethi
like a kid at the back of the class. But Lujza had already turn
away, heels tapping into the distance, breaking from a bri
walk into a run and back again, the suitcase knocking agai
her leg.

∎

Sargis was constantly off-balance in the year that followed, r
knowing what to count on next, and then, in the years aft
locked into a certainty so iron-clad it rusted into a coco
around him. Stalin's death brought everything to a dead h:
as if he'd been excised from the official register, though eve
so often the secret police, the ÁVO, would pay him a visit aski
questions he had no idea how to answer, terrified to respo
in any way, for as low as he'd sunk there were always plac
lower — Csillag Prison, Recsk, Andrássy út — jails and cam
where prisoners lost fingers and eyes, where their skulls we
fractured, ribs broken, psyches so pulverized that even tho
who didn't actually die emerged dead nonetheless — walking
sure, eating, even talking and sleeping, but with a sense of s
shrunk to the size of a coffin. What happened to Sargis, thou;
was something else, creeping and incremental, the slow deleti
of happiness and desire, everything except the monotony
survival, as dull and gray as the same walk every day at the sa
hour in the same park. The ÁVO were watching, hoping that
by bit, year after year, Sargis would do their work for them a
build his coffin himself.

But their visits were just the tip of Sargis' misery. Worse w
his loss of privilege, starting with the rooftop penthouse h
shared with Lujza, down the long, steep slide into commun
housing. They said they needed to "transition" him to "differe
quarters," where he'd be "put up for a few days before getti
a new place." Well, those few days lasted forty years, stuck
apartments that were once the glory of Austro-Hungari

housing — motifs of flowers and arabesques on the facades, sixteen-foot ceilings, wood floors cross-hatched in dark and light grain — single-family dwellings now divided into quarters or eighths — makeshift walls butting up against fireplaces, run through the middle of French doors, bisecting bathrooms so one tenant got the sink and another the toilet — two rooms apiece for families of five, the kitchen communal. Sargis drifted through these places like a phantom, an aging tenant with bad Hungarian and patched clothes and a bitterness so wild he often cried in public, though he'd been famous once, famous enough that the other tenants could witness his disgrace, how meek he was when the ÁVO came to visit, like a cautionary tale planted in their midst.

Then there were the letters from home. The censors in the post office who regularly opened mail always allowed Rebecca's letters to get through — pages upon pages from a betrayed wife and kids damning him with their kind words. They arrived in batches at first, sometimes every day for weeks on end, forceful reminders of his crime when he'd most needed to be reminded of it, so powerful was his indifference to what he'd walked out on. Those letters were in fact the only stain on those otherwise flawless first years. Then, once Lujza left, and Sargis' face stopped appearing in newspapers, and the publishers started rejecting his work, he began writing back, responding belatedly to those early pleas and I-miss-you's, his pen poised above the page as if he had no specific thing he wanted to say and was just trying out the variants — apologies, explanations, promises — to which Rebecca responded more and more slowly, down to a creeping pace, from two letters of his to one of hers, to five of his and one of hers, to ten to one, twenty to one, and finally none, as if the intervals between her responses were a Morse code finally resolved in a silence three decades long, a silence that said all that was left.

Whatever else came and went through those years — books lost or discarded, scholarly projects left behind during late-night

evictions, notes filed in a suitcase until they lost all meaning
there were always those boxes stuffed to bursting with his fa
ly's letters. Sargis couldn't let go of them, even if he rarely if ev
lifted the flaps, took out the mail, the drawings, the birthd
cards. The fact was they reminded him less of his family th
of Lujza, even if they contained nothing of her except the pri
he'd paid for their three years together, the loss and dama
of it all. This was why the censors had let the letters through
Sargis was convinced of it — maybe even written some of the
knowing that his pain and remorse were entirely contained
the woman who'd left that day in 1953. What do they still wa
from me? he thought. What do they think I still have left to gi
He couldn't read the letters; he couldn't throw them away.

But there was more, and this was the worst of what they c
to him, letting Sargis glimpse Lujza now and then, making su
their paths crossed in the most unlikely of places, such as t
Széchenyi fürdő, where a woman rose out of the thermal wate
and disappeared into the steam a second before Sargis re
ized who she was; or the archives, where he'd sometimes fin
picture of her in the fonds they'd once looked through togeth
the librarians saying they had no idea how it had gotten there;
the Hungarian National Gallery, glimpsed disappearing arou
a corner of the retrofit palace, Sargis not sure if he should gi
chase or run away, and when he finally made up his mind a
rushed around the corner, and another, and another, arrivi
at the top gallery, under the cupola, there was no one there b
the giant statue of Dózsa György, leader of a peasant rebelli
long ago, in the agony of his execution, seated by his captors
a red-hot iron throne with a fiery crown forced onto his he
howling as the shreds of his flesh burned down to bone. Luj
was both his escape and imprisonment.

Sargis wasn't sure why they were doing this, her appearanc
diminishing more or less on pace with the letters from Rebec
until both stopped dead in 1956. It was then, with the upheaval
the anti-Soviet revolution that October, and the brutal suppr

sion that followed, that Sargis realized everything had been preliminary to this: Lujza was as unattainable as his past life. The end logic of his defection, what they'd planned for him all along, was a Thomas Sargis defined not by what he couldn't have, but by *not having itself*, a deprivation so acute there was no longer anything he even wanted.

For a decade he ran from this idea, finding refuge in false sightings of Lujza, following a familiar dress around a corner, or glancing under a hat brim, or waving his arms to clear the steam at the *fürdő*, only to discover it was someone else, always a different woman, and that the best thing was to stop the chase and just believe it was her, truly Lujza, and that he was strong enough to let her go. But he wasn't strong, he was lost, isolated, bereft, and in 1969, the year of his great hunger, deprived of the dribs and drabs provided free to everyone the state cared for, Sargis became a thief. He had no other choice. They'd abandoned him completely, he hadn't published in years, and that September he was relocated to a leaky one-room "apartment" that was once a railway switching shack in Óbuda, with winter closing in. He was already stealing anyhow, coal from the rail yards, to keep the fire burning in the iron stove that was the only source of heat in the place. When Sargis looked at himself naked in the mirror he saw an old man, bearded for the first time in his life, like some itinerant prophet, one of those ranters he'd seen a lifetime ago in Western cities, clad in sandwich boards quoting Revelations, a shock of white hair sticking up from his leathered face, his nose too large now, as if it were stealing flesh from his receding eyes and lips and cheeks. The ribs poking from his skin were so sharp he was afraid they'd scratch some final word into the glass.

For a whole week Sargis spread the keys on the table he'd built from scrounged bits of lumber, many of them covered in creosote, black circles burned into the boards by his cast-iron frying pan. There were dozens of keys — saw-toothed, skeletal, gray, silver, gold — one for each of the places he'd lived in since 1953.

He wondered if it was a trap, another idea they'd suggested
his brain, still communicating with him through Lujza. For wl
was the mystery of her disappearance if not the demand fo
key, no less insistent than an old lock defying you from a do
you've always wanted to open?

But he was desperate. Sargis looked at the keys trying
remember who lived where, what kind of jewels they still h:
family heirlooms left over from an Austro-Hungarian heyd
stashed in the first places he'd check — those tiny apa
ment-sized fireplaces hidden behind an iron plate; taped
an envelope to the undersides of armoires; secreted betwe
Munkácsy reproductions and the crinkled paper on the back
the frame. He was fairly sure he could eventually match up
the keys with street addresses, as if each one carried with it t
memory of each time they'd trembled in his fingers as he sl
back the bolt expecting to find Lujza waiting inside, telling hi
she was sorry.

When he'd matched up as many as he could Sargis chose o
at random. It belonged to Anikó Kovács, an old lady he'd liv
with for three months in a two-bedroom place in the Eigh
District. She went out every Wednesday to the market, comi
home just before dinnertime, and played bridge every Thursd
morning at a neighbor's across the hall. If someone else w
living with her, and someone probably was, it was a safe bet th
wouldn't be like Sargis had been — out of work, bored, nowhe
to go but into his notebooks. And if he got caught, he didn't ca
not anymore, because Sargis knew he was already in prison
solitary confinement as deep as you could go.

He set off the following Wednesday, fully aware of how insa
the plan was, but carrying it out anyhow, a decision that,
realized, was as indicative of insanity as any he'd heard. Ten f
into the Eighth District he was already bumping shoulders wi
the lumpenproletariat. Roma scowled at him thuggishly. C
widows with canes and rosaries moved at half a kilometer :
hour. Drunks staggered along muttering angrily. Young mothe

herded three, four children ahead of them. Sargis was harassed by beggars, most of them kids, though they stopped short when they got close and realized he was as hungry and bedraggled as they were. He entered the courtyard of Anikó's building, cool and elegant despite the fallen masonry and garbage, the rust along the railings of terraced walkways, pigeon shit patched over exterior mosaics of faded orange and gold. "Hello," said a young boy, huddled in a corner. He was five or six, in worn boots, a too-small overcoat belted at the waist, a watchman's cap clinging, wet, to his head, streaks of dirt down either cheek like a full beard. "Do you have any money?"

"No," said Sargis, shaking his head at the idea of this city, this country, this Eastern Bloc supposedly free from all want. "No money." He gazed up at the third floor, made out the door of Anikó's apartment, then swung open the double doors of an old wooden elevator the size of a telephone booth.

"What about a sandwich?" the boy asked, trailing after him.

But Sargis closed the door, pressed the button, and rose to the third floor. He listened a while at Anikó's mail slot, then inserted his key and crept in.

There was a new tenant living here. He could tell by the boots on the floor, a big man's jacket hanging on the coatrack. But Sargis didn't have too long to inspect the place because there were footsteps outside. Looking around frantically he ran into Anikó's room and wriggled under the bed, grateful for the weight he'd lost over the last ten years.

He lifted the lace edging around the mattress and peeked out, hoping the noise had only been someone passing by. Sargis had seen Anikó's room once or twice when he'd lived with her, the times he'd knocked on the old lady's door to repay one of her loans. It was crammed with antique furniture, paintings, vases, boxes inlaid with mother-of-pearl, Murano glass, Zsolnay porcelain, a small villa's worth of stuff stacked to the ceiling, covered with sheets, too much for this place though not nearly as much as there'd once been. She was obviously selling it off bit by bit,

a little more every month, in fact much of the good stuff w
already gone. Sargis waited, hearing more footsteps outsi
and then the door opened, small feet shuffled over to the b
and the boy bent down, lifted the skirting, and peered at him
"Get out of here!" Sargis hissed like a scalded cat.

"What are you doing down there?" the boy asked, and at t
same moment there was another sound at the door, this o
heavier, and the boy quickly crawled in beside him. The
was barely enough room, their bodies were pressed togeth
and Christ the kid stank. Glancing out, Sargis saw a pair
work boots below dirty trousers — he couldn't see higher th
the knees — as someone, the other tenant he guessed, walk
a few feet through the door, turned this way and that, th
backed out.

"You don't live here," the boy hissed. "I've seen the old la
and that man — Imre Bácsi, he gives me money sometimes
coming in and out of this place, but never you!"

"You don't live here either!" said Sargis, exasperated.

"I live . . . in the courtyard once in a while," the boy said. Wh
ever, thought Sargis. What the hell are we going to do now?

Very little, as it turned out. Imre Bácsi continued to mo
around next door, so the two of them stayed put, under the b
whispering accusations back and forth, and an hour or tw
later Anikó returned with groceries, then cooked dinner, re
prepared for bed, and fell asleep, the mattress barely flexi
under the featherweight of the old lady. By this point the b
— who thought to introduce himself after the second hour, "I
name is Elek, nice to meet you"— had to pee. But of course the
was nowhere to pee under the bed other than into his own par
which after an agonizing half hour he did, Sargis trying to ed
away from the expanding dampness on the rug only to reali
he had nowhere to go, and had to lie there, feeling the piss so
into his pants as well. "Sorry," Elek whispered. "At least I do
have to shit!"

Sargis wished he were dead.

Death, it turned out, would be the topic of the evening, as Anikó's dreams kicked in. Sargis listened carefully while Elek squeezed his eyes shut and put his hands over his ears. The old woman's voice started with a shout, and from there careened between every register from a hush to a scream to what seemed to Sargis the measured tone of someone trying to explain away a fear. Sometimes he lost the thread of the story amid the garble of phrases nonsensical and surreal. *"Please, she's only fourteen . . . Don't let go of my hand, Julia. Stop!"* Some of the cries were so heartrending it was almost a relief, but only almost, not to leave the story to his imagination, to realize the old lady was reliving what the Red Army had done to her daughter — done over and over again, with that mechanical indifference, like some assembly line, that proved to Sargis once again that Stalin really had managed to modernize the Soviet Union, replacing veins with wires and brains with steel and filling that empty spot once thought to be the soul with a little circuitry.

They listened all night long, crawling out early the next morning after both Imre and Anikó left. Sargis still had the old lady's dreams in his ears, and was sneaking out when the boy grabbed his shoulder. "Aren't you forgetting something?"

"No," said Sargis, his clothes crusty from being next to Elek for so long. He walked out, leaving the boy to steal what he could from Anikó, and, later, when he realized Elek was following him home — trailing three blocks back, then riding without a ticket in another section of the tram — and was now sitting outside, on the steps of the railway shack, Sargis let him in, if only to chase away the memory of Lujza that Anikó's dreams had awakened, so forcefully it felt as if she was in the room with him, as if they were wired together, the current always flowing one way, from her to him. Every time he moved toward opening the door for Elek, the charge lessened. When he went for the lock he felt the wires go slack. And when he finally invited Elek in they fell away altogether, as easy as her lips leaving his at the end of a kiss. Of course it didn't mean that Lujza had left. She'd stepped back

from him, that was all, kept in the room by some motive not
revealed. Elek smiled, he handled the soap as if he was worri
about getting it dirty, rubbed the blanket between his finge
handed Sargis the loot he'd stolen and stashed in a handkerchi
then settled down to gaze at the roof overhead as if it was t
most incredible thing in the world.

Elek would come and go from the shack over the next f
years, homesick for the streets, or drawn back to them by ha
whenever Sargis set him a difficult task — reading a bo
without pictures, long division, memorizing all that was irr
ular in the English language. But the trips out diminished as
became domesticated, used to regular meals, clean clothes, he
and fascinated by the old man who could speak entire books.

Some nights Sargis would go out — for food, on a solo robbe
to clear his head of Lujza's ghost — and return to find his box
of letters open on the floor, Elek asleep with one of his dau
ter's drawings clenched in his fist. It was always the drawin
the boy wanted, the ones Rebecca had made sure Molly and Ell
sent — "We miss you Daddy"; "When are you coming home
"Merry Christmas" — gradually devolving into "Why did y
leave?"; "Don't you love me?"; pictures of the family with l
figure crossed out in black crayon or cut out altogether; a
finally, at the end, two short farewells, both girls were teenage
by then, saying he was not and never would be their father.

He squatted by Elek, listened to the boy's snoring, and the
in his hands was something new — drawings Elek himself h
made, images copied painstakingly from the girls' letters, b
without the black X's and excisions, as if his name, Thom
Sargis, could stand in for the parents Elek would have liked
know, as if the girls' pain, in being able at least to put a name
betrayal, was already more than he could ever hope for. Sar
would pull the papers, drawing by drawing, out of Elek's finge
which pulsed weakly after them in his sleep, careful not to te
them not because the pictures meant much to him, but becau
they meant so much to the boy.

One time, Elek woke up, peering at Sargis as the old man continued to pull the drawings from his grasp. "Why don't you ever put yourself in these pictures, Elek?"

"I'm not there," the boy murmured, still half asleep. "I've never been there."

"You . . . we are never going to get there," Sargis replied, astonished that Elek could even conceive of anything like that.

"You don't think she will force us to leave this place?" asked Elek, rising to his elbows, struggling to throw off sleep. "She's not going to leave us in peace."

"You see her, too?" asked Sargis. He grabbed Elek's shoulder. "What do you see?"

"I only know what she looks like from the way you watch her," the boy replied. "She must be beautiful. And kind. And generous."

Well, one out of three wasn't bad, Sargis thought. Or was it even that high? Who was Lujza, really? Had he ever truly seen her? And wasn't this, her continued presence in his life, just part of the old plan, the one the ÁVO had made for him so long ago? They'd gotten inside his head so that he could continue to do their work even after the real planners and agents had retired, disappeared, died. Sargis shook his head, whispered for Elek to lie back down, knowing he could never let the boy leave, that if there was one hole in the ÁVO's plan, it was him, this chance encounter, this unexpected guest, this other voice that was the one anomaly in their logic of torment.

∎

Sargis taught Elek how to read and do research, in Hungarian and English; how to manipulate an argument; how to write when you had nothing to say; all the tricks he'd once taught to undergraduates at the university. He also taught Elek about the keys, and together they learned the finer points of theft, sometimes having to hide again under beds or inside closets or flattened behind an armoire. After the burglaries, Sargis was even kinder to Elek, trying to compensate for this one bit of

miseducation, as if there was some ministering spirit guidi
the old man — tucking the boy in, reading him a story, melti
real chocolate once in a while on the old iron stove and mixi
it with milk.

Sargis did calculations in the apartments they robbed. Hε
pick up a picture of the tenant (they never robbed families,
was a rule) and ask Elek how old they looked, and the boy wou
scratch his scalp and say, "Sixty-five, seventy," as if he knew, ai
then Sargis would check the pantry to see how well the tenant ε
looking around for booze or cigarette butts, going into closε
and bathrooms to check for running shoes regularly used, o
wet swimsuit, anything that suggested exercise. Then he'd pi
through the loot and take out an ivory brooch, a ruby neckla
a bundle of forints, saying, "This one's going to live for anoth
twenty years. They'll need this. No more stealing from here."
they left he'd drop the key they used back through the mailbε
sealing the promise, then turn and nod not at Elek but at sor
vacancy in the air, slightly above, off the edge of the balcony, aε
he was acknowledging a presence, though there was somethi
wary, distrustful, even paranoid about the old man's face.

On Sundays they went to sell what they'd stolen. It sound
more exotic than it was — "the black market" — meeting wi
their fence in a stand-up bar in Moszkva tér, the chrome aι
melamine tables filthy with the residue of green beer, car exhaι
settled from the air, the absence of anything suggesting a recε
clean, the floor covered in flattened garbage and cigarette buι
and reeking with the smell of piss. Despite this, Sargis alwε
dressed for the occasion, wearing the one suit he still had frc
the 1950s, though it sagged on his old man's frame, walki
there with a long-lost confidence, even flamboyance, as if thε
wasn't a thing to be scared of. Elek followed at a distance, havi
begged Sargis to dress down not up, the space between thε
growing and shrinking as he vacillated between fear for hims
and fear of losing the old man. If Sargis noticed he never sε
anything, never spoke to Elek's terrors or affection, as inc

ferent handing over the broach or earrings or watch they'd come to sell as he would have been handing over a carnation, his sense of security, even invulnerability, all part of what had originally been a theory, now a firm belief, that the ÁVO — never mind that it had been abolished in 1956 — were keeping him alive on purpose, this was all part of their original plan, Lujza had even lent them her ghost to prolong his torment. No matter what he did — squatting in the shack, thieving, participating in the black market — he was safe.

For the Christmas of 1983 Sargis bought Elek his first suit. They were still living in the shack, but they'd fixed it up, and Elek had come to appreciate the power of those clothes, how they helped you believe in your own performance. If he was seen, and sometimes he was, by a child or neighbor or roommate, he pulled his hat low and muttered something about being an agent of the state. All of them turned away. After all, who else would have a key? The suit was a graduation present, the awarding of a PhD, the passing on of the professorship, for Sargis was aged now, decrepit, still brilliant at meeting the fence, but not so quiet in the dark of breaking and entering, or robbery, his joints too arthritic from winters in the rail yard to lie all night under a bed.

Even lying *on* a bed was a problem. So he stayed up, fidgeting in the kitchen, drinking coffee since it made no difference with his insomnia, careful to avoid the eyes of the stranger in the mirror, so altered physically it was like he'd traded DNA with a gnarled tree. He lay in bed with a transistor radio pressed to his ear, listening to new words — *gospriyomka, glasnost, perestroika* — wondering if they meant anything at all.

What they meant, mainly, was access to information, though this would only come clear the day Elek returned home with photocopies from the National Archives, where he'd been looking into files recently made public, part of an assignment Sargis had set him on looking into "a major communist figure." He dumped what he found on the kitchen table, and the old man hobbled over and smiled at Elek's cheekiness, picking up

an interview with Rebecca conducted by the *Toronto Star* ba
in the day. He paused a moment at her picture, and despite t
yellowing of the newspaper, its spots and wrinkles, he reme -
bered how beautiful she'd once been. "Rebecca really let me ha
it in this interview," he said, sighing, recalling the crimes she
accused him of: "Leaving my department in the lurch; aba -
doning my kids; leaving my family penniless, just so I could . .
Hold on, hold on," Sargis said as Elek took the photocopy fro
his hands and glanced down the columns of print. "Don't tell m
Don't tell me!" Sargis closed his eyes and concentrated. "Oh
remember: 'So he could frolic around over there pretending to
a revolutionary.' Am I right? That's what she said, word for wor "
    Elek nodded. "She also said you have no integrity."
    Sargis thought about it a minute. "Well, not the kind of int -
rity she thought."
    "What other kind is there?" asked Elek.

■

For Sargis the big event of 1989 was not the departure of t
Red Army from Hungary, or the end of communism, but Elel
discovery, in the archives, that Lujza Galambos had left Hunga
in 1956. He sat there after receiving the news and tried to ke
the bits and pieces, the loose jigsaw, of his head together. "Th
whole time, she was gone?" Elek nodded. Sargis got up a
moved around the room wringing his hands, not quite su
how he should interpret the latest twist in his torment. Was
starting, finally, to admit that he missed his old life, the fam
he'd abandoned? Had he maybe, in some way, been wishing fo
all along, awakening at night with their names on his lips, afra
to consciously admit to his mistake, so enormous that the on
way to counter it had been to make his love for Lujza even bigge
    Elek laid out the documents he'd found—a Xerox of her pa -
port, the visa for a diplomatic mission she'd never returned fro ,
newsletters issued by an expatriate cultural center in Toron
called the Szécsényi Club citing her attendance at banquets a

dances. "She went to Toronto," said Elek, quietly, trying not to upset the old man, "the place you came from." He watched as Sargis held the papers with trembling fingers, and knew there was no choice for them now, not with Hungary's puppet government fallen into a heap of cut strings, the end of communism like the unplugging of some last life-saving device for Sargis, at once keeping him alive and denying him life, always with the promise of something worth waiting for — Lujza's surrender or release to the West. Except now that it had become available, now that they could actually go, and Lujza and the West had become one, Sargis was terrified that it was another ruse, that the way out was really the final closing of the trap, the moment when they showed him once and for all that the life awaiting him was only the waiting his life had become — no job, no country, no home.

"We can get the money to go," said Elek, sitting him down. "I could get it. Easy."

He looked at the boy, and realized he'd have to go. It was for Elek. And then he knew the boy had not been an anomaly after all, that their attachment, what he'd come to feel for him, had been engineered from the start. "It's a message from Lujza," he finally said. "I find out she's gone West just as the border reopens. It's what she wants us to do."

"Why would she want that?" asked Elek, though he was no longer puzzled by the old man's illusions, knowing for years now who was truly in charge of their lives. His only worry was whether Sargis would survive long enough to get them to Rebecca's door.

They left six months later, after a string of so many robberies Elek joked that things had changed, capitalism had finally arrived, proving it to Sargis by opening a suitcase stuffed with dollar bills. But it was the old man, seventy-one years, who led them off the plane at Pearson airport, landing in Toronto for the first time in four decades, guiding an orphan boy of twenty-five, his hand clutching a suitcase full of letters.

They took a room in a cheap hotel in the East End, Sarg
explaining to Elek that they had to look after their money no
there was no ÁVO here to protect them from their burglari
to keep them imprisoned in poverty rather than jail. Here th
would be sent to jail. Elek just shook his head at the old ma
delusions and decided not to argue. In the morning they we
out to find Rebecca and Molly and Ellen, Elek twirling in t
street as they headed west along King, pausing on Bay to ga
at the vertical rise of towers, their tops forming a crown ju
under the sky.

As expected, nobody in the old neighborhood remembered t
three women, much less where they'd gone — much less hi
Sargis even got lost trying to find the right block, the right pie
of property, the right house, and at the end of the day he a
Elek dragged their feet back to the hotel and sat on their be
drinking wine, Elek scouring the letters for clues to the wome
whereabouts while Sargis lost himself in reveries of what mig
have been had he come back in 1950 like he was supposed to.

"Don't you . . ?" Elek turned to Sargis, thinking of how to fini
the question.

"Don't I what?" asked Sargis.

"Don't you want to look for Lujza?"

"She'll find us." The old man shook. "Don't you worry."

Elek stared at him a while, then shuddered as well, and pull
up the covers.

■

Three months — that's how long they searched — Sargis
driven it was as if Elek didn't exist, as if he wasn't even the
while he went door to door asking questions, or comb
through addresses in the Toronto libraries, or scanned re
estate holdings.

In 1990 they found themselves in, of all places, a suburb
Buffalo. Sargis had managed to track down Rebecca followi
the faintest of traces — marriage registries, forwardi

addresses, interviews she'd once given in yellowing newspapers about her ex-husband's "character" and "political sympathies" and "betrayal" — to a spacious bungalow, where she'd settled in the mid-1960s with her new husband, Edgar Mansell, after several years of grinding single motherhood, double-shifting secretarial work in a series of Toronto law firms, and working nights as a waitress.

The trip to Buffalo took a whole day, since neither of them could drive, which meant a bus to Niagara, then hours of waiting — Elek wandering into casinos with a couple of bills and wandering out with more — then another bus to Buffalo, and checking in at a dingy bedsit. As bad as the place was — as bad as any of the rooms were during those three months — they were all better than the railroad shack, at least for Elek.

Sargis thought he had it worked out, what he'd say to Rebecca. He'd written down the words, memorized them, practiced in front of a mirror. But when they arrived at the bungalow, Sargis got out of the cab only to get right back in again, staring out the window and sweating. Within half an hour he'd gotten out again and was almost to the other side of the street when he hobbled back, Elek putting his arm around the old man's shaking shoulders and saying maybe they should try another day. "It's a stupid speech, an idiot speech," Sargis said. The more he thought about it the more it became clear that nothing he said was going to get him inside, much less stand as an apology, and in absolutely no way make up for what he'd done.

"The problem is Rebecca," he finally muttered, thinking of his daughters and the grandchildren he knew they had, having looked it up, nothing left to chance. "In three days it'll be March 3rd," he said excitedly to Elek. "We need to wait three days." When Elek asked why, Sargis laughed, he couldn't believe he'd remembered, maybe there was something to this homecoming business after all. In three days it would be Ellen's birthday. "They'll all be here together." He laughed again.

■

They waited three days. Elek wanted to use the time to "ma
money." "While I admire your work ethic," Sargis said, "it's wo1
remembering that we're not even in Canada right now." I
patted Elek's shoulder. But it was a false gesture, his confiden
was shot, and Elek knew it, listening to Sargis talking in l
sleep, desperate for a way out.

Sargis pretended it was preferable, facing them — his wi
daughters, and grandkids — all at once, but by the sixth day
was terrified, so enfeebled that Elek had to walk him across t
road and up to Rebecca's door. Sargis had bought a cane, and
wondered if he'd have to use it to defend himself, ringing t
doorbell and listening to the voices of adults and children in t
back yard, the heavy tread of a man's feet coming to the door.

It was Edgar Mansell. They were the same age, Sarg
knew, but he looked at least a decade and a half younger, ha
silvery, cropped close; a smooth shave; still trim around t
middle, and not in the starvation-diet way Sargis was b
muscular, a man who could still hold in the weight of hims(
Here's my replacement, Sargis thought, Rebecca's prize f
all she and the girls had gone through, filling the void Sarg
left with a presence that was trustworthy, generous, subst;
tial — a male presence, in other words, one that actua
lived up to its billing. And Sargis had to admit it was a go
thing he'd left when he did, making room for the sort of m
Rebecca deserved.

"Can I help you?" Edgar asked, head cocked to one side,
open beer in his hand, not threatened in the least. He was givi
both of them the look you'd give a beggar.

Sargis wrung the end of the cane in both hands. "I have
message for Rebecca."

"Can I tell her who it's from?" asked Edgar.

"Hm," Sargis said, thinking. He looked at Elek for help, but
just shrugged. "Tell her it's a message from Thomas Sargis."

Edgar paused a long while, looking at him, stunned. "You know Thomas Sargis?" He seemed to doubt it, but before Sargis could say anything else, he motioned for them to come in, and while Sargis hobbled into the front hall, Edgar walked down to the back door and yelled for Rebecca through the screen: "Becca, there's someone here says he knows Tom!" The voices in the back yard went quiet, almost silent, then Sargis heard the back door swing open and there she was — Rebecca — looking like his departure had made no mark at all. She was older, her face more lined than he remembered, but still somehow fresh, even vivacious, glowing with the presence of her children and grandchildren. She looked at him a moment, then extended a hand, and he took it gently. "Can I help you?" she asked. Whatever surprise she'd felt on seeing the old man, on hearing the name Thomas Sargis, it was gone now, replaced with a genuine concern over how weak he seemed, how frail, and for a second Sargis felt as if he was built of sand and blowing apart with every word she spoke.

He tried to respond, his mouth opening and closing, until finally Elek took his arm and said to Rebecca, "Could we get a glass of water?" Rebecca glanced at Edgar in a way that overruled his obvious concern, then she took Sargis by the other arm and led him down the hall, out the back door, and into the garden. There, in the afternoon sunshine, Sargis saw the birthday cake and fresh-cut flowers and his daughters and sons-in-law and all his grandkids. Rebecca and Elek helped him into a chair.

He drank a glass of water. Rebecca waited. Everyone gathered around. And finally she asked, "You said you knew something about my ex-husband, Thomas Sargis?"

It was the reaction he'd least expected. Sargis looked around, eyes narrowed against the brightness of the garden. Rebecca didn't recognize him. None of them did. He was so wasted with the poverty and hunger of the last forty years there was no way they could make the connection, not even if he admitted to who he was. And yet, most surprising of all was that instead

of despair Sargis felt relief, absolute, wash over him. "N
name is Lajos Galambos," he said, glancing quickly at Elek.
was Thomas Sargis' chief in the Ministry of Culture." He ev
managed to fake a Hungarian accent for them, not too diffici
with how little he'd spoken English since 1950. "You can call n
Louis," he smiled, showing off his missing teeth.

Everyone was listening, even the grandchildren, even El
with his eyes wide, not sure how to respond, as "Louis" explain
how "Sargis" had abandoned his family for the love of Lujza, he
beautiful she'd been — he left nothing back, he didn't need
losing himself completely in reverie — how they'd lived togeth
through the 1950s, '60s, '70s. He was lying now, imagining the l
that could have been, he and Lujza right at the top of the cultu
heap, as if he'd never been diminished, never lost esteem in t
eyes of the state, continuing on with the invited lectures a
symposia and champagne dinners with Lujza by his side rig
to the end, the two of them growing old together.

"They had a son," said Sargis. "His name is Elek." He turned
the young man now, trying not to wink, then looked back at l
daughters. "Both his parents are dead."

Rebecca was looking at him strangely now, no longer
kind as she'd been, and Sargis knew he'd have to leave, that
couldn't keep speaking. There was something in his voice,
thin and cracked as it had become, in his mannerisms, that w
keyed to her memories. "Maybe it would be better if we le
he said. "I promised Sargis I'd do this, but I never thought it w
a good idea."

"No," said Rebecca, and she stepped to Elek and took his han
Here was the Rebecca Sargis remembered — high on repris
sin, just deserts, but also loyalty, aid, the importance of fam
"We are happy to have you." Elek nodded at her, though there w
a hardness in her eyes even worse than what Sargis had seen
Lujza that last day.

Is this what Lujza had wanted him to come back to? No, Sarg
closed his eyes and felt the full tiredness of the last four decad

Lujza wasn't here, she wasn't anywhere, she was dead. He could have left Hungary whenever he wanted, Sargis admitted that now. He didn't need to wait for the fall of the Iron Curtain. He remembered the years — 1956, '57, '58, and after — when they weren't trying to scare so much as force him out, but he'd stayed on, thinking Lujza was still there, still after him, still needing him in some way for her work. The truth was, they'd have happily let him go.

When he opened his eyes again, Elek was shaking hands, smiling, all the family around him. But Sargis didn't want that. He hadn't wanted it then, in the 1950s, and he didn't want it now. All he'd ever wanted was Lujza, only he'd met her at the wrong time, ten years too late, when there were too many other commitments and promises made, too much damage, too many casualties in the way. But he'd throw it away again, just watch, it didn't bother him in the least. He would not give up Lujza even if it meant grasping after as little a thing as memory — what it had been like on the streets of the old capital, always waiting, at least once a day startled in some courtyard, frozen in the midst of picking out apples at the market, wide-eyed in an alley off Moszkva tér, as if he'd really heard it, the sound of a woman's feet moving in reverse, the suitcase swinging against Lujza's knee, those high heels tapping their way back to him.

Nom de Guerre

*C*hronology *for a critical biography of Nikolas Blackman, of* Harlc
Sequence, Oxley's Barely Legible Signature, The Anti-Froli
Terrorist Missal, *the posthumous* Dyschrony, *and numerous* otl
minor works.

1969   Born Nikolas Hencher Blackman on August 26, in Pa:
        to Earl Hencher Blackman, Canadian Department
        External Affairs, and Nadia (neé Solukov), ballet danc
        Italian composer Luciano Berio creates ten-minu
        imagistic piano duet, *Memory*, punctuated at unpredi
        able intervals with jarring discords.

1970   Earl makes a list of the men he knows, crossing o
        those Nadia's *not* fucking, until there's only thr
        left. He thinks for a while, crosses each one out, th
        erases the X's over the names, doing it again and aga
        until the paper is like onion skin. He sure is lucky,
        thinks, to have a bottle of Aberlour 18 to help him with th
        a man like him needs all the help he can get. Germai
        Greer (b. 1939), Australian academic, publishes *The Fem*
        Eunuch, insisting on women's rights to vaginal pleasur

1971   Nikolas is weaned. He cries for seven nights. Earl accuses Nadia of breastfeeding for so long as a means of birth control with all her "boyfriends." On the eighth day, he wakes to find the bed beside him empty. In November he is transferred to the embassy in Buenos Aires. In Haiti, François "Papa Doc" Duvalier dies and is succeeded by his son Jean-Claude, "Baby-Doc," under the guidance of Simone Duvalier, "Mama Doc."

1972   Nadia, now Solukov again, performs in *Deuce Coupe* in Chicago. Earl hires Itati "Tati" Olivo Calzada, a member of the embassy janitorial staff, as caregiver for Nikolas after repeatedly observing her playing with and reading to him in the courtyard garden. "He is left alone here too much, for too long," she says, and Earl, drunk as he is, is impressed by her bravery, risking her job at the embassy to criticize one of her superiors. He is impressed too by the image, indelible forever after, of his son's dark attachment to this woman, holding her hand as if he means to drag her away from life at the embassy, as if it is Tati whom Nikolas is rescuing, rather than the other way around. In November, Earl requests transfer "to anywhere," ostensibly over concerns arising from the recent incident at Trelew airport, but really in an attempt to escape his worsening alcoholism, and in December the family relocates to Ottawa. A team under surgeon Harry Buncke (1922-2008) performs the first toe-to-thumb transplant at San Francisco's Franklin Hospital.

1973   Nadia gives birth to Sophie Solukov in New York. Writes letter to Earl begging to be allowed to return, saying Sophie is his daughter. Earl counters that it's impossible. They haven't seen each other in two years. He isn't an idiot! Nikolas experiences his earliest memory: He and his father are crossing railroad tracks in the family car, a

1973 Cadillac Coupe DeVille in St. Tropez Blue Firemi
He looks out the window, and there in the distance, (
a parallel street, at the same spot on the crossing,
another car identical to theirs, a face gazes back at hi
from the back seat. Except this boy is smiling. Gord(
Gallagher, aged nine, stumbles across and explodes
IRA bomb while playing in a Londonderry backyard.

1974 Earl returns to the embassy in France, where he discove
with no small delight, that the French make whiskey t(
Nikolas is enrolled in the International School of Pai
His earliest memories will be from this period, a
they have the duration of sudden shocks — his fathe
drunken rage glimpsed from a hiding place under t
bed; a hummingbird diving for the plastic flowers or
woman's hat; Tati telling him hello in a way that seer
goodbye. Later in life it will make Nikolas feel that wh
he comes across a good memory, and he rarely does, i
like finding a letter dropped in the street by a strang
An Advisory Panel on the White House Tapes determin
that an eighteen-minute gap in one of the Waterga
tapes is due to erasure and of no consequence.

1975 Nadia and Earl reconcile. The first time Nikolas picks
his sister, she slips through his arms, and he thinks
the black circle at the core of every zero. Sophie spen(
five weeks in Pitié-Salpêtrière Hospital for the effe(
of dehydration and malnutrition. Earl exploits politi(
connections to defuse potential investigation by Cl
dren's Services and the police. Mattel manufactures t
"Growing Up Skipper" doll, whose arms, when twist(
increase the doll's height and size of her breasts.

1976 Sophie's first word is "Nikolas." She says it once and do
not say it again, or anything else, for a year. The little gii

eyes always seem to be misrecognizing him, he thinks, or looking for a Nikolas who isn't there. He lies on his bed and puts her face next to his until the caress of her fingers traveling across his lips and cheeks and eyes makes him sleep. Werner Heisenberg (b. 1901), physicist and Nobel Prize winner, dies in Germany.

1977   Earl relocates to consulate in New York. Once there, Nadia absconds with Joachim Haber, surrealist painter. Earl's first suicide attempt (pills), handled discreetly, and kept from his employer, by private physician Kent Phillips at Mount Sinai, who invokes "client-physician privilege" in return for promise (never kept) from Earl to seek treatment. Nikolas reunites with Itati Olivo Calzada, flown up from Argentina in the midst of the medical emergency, after Earl makes a personal request for her services to Ambassador Dwight Fulford, citing "her established history with my son dating back to my brief placement in Argentina, and my inability to vet a new caregiver due to the crisis brought on by the sudden dissolution of my marriage and solo-parenting of two young children." Activist Elisabeth Käsemann (30), a German sociologist, is abducted in Argentina, and her bullet-riddled body dumped on the outskirts of Buenos Aires.

1978   *Tati tells me we choose every path we are faced with, even those that diverge. Somewhere else, father is not drinking; somewhere else, he smiles to see us. Sophie asks why birds try to fly through their own reflections. Tati is horrified by the question, and refuses to answer her. She just kisses Sophie instead.*

1979   Nikolas publishes his first essay, "Evangelion," in the *Saint Pat's Yearbook*, a reflection on differences and similarities among the New Testament gospels. In an introductory

note, he explains that the class assignment asked hi
to reconcile the accounts, but in the finished essay
says that their "reconciliation occurs precisely in th(
differences," stopping just short of saying each gos[
took place in a distinct world. The last sentence is alm(
a snarl: "To attempt to reconcile these versions seer
to me not only to miss the beauty of the variations
Christ's life embodied in the gospels, but quite possil
what is meant in them by salvation. To pass over th(
differences and inconsistencies, rather than celebra
them, is in fact not only an error but a grievous sin." E(
and family end the year by being transferred, desp;
Earl's protests, back to Buenos Aires. In Northern Irela1
Robert "Basher" Bates, a member the Shankill Butchers
Protestant gang notorious for the kidnap and torture
Catholics, pleads guilty to ten murders.

1980 Experiences Argentina's Dirty War first hand, to whi
Nikolas will subsequently attribute his political aw(
ening. Earl launches lawsuit against Nadia for f(
custody of Nikolas and Sophie, ostensibly out of fathe
love but mainly in order to leave the kids in Tati's custo
and return frequently to Toronto for legal meetings a1
court appearances, which are themselves excuses f
missed appointments and drunken binges. In the e1
Nadia fails to show, forcing her lawyer to plead no conte
In August, Earl is admitted to the Hospital Británico
Buenos Aires with acute alcohol poisoning. In *Oxle*
Barely Legible Signature, Nikolas will refer to this episo
as, "Father's second suicide attempt, three years in t
making." California millionaire Robert Graham ope
"The Repository for Germinal Choice," a sperm ba1
from Nobel laureate types, which stays open until 19(
producing 215 children.

1981   Sophie begins to refer to Nikolas as "Oxley," a nickname she will use for him until her disappearance (and possibly even after it). In August, Earl's car is found abandoned on an embankment in barrio Núñez. Embassy staff find a last note scrawled in his appointment book, which reads: "Serge Boliveau, rep. Canadian citizen? Detainee at Navy School of Mechanics????" John Lennon's single, "(Just Like) Starting Over" and the album *Double Fantasy* top the pop music charts just weeks after his murder on December 8.

1982   Permitted to remain, temporarily, in Embassy with Sophie and Itati Olivo Calzada. Authorities try to make contact with Nadia. Argentinian-led police investigation into Earl's disappearance proves inconclusive. When the Canadian authorities announce that the children are to return to Canada, Tati absconds with them. For the next year and a half they live among her acquaintances and relatives in various towns and cities in Argentina. During this time, Tati introduces Nikolas to "a game whores play in the barrios, for when their time is over," which will form the basis of his first treatise, *Harlot's Sequence*. The jellyfish-like creature, *Mnemiopsis leidyi*, arrives to the Black Sea in the ballast water of a cargo ship, and begins to devastate the almost-closed ecosystem.

1983   *On five strips of paper Sophie writes out five different people she might become. Tati places each strip between the knuckles of her hand. "Who will you be today?" she says. "A princess? An astronaut? A dancer?" Sophie holds up her hand, giggles, and says, "Why not ten? Why not twenty?" So Tati has her write out another fifteen fates, and puts the strips between all her fingers and toes until we laugh. She turns and asks me to pick one of the papers, but when she reads it her smile fades and she throws it into the trash and picks another, only to throw that away too as*

she gets up and says to Sophie, "Enough of silly games, especia
if you aren't going to play them properly." Afterwards, I p
the strips from the garbage and read them. The first one sc
"Sophie Blackman is the daughter father took with him." 1
second says, "I am Herald Oxley's beloved sister."

1984   In early January Tati is arrested by Argentinian poli
      Sophie and Nikolas return to Toronto in the care
      Joseph and Sherrill (née Blackman) Gordon. Joseph wor
      in international investment banking at the Canadi
      Imperial Bank of Commerce. In protest, both childr
      refuse to speak anything but Spanish. San Francis
      voters approve Prop. K, prohibiting towers from casti
      new shadows on city parks.

1985   Two-week visit from Nadia (surname now Irwin), w
      has been living in Chicago since 1980. She stays
      Toronto two weeks, at the request of Joseph and Sher
      Heated discussion around the future of the childr(
      including Aunt Sherrill throwing a few glasses a
      plates against the walls, frantic with having "to host tl
      whore who betrayed [her] brother in [her] own hon
      but when Nadia discovers that Earl left behind little or
      money for Nikolas and Sophie's upbringing she refus
      to take them. Nikolas publishes "New Ruins" under t
      pseudonym "Herald Oxley," in *Discourse/Politics*, argui
      against "the carceral system of statist identity," and
      favor of "selfhood as debris — dispersed, half-form(
      salvaged." Loses his virginity to classmates, Susan a
      Merry Blakely, identical twins. Begins to experiment wi
      combinations of marijuana and "shit mix" (made of equ
      parts sherry, Southern Comfort, Lonesome Charlie, a
      Curaçao stolen from "Uncle Joe's" liquor cabinet). Af
      being sentenced to death for a Florida murder spr
      Daniel Remeta is found to have the mental age of a chi

and before his execution years later orders snow cones for his final meal.

1986   On strength of "New Ruins" Nikolas receives an invitation from Richard Rorty to take part in the three-month "Prospect Recovery Seminar" to be held that summer at the University of Chicago. Unwilling to leave Sophie alone with Auntie Sherrill, he writes back revealing his true age and pseudonym. As expected, Rorty rescinds the offer. Bitter with the decision, Nikolas reads Rorty's letter to Sophie, who locks herself in her bedroom for a month, refuses to eat, and is finally removed to a hospital in a near catatonic stupor. Nikolas graduates from Upper Canada College a year early because of advanced placement. His nickname in the yearbook is "The Drunken Whoremeister." On April 13, Phillip Hallford forces his sexually-abused daughter, Melinda, to lure her boyfriend, Eddie Shannon, to an isolated area in Daly County, Alabama, where he shoots the boy once in the mouth, drags him to the side of a bridge and shoots him twice more before throwing his body into the river, afterwards forcing Melinda to wear a necklace made from shell casings used in the shooting.

1987   *Sophie says that even when I'm gone I'm still here. Sophie never cries — not when mother fails to call, not when the girls in school make fun of her accent, not when she isn't invited to their birthday parties or they cancel a playdate at the last minute, not when Auntie Sherrill accuses of her being just like mother and then hits or kicks her. She never cries. She says I am always there, even when I am not. When Sophie looks at me she always seems to be looking at someone else — far in the distance, off to one side, or standing between us. She says it makes no difference whether I think I'm there with her or not, because I am always there. Does she want me to prove her wrong?*

1988 Nikolas delays Rhodes Scholarship to Oxford for a seco
year to stay with Sophie. Spends his spare time writi
early draft of *Harlot's Sequence*, which he burns at the e
of the year (he will not return to it until 1993). Take:
junior position at Uncle Joe's bank, an experience h
journal describes as "attempting to build the Tower
Babel with a single stack of pennies." His favorite part
the job is highballs at the Zanzibar or Big Brass after fi
especially those nights when he scores with one or mo
of the strippers. First recorded instance, in his no
books, of Nikolas suspecting that he has an "addicti
personality." Belgium passes a law forbidding the ritu
execution of animals in the home.

1989 Against Nikolas' protests, Sophie is sent to the Surv
Montreux finishing school in Switzerland. She leaves
silence, face blank, body rigid, and a panic behind t
eyes, as if a thousand pleas and apologies and promis
were being smashed to pieces against the sight of Aun
Sherrill and her quick handshake, impatient at how lo
it's all taking — getting to Pearson airport, marchi
Sophie to the gate, waving her a dismissive goodbye.
Nikolas, unable to take his arms from around his sister
feels as if he's holding a trembling stone. With "this i
tating impediment to [his] success removed," as Aun
Sherrill puts it in the car ride home, both she and Un
Joe insist that he immediately take up his Rhodes Sch
arship. Publishes article, "Wire Knot," in the *Internatio*
Journal of Political Science, under the Oxley pseudony
the first of his writings to adapt Hugh Everett and Bry
Seligman DeWitt's "many-worlds interpretation," fro
quantum physics, to political ethics. In South Afri
Reverend Frank Chikane almost dies after his underwe
is laced with poison.

1990 First year at Oxford. Recognized for outstanding undergraduate achievement with the Henry's and Falk Fellow-
ship for Academic Merit. Rorty writes to congratulate
him on "Wire Knot" and forgive earlier deception, though
criticizes Nikolas for continuing to use the pseudonym.
Re-invites him to the Prospect Recovery Seminar that
summer. In the fall, Sophie disappears from Surval
Montreux. Uncle Joe refuses to fund Nikolas' travel to
Switzerland to assist in the police investigation, forcing
him to borrow money from classmates, though by the
time he arrives the case has concluded in a finding
of suicide. Nikolas breaks down upon seeing her body,
refusing to acknowledge that it's Sophie. Accuses lead
inspector, Franz Allmendinger, of substituting the corpse
of a lookalike runaway for his sister. Spends two dissolute
weeks blowing the remainder of his borrowed money
at the Zähringerstrasse brothel until being admitted
to the Stadtspital Triemli for acute alcohol poisoning
and "afflictions of an intimate nature," after which he
is wired return air fare to Oxford by Uncle Joe, who's
severely pissed. The shrinking Aral Sea between Kazakh-
stan and Uzbekistan splits in two, creating a patch of
desert in between.

1991 Second year at Oxford. Majors in Political Science and
Philosophy. Engages in extensive correspondence with
Rorty (published posthumously in an appendix to *The
Nikolas Blackman Reader*) on "manyworlds ethics," about
which Nikolas writes: "Given the global effects of the
ceaseless activity of the human species — where activity
itself (and not, as Marx would have it, the *products* of that
activity) is perhaps the very definition of that species — it
might, in fact, be high time for a little paralysis, perhaps
even a utopianism based on inertia." Meets Lady Cecily
Langdon, 22 years his senior ("Not that you'd know it,

looking at her smoking-hot bod," he writes to Rorty, w]
does not respond to the comment, or other commer
like this, in their correspondence), at The Boat Race, w]
shocks Nikolas by challenging him to "henceforth publi
under [his] own name," and to "shoulder seriously a:
responsibly the demands of [his] talent," and generou:
agrees to pay off his debts. Hiking Hauslabjoch Pa
Erika and Helmut Simon find a preserved corpse fro
3300BCE, later nick-named "Frozen Fritz" by investi:
tors, who also discover that he is carrying the woody fr:
of a tree fungus as a remedy against internal parasit
as well as tattoos on his skin over areas of active arthri
and a flint arrow in his back.

1992   *Who keeps sending me these postcards? Is it Sophie? The fi*
one arrived a year ago, but there have been many more — Ju
23, 1991, Beijing; June 24, 1991, San Francisco; June 25, 19
Valparaíso — always in the same hand and always addres:
to Herald Oxley, bearing that one string of information —
date, a year, a place — and nothing else. It would take an ar:
of Sophies to board that many planes that fast, to find the ti:
between takeoffs and landings to buy and write and mail th:
postcards. I mark the places in my atlas, but it seems to me ea
postcard deserves an atlas of its own, impossible with th:
dates to connect them along a single grid, as if each one was s:
from another world, another timeline, another Sophie alive l
impossible for me to get to. I mentioned them to Dick and
insists I'm being hoaxed, probably by some enemy, most lik:
a woman I screwed over or owe money to. "Forget about it,"
writes. "It'll just throw you off your work." I don't tell Dick t
postcards actually give me more ideas.

1993   Leaves Oxford abruptly in the middle of winter ter
Whereabouts for the next six months unknown, presum
to be continental Europe, on a trip bankrolled by La

Langdon. Hospital records — including prescriptions filed in Switzerland, France, Germany, Austria, Italy, Spain, and Switzerland (again), in that order, for ceftriaxone, penicillin, and ophthalmic-grade petrolatum — suggest rough itinerary and general activities. In September, Nikolas sends blank, unsigned postcards to Uncle Joe and Auntie Sherrill from Montreux and other towns and villages in Switzerland, hoping to test them as his hoaxsters, and, if not successful, then at least to make them feel guilty for what they did to Sophie. When Sophie's trail runs dry, he revisits the Zähringerstrasse brothel, where they greet him like an old, incredibly wealthy friend. Nikolas trains one prostitute, Fabienne Gallman, to deliver memorized passages from "New Ruins" and "Wire Knot" and even "Evangelion" to increase his arousal. A fifteen-year-old girl, later identified as "FWS-87" by the UN Hague war tribunal, is enslaved, raped and tortured by soldiers in the town of Foča in Bosnia-Herzegovina, then sold for 330 dollars.

1994 Publishes *Harlot's Sequence* under his real name as part of the "Prospect Institute Theories in Politics" series. Dedicates the book: "To every Sophie Blackman there ever was or will be." With the agreement and financial assistance of Lady Langdon, he transfers to the University of Chicago to finish undergraduate degree. In Liberia's civil war, Roosevelt Johnson recruits Joshua Milton Blahyi, a.k.a. General Butt Naked, who prepares for combat by ritually killing and sometimes cannibalizing a small child — i.e., "someone whose fresh blood will satisfy the devil" — and who sends his stoned, drunk and crazed boy soldiers into battle wearing either women's clothes or — like the general himself — nothing at all, in the belief that this will protect them from bullets.

1995 Completes degree in Political Science at University
Chicago. *Harlot's Sequence* wins prestigious Connac -
er-Michaels Prize for Political Theory, but incites criti(
controversy. Nikolas' fiercest critic, Bernard J. Friesen,
the *Quarterly Review of Political Philosophy,* writes: "Bla -
man's theory of an 'infinite ethics,' taken in equal pai
from quantum mechanics and barrio whorehous ,
makes for compelling if not unorthodox reading. T
idea that each possible outcome of every possible choi
does in fact come to exist, that we become the sum
the infinite possibilities enacted by multitudinous selv
in countless parallel worlds, certainly finds assuran
in the scientific theories Blackman cites, as well as
the practices of subaltern peoples he carefully chai
through history. Such 'imaginative games' may inde
have inspired 'the proliferation of possibilities' that is t
precondition of any revolutionary break with 'the perm -
sible reality enforced by conservative and worse gove -
ments.' Missing here, however, is the practical con -
quences of the 'voluntary vacillation' he recommends
the face of this, a utopian vision so radical one wonde
if not just western civilization, but human civilizati(
as a whole, would survive it. One wonders, as well, at t
personal trauma, or guilt, underlying this *wunderkin(*
scholarship." Colombia is rocked by fraudulent insuran
scams, whereby criminals buy accident and life insuran
policies for unwitting beggars, prostitutes and peasan ,
who they then maim or kill to collect the money.

1996 Granted direct entry to Harvard's PhD program
Political Philosophy. Contacted by Fidele Carrizal ,
lawyer, requesting participation in class-action lawsu
against Argentinian government for his father's dis; -
pearance. Carrizales' refusal to name other clien

precipitates emotional break with Uncle Joe and Auntie Sherrill, whom Nikolas accuses of "trying to profit from [his] father's tragedy-slash-hoax." Still, Lady Langdon encourages him to sign on. She and Nikolas are married in a small ceremony in Boston. A few weeks later, Nikolas resumes affair with Marina Matveev, soprano with the Met, a woman, as he writes to Rorty, "whose presence in my life nicely complements that of my wife, at least in terms of temperament, the shape of her body, and, most significantly, sexual preferences. Cecily agrees with this assessment, except for the 'sexual preferences' part, and accuses me of 'compartmentalizing' my lusts after certain 'assumptions' and 'stereotypes' in order to 'vacillate among the endless variety' as if that were a 'substitute for a real relationship.' Not that she minds! It's a diagnosis, that's all. She goes on to suggest that I am trying in some way to enact, 'between the sheets' as it were, my political theories, as if what was important to me was not recognizing that each woman was different but rather experiencing the action of difference itself, which has nothing to do with them and everything to do with me — this appetite for a neverending movement that keeps me from having to settle on anything or anyone. She says I prefer the idea — unconsciously of course — of infinite worlds, and their endless options, as if an awareness of this might solve all of our problems, rather than facing up to the hard work of perfecting any one of them (which also means, of course, that I have to come to terms with, and accept, the ultimate failure of any such project, even as I'm morally obliged to keep striving to attain it). The infidelity, she repeats, is not the problem! Well, maybe she's right." Rorty does not respond. On a Mexican Ranch owned by Raúl Salinas, Francisca Zetina — a.k.a. "La Paca," a self-proclaimed witch — leads police to the site of human remains suspected of belonging to Manuel

Muñoz Rocha, a federal congressman who prosecuto
say conspired with Salinas in the September 28, 19
slaying of Ruiz Massieu, and who disappeared shor
thereafter, only to find, after an official autopsy, that t
remains had already undergone a *previous* autopsy, wi
the *later* examination revealing that they belong not
Muñoz Rocha, but to La Paca's father-in-law.

1997   Begins work on doctoral dissertation, a manuscript th
will eventually become Nikolas' second book, *Oxley's Bar*
Legible Signature. Increasing obsession with the Carriza
lawsuit leads to binge-drinking and near-breakdov
late in the year, followed by several months at the Sa
James Psychiatric Center in Cambridge, Massachuse
from which, upon release, he declares himself "cured
my recurrent obsessions" in an email to Lady Langd(
Spends a week "preparing for reentry to marriage" (
he writes in an email to Rorty) at Matveev's Greenwi
Village apartment, at the end of which he terminat
their affair. From Angola it is reported that UNITA
demobilizing its soldiers and getting the UN to retu
them to UNITA-held territory, where they are promp
re-mobilized and sent right back to fight the MPLA.

1998   *It happened every Wednesday between 1977 and 1978. Af*
being tortured for days, weeks, months, the prisoners at the Na
School of Mechanics were told they were going to be releas
Music was played, the liveliest tangos and milongas. They w(
made to dance, to express joy at their impending freedom, sh
fling sliced feet across the prison floor. The doctors who again a
again had brought them back to consciousness, who'd kept th(
alive, healed with antibiotics and saline drips and adrena
so they could be beaten and cut and electrocuted and burned
over again, gave them what they called "a vaccination." Rea
it was a sedative. Then, drugged but still conscious, complic

*but terrified, they were herded into convoys, taken to an airfield,
and invited onto planes where they were stripped naked by
soldiers and one by one shoved from the hatchway at an altitude
of 10,000 feet. Sent in screaming freefall into the Atlantic, the
Río de la Plata, bones shattering on impact, lungs filling with
the sea. Every one of them disappeared, unrecorded, kept from
newspapers, official accounts, even the memories of the men
who did it, either by denial, the intricate excuses of politics and
religion, the bottle, suicide, anything at all that would stop them
from remembering the particulars of a face or a name. My father
wants us to believe that he was one of them — washed up on an
Argentinian beach, face and fingertips eaten away, unidentified,
tossed into a mass grave — instead of escaped from Sophie and
me.*

1999 Nikolas finishes and defends dissertation, graduates with
distinction. On Lady Langdon's advice he decides not to
pursue teaching, and focus his attention exclusively on
research and writing as an "independent scholar." Moves
to London. Publishes *Oxley's Barely Legible Signature* at the
end of the year, and dedicates it, "To the Many Irreconcil-
able Memories of Sophie Blackman." Book receives rave
reviews, though its primary champion becomes Lady
Langdon's brother-in-law, Geoffrey Cox, in the *Guardian*:
"On the surface a scholarly study, Blackman's work is
really a genre all its own. Between his study of the blank
pages published in Galician newspapers during the 1920s
in place of news articles suppressed by state censors, the
erased photos on missing persons posters on the walls of
Ciudad de la Guirnalda in 1947, the blacked-out 'reports'
of government work camps in the 'redacted leaflets' of
Dzembe's Invisible Insurgency in 1957-66, Blackman
inserts his own peculiar meditation on the history of the
pseudonym (including his own, Herald Oxley) as a form
of 'subversive erasure,' a life found amidst the death of

our 'state-enforced identity.' Blackman's connection
identity with private property (owned by the corporat
state rather than the individual citizen) raises importa
questions about the ways in which the western con:
tution of selfhood is itself a 'preemptive prison' det
mining the limits of individual possibility." Charisma
fails to win racing's Triple Crown, finishing third in t
Belmont Stakes behind Lemon Drop Kid and Vision a
Verse, due to fractures in the lower left front leg.

2000   *Today I found a stack of blank postcards, from places as far af*
as São Paulo, Shanghai, Anadyr, the Sandwich Islands, a
others, in a box under a stack of old underwear in Cecily's clo
I sat with them in my lap in the late afternoon sun, and thou
about Carrizales and his refusal to meet with me, to speak
the phone, the "settlement" money he sent late last month. A
I thought of my first meeting with Cecily so long ago now and I
smile and the way she said, "You must be Herald Oxley," as s
took my hand, her insistence on our pre-nuptial agreement, i
general mystery over the size and reach of both her finances a
connections. I took out my old marked-up atlas and dumpe
in the trash, and wondered what it was Cecily wanted: for me
believe there could be Sophies out there somewhere, or to give
on her once and for all by confronting me with the absurdity
my obsessions? Was it an accident that I found those postca
or something she'd been building up to all along? Or are th
buried in her underwear, just a bunch of postcards, with
connection at all to those I've been receiving?

2001   After half a year of what Cecily describes in a letter
Cox as "Paranoid rages, wild accusations, black depr
sions, and a regimen of self-medication that includ
liquor, drugs, and women paid for and *gratis*, Nikol
and I have decided to separate. Or, rather, *he has*, thou
I refuse to grant him a divorce because I do believe in t

end that his intrinsic intelligence will win out." Nikolas publishes "Honeymoon and Forensics" in the *Chronicle of Political History*, a study of the dystopian underpinnings of the institution of marriage, "particularly the ludicrous notion of couverture, which assumes that any wife could ever possibly be 'subsumed by her husband,' literally or figuratively, for any appreciable length of time." Returns to Boston, briefly, to take up the Hallman Research Chair in Political Theory at Harvard, but since the position excuses him from teaching (which, in Nikolas' opinion, "is what all professors want, including the liars who pretend to like it"), he settles permanently in New York. In Rotenberg, Germany, Armin Meiwes is sentenced to a mere eight and a half years in prison for killing and eating Bernd Jürgen Brandes, though a later court overturns the conviction, throwing out the defense argument that Meiwes acted at his victim's request.

2002   Begins work on *The Anti-Frolics*. Begins, also, to experiment with drugs — cocaine, crack, heroin — in earnest, buying from dealers under the name Herald Oxley. Invited to give lectures in Berlin, Moscow, Geneva, Los Angeles, Toronto. Stages reconciliation with Uncle Joe and Auntie Sherrill in order to berate them, over several hours, for "engineering the type of Sophie it would be easy to dismiss before she was even gone," and for preventing him from going after her until it was too late. Is particularly vicious toward Auntie Sherill, whom he accuses of "conflating Sophie with your sister-in-law, my mother, whom you justifiably hate, when all Sophie really needed was a chance." "Who's stopping you from looking for her?" Auntie Sherrill replies. "Go ahead and look. You'll probably find her turning tricks on the nearest street corner. Or dancing naked in some loony ballet while her children and husband starve, *literally*, of neglect." Later, Nikolas

will remember telling Auntie Sherrill that she was "sic "
"diseased," "with a personality like a cancer," when the c
woman dies in December from an undiagnosed bra
tumor. He refuses to attend her funeral, but does senc
short note, which Uncle Joe, stammering and breaki
down at the reception, ultimately finds impossible
read. A panel of US Roman Catholic bishops calls fo
zero-tolerance policy against priests who molest cl
dren in the future, and a two-strikes-you're-out policy
those guilty of abuse in the past.

2003   Contacts Leslie Saunders, head of security at Canadi
        embassy in Argentina, to investigate his father's dis
        pearance, and also the authenticity of Fidele Carrizal
        whom Nikolas suspects "of being a pseudonym for r
        ex-wife, Lady Cecily Langdon." Nikolas writes furth
        "He disappeared too late, in 1982, four years after t
        death flights took place. Besides, why would *la últi*
        junta militar take the risk of killing a Canadian diploma
        No, he set the whole thing up — including the note
        his schedule about the Navy School of Mechanics —
        order to walk out of one life and start another. (
        perhaps countless others, since once you've done it w
        stop? Appalling to think, isn't it, that the old drunk cou
        use the Dirty War, the suffering of a nation, one th
        wasn't even his own, to enable his personal freedor
        And freedom from what? A failed marriage? A couple
        kids who loved and needed him more than anythin
        The search for Carrizales locates an old man, a lawy
        disbarred in 2001 for taking bribes from the governme
        during 1970s and '80s, and whose memory since th
        has been scoured clean by a thousand bottles of fern
        The Parisian doll-making company, LeComte & All
        & Lanternier, produces a limited-edition run of acti
        figures called, *Les étoiles de la théorie des 20e et 21e sièc*

which speak their most famous phrases — "Der Fokus der Subjektivität ist ein Zerrspiegel"; "Ne me demandez pas qui je suis et ne me dites pas de rester le même: c'est une morale d'état-civil; elle régit nos papiers"; "L'essere che viene è l'essere qualunque" — when their heads are twisted counter-clockwise.

2004 Publishes *The Anti-Frolics*, a treatise on "the use of games in torture." Dedicates it: "For Sophie, lost before she was lost." Wins the Lohft-Neibling Prize for Political History, The Lieutenant Governor's Award for Nonfiction, the Lansing-Tate Gold Medal for Exemplary Work in Human Rights in a Given Year, as well as being shortlisted for a number of other prestigious awards, and spends three weeks on the *New York Times* Best Sellers list. Gerald F. Keegan writes in the *New York Review of Books*: "Each chapter devotes itself to a particular type of 'torture game' according to Blackman's genealogy. There is of course the predictable list: Russian roulette, mock executions under Nicholas I, Stalin's show trials, the 'white torture' of Evin Prison, gaslighting, the 'Five Techniques' used in Northern Ireland, the more recent 'kidnap game' of children in Chihuahua, Mexico. To these, however, Blackman adds arcana scoured over countless hours in archives, many of them owned by collectors so private one wonders how he discovered them in the first place, never mind gained access. Here we find the 'absence games' of extreme deprivation brought to their highest refinement in the short-lived commune of Simon Le Gac in the 1830s, where immediate family, friends, and business partners were jailed with the prisoner and then executed in front of him on a schedule determined by dice throws; the 'multiplication game' theorized (but never implemented) by the 19th century Veronese lawyer, Ottone Carlevaro, in which the prisoner's identity is given to various (in

reality nonexistent) men who continue on with his wiv ,
children, mistresses, colleagues, friends, etc., sendi
back reports (penned by poets) of the joys, triumpl ,
affections the prisoner will never again experience; t
'pointless games' of the Kerbecz Regime during the 192
in which the vital information at first withheld and th ,
after great pain, provided by the prisoner, is seconda
to what the torturer truly wants — conflicting rum ,
outright nonsense, outdated news, random observati
— with the prisoner having to tap ever greater reserv
of imagination to satisfy the conditions of his relea:
and the 'reversal game' played by Hals Mariën at Chate
Fortier in 1782-83, in which the prisoner, jailed for
apparent reason, must correctly guess the questions
the minds of his otherwise silent tormentors, most
which have to do with his favorite color, or dessert,
weather conditions. In the end, torture becomes Bla -
man's metaphor for the perversity at the heart of
authority: 'Where suppression requires another disc -
sure, where censure insists on another blasphemy, whe
limits demand another transgression. What we see aga
and again is a need for information at once contained a
endless — as if the only real question were, "What else ,
and the only rule another neverending throw of the dic "
Middle Eastern TV stations broadcast graphic phot
of naked Iraqi prisoners being tortured and humiliat
by smiling US military police, forcing President Bush
declare that such treatment "does not reflect the natu
of the American people."

2005   Initial positive reaction to *The Anti-Frolics* gives way
       critical backlash led by Thomas Korvin, who writes in 7
       Times: "It appears Blackman has veered from his foc
       on utopianism and human rights into highbrow porn -
       raphy. This book has little to recommend it other than

voyeuristic fabulism." The postcards from Sophie stop arriving. Nadia arranges a meeting at the Metropole, and requests Blackman's permission to stage an "interpretive dance sequence" based on *The Anti-Frolics*, as well as a personal loan of $250,000. Blackman subsequently jailed for assault, uttering threats, possession of controlled substances, public intoxication and indecency. While awaiting trial he is contacted by documentary filmmaker, Lester Saul, over a possible collaboration on Blackman's life and works. Blackman refuses, and hangs up when Saul asks a pointed question about his "history of paying for sexual services." Gregg Miller sells more than 150,000 Neuticles — prosthetic testicles made for neutered dogs, which come in a variety of sizes, shapes, weights, and degrees of firmness — easily doubling his initial investment of $500,000.

2006   Spends six months at the Rusk Rehabilitation Center as part of release and probation conditions. Nadia files restraining order, agrees to be interviewed as part of biographical article written by Korvin in the *New Yorker*, suggesting that Blackman inherited his addictive traits from "that old drunk, Earl, his father." "But where he gets his penchant for loose women and promiscuity," she adds, "is utterly beyond me." Spends the spring, summer, and fall recovering in Berlin, attending NA meetings in German, a language he barely comprehends, never mind speaks. Extended Christmas visit by Lady Langdon, who proposes a reconciliation. A Turkish court acquits 92-year-old archaeologist Muazzez İlmiye Çığ for claiming that Islamic-style head scarves date back more than 5,000 years — several millennia before the birth of Islam — and were worn by Sumerian priestesses who initiated young men into sex.

2007 *Cecily sits in my living room overlooking Oranienstraße, l*
in a glitter of light. When the phone rings she tells me to
it, and there's her voice on the other end, asking if I'm "ok "
with her visit so far. I pull the phone from my head and stare
her. "Do you think it's a recording of me on the other end?" s
says. "Go ahead — ask me a question." I look at the phone,
it to my mouth. "Where are you?" "Oxford," is the reply. "Bro
Street." The Cecily on the phone and the Cecily in front of
laugh. "Or Berlin, Oranienstraße," the voice continues. I wa
to throw the receiver over the balcony, but settle for dropping it
the floor. "That's not really your voice," I say, "who's helping y
prank me this time?" Cecily shrugs, fumbles for cigarettes she
longer smokes, finally rests her hands in her lap. "What if I cou
put you in touch with Sophie?" she asks. "With all the possi
Sophies?" I shake my head. As if reading my mind, she contini ,
"The postcards didn't come from me. I tried to explain that to yo "
She taps her knee. "I fished as many of them out of the mail
soon as they arrived. But there were too many for me to get the
all. I was trying to protect you. You always got so agitated af '
reading them!" I don't believe her, I don't believe any of it, sh :
manipulating me again. "I wonder how Sophie managed
send so many postcards from so many different places?" Cec '
wonders, pretending to be speaking to herself rather than .
"She must have known, I mean she must know a lot of . . . tr -
eling men." She waits for me to say something, but when I do
she looks around the apartment. "You're broke again, aren't yo "

2008 Returns to London. In May, moves into the Langd
property on Broad St. in Oxford, following Cecily's of
to again bankroll his career. Begins work on *Terror*
Missal, frustrated by unsatisfactory progress. Begins
call his mother, Nadia, every day, always asking the sar
question: "Have you heard from Sophie?" Blackman li -
wise receives daily calls from Lester Saul, who, lacki

his subject's consent, has begun an "unauthorized documentary." He asks about illegitimate children, and, specifically, whether Blackman's seen Marina Matveev recently. As per Islamic law, an Iranian court gives Majid Movahedi (27) a choice, either pay two million Euros or have his eyes put out, for the crime of blinding his love interest, Ameneh Bahrami (24), in an attempt to keep anyone else from marrying her, only to be then forgiven by Bahrami while waiting on his knees for her to drop acid into his eyes.

2009   Enraged by Saul's constant phone calls and requests, Blackman burns draft manuscript of *Terrorist Missal*. Departs Oxford on invitation to Monaco from Marina Matveev, who introduces him to her daughter, Sonya, born seven months after their affair. Demands that he acknowledge paternity. Cecily registers him with police as missing person. From July to December whereabouts unknown, presumably working on fresh draft of *Terrorist Missal*. Turns up in Marseilles, contacting Cecily to wire money, then fails to arrive at bank to receive it. Jia Yinghua's *The Last Eunuch of China* is published, describing the only two memories that brought tears to Sun Yaoting (1902-1996) in old age: the day his father cut off his genitals with a razor, and the day his family threw away the pickled remains that would have made him, in death, a whole man again.

2010   Elizabeth Kunkle, Nikolas' editor at HarperCollins, receives final manuscript of *Terrorist Missal*, without return address. Nikolas, however, turns up in Toronto at Uncle Joe's. They celebrate his 80th birthday, just the two of them. Blackman spends long hours reminiscing by organizing pictures of Sophie taken out of the family photo albums by Aunt Sherrill into an album of their

own. Marina launches lawsuit for paternity paymen
though what she really wants is public acknowled
ment that the famous Nikolas Blackman is the fatl
of her daughter. "Hey, that name, 'Sonya,' it's a Russi
diminutive for Sophie!" says Uncle Joe in the midst
eating his birthday cake. The phone rings. It's Lester Sa
asking if Blackman ever bothered searching for his sist
in Argentina. NASA researcher Felisa Wolfe-Simon (
issues a controversial report on the strange bacteriu
the GFAJ-1 strain of *Halomonadaceae*, found in Californi
Mono Lake, which redefines life as we know it by not oı
eating and thriving on arsenic, but incorporating t
toxic element directly into its DNA.

2011   Terrorist Missal *confounds the critics. The reviews make*
laugh. "I'm not sure what this is," writes one of them, "a spiriti
primer for mass murderers?" They don't know what to do w
it. Is it history? Theology? Biography? Self-help? Is it a jol
"What Blackman's latest book really is is a catalogue of ritu
behavior — one for every day of the year (including an en
perversely, for leap years) — carried out by hundreds of the m
notorious terrorists in history. Does Blackman expect read
to pick it up every day as some form of 'spiritual practice'? D
he expect readers to emulate these behaviors? For instance, t
third Wednesday in October is dedicated to Luigi Lucheni, w
the recommendation that readers hang themselves from a b
as long as they can bear it, or even longer. The second Thursd
of March belongs to Heinrich Cibo, with the recommendati
that readers swallow a pfennig, or at least a penny. Each en
also provides paragraphs of historical context: Lucheni's ass
sination of Empress Elisabeth, Swiss law denying him t
death-penalty he craved, his determination to become an an
chist martyr even by his own hand. Cibo's attempt to bankrı
Prussia through mass counterfeiting operations, his failure
produce a credible replica of the currency, and his attempt

evade arrest by swallowing the evidence. The point of all this, somehow, goes missing." I read the reviews to Uncle Joe and together we laughed and laughed, though he had no idea what it was all about, the demented old idiot. But he stops when he gets to the dedication. "Sophie," he says. "We failed her. I failed her." He shakes his head. The sound he gives those sentences — as if she's still alive. "We used to receive these letters from her . . . postcards, actually. Unsigned." Bewildered, I ask him to show them to me, but he says Aunt Sherrill burned them all, every single one. "She was dead set against Sophie from the start," he says. "She decided early on, even before Sophie came to live here, just what kind of girl she'd become out of the kind of girl she'd come from." The old man's face quivers, maybe pushing back a wave of tears, or maybe it's just age.

2012   Despite mixed reviews, *Terrorist Missal* becomes Blackman's most successful work to date, winning the Charles Naylor Prize for Historical Nonfiction, the North American Booksellers Consortium Readers' Award for Creative Excellence, the Governor General's Award for Nonfiction, the Commonwealth Prize for Political Writing. For the first time in Blackman's career, the words "Nobel Prize" are mentioned. The book spends eight weeks on the *New York Times* bestseller list, and goes into five printings. He sends all of his earnings, and signs over royalties from the book, to Marina, as well as publishing an "open letter" affirming his paternity of Sonya. The letter, in the *Monaco Register*, becomes the subject of a lawsuit brought by Cecily Langdon against Matveev and Saul. Blackman refuses direct contact with either of the two women. Takes up with Ruby Ellis, barmaid at the Black Bull Tavern on Queen St. in Toronto. Also with Thalia Katsaros, flight attendant; Judy Alsop, weathercaster on CityTV; Marianne Curtis, nutritionist. Thai police arrest Chow Hok Kuen (28) after finding his luggage contains

six human fetuses that have been roasted and covered
gold leaf as part of a black magic ritual, and which he
planning to sell for $6,600 apiece.

2013 Contacted by Saul, who mentions ongoing research i
his documentary on Blackman, including the recen
discovered grave of "Sophia Olivo Calzada" in the La Bo
barrio of Buenos Aires. Long pause on the telepho
Blackman hangs up without another word. He will nev
speak with Saul again. In a landmark case, a Dani
man is acquitted of molesting two seventeen-year-c
girls after he is found to suffer from a rare sleep disord
known as "sexsomnia."

2014 *She returned to Tati, and then Tati died, and Sophie ended
in one of the few occupations left to her. Dead now these p*
*ten years, buried beside the one mother she'd known, who
name she'd taken, the care and worry and love they'd shared
interred and dead now as well. I think of the postcards she so
my arguments with Cecily, the conspiracy theories spun out
cobbled logic, as if the leap from one idea to the next was nothi
but reflex, the quickest escape route, the panic of flight. So ma
Sophies I devoted myself to. But she knew there was only ever c
that lone signal, postcard after postcard, waiting for someo
to recognize them for what they were — nameless, no retu
address, empty of content — waiting for us to supply these to I
to acknowledge she was there, to not abandon the search. Bu
gave up looking for her. I never even set out.*

2015 Blackman disappears from Buenos Aires, and is presum
dead. Uncle Joe is contacted three times over the next s
weeks, each time by a different coroner, identifying thr
different bodies as belonging to Nikolas Blackman. Ea
body is eaten away unrecognizably. Authorities can't id
tify the sex. But the fingerprints, each time, are a part

GHOST GEOGRAPHIES

match. Sends response to third coroner: "For fuck's sakes, how many Nikolas fucking Blackman's could there be?! You fucking inept retards!" Sends apology for "word choices" two days later. Blackman's literary estate passes to Lady Langdon, who finds his final work: a 46-page list of historical events, one per page, and one for every year of his life plus seven, under the heading *Dyschrony*. She publishes it, with a dedication to herself. It does not sell well. The introduction, written by Thomas Korvin, calls the work "The end logic of Blackman's thinking: total obscurity. The blankness of the page around each brief, present-tense event in a given year seems somehow more telling than the events themselves. Random, arbitrary, and sometimes, it seems, chosen for precisely this effect, they force us to cast a backward glance on the entire *oeuvre* and wonder at what Blackman spent his life — certainly his intellectual life — avoiding, as if the elaborate theories, the intricacies of research, were there not to take us anywhere, but only to get lost in." Hector Mansell, on Fox News, blasts Blackman for completely ignoring the events of 9/11 in *Dyschrony*, "as if the United States had never even been attacked by Muslims," and including only "the sort of trivia the over-educated liberal elite would be interested in." Other critics, notably Susan E. Swanson, in the *New York Review of Books*, discover in *Dyschrony* "a vein of misogyny that, in retrospect, seems to grow more and more visible from book to book, and which we are certainly justified in noting, especially if Lester Saul's documentary from a few months ago, *The Time in Toronto, The Time in London, The Time in Buenos Aires*, is even marginally accurate." Others, such as Paige Donnelly in the *New Republic*, argue that *Dyschrony* was "never a book, but a riddle sealed in its own privacy," and that "it should have remained there." "What, for example," she asks, "are we to make of the following entry for 2015, presumably

written before Blackman's suicide: 'In Lesotho, the w
of a Danish man — who was caught in South Africa l
month with twenty-one pieces of female genitalia in l
freezer — was killed outside her home in the Maseru'? B
more importantly, what are we to make of the entries f
2016, 2017, 2018, 2019, 2020, 2021, 2022 and, lastly, 2c
— the years, some of them yet to take place, followi
Blackman's death? What was he, precognitive? Frau
lent? Or is this meant to make us think of another Niko
Blackman, reporting back to us from an alternate li
And is this not, in the end, only there to make us refl
on how unimportant Blackman's life was in the scher
of things?"

2016   Wins a Merriss-Baker Citation for Lifetime Achie
ment. Wins the International Association of Philo
pher's Medal for Sustained Excellence. Is named to t
Osakhira List of Intellectual Achievement (the $250,0
prize money is donated by Lady Langdon to the Inter
tional Coalition Against Trafficking in Women). Receiv
a Cowper-Durant Professorship (posthumously, needle
to say), a Yale Honorary D. Phil. and a Chair of Politi
Philosophy at Harvard (held in absentia). Receives lengt
obituary notices in the *Globe and Mail*, the *New York Tim*
Time, Figaro, the *Guardian*, among others. Ladbrokes off
four-to-one odds of Blackman winning the Nobel Pri
for Literature, even posthumously (which Korvin writ
"is not as laughable as it seems, given that most of l
philosophy, if not his life, can be considered pure fictio
Lady Langdon receives a postcard featuring an image
Cristo Redentor, and the words, "July 5, 2016, Rio de Janei
on the reverse. Sri Lankan authorities begin destroyi
a shipment of African ivory seized three years previo
following a ceremony at which Buddhist monks give t
slaughtered elephants blessings for a better rebirth.

2017   *I have waited a long time for my posthumous awards. They are the best ones to win, because the winning is also a dismissal, because each one pushes you further into the earth. I did not die at sea. I died long before. This is my prize.*

2018   Professor Anne Polish, Department of Languages, Stanford, publishes lengthy condemnation of the entirety of Blackman's *oeuvre*. Accuses him of "peddling cheap cynicism — as if uncertainty were saintliness, and conviction a curse — when what is so desperately needed on the left is an unbending conviction equal to that of the right, whose unstinting belief in absolute truth is precisely the catastrophe defining our political moment." She is joined by Korvin and Swanson in *The Times* and *NYRB*, respectively. The lone voice of dissent is Geoffrey Cox, who writes in the *Guardian*: "Is it just me, or is Polish's criticism the most obtuse and self-contradictory thing I've ever read?" Lester Saul manages to have lawsuit brought by Lady Langdon for defamation thrown out, though not before "mistakenly" playing a bit of recording during the trial (which Lady Langdon will in a statement call "not a mistake at all, but rather a strategic error to further undermine Nikolas' legacy") purportedly from Sophie. The recording sounds as if it were taken during Carnaval. There are trumpets and drums in the background, a crossfire of voices and laughter, a distant bullhorn delivering instructions. But the voice also sounds slightly garbled, as if it were arriving through a cellphone. *I don't know that Nikolas. We were separated so long ago. No, I'm not disturbed by his fixation on me. I feel sorry for him. It happens with these narcissists — they turn some lost girl into a reflection of their inner torture. But I'm not lost. Not this Sophie Blackman. She found her way. She knows exactly where she is.* It is reported that England's Freemasons will admit women to their secretive society, but only if they were previously male masons.

2019   Shouhei Watanabe releases *Blackman's Blips*, a sh⸱
animated feature, five minutes in length, showing
crudely drawn Nikolas Blackman laboriously peeling ⸱
his skin with a thumbnail. The final piece of skin tea
away, it rises entire, in the shape of Blackman, and wal
off. Then Blackman begins peeling all over again. T
voiceover either sounds like Blackman mimicking a Ja⸱
nese accent through autotune or someone with a Japane
accent mimicking Blackman through autotune. It delive
a crude sales pitch for each of Blackman's books — *Or(*
now and we'll deliver straight to your door! $14.99 each, or f
for $74.95! Interviewed in *Interview* magazine, Saul adm⸱
the snippet of conversation with Sophie was a telepho⸱
interview. Unable to confirm her identity, he ackno⸱
edges it could have been faked. "But, then, everythi⸱
about this family was so fake that the fake itself could
the real thing. Did you know that we tried to track dov
the guy, this Serge Boliveau character, that Blackma⸱
father went after at the Navy School of Mechanics? ⸱
birth certificate. No passport. No citizenship. No reco
of him anywhere." Lady Langdon receives postcard fro
the 67th Annual Las Vegas Car-Show featuring a 19
Cadillac Coupe Deville in St. Tropez Blue Firemist, t⸱
words "November 3 2019" written on the reverse. Po
Francis ushers in the New Year with an ode to moth⸱
hood, reminding the faithful that a mother's example a⸱
embrace is the best antidote to today's disjointed wo⸱
of solitude and misery.

2020   DVD release of *The Time in Toronto, The Time in London, 1*
Time in Buenos Aires features "Bonus Scenes," includi⸱
surreptitious recording of argument between Blackm⸱
and Lady Langdon backstage at the 2012 Comm⸱
wealth Prize for Political Writing. "Look at you, ⸱
these people here to celebrate your work, and you c⸱

barely stand up, and you smell like a garbage bag filled with whore secretions. You have no respect for anyone or anything — not even your own work." "Correction," Blackman responds, belching, "I have no respect for the *product* of my work." "Whatever!" she yells. "The *process*, though," he mutters, "well, that's some pure possibility shit . . ." "Whatever!" "That's infinity." "Whatever, whatever, whatever!" Uncle Joe, now aged 90, cuts deal with the *Paris Review* to publish "Blackman's Bad Years, 1969-2015," based on a series of Post-it notes written in the first person, purportedly left by Nikolas in the photo album devoted to Sophie. The entries are short, never longer than a paragraph, and pertinent only to the years 1978, 1983, 1987, 1992, 1998, 2000, 2007, 2011, 2014, 2017, 2022. Most critics refuse to accept their veracity — "for reasons of the maudlin style," writes Geoffrey Cox, "but also, naturally, because, first of all, there are entries for 2017 and 2022, when he guy's supposed to be dead, and, second of all, because where are the entries for all the other *bad* years?" — and they are not included in the 2020 revised edition of *The Nikolas Blackman Reader*, which sells poorly in any case. Uncle Joe uses money from *Paris Review* sale to buy himself "a vial of Viagra, and one last good time, in honor of Nikolas." Senator (R-MS) Susan Sappington blames two consecutive years of record flooding in Manhattan, and the failure of efforts to save Venice and the Maldives from submersion, on gay marriage, pointing to "fact-based data" proving that ocean levels have risen for every year since the Supreme Court upheld the rights of gays to marry.

2021   Anne Polish publishes her omnibus review of Blackman's works, "Bullshit Factory," in the *New York Review of Books*. "What to make of this intellectual adventurer with no actual beliefs," she writes, "hopping from one idea to the

next as they occurred to him, like stepping stones over
abyss, as if movement itself was sufficient to thought?
course, there is a trick in this, one he was either hoping
wouldn't notice, or thought we were too stupid to see
one is ambiguous enough, or scattered or encompassi
or indeterminate enough, one can, by generating a cert
mystique, keep the critics interpreting. In fact, this see
to be Blackman's definition of intellectual and artis
success: to contain a multiplicity of interpretive po
bilities, including contradictory, diametrically oppos
mutually negating ones. And it is this capacity for pro
erating interpretations, year after year, that he hop
would keep him alive — instantiating endless resurr
tions, endless inner worlds, endless Blackmans. Even l
purposefully provocative 'dateline,' *Dyschrony*, is mea
to keep critics parsing for connections to his biograp
But the truth is, he had nothing to say. There is nothi
to interpret. On Blackman, therefore, we must rema
silent." The critique is picked up and furthered by Thom
Korvin in the *Journal of Speculative Philosophy*: "It see
utopian, if not infantile, to expect that Blackman wo
be any different from us: a mass of incommensural
impulses, desires, fetishes. Sadly, this is exactly what
was: average, banal, ordinary." But the most damning
Susan E. Swanson's "Nonsaint Nick" in the *New Repub*
"*Dyschrony* is the culmination of a sick and superfic
fascination with the horrors perpetrated by humans
other humans, especially men on women. Humanity v
nothing more for Blackman than a hilarious home mov
Joseph Rogers Pitts, CEO of Lutik Entertainment, hol
press conference denying nonconsensual sex with
to a dozen employees, stating that he has nonethele
decided to resign "as a martyr to #metoo:" "For althou
I regard the movement's collateral damage in innoce
victims, such as myself, as inevitable, this is a negligil

consideration in its greater mission of a much-needed reform in gender relations."

2022   *What was that other boy looking at, in the car that day, in 1973? What did he see? His life inverted, distilled to misery? Did seeing me make him feel as relieved as seeing him made me feel distressed? Or was he sending me a gift on the end of his gaze — the sense I had even then, perhaps not fully formed or consciously apprehended, that at least somewhere out there I was, or many of my "I's" were, better off, happier, that their lives had diverged at just that right moment, that decisive point on my timeline, to set them on a path of promise?*

2023   On a wet afternoon in October, a fifty-four-year-old man sorts through old plates, silverware, needlepoint, stamps, vases, jewelry at a *vide-grenier* in the Ninth Arrondissement of Paris. Beneath a bouquet of plastic flowers, he finds a doll. No, he realizes, not a doll, an action figure, six inches high, old and naked and missing an arm, its skin faded to a plastic grey. The manufacturer's stamp on the inner right thigh says LeComte & Alliot & Lanternier. He peers closely at the face and remembers, or perhaps misremembers, glimpsing an unhappy boy on another continent in a car long ago. Seeing his consternation, the old woman who is running the market stall gently reaches over and takes the action figure from him. She speaks in Spanish: *tienes que girar la cabeza.* When the man does not understand, she twists the doll's head, and a high thin stuttering sound comes from a speaker in its back. They lean in to listen. She twists the head again. The recording is broken inside, its syllables fractured into multiple sounds. She twists the head again. But there is no point. He'd have to listen to it forever to make it out. The man buys a piece of Delft Blue instead.

The New Improve

Oscar Telel

The old man was Joseph Fisk, but he said his name was Oszk
Teleki. And the way he said it, the accent he had, made y
wonder whether he could hear himself speak.

He sat in the hospital room with a blanket around his sho
ders, hands resting on a cane planted between his knees, a
repeated the key moments, as he saw them, of "his" life: bo
and educated in Budapest during the 1920s and '30s; his br
and absurd directorship of the Budapest Zoo; surviving t
siege of the city 1944-45, when he was captured by fascist forc
while trying to flee west from the advancing Red Army, press
into military service, captured again this time by the Sovie
pressed into *their* service working for the secret police; fina
escaping Hungary in 1956 and settling in Canada in return f
providing information to NATO; finishing a doctorate in histo
at the University of Toronto specializing in "state repression"
the Eastern Bloc, tons of publications, fame both national a
international; married, divorced, no kids.

More than half of this — the things he told them — w
unknown information, for Teleki had been a very private m
Besides, his face, his DNA, the few acquaintances called in
said he was Joseph Fisk, an account manager living out his reti
ment in a room right next to Teleki's at the Happy Meado
Extended Care Facility.

They called in Teleki's ex-wife, Eva Makó, thinking she'd know him best, and she reluctantly agreed after it was made clear she was dealing with the police. She took one look at Fisk after she went into the room and snorted so loud they could hear her outside the door, but then Fisk whispered something into her ear that made Eva turn white and run out of there, and after that she refused to answer the phone or open the door, not even for the police. The whole thing was ridiculous. And creepy.

■

With Eva's refusal the officers called in another Hungarian, oddly enough, on Fisk's request. "Call up Professor János Varga," he told them, "he'll prove I am who I say I am." Not knowing what else to do, they did. Varga had long ago been a star graduate student of Teleki's — favored, mentored, invited for drinks at the faculty club. As the years wore on, and as he went from student to colleague to acquaintance (but never friend, Teleki had no friends), he'd even received half a dozen or so invitations to come over for dinner, to meet Teleki's wife, to retire to the study afterwards for expensive brandies, learned conversation, and impromptu piano recitals by the esteemed professor himself. He even had the not so rare honor of having some of his research ripped off by the old professor back in the 1970s, but the police didn't know that. Nobody did.

"So your father was Boldizsár?" János asked, and Fisk said that's right, his father had fought in World War One under Admiral Miklós Horthy de Nagybánya, barely escaping with his life from the Battle of the Strait of Otranto in 1917, along with Horthy himself, who was seriously injured in the fighting. Fisk said Boldizsár was also there the following year, during the raid on the Barrage, watching from another ship as the dreadnought *Szent István* went down, torpedoed by an Allied submarine.

"You know what my father's big word was?" Fisk asked. When Varga said nothing, he continued: "*Loyalty*. The most important virtue, he said." He stood by Horthy after the war too, in 1919 and

1920, when they formed the National Army to fight the comn
nists Béla Kun and his "gang of Jews" — yes, that's the phra
Fisk used, quoting Boldizsár, with the same curl of lip Var
had seen whenever Teleki said it — along with their Hungari
Soviet Republic and its 133 days of Red Terror. Of course, it w
the Romanians who really drove Kun from power, but Boldiz:
would always skip that part when telling his story, preferri
to concentrate on the National Army's "triumphant" entry in
Budapest, with Horthy at the head and Boldizsár only one
two men behind.

"Did your father ever mention the White terror that follow
upon the Red? "

"After Horthy became regent, it was necessary, my father sai
Fisk was sneering again. "To get rid of 'elements disloyal to th
own country.' He said it was another chance for him to prove l
loyalty by making sure that the orders for beatings and arre:
and murders ended with him, that nothing could be traced ba
to Horthy. He took me along one or two times . . . to see what
did, what had to be done."

"You remember?" asked Varga.

"I was six years old," said Fisk.

■

After the interview, Varga left the room and spoke with t
officers from the OPP Missing Persons and Unidentified Bodi(
Remains Unit, and said, "Other than the fact that he looks tota
different, that man's Oszkár Teleki. No question."

"We found this guy about fifty miles down, by the Grand Riv
one of the officers said, frowning at him. "The funny thing
he scratched his head, "before Teleki disappeared from Hap
Meadows, he was telling people — anyone who'd listen — abo
how depressed he was, going on about his experiences in t
siege, his failed marriage, how nothing worked out for him, a
now he was sick and old on top of it all. He also talked abo
taking off to Florida! Said he wanted 'sun and fun': drinki

margaritas, all-you-can-eat buffets, fishing for marlin, Oriental massage. Oriental massage! So one day Teleki leaves Happy Meadows — 'for a walk,' he says — and the next day someone finds his wallet on the riverbank. All that's inside it are pieces of ID, no cash, like he was leaving us a suicide note or something, leaving himself behind. And around the same time Fisk disappears, too, except we find him a week later wandering beside the Grand."

"What do you expect me to do?" asked Varga.

"How about getting him to tell us the truth, as in where the real Teleki is?"

"Why don't you look in the river?"

"Are you kidding? You know how many people disappear into that river every year? There are bends in there, deep stretches, rapids. We've already spent a week dragging the water. We almost never get a body."

"Well, maybe this is the real Teleki," Varga smiled.

"This guy is Joseph Fisk. An accountant. He had the room right next to Teleki at Happy Meadows, and they obviously talked and Fisk obviously ripped off Teleki's memories. If he was Teleki he should be able to speak Hungarian, shouldn't he?" The OPP officer was not smiling, and so Varga shrugged. The officer then opened up Fisk's file, and showed Varga how little there was inside it. "Look at this," he said. "The only thing this guy ever did was hit on old ladies at Happy Meadows." He handed the file over to Varga, who read the list of "minor infractions" handed down on Fisk: "Daily delivery of roses to Mrs. Delazney in #312, despite being asked to desist"; "Uttering suggestive remarks to Patricia Gracie in #400"; "Repeatedly having to be told that Claire Winston was not available for a 'get-together.'" The officer looked at him. "Just another crazy, lonely old man. He was nothing like Oscar Teleki,"

"I don't know, it sounds like him to me. Teleki was quite the womanizer."

■

Two nights after that Varga got a call from the front desk of l
hotel saying there was a man by the name of Oscar waiting
see him, and going down he found Fisk in the lobby runni
his hand over a table. "We used to sit at a table like this," he sa
when he saw Varga. "Minus the plastic flowers and brochur
This was before the war. We had a big house in Rózsadomb
would sit at the table and my father would pound it and pou
it during dinner. Loyalty was always his theme. Ranting ho
Hungary was 'drowning' in enemies. Those who were outside t
country — the Romanians, the French, the British, the Russia
the Americans, the Slavs — and those inside it — the Jews a
gypsies, the communists, the people who would have preferr
the return of Charles IV or Count Apponyi instead of Horthy
all those people, he said, who weren't 'real Hungarians' even
they'd lived in Hungary for generations and spoke the langua
and paid taxes and contributed work and even had Hungari
names and ancestors." Fisk shook his head. "Pounding a
pounding the table. And I was quiet, I'd learned to be quiet.
look out the window and down the hill toward the Danube a
think what it would be like to float out under the five bridg
down through Hungary, Croatia, Serbia, Romania, Bulga1
Moldova, Ukraine, out to the Black Sea. I loved the East, As
where the Hungarians had once lived, before wandering into t
sinkhole of Europe. Before, when they were still nomadic, op
to change, able to accept transformations . . ." he shook his he
"But every once in a while I'd ask about my mother. I would a
my father if she was coming back.

"Then my father would stop, collapse into himself, befo
pounding the table harder than ever, saying her disloyalty h
been unforgivable, consorting with an enemy so terrible that
cross over to him once was to cross over to him forever. He nev
told me which enemy, of his long list of enemies, it was, I o1
remember waking to my father's murderous yelling, on the la
night I saw my mother, the sound of someone falling, son
thing shattering, a hand clutching the doorknob to my roo

torn away. I never saw my mother again, except maybe once in a while in nightmares, where it felt like I was running *toward* what scared me rather than *away*. My father said he would help me with those nightmares by never granting my mother another second with me. Not even the sight of my face. Not even so much as passing on a letter saying goodbye."

"Mr. Fisk," Varga said. "I'll take you home, okay? It's quite late now."

"Home?" He laughed. "Oh, you mean that place. Full of old people." He waved his hand. "I left two nights ago. I'm not going back there."

"You left?" said Varga. "Why?" And when Fisk shrugged he said, "But where did you go? I mean, where will you live? And what about the police?"

Fisk shrugged again. "Do you have my article? I sent it to you."

Varga stepped back from him then. Something started in his throat, stuttered there, died.

"I think we need to discuss my article," Fisk said.

From here it was a long elevator ride, Varga trying to fight off the dizziness he felt, Fisk still rambling on about old Boldizsár and how happy he was to announce, after Teleki graduated from Pázmány Péter University, that in reward for his loyalty to Horthy he'd managed to get his son *protekció*, namely, the position of director of the Budapest Zoo. The zoo! Teleki had been incredulous. He was a student of history, what was he going to do in a zoo? But it was actually a pretty good job, he was to learn, delegating anything that required expertise to biologists and keepers and reserving for himself the job of showing dignitaries and their families around, attending government functions, and being responsible for the proceeds from ticket sales, which meant outfitting his office with the right books, furniture, cigars, alcohol, just in case the dignitaries wanted to socialize after seeing the animals, and otherwise enjoyed by Teleki alone, as he paged one more time through the *Gesta Hungarorum* laughing his head off.

By the time they got to Varga's room, Fisk was starting
on the events of late 1944, the deposing of Horthy by Hitl
who wasn't too happy with the admiral's rather *disloyal* (Fi
emphasized the word) decision to break their pact and ma
peace with the Allies, and the subsequent installation of t|
super-loyal Arrow Cross Party, who'd choose suicide — persor
and national — over breaking faith with the Nazis. By this tir
with Fisk starting in on the arrival of the Red Army in Decemb
Varga stopped in front of his door and yelled: "My God, wou
you please shut up? Please?!"

Fisk, to all appearances innocent, stepped back, "But this
the best part!"

Varga stared at him. "I'm not here to listen to stories, Mr. Fi
I'm here to figure out how you got hold of this information, a|
where Teleki — the *real* Teleki — is."

"Ah," said Fisk, faking an epiphany, "the *real* Teleki. Well, you
have to let me know when you find him. There's a couple of thin
about him only I know, and which I'm sure he'd like to hear."

"You wait right here," said Varga, "Right here! Don't move," a|
went inside, grabbed an envelope out of his suitcase and car
back. "Now," he said, showing Fisk the envelope, "you tell r
what's in here."

■

Varga had received the envelope shortly after news of Te
ki's death. It contained a cover letter supposedly from Tel(
asking Varga to consider an enclosed article for publication
the *Central European Review*, a history journal Varga edited. T
return address was a street in Key West, Florida, a suggesti(
so ludicrous he was considering throwing out the envelo
when the police called saying they'd taken custody of Fisk, a|
needed someone with "intimate knowledge" of Teleki to che
him out.

Fisk stood in the doorway, staring at the envelope. "You kn(
I'll bet that was sent to you by another one of us. Florida, huh

don't know anyone in Florida, but that doesn't mean anything. Nice place to be right about now, late summer . . ."

"Another one of us?" asked Varga, again feeling that terrible choking.

"Do you have a telephone?" asked Fisk, nodding toward the room.

And so, just like that, Varga was talking to a woman, about the same age as Fisk from the sound of her voice, who was recounting, in a halting way, as if she was reluctant to say it, about how in December 1944, with Soviet guns booming off the eastern edge of the city, Teleki received a note from Boldizsár claiming he and other supporters of Horthy had been rounded up by the Arrow Cross, and commanding him to go, without further delay, and warn General Kiss and Bajcsy-Zsilinszky, who since Horthy's removal had been working against the Arrow Cross, that they were coming for them as well.

"It was then," she said, as if she too was Oszkár Teleki, "that I thought about the anti-Semitic laws Horthy passed. Did you know Hungary passed the first such laws in Europe after the first war? 1920, law XXV, limiting the admission of Jews to universities." She paused, but Varga said nothing. "Of course, Horthy would pass other such laws, and later Hitler returned some of the territory Hungary lost in 1919. So there I was, note in hand, thinking these thoughts and wondering, Who were these men loyal to, really? The Hungarian monarchy? No. The Hungarian people? Only those that agreed with them. To their allies? Nope. Their children? Obviously not. I'll tell you who they were loyal to: *themselves*. Only themselves. And the second I realized this I threw away that note, and headed west, *away* from the Russians . . ."

Varga slammed down the phone.

∎

"So you just kicked him out — an eighty year old man — just threw him out?"

Varga was talking to the OPP again, wondering whether t
men he was looking at were the men he'd been looking at the l;
time, glancing around the office at the metal tables, the sta
white of fluorescent lighting, the featurelessness, thinking th
well, he'd been infected, breathed into by Joseph Fisk, and n(
everything in the world was becoming interchangeable, san
ness replicating as a virus might, making ever more copies
itself. Varga was so scared he almost told them about the wom
on the telephone, and, after that, how he'd been so angry
tossed Fisk out, and stood there afterwards panting on the oth
side of the door looking at the envelope and realizing Fisk had
answered his question about what was inside.

By the next night, Fisk had still not returned to his room
Happy Meadows, and the OPP were looking at Varga and sayin
"So, to get this right, he came to your hotel and you had an arg
ment, and in your words you just 'clicked,' and tossed him ou
Varga nodded. "I had enough of him impersonating Teleki
lost my patience."

"So you and Teleki were that close?" asked one of the police.

"I guess so," said Varga, uncertain of how he should answer.

The officer glanced at his partner. "Because from what Fi
told us, Teleki went out of his way to put other professors out
business," he said. "In fact, from what we've gathered, he did
like other professors very much at all."

The first officer opened his notebook. "Jerome Antheil. 19
Teleki delivers a 'keynote address' at some big conference
London, and he spends the whole hour taking apart this g
some kid fresh out of graduate school who's just published l
first book. According to Fisk," the cop said, "Teleki did son
thing quite similar to you."

"Well, you said it yourself, Fisk is just a crazy old man," repli
Teleki.

"Maybe you should stick around for a while," the officer repli(

■

Teleki had blasted Antheil for daring to suggest that the Allies had "sold out" Eastern Europe to Stalin and the Red Army. "Antheil's thesis," Teleki thundered at the lectern, "is little more than moral relativism that would make the governments of Britain and America no better than that of Hitler or Stalin." Of course, that was fifty years ago, when few were brave enough to be seen listening to what Antheil said, much less agreeing with it. And now, when it was in fact generally accepted, where was Antheil? Embittered? Trying to regain a lost reputation? Swallowed, like so many of Teleki's victims, by some technical college, teaching Canadian history to university transfer students, dusting off the same note cards for lectures delivered year after year between interruptions from sewing machines and table saws and welding torches from the shop classes next door, while all those ideas for talks and articles and books dried from a torrent to a trickle, to the tracks of grief felt most acutely at 3 a.m., burning down your face, a desire you thought you'd exorcised, purged from your system, for fear of what it might do to you now that it could not be appeased. Teleki had done it to so many, to anyone who trespassed on his area of specialty — using his knowledge if he could, and his connections if he couldn't — to bring them down as he'd almost brought down Varga.

Except that Varga had come through. For he'd seen enough of Teleki's victims to know there were no second chances once he got the hooks in. So he let him get away with it — ripping off the best bits of a dissertation Teleki was supposed to have been *supervising* — as if there'd been a moment of grace, a message telling Varga there was more to be gained in being Teleki's friend and collaborator than in trying to expose him. And in return Teleki wrote him phenomenal reference letters, and Varga's career was launched. In time, of course, the old professor would reveal just enough of himself, to the tinkling of piano keys, that Varga came to believe it was even the better thing to do, helping that poor damaged man, and he continued to share his research with him once in a while, out of pity he supposed, which Teleki always

appropriated as his own, granting Varga secondary authorsh
as if it was a favor handed down, and which in turn made Var
wonder if his motive was really compassion or only cowardic

■

Fisk was waiting in the lobby when Varga returned to his ho
from the OPP, sitting in the lobby as Teleki always had, ari
extended along the back of the couch as if no harm had or wou
ever come to him, as if he'd lost so much once, long ago, th
nothing could threaten him again.

"The police are still looking for you," Varga said, sitting dow
Fisk shrugged. "I learned how to get by. I don't need a roof ov
my head." He nodded toward the piano in the centre of the lob
"I'm thinking of playing something," he said. He got up, crack
his knuckles with an eighty-year-old sound that made Var
wince, moved through the ferns to the baby grand, and witho
the slightest pause for memory began effortlessly movi
through Fauré's Impromptu no. 3, as Varga had seen Teleki d(
few times at dinners and parties and even, once, in Varga's livi
room when he'd been visiting. That time, as now, Varga h
walked over to stand behind him, and then, as now, Teleki h
sensed him there, over his shoulder, and began to speak: "The
were two children there . . . all the other bridges over the Danu
had been blown up. Some by the Allies. The Nazis destroy
the others in order to stop the Red Army getting from Pest
Buda. There was only one left, and two children, among all th
crowd of refugees fighting each other to get across. Two childr
waiting for parents who would never again arrive. Sitting
the bridgehead; and the second I saw them I realized it was o
one chance . . . for all of us. I told the guard there that they we
mine. I took their hands. And then, once we were on the oth
side," Teleki shrugged, but his hands continued playing, "I l(
them there. I looked back at them, the two boys standing the
hand in hand, watching me go, and I kept on going. And lat
after I'd been captured by the Hungarian forces, not a hundr

yards from that bridge, and forced to fight for the Nazis, and after that captured by the Red Army, and forced to work for the Soviets, and then given a second chance to escape, in 1956, and met that man in the Austrian DP camp, he was British — what was his name?" Teleki's eyes were closed now, his body trembling. "After all that, I used betrayal again. Told him what I knew, the people I'd worked for, the things we'd done, and in return he got me here." He frowned, eyes still closed. "My second life." All the while the music poured from the piano, his hands moving as if he didn't need to spare them a single thought, mechanical but for a feeling there, a register of emotion no one had seen in Teleki, for it appeared to be sorrow, even regret.

"Eva," Fisk continued, "was the daughter of Antal Makó, the designer. I married her knowing she had an empire behind her, in case the empire I was building didn't work out. She saw it every day — that I was running around, that I wouldn't stop." The piece had come to the end, but he continued, returning to the start and playing on. "One of my old mistresses, her name is Andrea Gerő, she comes and visits me sometimes at Happy Meadows. She sits there knowing what you know."

Fisk turned to Varga, his hands still moving, and Varga finished it for him, what Teleki had thought, what had gone through his mind, receiving that note from Boldizsár, sitting in the zoo thinking of where all that loyalty had gotten them — not just his father, but Washington and Berlin, and Moscow, London, Tokyo, Salò, Vichy — and as he stuffed the money from the zoo's safe into a suitcase he wondered what would have happened if they'd just broken faith, all of them, just like that, from whatever allegiances they'd sworn: to nation, to race, to family. Would it have silenced the guns thundering to the east? Would it have stopped the flood of refugees — the orphans, the wounded, the homeless? Or was it in fact the logic of loyalty, its outcome followed through, to produce its opposite: migration, suicide, desertion? For this would be the distorted utopia Teleki held to all his life, the one visionary claim in a work otherwise dedicated

to practicalities — to demonstrating his gratitude to the W
— though there in subtext only, so faint you would have had
know him as Varga knew him to see it: a world where no pro
ises of allegiance were made, none kept, to ideology, to faith,
love itself, a place where no one made so much as a move, eith
in aggression or defense, for at any moment it could all swit
around, friends become enemies, enemies become frien
— a society perfected by indecision, disorientation, passivi
Though the way Teleki had lived it, it was just selfishness.

Fisk watched Varga's face as if he was capable of hearing wh
was going on inside him, and then said, "She thinks I loved h
the most, you know, Andrea. She used to come visit me at Hap
Meadows, sitting there staring at me. She came back eve
single day, as if to prove me, to prove what I've done all my li
wrong. As if there's still time for that kind of thing." He shift
his gaze back to his hands. "But it was only Eva I ever loved. Ev
really loved." Teleki started up the piece for the third time. "S
refused to read my work. She sensed the lie in it — that I cou
turn what I'd done into a good thing — though I believe I w
pretty glamorous at first, when we met. She was all of eighte
I'd just published *Refuge West*."

"I remember that book," said Varga.

"It was about Stalinists who'd cut deals after Stalin di
spilling state secrets in return for being set up in the West. Th
were right to fear reprisals, especially once Khrushchev came
power. But of course they didn't realize — especially not poor c
Péter Szabó — that there were people out here who hated the
just as bad."

"Yes, I'm aware of the Szabó incident . . ." started Varga.

But Fisk plowed on: "And when the book came out, and t
information inside it helped one of Szabó's old victims track h
down. What was his name?"

"You don't know his name?"

"Yes, Rudi Bálint, thanks," Fisk winked at Varga. "When Ru
killed Szabó my book became notorious, or famous if y

prefer. And Eva's father — always a lover of right-wing dissidents, which is to say a hater of leftists — held that party, and I met Eva, and fell in love with her money . . . what was I talking about?" asked Fisk.

"But you're not you," Varga jumped in. "You're not Teleki." He stopped, feeling that terrible pause he'd had days ago in the same lobby. "Teleki even managed to run out on himself, didn't he? He left you to clean it all up."

"The article," Varga muttered, "it's called 'The War's Orphaned Memories.'"

Varga rose then, nodding his head like he'd known this was coming, and walked out of the hotel and along whatever streets opened to him, always for some reason picking the path of least resistance, and so, going downhill, it wasn't long before he came to the river and stopped, unable to go further. And Fisk caught up to him. "You really loved me, didn't you?" asked the old man, standing beside Varga and following his gaze out along the Grand. "If that's the case I'm glad I came back."

"After that day by the piano . . ." Varga shook his head. "God that was a long time ago." He shook his head again. "After that day, I felt like I'd been there, where he'd been, in the siege. He needed someone to know. But more important than that I think it was his way of trying to explain it, what he'd done to me, to everyone. It was as close as he could come to an apology, and as far as I know I was the only one who ever heard it."

From the look on Varga's face, you'd have thought he was going to go silent, but he didn't, recalling instead the high tone Teleki had always taken against the Soviets, not only, Varga thought, to prove his loyalty to the West, but because he was afraid, as if the whole thing might collapse again and he would be back there, everything fallen apart, his mother disappeared, his father arrested, his city in flames. Bombs falling. Armies firing rockets and bullets and mortars at one another over and through crowds of civilians. Streams of men, women and children on the streets; wagons, pigs, chickens; belongings heaped

in wheelbarrows sliding this way and that in tracks churned
muck by tanks; the wind carrying away the heirloom weddi
dress, the daguerreotypes, the table setting handed down acrc
generations, all swallowed up, gone to feed that terrible win1
Bodies dismembered. Women raped. Jews shot and kicked in
the Danube. Children forced to march on ahead of the invade
carrying their ammunition.

All this, and the thought of his father taken by the Arrow Cro
clear enough from their rhetoric what they'd do to him, w
another thought to run from, and to keep running from alo:
the landscape Teleki never ran clear of, where any feeling
security was regarded as a lapse or forgetfulness, often fat
that any moment on any street is separated from what he'd se
in Budapest over that hundred days only by this: the mutu
agreement to let things go, unnoticed, unspoken, except in t
most private of moments, nighttimes rolling in bed afflicted
what can no longer be elided with the busy-ness, the pleasa
ries that pass for friendship, the diversions of nine to five, a
which must finally be faced: the indifference in a cashier's e
as you beg for a refund because it broke and you can't affo
another one; the colleague whose entire job, it seems, revolv
around sabotaging the group effort; a terrifying remark fron
girl of sixteen — replayed over and over until the sun comes
and it's easier to believe that all this, the fixations that keep y
awake, are only a childish fear of the dark, the mind fasteni
onto whatever comes to hand, and not at all signs that wh
happens elsewhere might happen here, for the neighborhoo(
too friendly, the race too sensible, the government too den
cratic. But Teleki's sun never did come up. He couldn't forg
And his streets remained the streets of the siege — burnir
lined with bodies, perforated with bullets, crushed, straf(
looted. That was what he navigated, no less after the war th.
during it, everyone an enemy and love and innocence and am:
all luxuries or entertainments to while away the time in betwe(
while you waited for the next one.

That's how Varga had thought of him since that day by the piano, and why, all these years, he'd continued to take his phone calls, publish his articles, invite him to give guest lectures, attend colloquia, deliver the keynote, and why too, perhaps worst of all, he found himself entertaining Fisk, if not in fact starting to believe him, not because of what he seemed to remember but because Teleki would have been overjoyed to have someone else remember it, to spend the last years of his life in Key West, or wherever, no longer frightened of staying in one place — watching sunsets, eating fresh crab, asking for an extra twist of lime — an amnesiac, for all intents and purposes, cradled in the pleasures of the instant. If Teleki could have expelled his memories — "orphaned" them, as the article had it — then he would have done so, Varga was sure of it, and to the first person who came to hand: a student, an ex-wife, his next door neighbor at Happy Meadows. The only question remained as to why Teleki would write an article about it, much less send it to him, unless the impossible had happened and Teleki felt guilty.

"So what are you going to do now?" Varga asked, turning back to Fisk. "Try rafting your way to Florida again?"

"Get to Florida?" Fisk said. "Hell no! When they picked me up I was trying to get *back*." He laughed. "The cops more or less did my job for me."

"You're telling me you were in Florida? You were paddling *upstream?*"

"Oh, I wasn't coming back to stay," said Fisk. "Don't think that. I just had some unfinished business is all. Something to take care of."

"Like what?" asked Varga, at the same time as he asked himself if he was really doing this, really buying into Fisk's story.

"Well," Fisk said, "it's got nothing to do with Oscar Teleki. I'll say that much."

∎

Fisk would tell him nothing else. Not that night. They walked

back to the hotel, and Fisk bowed slightly saying goodbye, Var
stifling an urge to ask where he was going, under what ro
spending the night, but he just stood there feeling as if the aft
noon they'd spent together had not been part of Fisk's plan. I
wondered if he'd see him again.

To console himself Varga re-read the article on what Tele
cribbing from a scholar called Ross Chambers, referred
as "orphan memories," sitting in bed going over what mig
well have been Teleki's last public act, these words he want
published, circulated for all to see, as if what was required f
his vanishing was this sudden flaring into fullness, a disclosu
to distract them all, allowing him to slip out the back way.

So was that it? Had Fisk shown up to console him, to tell hi
he'd done right, letting Teleki off the hook year after year, i
matter what crimes he'd committed, wrongs done to othe
because Varga had felt for him as another orphan of the siege

They were there in the article too, the other orphans, tho
who remembered the worst places of the war — Stalingra
Ukrainian shtetls, the Battle of the Don, camps, ghettoes, ma
graves innumerable — all of it in their heads in photograph
detail though they'd not been there, not seen any of it, as dista
from such places as refugees already driven out, on roads clott
with others also in flight; or holed up in cellars far remove
waiting for an end; or not yet born. Yet they remembered,
if the memories of the dead had nothing to do with the firi
of neurons, with what stirs only in the sealed rooms of an in
vidual psyche, buried with the bones and heart and what el
as if there might be a material trace of what these people ex
rienced — though nothing for you to hold — tangible as air
breeze that somehow blows against the spin of the weatherva
and enters you, and settles there, until you speak all that it nee
you to, all that must be told.

But if Fisk was a host for one of these — and consoling Var
as he'd admitted, was only a happy accident — then who did
want to speak to?

■

It would be another day before Varga figured it out. Another day of reading the article — wondering if it was Fisk or Teleki who'd sent it to him — then reading the file on Fisk until, going over his "infractions" for the hundredth time, he sat up, remembering the voice he'd heard on the telephone, the woman reciting Teleki's memories as if reading from a script. "Eva," he whispered. "Eva Makó."

By the time he arrived at Eva's place, Fisk was waiting for him on the sidewalk across from the house, shaking his head. "It took you long enough," he said.

"So this is where you've been staying. How'd you get her to take you in?"

Fisk frowned, suddenly humorless. "It wasn't a question of her letting me in. She's in no shape to . . . If you saw her, you'd know." Fisk was tired, looking like every one of his eighty years. "I can't do it without you," he murmured. "I've been trying for days, but she won't believe me when I tell her about my past. She thinks I'm making it all up."

"But that is your past. I mean Teleki's past. How could she not know about it?"

"I never told her," said Fisk. "About before, when I was in Hungary." He let out a small laugh, managing it without smiling. "I didn't want anyone, especially her, to know what I'd done back there — betraying my father, working for the secret police. All I said was that I'd fought to get out, and then *dedicated* the rest of my life to toppling the regime." He glanced across the street at Eva's place, the streetlight overhead flickering with moths and nightflies. "You were the only one I couldn't keep it from." He looked at Varga for understanding. "I had to tell *somebody*. And after what I did to you, stealing your work, and you let it go, I trusted you." Fisk shook his head. "I thought if you believed me, if you verified what I was saying to her, then Eva would believe me, too. That's why I played that joke on you, got you to call her

from your hotel room. If you listened to what she said and did
contradict it, she'd finally believe it was true. But she didn't. S
still doesn't. And unless I can get her to, she won't understanc
"She won't understand why you cheated on her all those yea¡ "
said Varga, incredulous, all of it coming clear. "Why you could
keep faith."

By the time they'd walked across the street they were looki
at Eva, standing frail in the doorway, dark rather than lumino ,
as if the light buzzing down from streetlamps ended inch
from her skin.

"Oh, you're still here," she said, looking at Fisk tiredly, "Osc "
pronouncing it on purpose in English. And she stepped aw
from the door without the slightest sign of resistance, and Fi
grabbed Varga's arm and brought him across the threshold
if he was necessary to the crossing, as if he was the ticket. A¡ l
once inside, Varga saw the house as he'd never seen it — empti
of all it once held, furniture, paintings, even chandeliers, E
standing in the corner in clothes so new Varga wouldn't have be
surprised to see tags still attached. "What happened?" he ask ,
remembering how filled the space had once been, heaped wi
Austro-Hungarian antiques, with books, fine wines, beauti
bodies, brilliant minds, a collection of everything that was be
"I've gotten rid of it," she said absently, to no one in particu]
"I thought there was nothing left of what Oszkár had done to r
But when he disappeared, I looked around and realized it was
still here." She looked up as if seeing Varga for the first time, a¡
Eva brightened. "Hello, János," she said. "It's been years since I'
seen you." Varga started to say something, but couldn't figu
out what it was supposed to be, and instead stepped forwa
and kissed her on both cheeks and whispered hello. "We used
be such good friends, didn't we?" she said.

She looked at Fisk. "Close the door, Oscar." And when he d
she turned to Varga and whispered, "He thinks he's Oszkár," a¡
she laughed, but there was something trembling in it, and Var
realized Eva was starting to believe it too.

"Eva," Varga said. "I don't think you should be letting him stay with you."

"Oh," she fluttered her hand at the house. "This isn't my place. I thought it might be, but it never was. Oszkár dumped it on me." She looked back at Fisk. "Whoever wants to stay here can stay here." And then she leaned forward and whispered again into Varga's ear. "I thought that if I could get angry enough with Oszkár for what he did to me I would stop being in love with him. And it seemed to work. By the end I was so mad it seemed like it had blotted everything out. But then he disappeared, and all that rage, it was nothing but still being in love with him, only . . . well, it had turned inside out. But we're all done with that, aren't we, Oscar?"

Fisk looked at her, and then at Varga, silently begging him to do something. "No," Fisk finally said, "we're just starting." He had a terrible smile, false right through, trying to appear confident. "We'll fill this house back up again."

"Oh! Oh we won't, Oscar. No, no." Fisk looked at Varga again for help, but Varga shrugged. "No, I sold the house today, Oscar," said Eva.

"You what?"

"Yes, I sold it. Oh, there's no use crying about it, Oscar."

And for the first time since his arrival, Varga felt sorry for Fisk rather than Teleki, standing there as if whatever spell he was under, whatever Teleki had cursed him with, all those memories he'd done nothing to deserve, the rending emotions they brought on, could only be broken by Eva saying "Yes," forgiving him for what Oszkár had done and thereby granting him release, returned to the simple pleasures Fisk had enjoyed before — sending roses, offering to walk old ladies down the hall, flirting with the receptionist. "Please," he said to Eva, and it sounded like the air was coming out of his lungs.

"Oh yes, nothing to be done, Oscar. It's over. Here," she produced a sheaf of papers from her pocket and handed it to him. "It's all there."

Fisk stood there trembling, not daring to open the papers. I moved to slip his thumb under the manila tab, and then pull back. He seemed for the first time truly at a loss, almost stu bling as he walked around the room with the papers in ha and Varga stifled an urge to reach out and get him to stop. "Y know," Fisk said, laughing quietly, speaking to Eva, "I came you because there was something I'd forgotten, somethin hadn't remembered since it happened." He looked around t echoing house. "And I thought maybe if I told you I could pu stop to it."

"A stop to it?" asked Eva, but Fisk put up his hands so he cou continue.

"There were some people, during the siege, I remember the now, who tried to help. You have to understand what it was lil He looked at her, at Varga. "You can't imagine. No electric No water. No food. Fighting and fire and bombing. Shelte meant to hold people for an hour, the length of a bombi run, now being lived in for weeks. Civilians and soldiers de by the thousands in the streets. The injured crammed in makeshift hospitals in the Parliament, the Museum of Milita History, the State Printing Press, the Castle District — bod naked, dying of thirst, often with limbs missing, so little roo they were sometimes stacked on one another, unbearable h and cold, lice everywhere, piss and shit. Doctors operati through the night being interrupted by drunken soldie coming in shooting at one another." He waited. "But the o I remember — *now I remember it* — was the hospital where t babies were, the ones whose mothers never came for them cut off by the Soviet advance, by the bridges blown up alo the Danube, by the collapse of buildings, rape, murder. A the nurses held them to their breasts thinking they mig give them that — at least that — before they died. And one one the nurses started producing milk." He paused, waiti for her reaction. "I remember that now! It's what I came ba to tell you."

Eva opened her mouth, but it was Varga who spoke: "You never told me that," he said, suspicious and amazed. "You never once mentioned that." And now it was Eva's turn to appear distraught, unsure of herself.

She stood there. And when she finally spoke her voice was cracked. "You're not really Teleki, are you?" she said, unable to hide the hopefulness in her voice.

"I'm Joseph Fisk," he said. "You know, there were memories Teleki ignored. Ones he couldn't use to his advantage. Because even that, the siege, his suffering, was something he used." And when Eva smiled again Varga finally saw where Fisk was in all this, having spent those weeks listening to Teleki talk and talk and talk about himself. For Fisk had not been passive in that — content to echo the professor — but had latched onto Teleki's memories and combed through them for those that would prove to Eva you could be Teleki, you could have gone through what he did, and still come out of it believing in something other than the inevitability of ruin — narcissism, cowardice, infidelity, depression, suicide — and know that it was finding her that was the end of it.

"Joseph," Eva said. And when Fisk nodded she reached up and touched his face.

■

But, of course, what was easy for Eva to accept — what she wanted more than anything, even truth — would not, ultimately, be so easy for Varga. And whenever he thought of them after that, wherever they'd gone, he couldn't help but wonder if Teleki wasn't laughing somewhere, maybe even at the fact that Fisk thought himself responsible for figuring out what was needed to get Eva back. And Varga's role in it, the need for his presence, was not for what he could corroborate, but for what he *couldn't*, for what Teleki *hadn't* told him. Because if Teleki had managed to remember the doctors and nurses — and how else would Fisk have known about them except from Teleki? — then maybe the

Siege hadn't left a mark on him, maybe what he'd told Varga th
day at the piano was only to lead him on, to make him feel sor
for Teleki, using the siege to his advantage as Fisk said. In fa
maybe Teleki had never lost sight of human goodness: that
matter what is done, what happens, it all turns out for the be
in the end — for him in Key West reaping the rewards of a l
lived in perfect selfishness; for Eva finally free of the home the
shared; for Fisk no longer lonely; and even Varga, knowing l
sacrifices for Teleki had finally been acknowledged and put
positive use. And although Varga doubted it — for he too need
to believe in something better than what he suspected —
couldn't help but remember the smile Fisk had given him th
night over Eva's shoulder. It was a smile of victory, one he'd se
many times. It was pure Oszkár Teleki.

Spire

One afternoon the twins disappeared. Maris looked for the
everywhere — in every room, the crawlspace under t
house, the cave in the split boulder in the back yard, hacki
her way through ferns, salal, blackberry to the sunken mead
where she found Tommy with his wooden gun, Clara wi
her bow and arrow. Hunting bear, is what they said. Tomr
pointed to a rotten log that had been clawed apart, fragments
a beehive inside, bits of shredded honeycomb trailing into t
underbrush. There were a few bees still squirming in the wo
whether salvaging honey or larvae or numbering the dead Ma
couldn't tell. She grabbed the twins' hands and raced them ba
through the trees.

Two weeks later, Tommy screamed "Bear!" inside the hou
and Maris came rushing out from the kitchen. The bear w
up on its hind legs, ten feet tall, so black Maris thought she s
stars glittering in its fur, as if she might fall inside, spend t
rest of her life drifting in space.

When she opened her eyes Tommy and Clara were standi
there, plunging their plastic knives into nothing.

After Paul came home from work he'd hunt bear for fifte
twenty minutes, until finally he had enough. The twins wou
grab his hands, but he'd shake them off, irritated. It was alwa
like that — furious play, then a dead halt.

Paul was like that with Maris too. It was how he disarmed her — "I promise when we're ready we'll move away from here and buy a house and get you a bank account" — but the minute there was an actual opportunity, action to be taken, he was paralyzed. When she made an appointment with a real estate agent or bank manager he grew sullen, resistant, and finally enraged, staring her down and shouting: "Why do you want to move us into town when we can live here for free? This is a perfectly good house. Why should I go through the trouble of getting you a bank account when it's easier to just hand over the money?"

If Maris persisted he used the kids. "Don't upset Tommy and Clara," he hissed at breakfast and dinner, on Saturdays before he went off to hunt or fish. "They don't need you attacking me, they've gone through too much already." But the yelling drained him. There was too much risk, too much work, in rage. "Later, later," he said, waiting for her silent treatment — short and fierce — to soften into despair, helplessness. Then, late at night, with the bedside lamp throwing their shadows against the wall, he would present more reasonable objections, his voice going from a rasp to a murmur: A promotion at the company if he stayed put and did as he was told; the bad schools — full of Indians and rednecks — the kids would have to go to in town; the transfer to head office in Vancouver that was just around the corner, where they could really settle down.

"We've been in this place two years already," Maris said, turning away from him and glancing out the window in the direction of the bay, the waves black except for where they curled silver under the lights of a distant dryland sort. "Nobody stays in these houses for long," she said to herself. Paul was already asleep.

■

Some days the kids would go into the other Company houses — there were only four, down the dirt road at the edge of Stillwater Bay — through a broken window or a door left creaking. Maris found them up on counters, fingers reaching for the high

cupboards. They discovered a glass door etched with Chine
birds. Someone must have brought it with them, installed
then left. They found a torn note under a light switch cov
hanging from one screw: *I spent a winter here in 1959, driven
see* . . . Why had they hidden it there, and what was the rest of t
message? They found a bottle of blackberry wine hand-labell
1945. She shooed them out, said the places were private propei
Clara asked if that was so, then why did no one live in the
"Sometimes they do," said Maris, thinking of the people whc
been here when they arrived, the woman, Julie Locke, taki
her aside, "Listen, Maris, we've been here nearly a year and \
should have left months ago. It's free rent, but it's a trap. Y
can't sit around month after month with no one to talk to b
kids. At least get Paul to buy a car so you can go into town."

Sometimes the children said they could hear voices off the s
They interpreted every shriek of the wind as a message beari
news of kings and Turks, the Tartar invasion, palace intrig
wheels of fire rolling through armies — all the things Maris re
to them at night. There was no reason for them to learn Engli:
They never spoke it, mute in the company of a rare visitor tryi
to piece together Maris' broken grammar.

She waited for Paul to get transferred. What was the long
the Company stationed you in one place? Three years? Oth
families came, sometimes for as short as eight weeks — t
men off into the bush with their pickups, surveying tracts
forest, engineering roads and bridges, making sure the l
booms left on time to mills in Port Alberni, Crofton — th
they left and the houses were empty again, stovepipe chimne
silver in the rain.

Sometimes feral cats got into the houses. They screech
and growled and hissed all at once, as if sound was a sheet y
could rip into pieces. There were a lot of cats in the forest. Peoj
stopped along the nearby highway and tossed them into t
ditch. They gathered in the middle of the road like a carpet th
suddenly unravelled in every direction. Tommy and Clara we

fascinated, pulling fish bones out of the garbage to feed them, until they were bitten or scratched. The cats liked to give birth on the verandas and in the abandoned rooms, the children trans-fixed by the fetuses being pushed out, the mother licking them clean, eating the afterbirth. Whenever a cat came too close, or Clara and Tommy got hurt trying to grab one, Paul would pull out his .22 and go outside. He said that killing a cat once in a while made them respect you. Animals stayed away from places of unnatural death. He was a good shot with the .22, resting the barrel on the hood of the truck, taking his time to sight the scope. Usually it only required one bullet, and Paul was back inside within minutes, but one night a few months ago the first shot was followed by another, then another, and another, and Paul was gone upwards of an hour, returning with leaves in his hair, scratched by brambles, too angry to talk, locking himself into the bedroom for the rest of the evening. After breakfast, the children followed the red spots from leaf to leaf, before they found the injured cat, bringing it back over the pinecones and rocks and fallen branches in their wagon. Maris promised she'd fix the animal, but after the children went for a nap, she took it down to the bay. The next morning, drawing the rope in, unknotting the sack, she looked at the glossy fur, ran her fingers through it, and felt a strange peace.

It was a feeling Paul never had. He still walked as he'd done in those taut hours when they snuck across the border in 1956. He'd gone ahead of her and the children. The guard towers were darkened on purpose, he murmured. It made you think snipers were present when they weren't, or absent when they were there. He ran beneath them, hands over his head, as if the tiny bones of his fingers would stop bullets. He parted barbed wire with old mittens brought along for the purpose, then snipped them with pliers. Maris followed when he indicated it was safe, trying to keep the children quiet and in line. He spent what felt like a lifetime moving to the left, to the right, in fields he thought were mined. He approached the Austrian guards on the other side;

battled with the English language, paperwork, passports, t
big decision on where to go — Australia, Canada, the US; th
struggled up the job ladder of the logging industry. He'd done
all, under duress. Now he refused to move another inch.
Every three weeks a letter arrived from his sister, Anna,
Budapest. They hadn't even told her they were going. The rac
came on that morning, reported that Soviet tanks were enteri
the country to beat down the "reactionaries," and in th
moment the decision was weighed and taken. Anna's lette
detailed, repetitively, how she was paying the price for Pau
treason. The state made public examples of people like her, t
family left behind, as a warning to others thinking of esca
Her name was at the top of every blacklist ("class traitor" was t
official designation); she'd been fired from her job, barred frc
Party membership, relocated to a coldwater flat on the ind
trial island of Csepel, sharing it with a couple of factory worke
young men, illiterate, sexually explicit, farting in front of h
She was a trained chemist with a PhD! She was the daught
of the conductor of the national symphony! She'd looked aft
Paul when their parents disappeared, carted off along wi
the other dangerous hordes of middle-class citizens after t
Red Army arrived. She'd found them an apartment, worked f
three years in a tire manufacturing plant to prove her loya
to the proletariat. Until then they'd both been classified as
citizens," inheritors of their parents' crimes, unable to get go
jobs, Party membership, or, in Paul's case, entry to university.
was her sacrifice that changed that. Paul had been able to nar
her, this factory worker, this proletariat, as his "guardian," a
in that moment, with that one alteration, he had gone from
criminal to favoured son, picking his university from the li
They'd lost it all, she reminded him, the villa in Hűvösvölgy, t
Bösendorfer pianos, gala dinners, ancestral portraits in oil, t
peace of the vine-shaded arcade. Now he was out in the We
where he could start over, while Anna was still at the factory,
an even worse apartment than the one they'd shared, collecti

tinned sardines, underwear, looking for that perfect pair of boots for when they finally took away what little she had and kicked her into the street.

Paul sat with the letters as if they were maps that would keep him from getting any further into Canada.

"I'm so tired of escaping," he said to Maris.

"We have escaped, Paul. We made it."

"They're still shooting at me from over there."

He thought he was the victim in all this, Maris realized, looking at him slumped over the letters. Maybe he was. He'd used up all his courage surviving what happened to his parents, getting her and the kids out of Hungary. He was beyond repair.

■

Clara found a scaffold one day, buried in ferns. The forest was filled with things like that — discarded furniture, cars without wheels, a bullet-riddled radio. People left these things behind when they moved away, dumping them in the ravine south of the main road. Sometimes Tommy brought her pieces of silverware — they looked silver, but how could they be? — a knife with a rose on the handle, a soup spoon shaped like a shell.

The children ran to get Maris, dragging her along to the scaffold, ignoring her as she yelled at them for playing unsupervised in the forest. "Can we use it, Mom? Can we?" Clara was already straining, trying to lift the structure to its feet. Stepping carefully between the ferns, unsure of what they might be hiding, Maris examined it. The pipework was rusty, some of the boards needed replacing, but it was still solid, and small enough that she could haul it disassembled on the kids' wagon. When she made it to the house, Tommy had a blueprint unfurled, flapping in the breeze, along with his father's hammer and nails, new planking. Maris dropped the rope from her shoulder and gathered up her drawing, fighting the wind to get it furled up again, then turned on Tommy. "Did I give you permission to go into my things?"

Tommy looked at her, then at Clara, who took her mothe
hand. "You look at them at night," she said, "Dad says you want
to be a builder, a long time ago."

Maris reached up. Her hair was thick with sweat. "No
'builder,' an architect," she said, flicking the blueprint at the cl
dren as if it was useless, a worn poster. "But I got interrupted
. . ." Neither Tommy nor Clara understood. Maris squatted a
rolled out the drawing, a project for architecture class, wh
lines on blue, a design for an observatory, and fixed the corne
on the grass with rocks. Then she took a hammer from Tomm
hand. "Let's build it," she smiled.

They worked all day. The bottom level was the engine roo
The middle one was the lab. Up top was the observatory, a
they sat there until night, Maris bringing them food for a picr
Paul's voice crackling on the CB radio in the open window sayi
he was stuck at camp and wouldn't be home before mornin
The stars were painfully bright, uncut by the lights of a city, li
the ends of needles on Maris' eyes. Tommy and Clara called c
to them to fall, their fingers tracing new connections betwe
the points.

She worried that the children would learn nothing out he
Once in a while they went to town in the Company pickup loan
to Paul. The town was a ribbon of houses stretched along t
coast, bulging around the pulp and paper mill, thinning out
it hit the fishing community at the furthest point north. Ma
spent a day figuring out which dress to wear of the three sh
managed to bring, which pair of heels, the matching moth
of-pearl earrings her mother had given her at the wedding
the secessionist locket handed down by Paul's grandmother.
was probably all out of date already, she imagined, thinking
the women in the latest fashions on Váci Street. She comb
Tommy's splayed hair, drew a necktie tight around his thro
She put Clara into a dress, French braids. In the driveway, Pa
looked at them and shook his head, but otherwise stayed sile
They climbed into the truck and bounced into town.

Maris was cautious in her high-heeled shoes, careful to avoid turning an ankle in the gravel parking lot when she got out. They stood for a second in the old townsite, the place where the first homes had been built, for workers, around the pulp and paper mill in the early 1900s. She hobbled to the edge with the children, gazing downslope at the beach, the campsite farther on, the pulp mill a kilometer up the coast, billowing smoke. The sea stretched onward from there past islands and mountains and unbroken wilderness. Paul waited by the truck, smoking a cigarette, looking at the ground. When they came back he walked a few paces behind them in his woolen coat, workboots, the logo on his cap advertising a hauling contractor.

The main part of the town was one road, six blocks from end to end, filled with a stationery store, bookshop, Chinese-Canadian restaurant, boat and outboard motor repair, donuts, used cars, bank, liquor and grocery store, and the strip bar. They walked up one side and down the other in half an hour. Maris was stared at in the bookshop, the woman behind the counter whispering to the proprietor while their eyes were like fingers poking at her clothes. Tommy and Clara were befuddled by the books they couldn't read. Paul stood by the door, ready to leave at any second, wincing whenever she pronounced his name "Pál." There was something different about how the women dressed here. Maris couldn't quite sort it. The fabrics were different, stiffer, more opaque. The cuts were definite, square.

On the way back to the parking lot a man rolled down the window of his truck, leaned out and glared at her over his mustache. "How much you asking, baby?" He sneered at Paul, who stared at him for a few seconds then looked away. "Faggot," he said, rolling up his window and rumbling off.

When they got home, Maris sat at the bedroom desk, staring at a blank sheet of paper. *Kedves Édesanyám*, she wrote, and then it poured out of her. It was the first time she'd use the phrase, "My pushed-underwater life."

Paul was drinking a beer and listening to Leo Weiner. T
groceries were still on the kitchen table where she'd left the
Clara and Tommy sat sleepy-eyed in the kitchen watching
mouse edge closer to a trap behind the fridge. Clara was aimi
her slingshot loaded with a marble, and there were already
few dents in the side of the refrigerator. Maris stared at the
a minute, then began pulling cans from the shopping ba
She cleared the table, set them down. Here was Buda Cas
That fold in the embroidered tablecloth was the Danube. He
was Mátyás-templom. Big can, big can, little can. "Wat
the spires rise," she said, Clara and Tommy edging closer
the table. "Here's the Lánchíd," Maris said, lining up a seri
of matchboxes, "across the Duna." More cans, and then sh
built the white towers, fine as fish bones, of the parliame
buildings. Then Saint Stephen's Basilica. The Academy
Sciences. The kids were helping now, fishing cans out of t
cupboards, carrying them to her. Maris then went on to descri
the city as if they were walking through it. She told them t
story of the architecture, how the stone set aside for the par
ment was stolen, and the one the architects replaced it with w
softer, more porous, sponging the grime of pollution from t
air. Paul looked in on them and smiled, the music soft in t
background. Clara was lost in the streets. She didn't even noti
him. "It's time for the children's bath," he finally said.

The haze across her eyes faded. Maris stepped straight out
the city. It seemed to come with her, trailing behind in a seri
of fading images, as if she was as quickly stepping into a frar
as leaving it behind. She nodded at Paul as if she didn't knc
who he was. The children followed her traipsing up András
Boulevard, through Heroes' Square, straight to the entrance
the Széchenyi fürdő, steam rising off the waters.

■

Every day after that she walked them along the streets of t
capital. Tommy always wanted to go to the Nemzeti Múzeu

and see the crown with its tilted crucifix. Maris peered between the pillars of split pea and cream of broccoli soup and described what they saw in the glass cases of the exhibits: coats of arms, chain mail, swords unearthed at Mohács, the shifting borders of the kingdom. Clara wanted to stand spinning beneath the secessionist motifs of the Iparművészeti Múzeum, ceilings of ceramic tile, all flowers and arabesques. Mother and children, they walked through the old city for miles.

In fact, they never left. In the forest near the house they were on the Kiskörút, farther away it was the Nagykörút. Maris carefully corrected the children as they listed the streets: Szent István, Teréz, Erzsébet, József, Ferenc. The old logging road met with the abandoned spur met with the new way to the dryland sort met with the long driveway to the towed-away house met with the gravel track that led home again. They circled around and around, stopping at famous places along the way: the West Station, the Comedy Theatre, Hotel Royal, the New York Café, the twin towers of the Józsefváros Church, the Oktogon, Batthyány Palace. They dined with artists and faded aristocracy and the apparatchiks whose evil Maris taught them to recognize on sight.

Letters arrived from Maris' mother, filled with news of the family, the events less important to Maris than where they took place. She closed her eyes and imagined taking the HÉV to Gödöllő. She thought of the seven hills of Veszprém. She could see the waters of Lake Balaton, iridescent green, from the dry forests of Balatonalmádi. She could smell the waves on the breeze.

The children started calling Stillwater Budapest. "Stay with us in Budapest," they said to Paul, the next Saturday, as he got into the truck.

He looked at Maris, then squatted to speak with the kids. "I have to go to work today," he said. "Just until lunchtime, then I'll be home. And all day tomorrow." He looked back at Maris, who was holding out the hem of her dress and swaying slightly, like a young girl hearing a waltz for the first time.

"We're going for a walk to the castle today," said Tommy.
"We're going to look out from the Halàszbástya," said Clara.
"I'll be back in time for lunch," said Paul, frowning.
He finally caught Maris' eye. She smiled and whispered
him to come back soon. She told him he should stay. She sa
whenever he came back was okay.

■

Paul sat in front of the stereo and watched her, Bartók's Stri
Quartet no. 4 jabbing at his nerves. Maris was making *madár*
— bird's milk — for dessert that night, describing, plot poi
for plot point, the first time her mother had taken her to s
Bluebeard's Castle at the Opera House. The children were sitti
in the aisles with her, desperately waiting for intermissic
Tommy unwilling to break from the story to go pee. Mai
would not pause. "We're at the opera," she hissed. "You ca
just get up and disturb all these people because you forg
to go beforehand like I told you." Paul turned over the reco
and reset the needle, pausing to push a loose floorboard wi
his toe.
"Do all the wives die?" asked Tommy.
"When I grow up I want to be Bluebeard," said Clara.
"You can't be Bluebeard. You're a girl."
"Yes I am. And you're going to be my wife."
Outside the door cats were fighting. Paul went into t
cabinet and pulled out the .22, happy to have a problem wi
an easy solution.
When he came back, they'd barricaded the door. Maris w
whispering to the children about the defense of the city. Pa
could hear her through the frame. One minute it was 1848, wi
the Austrians and Russians entering Budapest. The next it w
1918 and the French and Romanians threatening to bring the
down. Then it was 1945, with the Soviets on one side and t
Nazis on the other. "Someone is always threatening the beautif
city," she said, and Tommy and Clara looked at her with wond

but also uncertainty, glancing at the front door every time their father hammered it with his fists.

"This isn't going to work, Maris. I don't think you're crazy." No, Maris thought, you're the one who's crazy. You with your fear of change. She brought out the soup cans again, giving the kids directions. Tommy had to build the cathedral. Clara was working on the spires of Mátyás-templom when Paul finally kicked in the door and stormed into the kitchen knocking everything over. He glared at her a moment, then shook off his boots, put away the gun, and tried to sit again by the stereo as if nothing had happened. Maris helped the children re-stack the cans, telling them the city was a maze. You could get lost in it. There were a hundred places where you'd suddenly come across beauty — a stained glass window filled with flowers, a tiny café no one had heard of, a chapel left alone by the government, two old men on a bench reciting banned poetry they knew by heart. There was too much in it for anyone to control. There were perfect moments, she said, kept secret.

At this, Paul got up and ripped the needle off the record. They could hear it score the vinyl, like a rusty zipper. He cursed, fumbling with the record and the paper sleeve, and finally just left it there, half stuffed into the jacket, when he went to the bedroom and slammed the door.

■

It was Tommy who ran up to the house the next day saying he'd discovered the garbage. He didn't use the word "garbage." It was treasure, an avalanche of it, he said, down the hillside into the field where the Lockes used to live, and it had appeared magically after a night of rain. He was tugging Maris' hand, pulling her along, trying to get the story out of his mouth, talking about the Avars, the Romans, ancient tribes in the Carpathian basin, the relics they'd left, rituals they'd enacted, like a mash-up of the exhibits Maris had described during their many walks through the Nemzeti Múzeum.

The two of them walked along the ridge above the Loc
property. Clara was waiting for them a half kilometer off, h;
blowing around her face as she stared down at the fallen tre
drifting clumps of wild grass, and the steady flow of the St
water River, swollen with rain. When they arrived, Maris s;
where the earth had washed away, a scar, and inside it we
old TVs, chairs, throw cushions, toasters, hubcaps, rusted s;
blades, best-sellers, and under these the occasional china tea
and ceramic dish and glass vase and rotted leatherbound boc
"Look at it," said Tommy, wading into the river before Ma
could stop him, reaching down, water wicking up his sh
sleeve, and pulling out a scalloped plate fringed with curli
vines and gold leaf. Maris took it into her hands as if the rest
the world had faded. Tommy fished through the garbage a
handed her something else — a ceramic ladle, white, with de
blue tracery, only a few hairline cracks to show for being buri(
How had it survived? By now Tommy was in the river up to l
thighs, one hand gripping a long branch from a tree along t
shore, reaching down to bring up a photograph in a steel frar
of interlocking birds. It showed a woman in a ball gown.
Maris gazed down the hill. "Clara, go back to the house a
get some rope out of the shed." All afternoon they worked, ro
knotted around their waists, though by afternoon the level of t
water had fallen to their ankles, and in some places was alrea
gone. Buried in the muck was a gilt mirror, a bone hairbrush
Lamprecht No. 36587 medicine bottle. They were finding few
things now, but still finding them. They seemed to be mo
precious the deeper they went beneath the trash on the surface
a cameo locket filled with hair, a cut-steel necklace with cryst;
in the shape of daisies, a belt buckle that was a butterfly wi
enamel wings.
They piled what was valuable on the solid earth at the edge
where the river had been. Maris was so obsessed with the wo
she didn't notice the afternoon become evening then night,
the arrival of Paul's truck in the far-off driveway. The kids saw t

headlights and stopped, but she urged them on, saying they had to get it all out before it was too late. She looked up, expecting clouds, more rain, the possibility of the hillside washing away.

"Mom, it's Dad," said Tommy pointed along the ridge, where Paul was striding, swatting aside branches, fronds, blackberry. "Maris, what are you doing?" He was yelling. Normally at this hour he'd be opening the front door, the smell of dinner rising from the kitchen table, part of the predictable, routine life he demanded.

"There's all these things," said Maris, gazing into the seam. "These beautiful things." She pointed them out to Paul with a finger, though there seemed less of them now than an hour ago, as if they were burrowing back into the earth. Maris was trying to explain it to Paul with her hands. She kept turning them, knuckles up, palms up, unable to decide, tracing in the air the contours of the bank as the rain washed it into the river. "Why would they — " She was looking at Paul and the children for an answer. "Why would anyone bury such things?" She wiped at her cheeks and forehead, leaving streaks of dirt on her skin, her hair wisping around her face. "Why wouldn't they keep them safe?" She was crying. "Who would do something like that? What kind of people?" She was holding a tiny wooden barometer, intricately carved, and waving it around in the air as if she might summon whoever had once owned it.

"It's just a bunch of old garbage," said Paul. "Someone probably threw it out when they moved away. You shouldn't be playing with the kids in a place like this."

"No," said Clara, bending down to pick up what was either an ear trumpet, or the horn from a wind-up turntable. "They didn't throw it away. They buried it. They wanted to be able to come back to get it."

Tommy nodded in agreement. "They wanted us to find their treasures. They put it here so after a hundred rains it would come up."

Clara said, "It's on our map. Right here." She pulled a piece of

paper covered in crayon scrawl from her pocket and showed
to Paul, who took it and shook his head, then looked up at h
daughter and went back to the map, slowly, almost imperc
tibly, starting to nod in thoughtful agreement.

"I'll bet you there's more!" said Tommy. "That's not our or
map."

Paul looked at him sadly, still nodding. "You could be rigl "
He didn't yet sound convinced of his own words.

"There could be treasure everywhere!"

"Everywhere here," said Paul again, his voice firmer now, as
he knew what he had to do. He winked at Maris, who looked
him strangely.

"In our city!"

Was it Clara who had spoken or Tommy? Maris couldn't t
Paul was squatting in front of the children now, as if he w
addressing them, but really he was speaking to Maris. "Ma
ancient cities were built on top of older ones," he said. "It go
deep. City upon city upon city. There's no end to the traces . . .
what you might find. They're all there, underground, waiting f
you." He drew an X on the ground as if they could start diggi
right there, as if they didn't need to move an inch.

The children were looking back at Maris and smiling, as
victory was theirs, as if Paul had finally come over to their w
of thinking. But Maris' hands and face shook. She knew wh
Paul was doing. "Your mother is right —" he continued, "the c
goes on forever." His voice was hard with false conviction, t
rage of teaching her a lesson. Tommy and Clara were in his arr
now, they looked like three children babbling excitedly, buildi
Maris a prison out of her own glittering words.

Crossword

The first bad Remembrance Day was 1984, the year Fra
turned seventeen and his mother, Juliska, passed aw .
The old men came up the front steps in their berets and dre
uniforms and polished medals, and Feri, Frank's father, m
them at the door and told them to go away—"Get lost, murdere "
is what he actually said—and then they were arguing over wh(
fought for who and which government you should be grateful
and whether or not Feri should maybe just pack up if he rea
felt that way and go home to whatever fucking country h(
come from.

Those old men really knew how to swear. It was, in fact, t
main reason Frank believed they'd fought in the war, dov
in the dirtiest trenches, in conditions so extreme everythii
— every moral lapse — was permitted. "Go home to whatev
fucking country you came from" was actually one of the ni(
things they said. Sooner or later, as Feri railed against them, t
veterans would get to words like "jackass" and "selfish basta "
and then, eventually, "goddamn Nazi asshole," which for F(
was the worst insult of all.

"Hungary was not a Nazi country!" he shouted.

"Goddamn Nazi asshole son of a bitch," the old men said.

"The Allies spent the war shooting and bombing Hungaria
and you want me to give you money for your stupid plas`
flowers?" The vets glared at him. "What else do you wan "

Feri said. "Maybe I should dance around and clap for you like a monkey?"

"We fought so you'd have a country like Canada to come to."

"If you hadn't fought I wouldn't have *needed* a country like Canada to come to!" The veterans had this fidgety look, like they were still obeying some old reflex, patting their hips for service revolvers no longer there, reaching for rifles that used to hang on their shoulders. The movements made no impression on Feri. "Or," he shouted, "if you'd fought a little *harder* and pushed the Commies back to Moscow instead of being so friendly with Stalin you gave him half of Europe, I *also* wouldn't have needed a country like Canada to come to." At this point Feri hauled back the door as if he was inviting them inside, but really just so he could slam it that much more forcefully in their faces.

Frank watched the old men stumble out of the driveway that rainy November day. There was the lanky one he'd come to know as Lester, the barrel-chested one, Harlan, and there was of course Hank, who'd done all the swearing and finger pointing and stomping of feet. Frank took out his sketchbook and drew a cartoon of the three of them, Lester and Harlan with their arms around Hank like he was some comrade they were carrying home from battle, and the following year he went back and wrote "No. 1" beside it.

■

By 1985 Frank was sketching more than ever, something he did when he was nervous, watching Feri disintegrate, the house dirtier with each day since Juliska's death, their lives unraveling. He pulled out the big black hardcover and flipped to a blank page, dreaming of getting out of Mr. Simpson's art class with a portfolio good enough for university. He was so lost in it — drawing the changes to his father's face — that when the doorbell rang he jerked and chiseled a line through Feri's mouth.

Frank got up, his face already lined with the strain of getting Feri to work every morning, rolling the old man out of bed in

that tiny guest room he'd taken to sleeping in after the funei ,
so narrow and stuffy in there you could get loaded off the boo
fumes he exhaled. Then Frank would go to school, trying
finish grade twelve, shopping for groceries afterwards, drivi
to work to pick up Feri, coming home to make dinner, do lunch ,
laundry, then whatever homework would still fit into the day

At night he'd get calls from Arlen Hassburger, Feri's bo ,
about how he'd caught him napping in the supply cupboard,
drinking on the job, or letting the other guys on the rigging cr(
pick up the slack, and Frank would have to talk Arlen out of firi
Feri. He'd have to beg for sympathy — after all, who would
fall apart after the death of his wife of nineteen years? — a
then lie about how Feri was making "visible signs of progre "
(Frank had learned this language from the high-school cot -
sellor who'd helped him with his own grief.) If Arlen could o
give him another month of grace things would improve.

"Your father was always my go-to guy," Arlen said. "It hurts r
to see him like this. But I've got to hold up my end, too, you kno "
"He'll be your go-to guy again, I promise," said Frank.
"What about you, Frank? If things don't work out wi
Feri, I could use someone like you down here. There's alwa
openings . . ."
"I don't know," said Frank. "My plan was to finish high schc
and go to university." He stopped, realizing he'd used the wo
"was" instead of "is," and wondered if it wasn't too late to take
back, to stop whatever the word had set into motion.
"To study what?"
"I was thinking fine arts."
"Waste of time. You'll blow four years in university and yor
be good for nothing but what you should have done in the fi
place. Take it from me — I wrote an honors thesis on Alexand
Pope. Rhymed couplets, the 'incisiveness of satire,' all that sh
I've got friends who went to grad school and are serving mea
while I'm making eighty-five grand a year as supervisor. Uni(
wages. It's good money."

But it's not good *work*, thought Frank. Thirty-five years of it. Your whole life gone. He held the phone to his ear and said he'd get Feri to work on time tomorrow.

■

Now he came around the corner and saw them.

Hank was in front, just like last year, peering out from between his gin blossoms, pushing his face forward with every point he made, telling Feri about the war, his role in it, those of his friends Lester and Harlan, who stood to either side, agreeing with Hank's descriptions of how they'd suffered. And all the while he rattled the box filled with change, his lapels covered up and down, not an inch to spare, with the poppies he peeled off and gave away.

Feri looked at Hank like he was a freak. Feri was drunk. "You didn't fight for me," he finally said when Hank stopped to take a breath, "you fought *against* me."

Hank pushed his face even closer, as if he either couldn't believe what he was hearing or had already forgotten it. "Do you know what it's like to be trapped on some hill shaking with dysentery while mortars are raining all around you?"

Feri smirked. "Do you know what it's like to be ten years old, stuck in some cellar, while Allied bombers are blowing up the city over your head?"

Hank looked back at Harlan and Lester as if Feri's response was a prank, just the sort of thing old comrades would pull on their former sergeant, but they looked just as shocked and bewildered. So he turned back, head tilted the way a dog will look at humans who are doing something inexplicable. "Do you know what it's like leaving behind your family and country to go fight for someone else's freedom?"

"Do you know what it's like realizing that your country has been overrun by foreign soldiers, who are replacing the last foreign soldiers, who are replacing the foreign soldiers who came before, all of them promising freedom?"

Hank put his fists on his hips, not knowing what else to (
with them. "Do you have any idea what the nights were li ,
working on three hours sleep, covered in mud, bitten to shit
mosquitoes, waiting for the bullet that's going to end it?"

"Do you know what it's like for a young boy to step out of t
cellar to get water, and there's a Hungarian soldier lying on t
sidewalk, his head crushed flat by a tank, and the boy realizes i
the soldier who helped him get water yesterday?"

Hank's face was red now, furious. "Do you know what i
like holding your friend, some guy who's covered you, sav
your life more times than you can count, while he tries to t
you something, choking on his own blood, and you're not ev
praying that he lives, you just want God to give him a chance
say what he wants to say before he dies?" He stepped forwa
again, looking into Feri's face.

"Do you know what it's like when the Allied armies fina
arrive and the soldiers, *Allied soldiers*" — Feri poked Hank in t
chest — "come into the place you're hiding with your moth
and aunts and sister and take turns raping them in front of yo "

"You have no idea what it took for us to win that war!"

"You have no idea what suffering is!" Feri yelled back. "You sh
your way through Europe then came back to Canada and did
have to live with what was left!"

"And all of us died so you could come out here and enjoy it to "

"What makes you think I'm enjoying it?" shouted Feri. Ai
then he pulled back the door and slammed it in his face.

"We'll be back next year!" howled Hank.

"You can come back every year for all I care!" screamed F(
straight into the oak grain of the door, the words coming out ii
movement so violent it jerked his head forward, teeth bared li
he wanted to take a bite.

■

If the "No. 1" visit was unexpected, and "No. 2" a test to see ii
had been real, then "Nos. 3–10" were by design. Over the yea

Frank would see every variant on the argument, every tactic, every cheating attempt at victory, until November 11 became for his father a kind of Christmas and Thanksgiving and Easter rolled into one, the day on which he flickered briefly to life again. The veterans tried everything. They tried shame, telling Feri they were going to go to every house on the whole block, the whole neighborhood, the whole town, and let everyone know what an ungrateful bastard he was; Feri said he didn't care what others thought, and looking at him, breathing hoarsely, flashing yellowed teeth, in that old sweater with its constellation of cigarette burns, the vets knew he wasn't bluffing. They tried hostility, ganging up on Feri and yelling at him at once; but Feri was like some master fencer, parrying every point, patiently explaining why they were wrong, even remembering things they'd said in passing minutes ago, returning to refute each of them in turn. (This, from a father who no longer remembered to wish his son happy birthday.) They tried empathy, telling him he was right, soldiers had died on both sides, that Remembrance Day really was for soldiers all over the world; but Feri just snickered and said, "Don't patronize me." Did they really think he believed for one second that they'd be happy pinning poppies on the lapels of former Waffen-SS?

So the vets had to become creative.

"No. 6" took place on a weirdly sunny November 11. Feri was sitting on the front steps drinking beer, lining up the full bottles on his left, the empties on the right, and the ashtray on the step below, between his feet. He scowled when he saw the vets arrive.

Frank was up a ladder around the other side of the house, out of sight, but he could hear everything. He stopped to listen in the middle of cleaning the eavestroughs, his arms caked in muck and weeds and leaves up to the elbows.

By the time he'd climbed down the ladder and come around the corner, Feri had gone into the house and come out with their old atlas, paged forward to a map of Central Europe, and

began pointing to the scenes of historic battles: Stalingrad, t
Don River, and finally Voronezh, where the Soviets slaughter
100,000 soldiers from the Hungarian 2nd Army. He point
to each place on the map, then went through the invasion
Hungary, from county to county, city to city, ending at the Sie
of Budapest, listing off the numbers of the dead. "If Hit
hadn't been distracted by you bastards in the west," Feri sa
his voice slurring, "we might have been able to mount son
opposition to the Soviets. And then all our cities wouldn't ha
been destroyed."

"That's not our fault," Harlan said. "You picked your side."

"We picked our side as much as Canada did," Feri repli
"There was no choice. The only difference between your count
and mine was luck — yours good, ours bad. When Regent Hort
tried to make peace with the Allies, Hitler threatened his so
then kidnapped Horthy, then replaced him with puppets."

"Excuses, excuses," Lester said. "The Poles resisted. The Ron
nians managed to switch sides. The Greeks, the Serbs . . ."

"We had an underground, too," yelled Feri, "General Kiss a
Bajczy . . ."

"That's not all that's been going on underground, Mr. An
Canada," Hank said, speaking now as if he'd meant to spe
much earlier, totally out of synch with the conversation. I
reached into the rucksack he'd brought along and pulled o
a photo album that he opened with the pages facing Feri. "Y
say you're not happy with being forced to come here," Ha
said, sweating into the wool of his collar, "but these pictures s
otherwise." There they were: Feri and Frank sitting in a canoe
the middle of Freda Lake, mist rising off the surface, slash
around, whitecapped mountains rising on every side; Feri a
Frank down by the marina getting on board the *Princess Anne*
go salmon fishing in the Strait of Georgia; Feri — alone this ti
— sighting his rifle on the hood of the truck, a bottle of *pálin*
open at his elbow; Feri — alone again — squatting on the edge

Stillwater Bluffs while a storm front opened over the sea, sheets of rain dimming the islands along the strait, an image cold and miserable and solitary.

"You've been following him?" It was Frank now, cutting in, stepping between Hank and Feri, who was staring at the pictures open-mouthed. "You can't just follow people around and take pictures of them."

"I was just getting proof," Hank said, while Lester and Harlan turned red, and Frank realized they hadn't agreed with what Hank had done, stalking Feri, that he'd done it alone. "Go ahead and tell the police," Hank continued. "They're on our side." But despite his confidence he'd already snapped the book shut, and was backing away.

Why wasn't Feri saying anything? Frank turned back to his father and saw that the old man was swaying on his seat, still clutching his atlas, face wet with tears. "Juliska liked going out to Stillwater," Feri said, having such difficulty forcing out the words it was like a stage whisper. But Frank knew it wasn't true. His mother had never gone out there. Once again the old man was reinventing the past to make it look as if he'd had some insight, some intimacy, with the woman he'd been unwilling to know.

"Maybe you should go inside," Frank said, but he wasn't talking about the moment anymore, what was happening with the vets, but of something more permanent, watching as Feri tried to pick up the beer bottles, which clattered and rolled down the stairs — not a single one broke — the old man stumbling through the door, gone into full retreat now, from work, from the world, from any thought of the future.

When Frank turned back only Harlan was still there, holding out a plastic poppy. "I'm sorry about Hank," he said. "I don't know what got into him. He's kind of gone crazy with your father. I think . . ." Harlan paused, still holding out the poppy, its fuzzy petals trembling. "You see, things happened to Hank in the war. He came back from over there . . . Well, he came back

and he's been like this ever since." Harlan coughed. "Lester a
I try to make sure he doesn't do anything too crazy, though \
can't always . . . Look, I'm not trying to make excuses, and yo
father is as much to blame."

"I think you should leave," said Frank, not taking the poppy.
"It's not our idea to keep coming back here. It's Hank. \
come because he tells us to." Harlan blushed, looked aw
then mumbled, "Well, he's a sergeant and we're just privatɛ
Throughout it all Harlan held the poppy extended, but he a
Frank were too committed to their positions either to retract
reach out for it.

Finally, Harlan just let it fall between them.

It stayed there, on the ground, for weeks, for months, until t
spring, when one of May's downpours washed it away. Passing
every morning going out, every evening coming in, Frank wou
wonder about the flowers that had come and gone since the sta
and all the flowers yet to come, offered across the thresho
raining on the years of Feri's bereavement like some disin
grating bouquet. It would have been better if the old man h
just taken the first poppy Hank had offered, dropped a quart
into the box they held out, thanked them for the sacrifices they
made, then closed the door, tossed the poppy into the garba
and never seen them again. And if they'd come five mont
earlier, the night Juliska sat them down before dinner and tc
them what the doctor had said, how little time he'd given h
before that terrible scene between her and Feri on the last nig
any time at all during those four months it took her to die, th
maybe that's how it would have worked out — Feri too distract
by what was happening to him (because that's how it was, Julis
was sick, yet somehow the whole thing was happening to hi
to do anything other than nod, neither really seeing them at t
door, nor hearing what they were saying, nodding, noddii
nodding, absently dropping the coin into the box and th
standing there holding the flower wondering what it was f
He often looked at people — especially his wife and son — li

that during those four months, standing in the kitchen staring as if he couldn't figure out how they were put together, according to what design, what aim, and it wasn't until the vets showed up that Feri flickered back to life again, in a way he'd only ever do with them, every year on the anniversary of their first visit, summoning up that original energy, the man he'd been when he was still secure, before his wife's death, loss of job, before the cigarettes and bad food and booze took their toll — too soured on what Juliska's passing had done to him to notice that his son, Frank, was still there, looking in, attending to his father's needs, and to realize that if he *had* noticed they might have been in it together instead of alone.

■

For "No. 7" Frank was in the shower, early morning, and as usual Feri came into the bathroom, too lazy to use the one upstairs, dropped his pants, sat down on the toilet and lit up a cigarette. "Smells bad, doesn't it?" he said in Hungarian, always Hungarian when it was just the two of them, though his English, perfected from the gutter-speak of the rigging crew right up to the pseudo-formality of union meetings, was almost flawless, his accent only coming out once in a while and in the strangest of places — saying "shet" for "shit," "kwen" for "when," and "slot" for "slut."

Frank said nothing. It was just awful, the combination of steam, tobacco smoke, and his father's loose bowels, and the years had for some reason weakened rather than built up his resistance.

"I must say even I find it disgusting." The old man shook his head, completely bewildered. "And yet I am the source of the smell."

Frank wondered if this is what had killed his mother, not this specifically of course, but the slow accumulation of such incidents — the oncologist had told him that stress was a contributing factor with cancer — back when they still lived together in this house, when the place was clean, kept up, when he'd get home from school with the smells of his mother's meals wafting

through the place, when Feri would return from the mill havi
actually worked, tired but satisfied, having accomplished wh
was expected of him — back, in other words, when things we
relatively normal for Frank, when he could still look forward
the sorts of things sixteen-year-olds looked forward to: getti
his driver's license, girls, bootlegged beers, at least a decade
odd jobs and irresponsibility before work, marriage, and ki
set in — the rewards of a life kept on track.

The doorbell rang. Frank popped his head out betwe
the curtains. "Is that the doorbell?" he asked. But instead
answering Feri wiped himself, stood up, belted his pants ai
pressed the toilet lever. "Watch out, I'm going to flush," he sa
knowing that flushing always cut off the cold water to the show
though he always did it anyway.

Frank pushed himself into the corner where the scalding spr
couldn't reach, pressed shivering against the cold tiles until
knew the toilet had filled up again and the temperature go
back to normal.

By then, he could hear them shouting through the bathroo
door Feri always forgot to close as he left, the heat and stea
escaping with him, so that when Frank got out of the shower
was freezing. The veterans had brought along a woman, Franl
age or so, and he crept out at the sound of her voice, bare
remembering to wrap a towel around his hips.

She was beautiful, women were all beautiful, they got mo
beautiful the longer Frank was trapped in this house with F
— the women, the thought of women, the possibility of wom
receding from him as if Feri was a boat carrying him off to s
even though he could still make them out, all of them, throwi
confetti and lifting champagne bottles and waving from sor
distant pier for him to come back.

She had black ringlets down to her shoulders, a narr
face, cheekbones so high they ricocheted the sun right into l
eyes, and the pinkest lips he'd ever seen without actually havi
lipstick on them. She was already talking to his father wh

Hank, Harlan, and Lester stood behind her, arms crossed, like some geriatric bodyguard.

". . . moreover, if the Canadian and American soldiers hadn't come, my grandparents would have died there, along with the six million others," she finished.

Feri looked incredulous. "Are you kidding me?" he said to the three vets.

"Really. If not for men like these," she indicated the vets, "I wouldn't be alive."

Feri pretended to gag, though it could have been a cough.

"It's not like the soldiers of your country were doing anything about the concentration camps," Hank said, nodding along with the point she was making. "Or I should say — they weren't doing anything to *empty* the camps."

Feri turned to Frank, who stood there in the towel dripping wet, then rolled his eyes at his son's lack of social graces — even as he was still wearing one of the three sets of clothes the veterans had seen him in year after year — then turned back to the visitors. "Very nice. So if I agree with this young lady, then I might as well thank you all for fighting Hitler. If I say who cares, then it proves I was a Nazi." Feri crossed his arms and tapped his temple. "Here is what I say to you — what is your name, Elena? —" she nodded and Feri continued, "the Red Army did more to free the Jews than the British and American armies put together. So maybe you should send a thank you to Russia."

"It was the great Anglo-American alliance that won the war," yelled Hank. "It was the triumph of conservative principles over socialism!"

"Ha!" yelled Feri. "You remember nothing. The Red Army did most of the fighting and most of the dying." He lifted a thumb. "Their leader was a communist. The Americans came second," he said, lifting his index finger. "Roosevelt was a very liberal president, maybe the most liberal in American history. And the British third," he said, lifting his middle finger. "They didn't do as much fighting or dying as the other two." He shrugged. "And

Churchill was the only true conservative among the three."
dropped his fingers and chuckled. "One communist, one liber
It was actually the socialists who defeated Hitler." Here F
laughed out loud, not because he cared who'd defeated Hitl
or who was or wasn't a socialist, but because he was just so hap
to destroy the veterans' argument and see the look of hatred
their faces.

It looked like Hank was going to start jumping up and dov
in rage.

"He has a point," Elena said, though she was looking at Fra
as she said it.

"He has no goddamned point," said Hank, who then stopp
for a minute to think about what the point was. "The Brits foug
hard," he finally said, unable to come up with anything mo
concrete, but Elena cut in, saving him from the lapse.

"Yes, but Stalin and Roosevelt were both to the left, politica
Not to the same degree of course. But, I mean, if Roosevelt w
running for president today, with his policies, the Republica
would call him a socialist."

"Those people don't even know what socialism is!" said Feri
"That's not the point!" yelled Hank, responding to Eler
not Feri.

"I'll tell you the point," said Feri, getting into the old man's fa
"The point is you stopped the Nazis from killing people, then y
let Stalin kill twice as many." He pulled the door back shaki
his head. "No plastic flower for me this year, no thanks, no tha
you," he said, and slammed it in their faces.

Through the crack Frank caught a last glimpse of Ele
looking his way, and for a moment thought of putting his ha
out to catch the door and find out if what he saw in her eyes w
attraction or pity.

■

Frank was still drawing her picture months later, even thou
he'd tracked down her name, Elena Prager, and phone numb

which he was building up to call. Sometimes while Frank was drawing, Feri would enter the room and come up from behind and place his hand on Frank's shoulder and just stand there like that, breathing hard, with the rattle in his throat growing louder and louder as his daily dosage of cigarettes increased. "She was a pretty girl. Maybe she'll come back next year!" The old man laughed. But when Frank didn't laugh along with him, Feri lowered his voice, "Maybe I'll be dead by next year." Frank just kept working on the picture, ignoring him. The old man coughed, not too long, not like in the morning when he couldn't stop, standing by the sink as if he was going to heave up his lungs, but just once or twice, as a reminder. Frank looked up at him, put down his pencil, and asked Feri if he'd like a beer. Or wine. Or *pálinka*. "As much as you like," Frank said, angry now, pushing out of the chair, moving into the kitchen with his father stumbling behind him, locating the old man's stash, always shifting but never so well hidden Frank couldn't find it sooner or later, pouring the booze into a shot glass, holding it out for Feri, who just stood there pretending nonchalance, as if he could say no, as if he could resist. Then Frank remembered his promise and shook his head, angrier now with the hopelessness of it all, and in the last second, just as Feri was reaching for it, he turned and dumped it into the sink.

"You'll never call her," Feri snarled. "Never, never."

∎

By "No. 8," Feri was three-quarters rotted, breathing in rasps, too tired now for the effort of hiding his drinking or maintaining his dignity, to do anything other than sit in his chair with the cross-word puzzles his brother sent every week from Hungary, back issues of old *Füles* magazine bought at flea markets, relics from the communist era printed on cheap newspaper stock, black and white, though every issue had pictures of naked women posing seductively in the middle of the darks. If Feri somehow managed to finish one, which was rare, he always made sure to

rip it up and throw the scraps into the garbage in front of Fra
something he'd been doing for fifteen years, as if no time h
gone by since his son was ten. It was the demonstration of su
riority that mattered, not the naked ladies, because God kno
there were always enough unfinished crosswords lying arou
the house, sometimes for years. Nonetheless, Feri would sta
there, tearing them up page by page, smirking at Frank, who
longer had any idea what his father could be thinking, lost
another empty ritual, another idiosyncrasy the old man clung
— like his feud with the veterans, or his constant demands th
Frank drive him out to the places he claimed Juliska had lov
or the way he always said, "*Guten Morgen, mein Herr*" when
entered the kitchen for the coffee and eggs Frank made; or "s
bitte schön," once they'd sat to eat; or "*tostada, por favor*" when
needed another slice of toast — always the same, every morni
year after year.

There were other idiosyncrasies, of course, and far mo
malevolent. All of Frank's girlfriends had commented on h
Feri would sit around talking about how he was too old and tir
to help with cooking or cleaning up, but the minute the fo
was on the table he was there instantly, fast as teleportation
it didn't matter if he'd been in the next room, on the toilet,
the garden — and then complaining loudly for everyone else
hurry up so he could eat. He was too old and sick to get up fro
the couch for the TV remote control, five feet away, yelling
Frank to get it for him, but when it came to driving to the liqu
store for another week's supply of booze he was good to go, ke
in hand, shoes on, no help necessary. But what really bother
them was the way he stood and stared, never making clear wh
the stare implied — Melissa described it as a leer, Tara as a gla
Neve as a form of psychological blindness — except that the
was a kind of violence to it, as if Feri knew exactly who and wh
they were.

"Don't leave," Frank always said when the girls suddenly s
up, checked their watches, and said they needed to go, thou

he always said it low, under his breath, not wanting to beg. He was tempted to add that Feri wasn't going to live much longer, if they could just be patient, but he decided this might jinx it, his father's death, and the old man would somehow recover, his lungs turning pink and elastic, and he'd live to be a hundred.

The girls always smiled. "You're a great guy, Frank, but I can't sit around like this." They made it sound like they were waiting for something else — to move in together, get married, have kids — but Frank knew exactly what it really was: that even if Feri died tomorrow it would have taken too long. They'd seen Frank come home from a dead-end day with the riggers, driving Feri to visit doctors the old man never listened to, refusing to quit drinking or smoking or eating sandwiches slathered with chicken drippings, and all of them knew that every week Frank would peel the sheets off his father's bed, stained yellow with the nicotine the old man excreted in his sleep.

Worst of all, they'd witnessed the pride that kept Feri from admitting how much he owed Frank, which would have meant admitting how hard Frank worked for him, which would have meant admitting his absolute lack of gratitude, all of which was impossible since Feri was never wrong in anything he thought or did. He deserved it all, automatically.

No, it was easier to belittle Frank, Feri sitting with his crossword, asking his son's advice: "What is a four-letter word for the Greek goddess of victory?"

"Nike," Frank would say.

"Nike? That must be another of those goddamn Anglicisms." Feri stared at the page. "*Nikusz!* That's what it must be." He turned back to the crossword. "Wait a minute, that's six letters — too many."

"N-I-K-E. Four letters," said Frank.

Feri smirked. "It's a Hungarian crossword puzzle. I wonder what it is in the original Greek. Must be closer."

"Maybe it's spelled 'Nike' in Hungarian, too," said Frank, "only pronounced different." Feri just snorted. "What?" continued

Frank, coming from the kitchen carrying the long knife h
been using to cut up a chicken, "you think just because it's t
same in English it can't be right?"

"Hungarian and Greek are European languages. They're clos "

"English is a European language."

"No it's not. Ask the English if they consider themselves part
Europe. Go ahead — see what answer you get."

"It's Nike," said Frank. "Why can't you just admit it?"

Feri looked at him in total silence, which was the clos
Frank ever got to winning an argument — the old man sayi
nothing, not having a comeback but refusing to concede. And
the background, some girl or other, there only for the two wee
Frank ever managed to have any girlfriend, would sit in qu
witness, sometimes shaking her head, unable to understa
why Frank stayed.

"I promised I would," he would say later, after Feri had be
put to bed.

"Your mother couldn't have expected you to put up with th "
she'd answer.

She hadn't, Frank thought. She'd lain in that bed, a shawl ov
her bald head, and listened to Feri weep and go on about h
he'd look after Frank when she was gone, how he'd make su
their son went to school, studied hard, avoided the pitfall
getting an easy job in town rather than a university degree. Th
she'd leaned up on her elbow and motioned to Frank.

"Promise me you'll leave," she'd hissed, whispering into Fran
ear with the last of her strength. "He has no idea how far h
sink. Run away. Promise me!"

And of course Frank had promised, knowing it would nev
keep, that there would always be that other father — now dis -
peared completely into the wreck Feri had become, killed off
fact by the suicidal indulgences the old man permitted hims
— the one who'd taken Frank fly fishing as a kid; and hunti
and skiing and swimming at night, laughing as they jump
into the water off a log boom at Mowat Bay; who'd gone over

Harold Bosco's house when he complained that Frank had been trespassing on his property, running through his strawberry patch on the way to school, and set him straight in no uncertain terms; and who most importantly had seen to it that when he took sixteen-year-old Frank back to Hungary the kid had the freedom and license to get laid, something Juliska would never have permitted. None of these things had ever been presented to Frank as a debt to be repaid, and he himself didn't see it that way, only that looking after this terrible old prick was his last chance at communing with the dead, with that long-departed father who would have loved Frank looking after him.

Besides, he thought, holding his mother's dying hand, it was easy for her to ask for this promise now, passing off the responsibility for something she should have done years ago, if the security of being with Feri hadn't been less scary for her than the thought of going it alone.

■

When November 11 came around again Feri was at the door before Frank could react. The old man responded to the doorbell like he'd been waiting for it, shuffling along the carpet with the kind of speed he only ever used for dinner, or if too much time had gone by between shots of brandy. Frank buried his head in his hands, expecting another battle, voices yelling, drowning each other out, but it was quiet, so quiet that after a minute he lifted his head and saw that the scene had changed.

It was the veterans, as usual, but Lester was missing, and in his place were two young men, cadets, carrying clipboards and maps and handling the money and poppies.

"Where's my friend, Lester?" Feri asked, looking around as if he was truly bewildered by the vet's absence, as if they really had been friends.

"Lenny?" Hank rubbed the back of his head and looked at Harlan and the cadets.

"Lester's dead," Harlan said.

CROSSWORDS

In that moment of silence, Frank thought of Juliska, and wh
she might have said to all this, standing at the door telling Feri
stop teasing the old men, get back inside, mow the lawn, put u
shelf, re-roof the garage, all the chores Feri had hated but whi
ultimately kept him functioning, off to work, away from t
bottle, alive. "You'll all be dead one day," Juliska would have sa
"and replaced by other old men keeping to their wars." She'd ha
glided over to run a hand down the fuzzy faces of the cadets,
the while looking at Frank, "And enlisting boys like these to
your dirty work."

Feri looked at Frank, and then in the direction his son w
gazing, his own face draining of color as if he could see Julis
too. Then he turned to Hank: "See what you've done to my so
Do you see? It's the same thing you people did to me! It bro
Juliska's heart, having to come out to Canada, to this place. I'
never told you about that, have I? Back in Hungary she taug
literature. Do you realize what coming to a country like this
where you can't do the one thing you were born for — does to
person?"

Frank rolled his eyes. Feri had been delighted to tell Julis
there was no point in looking for work, that he was making mo
than enough to keep her at home doing laundry, washing dish
cleaning toilets, in what Juliska would, at the end, refer to
broken English as her "strangled life." But she'd done it, deprivi
herself, and the only time she complained was at the end, tryi
to keep Frank from doing the same.

"You did it to yourselves," yelled Hank, "you and your Na
government."

"We weren't Nazis!"

Frank turned and walked away from the door. By the time h
reached the kitchen, the argument was in full swing.

■

Feri lived another two years. By then he was attached to
oxygen canister, wheeling it along behind himself, covered

273

stickers that said "danger" and even one showing a huge skull and crossbones. Frank thought of it as his father's pirate flag cruising the high seas of the Uptown Mall, Hendricks Liquor, the Hollinger Hill Tobacconist Shop, and, of course, that last November 11 the old man would ever see, "No. 10" on the list, when he hobbled in sight of old Hank, who was more befuddled than ever, standing outside the liquor store in full military regalia, mechanically jingling a set of bells while three or four cadets stood around in camouflage and black berets handing out poppies. "I guess I'll see you at home later," said Feri, shuffling over, aggressive as always. Hank stopped jingling for a second as if he wanted to say something in return, but then a wave of blankness passed over his face and his hand resumed the side-to-side motion with the bells.

Feri looked at Frank, but it wasn't with the usual mix of rage and arrogance — that sort of listen-and-learn widening of the eyes Frank remembered from every November 11 — but a kind of withdrawal, even fear, as if Feri was asking for help. "I'm Feri Kovács," he said, turning back to Hank. "Your enemy."

The cadets stopped what they were doing and closed in, not yet alarmed but wanting to know what was going on. Hank's arm continued jingling the bells as if it were detached from him, some cartoon arm he could unscrew and leave hanging in space still doing its job while the rest of him turned to the cadets, uncertain, waiting for instructions.

"My brother stayed in Hungary," Feri said, verging on desperate. Some of the people coming out of the liquor store stopped, a small crowd forming. "I told you about him," Feri continued. "It was what the communists did to family who remained behind after someone got out. They made them suffer. Bad jobs. No promotions. Terrible places to live. The guilt was supposed to discourage people from trying to escape. My brother used to write me letters about how bad his life was, blaming me."

Feri stood waiting, wondering why Hank wasn't fighting back. It was as if his words were nothing but sound for the old vet,

rising and falling, glimmering for a moment like some firewo
at the top of its arc, then fading as if it had never been there.
Hank stopped jingling the bell again. "Feri Kovács," he sa
speaking as if there was a hair on his tongue. "Fuckin' bastard.
His voice trailed off.
"That's right," said Feri, smiling with relief. "Fuckin' basta
That's right."
Hank jingled the bell a few more times, then his eyes brig
ened, a phrase occurred to him and he spoke it: "Canada
your home."
"Canada is my prison!" said Feri, his tone light, relaxed, sl
ping into the old argument like a pair of slippers. "Canada
the place you forced me to live in. The place filled with my de
wife. The place I keep coming back to whenever I visit Hunga
and realize I don't belong there anymore, the country went
without me, when you people forced me out you forced me o
forever!" The phrases were so easy, streaming out of Feri, a
Hank seemed pleased by them too, smiling so wide his ey
crinkled at the edges, and he jingled the bell in time with Fer
syllables so perfectly Frank thought the crowd was going to st
clapping along. But one of the cadets stepped in.
"Better leave him alone," he said, straight and simple.
"Who are you?" asked Feri, and Frank knew that if this h
happened twelve years ago, when Feri was still in his prime, t
answer wouldn't have mattered.
"That's irrelevant," the cadet said.
"Dysentery means you shit yourself," interrupted Ha
sounding a flurry of jingles on the word "shit," and smiling li
he'd pulled off a complicated riff.
Everyone stopped, looked at Hank, and for a moment Fra
thought Feri was going to walk over and put his arms arou
the old vet, fold him into an embrace, but instead Feri ju
looked down, saying nothing. And so it was up to Frank on
again, whispering to his father that maybe it was time to
Hank watching them walk back to the car like he had no id

what country he'd just wandered into, the nature of the enemy he faced, standing there like some fresh-faced recruit at the moment of the landing in Normandy. Feri, gazing back at him, looked much the same. When they got home, Feri moved silently into his chair and picked up one of his unfinished crosswords. But he didn't read it, just sat there staring over top of the page mumbling about the time that had come and gone, his days wasting away, what little remained. The old man's voice rose and he began speaking in fits, between the fitting and removal of the oxygen mask. It was all nonsense, stories that hadn't happened, a past invented on the spot, romantic excursions with Juliska she'd never for one second entertained, not even in the most wistful of daydreams, and Frank would never know — speaking to the ambulance driver hours later — whether this fake history was just lack of oxygen in Feri's brain, or something the old man had come to believe.

"We — your mother and me — had a picnic once on Stillwater Bluffs," the old man said, the words exiting him like a breeze pushed through a pinhole. "You wouldn't believe the color of the ocean that day . . . like hammered gold." He coughed and whispered, "She loved me so much." He looked at Frank. "You, too."

Frank nodded, holding back his response. It was like swallowing a cactus.

"Night after night I sat with you and worked on the math, remember? When Juliska left the room I always had chocolate for us. I made it fun, didn't I?"

"Chocolate . . ." Frank said, his voice trailing off. "Math." But he couldn't quite bring himself to say, "I remember that."

"That time we all went out . . ." Feri said.

"We went out cutting wood," Frank broke in. He couldn't take it anymore. "Do you remember?" Feri's eyes softened. Here was something real. "It was winter. We still had the truck." Feri nodded. They'd been out cutting down snags, sawing the wood into rounds, splitting those into quarters, stacking them back

in the truck. They were on the edge of Cranberry Lake, in t
brush off a side road on A-Branch, keeping the cold away wi
the heat of work, the two of them so quiet they could hear t
snowflakes touching down, in a hush that seemed, that o
time, like an arrival, an understanding.

"I brought along some of your favorite beer that day," said Fe
"Do you remember? That beef jerky you loved. And afterwar
we stopped by the Beach Gardens and ate steak . . . Wow, wh
a day that was!"

Frank closed his eyes, shaking, wanting to strangle the old m;

When he opened them again Feri was looking at him sac
some word playing about his lips — what was it? "I'm sorry
"Thank you"? "Goodbye"? — trying to become sound, but Fe
couldn't quite form it, and after a while he put down the cro
word, got up, rattling the canister behind him as he went in
the bathroom for one last cigarette and a shot of *pálinka*. Fra
sat for a moment, then picked up the crossword his father h
dropped on the floor, finished years ago but for that four-lett
word still blank after the rest had been filled in, as if the nar
for victory was also the name for defeat.

Ghost Geographie

"You can think of Sándor's map as a nation made of all t
vacant lots in all the cities of the world." This is the closii
line of *The Ghost Geographies of Sándor Eszterházy*, a short ex
bition catalogue by Helga Bruin, who is a colleague of mine
Wilfrid Laurier University. She is trying to define Eszterházy
idea of utopia.

We all know the places Bruin is referring to — corner lots wi
faded for-sale signs sinking into mud; abandoned T-shirts ai
underwear driven by years of wind into chain-link fences ai
hardened in place; bits of wire and string hidden in the dan(
lions ready to snarl your feet; lost mementos you come upon –
locket with the face of a young boy, a bunch of letters bound
twine and warped with damp, a gilt-edged invitation to a silv
wedding anniversary, 1978.

Then there are the questions Bruin's book asks. If you we
to take these places and stack them end to end, would it bri
together some nation broken up and scattered, and wou
that country wave as its flag a sheet of frayed plastic? Or wou
it, finally, be better not to bring them together, since they
less about a country than a kind of placelessness, a nowhere
unclaimed, camouflaged from surveillance by being benea
notice, holes where you can safely step out of the ord
of things? What kind of government, if any, corresponds
the derelict?

The answers to these, if there are any, seem entirely contained in the artwork of "Sándor Eszterházy." I've put his name in quotation marks because historians such as Bruin aren't sure that this wasn't a pseudonym. There is, in fact, very little they are sure of regarding Eszterházy, except for the time and place of his death: November 13, 2002, in Fort Erie, a few miles from his favorite border crossing, the Peace Bridge. The coroner who examined the body said Eszterházy was somewhere around seventy, seventy-five, though of course without paperwork the exact year was impossible to determine.

Eszterházy spoke Hungarian, that much is certain, and the one or two people who knew him said he claimed to have been born in eastern Hungary somewhere, possibly Debrecen, and that he'd been orphaned during the war, and had come to Canada or the US in the late 1940s and long ago lost any real identity papers. He was truly stateless. For most of his life, he lived in two locations: the Warspite Hostel in Buffalo, New York, and Maja Horváth's Bed and Breakfast just off Roncesvalles Avenue in Toronto, Ontario. He jumped back and forth across the border so many times it would be impossible to say which place or which country he considered home, though I'm guessing that his answer would have been neither or both, which is the same answer either way.

His "artworks" — and again I'm using quotation marks because in all likelihood Eszterházy did not consider his life's work art, for him they were actual maps — are currently housed within the permanent collection of the Albright-Knox Art Gallery in Buffalo, which made a more convincing claim (not to mention financial offer) than the Art Gallery of Ontario. The works themselves became the property of the city of Fort Erie after Eszterházy died, and though there was some controversy over whether the city should retain them, or whether they should at the very least remain in Canada, financial gain eventually won out. Individually, the maps are astonishing, each one a beautiful object, but they add up to something much greater.

Eszterházy drew them on whatever paper came to hand — be
coasters, foolscap, the backs of postcards, even the waxy insid
of cut and flattened coffee cups — and there's no consistency
them in terms of style — some being standard topographic
surveys, some watercolors from a sidewalk perspective, sor
not pictures at all but paragraphs: "A fence, twenty paces, alo
the northeast corner, fallen over after that, the boards on t
ground half rotted, filled with holes, the rest of the lot encircl
by brambles roughly two hundred paces in diameter . . ." In l
maps, the areas around the vacant lots — and sometimes there
more than one lot on each map, as many as four in the drawin
of some of the poorer cities he visited — are left blank, and or
the vaguest understanding of streets and housing developmer
and rivers and forests can be made out by how that blankne
fits against the incredible detail of Eszterházy's neglected plac
The rest of the world just didn't exist for him.

Each of the individual maps are slotted, and the slc
numbered, so that you can fit them together into a larger m
as if it didn't matter that side by side you get an overgrov
orchard outside Cleveland adjacent to a fallen tenement
Manhattan. They might as well be right beside each other
Eszterházy's geography.

Put together like that, the little maps become the old ma
atlas, a country real enough in its details, but whose over
parameters are spectral. Only once has the Albright-Knox ev
mounted a complete exhibition, for which Bruin's book serv
as the catalogue, and which ran from June 30 to October 31, 20
Eszterházy's mapped "geography" does not lie flat but rises a
falls, with some of the smaller maps inserted into the ensem
vertically, while others come together to form protrusions,
that in the end the larger map is rendered in a kind of illusc
3-D. This is the landscape he spent so many years surveyi
traveling back and forth across the border, and for which
ultimately died, his heart failing for the homeland he'd ha
given anything to see rise not as some cardboard art project b

a new kind of country. Prior to the Albright-Knox exhibit, the last time the map was set up in its entirety was in a room in a condemned house at the corner of Heurle and Dorsey Streets in Fort Erie, rotten furniture and black mold and snowdrifts in the corners, windows broken open to the winter, and Eszterházy's bent corpse, wound in blankets with his cheek resting on the floor, frost on his lashes, eyes still open to what he'd spread in every direction before him across the windswept boards.

His death seemed so small beside the map itself, and it was undoubtedly the picture taken of it at the scene, and featured on the evening news, that caught the eye of the curators at the Albright-Knox and AGO. The map spilled across the floor as if it had been poured from Eszterházy's eyes.

■

I first heard about Sándor Eszterházy when I was a kid, well, not about *him* specifically, but it was the first time his shadow passed over my life. My mother would not have known who he was as an individual, but he would have featured, faceless, nameless, almost a cliché, among her cultivated fears. Whenever we were in trouble at school — not doing our homework, getting a failing grade, called to the principal's office for some misdemeanor — my mother would tell us about the *Hontalan*, "the stateless," those men and women who'd come to Canada from Hungary but failed to find a foothold (which for her meant a good job, a home, the means to start and sustain a family) and ended up "living like gypsies." It was a racial slur, I know that now, and though I hadn't at that time met a gypsy, I knew what she meant — people like Frigyes Bakó and Aurél Kalmár — men of a million odd jobs who would long ago have starved to death or been found frozen behind the liquor store if it wasn't for the support of the expat Hungarian community. Her opinion was that statehood, belonging, had to be earned, usually by listening to the teacher and working harder than was asked, and that not to earn it, to refuse to try, to fool around and be lazy, meant that

all we would ever be were Hungarians who'd lost one count
without arriving in another.

When I first heard Eszterházy's name from Bruin, I felt
though I already knew him, as if my mother's bogeyman h
stepped out of her head into history. Bruin had slides of Eszt
házy's maps, the bare bones of his biography, some theori
about the political and social and cultural implications of h
work. But it was only after the exhibit and the publication of t
catalogue, when I got a sense of the implications of her discove
and more importantly its mystery, that I came around to qu
tioning her further.

The biography of Eszterházy is nothing like what you'd expe
with a place and date of birth, names of mother and fath
where he'd been educated, the year he'd emigrated to Cana
All that stuff, Bruin said, was lost, if it had ever existed in t
first place. What she did have were the names of a few peo
who'd known Eszterházy, who'd arrived for the funeral or se
notice, as many of them from the US as from Canada, alm
all of them Hungarian, people who'd looked out for him or h
at least tried to. Bruin was kind enough to share these conta
with me. Almost all of them traced back to one or another
his "permanent" residences in Toronto and Buffalo, to oth
boarders like himself, or those who ran the places, or who we
connected with them in some way as volunteers or staff. N
one of them could say why he'd ended up in that empty roo
in Fort Erie, why when he was rejected at the border he had
simply come home as he usually did, waited a while, and th
tried again.

Eszterházy claimed to have snuck back and forth across t
border over two hundred times between 1950 and 2001. H
been doing it since he'd arrived in Canada as a refugee at the e
of the Second World War. He was only a child then, eight yea
old, and his time at Saint Xavier's Orphanage for Boys in N
York, and at the Toronto Home for Orphaned Boys, are the or
official documents testifying to his having had any childho

at all, or, more accurately, ever having been that age, since it's doubtful those years were experienced as anything resembling childhood. The pictures in the records of the two institutions are obviously of the same boy, though both cite him as being eight years old, the first in 1946, the second in 1948. The records from Saint Xavier's claim that he was transferred there from an institution in Montreal, though neither Bruin nor I were able to find any evidence of a Saint Boniface's Reformatory. In New York he was called "Andrew Astorhouse," and in Toronto, "Alexander Estherhaus." Both places are now gone, and the names of given janitors, administrators, and caregivers correspond to the dead or the disappeared. What the documents do show is that Eszterházy — and probably this name was something he picked out of the air, ironic or wishful, given that it belongs to one of Hungary's most famous noble houses — had lost his parents in the war, and was part of the numberless children who ended up alone, sitting amidst the rubble of bombed apartments, on suitcases in train stations, tagging along after some other family of refugees, all waiting, as Eszterházy had clearly waited, for someone to claim them, long after hope had turned to panic, after they knew the mother or father who said they'd return in a minute, just wait here, don't move from this place, had forever lost the way and was not coming back.

How Sándor came to North America is unclear, and I'm not sure whether he lost his parents back in Europe in the chaos of postwar migration, among refugees streaming West or East depending on what they were running from and what toward — ethnic homelands, family affiliations, visions of which countries would become postwar havens — or in America. But circumstances that should have led to a lifelong desire for home, either return to Hungary, or establishing himself in Canada or America, instead led to a refusal of citizenship in any sense but his own. It was as if places attached themselves to Eszterházy rather than the other way around, as if he possessed a thousand imaginary deeds to parcels of land as far south as the Carolinas

and as far north as Thunder Bay, all of them carefully detailed
the maps he drew and archived and preserved in the batter
leather suitcase he carried back and forth across the border.

■

There are a few photographs of Eszterházy — three, to be exa
— that Bruin retrieved from Canada Customs through t
Freedom of Information Act. You'd never know it was Eszt
házy in these pictures, what with each disguise, unless y
were specifically looking for him — that longing in the eye, t
lips that never seem to close over the teeth, the deep wrink
as if cut into the skin of his face with a razor, that no amou
of makeup could quite conceal. Despite his claims of illega
crossing over the border so many times, these three pictures a
the only evidence that he crossed over at all, though of cour
they merely document the times he was caught. According to t
stories Eszterházy told to the people he lived with, he roam
far and wide, going south at Fort Erie and then back throu
Washington State, hopping across in Maine and wandering t
length of the US until he wanted to be in Canada again, sneaki
back into Alberta. The few times he was caught — just outsi
Blaine in 1978, in Buffalo in 1986, in Windsor in 1999 — t
authorities didn't hold him for long, each time sending h
back to the country from which he'd come without realizi
they were just giving him a free ride from one place where
didn't belong to another. In transcripts of the interviews ma
at the times he was detained, Eszterházy complains about h
easy it used to be in the 1950s and '60s, when more often th
not you were just waved through the border, when almost a
piece of ID would do. Later, he said that the trick was "to belie
in your own innocence, to think you were doing nothing wror "
that no one would notice as you strolled past the kiosks, traf
backed up for miles, most of the customs agents too busy wi
the drivers, never for a second imagining an illegal would simp
stroll through like he had a right to it, free entry from country

287

country. Most of the time they probably thought he was one of them, some guy from management going to a meeting, carrying some message from one office to another. Often, in disguise, Eszterházy was carefully dressed, his silvery-gray hair short and neat, his beard likewise, carrying himself with an aristocratic elegance. But this description couldn't be more different from the eccentric, almost helpless man that emerges from the stories of those he came in contact with, mainly through the Hungarian cultural organizations that gave him occasional work and money.

Bruin wrote to many of them, phoned others, and in some cases, when there was grant money, visited a few and, with clearance from ethics boards, taped and transcribed their conversations. They read like a century of Sundays put into print. Details of the quietest of lives. Widows running BnB's, bachelors managing halfway houses, priests who make arrangements when the local drunk needs a room in which to dry out. These were Eszterházy's employers, as close as he ever came to a community.

Eszterházy worked when he had to — cleaning eavestroughs, mowing lawns, clipping hedges, painting rooms. He made few claims on the people he worked for. A typical meal, most of them said, was a cup of hot tea — no milk, lemon, or sugar — and two slices of bread spread with a thin layer of butter, which Eszterházy ate standing out on the veranda or porch or balcony, surveying the city as if he could see through the buildings, keeping his eye on something that was disappearing even as he looked at it, as if the act of looking might slow that disappearance, or at least save it in memory.

Whenever he got a bit of money he'd buy clothes — new pants, suits, shirts, and even dresses, wigs and false eyelashes, mustache, beard, makeup — and the next day he'd sign out of the home where he'd been living, wouldn't show up for work, gone.

His favorite thing, they said, was the arrival of mail. He'd grow agitated if it came late, if he had to wait on the front steps or by

the window for the letter carrier to stride up, flip the mailb
lid, and put the mail in. Maja Horváth recalls how she once to
Eszterházy that he could have received mail too, the postm.
could have been making deliveries for him, if he ever stay
long enough. But Eszterházy said he wasn't interested in wh
was inside the envelopes, that even if they came for him he
never read a word, that what he loved was only their arrival, th
moment, someone bringing news.

Maybe this is why whenever I look at Eszterházy's maps
see in every lot a mailbox of some kind: a pipe for groundwat
half buried in grass; a tin can pushed through the wires oi
hurricane fence; the branches of a tree twisted into a tube
river running off a pond like the post at the bottom of a count
letterbox, a stand of rushes sticking out the top like a raised t
flag. It's an easy temptation, linking Eszterházy to what's im
ined rather than known, to let that kind of conjecture speak f
him, and I guess this is where the work of an art historian li
Bruin and my own diverge, since I'm less interested in conte
fitting pieces into place and stopping there, than in what Eszt
házy was always moving toward, what was always lost for him
the haze of our precision — lines of latitude and longitude, hi;
ways and roads clearly delineated, the robot voice of onboa
navigation, Nexus clearance for ease of border crossing.

September 11 put an end to those travels. I imagine Eszterhá
on some street in Ottawa or Toronto or wherever, standing wi
a crowd in front of an electronics store, watching the plan
the towers, the explosions, falling bodies, dust clouds chargi
through lower Manhattan, and feeling around him in the sho
ders and positions of the crowd an alien solidarity, a hardeni
of positions that kept him from backing out even when
wanted to, when he turned and they refused to let him pa
either with a shove or a comment, as if what was on televisi
demanded they all stand together in witness.

After that, Eszterházy was stuck in Canada. He never ma
it across the border again, though he tried more than once, I

ruses and disguises failing in the new world of global security. He was locked up, he was interrogated, he was released, and after a while they turned him away the minute they saw his face. In Eszterházy's pocket, at the time of his death, was a sheet of paper folded twice with the word "Passport" written on it in black crayon, and inside a picture of Sándor from long ago, he must have been twelve, trying to smile into some institutional camera.

■

It's a smile I've seen on other faces in other institutional documents, though different in that while Sándor is making it under duress, my mother, father, and other relatives who'd gone through the war, who'd lost family, friends, loved ones, seemed to have emerged with a greater rage for government, for security, the need to know that someone of the right moral persuasion was always watching, and so their smiles are grateful, eager to please. It was as if the upheaval they'd experienced back then — when Hungary's rulers were replaced in quick succession by two quisling governments, the country burning, criss-crossed by tanks, bodies in the streets — was, for them, an experience of extreme statelessness, and why whenever my mother caught me or my brother in the acres of bush at the end of Fernwood Avenue, right where Ontario Street ran down to the beaches, she'd tell us both to get out of there, and we'd come out from the brush filthy from ankle to neck, having spent the day racing our bikes through a mud patch, or discovering a stash of *Playboy* magazines inside a huge overturned and burnt-out stump that was like a cave, or having stolen hatchets and hammers and nails from our father's workshop to cut down thick branches and saplings and try to build a spiral walkway between the trees, circling higher and higher toward the sky. She said we could get hurt in there. She said it was private property. She said it was no place for play. But what really scared her, I think, was simply that we were drawn to places of neglect, and what such places represented for her, how fragile and tenuous the social

order, how easily human beings abandoned it for ruin, and hc
quickly that ruin could swallow all of us. It might not even ha
been consciously realized, but the fear was there in every pra)
she whispered on Sunday, every vote she cast for the right-wi:
candidate, every time she shook her head at some group or oth
trying to bring about change. And it was there that time wh
I was fifteen and decided I'd had it and was going to run aw
spending a night in that abandoned lot only to come home
three in the morning wet and scared out of my wits — it w
there in the way she smiled, and her embrace.

■

In fealty to that memory, I took a trip last year to locate sor
of Eszterházy's lost country. My wife, Marcy, and I drove dov
to Fort Erie and across the Peace Bridge to Buffalo, the Niaga
River shimmering beneath us in the late summer sun. We m
with the curator at the Albright-Knox, Samantha Hoss, w!
took us through what they now call the "Eszterházy Coll   -
tion," singling out maps of those places we could get to in t
few days we had in upper New York State. I noted them wi
the promise that I'd send her details on what we found. Frc
there Marcy and I drove to the old Riverside section of the c
where a sizable Hungarian population had once lived, only
find that the lot Eszterházy described was gone, replaced b)
mini-mall containing a pharmacy, a liquor store, and a sex sh
— everything you could ever want all in one place. It was t
same everywhere we went. Nothing remained of the locatio
Eszterházy had spent his life documenting. Instead, there we
buildings — homes, government offices, malls, apartments,
one case a car wash. The only surprise came on the way ba
home, stopping in Fort Erie to look at the place where Eszterhá
died, only to find that it, too, was changed, except in this case f
the better, for the house in which they'd found him was gone
kid on the street explaining to me that the roof had caved in a
the building been declared too dangerous to leave standing. T

foundation was still there, charred and rubbled, half filled with water, graffitied with whatever slogans announced belonging in this neighborhood.

"You hear about that old guy?" the kid asked me. I looked at him. He must have been ten years old, no more, one of his nostrils caked in a tiny ring of blood. "I met a lady here about a year ago," he said. "She was asking questions about him."

"Helga?"

"Maybe, yeah," the kid smiled. "Him and me, we were friends, you know."

"Really?"

"Sure," he said. "He used to visit me here. Showed me some games." I stared at the kid, concentrating on his nose. He looked away. "Sometimes," he paused, "sometimes I get chased. He helped me." The kid shrugged. "One time he had this suitcase, the kind with the metal on the corners, and he hit Will Kantrell on the . . ."

I squatted down. "What kind of games?"

"Well." He looked at me suspiciously. "We used to build sails." When he saw me looking around the lot, he continued. "We'd find stuff. Plastic bags. Old shirts. One time a roll of toilet paper. We'd string it up between the trees. He said the wind could catch it and it would tear the whole lot free, and we'd go sailing into the sky." The kid's voice had risen, I thought he was going to let out a whoop, but then he calmed down. "Did you ever see his maps?" the kid asked, and when I nodded he relaxed again. "He said he was going to take me there. He set the whole thing up. Said he'd be waiting in the morning." The kid looked over at Marcy, who'd finally decided to get out of the car. "But then it snowed, and then it . . . it was winter," he finished, saying nothing more.

"I've seen the maps," I said, wanting to offer something hopeful, looking around the lot trying to spot a stray plastic bag, a shirt, a roll of toilet paper. "They're in the museum uptown. The Albright-Knox. You know where that is?"

"The maps are no good without him," the kid said, dismissing

me, already backing off in the direction of home, or wherev
he was going, the dirt on his clothes, in his hair, around his ne
suggesting it might be better if he just stayed here. "Mr. Eszt
házy was going to take me there."
I nodded, not wanting to tell him there was no country, n
anymore. There were only the maps. And it occurred to n
watching the boy disappear down the block, and recalling r
own failed escape at the end of Fernwood Avenue, that not ma
of us can bear statelessness, that something in us always lon
for home, even one that's imperfect, broken, harmful — exce
for Eszterházy, who spent his life traveling neglected lands, n
a caretaker at all but a witness to their disappearance, until t
lots were gone and there were only his maps. It was that dis
pearance he longed for, and why he lay down that winter nig
in the unheated room, gazing into a place where no one cou
travel — his scattered and unified utopia — that existed only
long as no one could say this was his country too. In the end,
never had any intention of taking anyone there, he *couldn't* ta
anyone there, even himself. But I didn't have the heart to tell t
kid that.

Krasnogorsk-

Papa Joe bought the movie camera on the black market Moscow in 1973. It came in a green plastic case with a hand , he carried it with him wherever he went, and when they fou his body he was clutching it to his chest. No one was quite su what killed him, but he was three days gone by the time h brothers went into the house, and one of his legs was rotted to the knee and smelled even worse than the rest of him.

The house was a mess. There were piles of old newspapers feet high, as if he were building pillars to nowhere. The kitch ceiling was crisscrossed with strings tacked to the walls li crooked rigging. Hanging from them were tiny squares of pap on which Papa Joe had recorded, day by day, the things h drunk and eaten; the side effects of the pills he was taking f his obesity, heart, blood pressure, arthritis; and how often h taken a piss or a shit.

Hidden everywhere — in the back issues of newspapers, t old books so heavy the shelves sagged under them, the ca - board boxes stacked in the kitchen — were family heirlooms secessionist locket that opened on a picture of a young woma a letter from the painter, Munkácsy, to some long-lost Dut relative; a brass mortar and pestle used by his mother to gri herbs a century ago.

It wasn't until day three that János, András, and Henrik fou the porno movies their older brother had made.

■

Even after he'd come to Canada—was forced to come, he insisted—Papa Joe continued to introduce himself the old-world way, last name first, first name last: "Papp, Joseph." It hadn't taken them long at the photo-developing lab where he worked to change that to "Papa Joe," but he didn't object, not even when they started calling him that in the family. In the days after his death, the name would become a cypher for his perversity.

The brothers found the films in a series of canisters, each marked with a Roman numeral, seventy-four in all, filed in numeric order in a large pile of boxes in the basement. The ones holding the pornography were conspicuously dust free. The brothers watched the films that night on Papa Joe's screen, the click and whirr and strobe of the old projector churning up memories of family picnics, car trips to the Rockies, summer vacations on return trips to Hungary, the cool villas of Lake Balaton. The images were staticky, a little too fast, women and children moving in and out of the frame, men waist deep in water, smoking cigarettes, clowning in the summer haze.

Then they came to canister thirty-one. Henrik flipped the switch, and a ghostly image floated on the wall, black and white, dust motes drifting in the beam.

She was naked, so pale it looked as if she'd covered herself in powder. Maybe that was why she was so blurred, tiny clouds rising whenever she shifted a hip or an arm. As they watched the slow gyrations they couldn't even be certain she was a woman, or a young man, and only when her breasts came momentarily into focus, or when she bent over, did the impression of sexlessness lift. As for Papa Joe, he wasn't there, neither as a presence nor a voice. The camera never moved, never shifted perspective, never panned back or zoomed. The woman wasn't concerned with it, moving slowly, as if seeing her own body for the first time, entranced by the tilt of a leg, trying to peer over her shoulder, down along the spine, bending over, running fingers

up the backs of her thighs, teasing the camera to come clos
It never did. It sat unwavering. She twisted in front of it like
sheet unwinding in a river. In the background, under the wh
of the projector, Henrik thought he could hear something like
broken music box playing the same four bars of the same tu
over and over.

No one spoke after it ended. The tail of the film slapped t
desk, going round and round before Henrik reached over, to
off the reel, feeling oddly tranquil, almost sedated, by what h
seen. It was a feeling he'd not often had, maybe once in a wh
from a piece of music or a book. It was as if the swaying wom
had taken him out of place, to a world no longer bound by I
way of perceiving it.

"Well," said András, the oldest remaining brother. "Well."

"I can't believe that Papa Joe — the eternal virgin — managed
get a woman to strip naked," said János. "It means that anythi
— anything — is possible in this world."

"But what kind of woman," asked András, "would help Papa J
make pornos?"

"One he paid," said János. "But if you ask me this isn't porn
raphy. It's not even that other crappy stuff. What do they call
'Erotica'? It's not even that." He kicked the box of canisters ligh
with a toe.

Henrik, the youngest brother, stared at the floor. "We should
watch any more." He put his hand into the light from the le
"Do you think she was Papa Joe's girlfriend?"

János laughed. "I'd bet my pension against it. Papa Joe loved
watch women. But the thought of being touched by one of the
that terrified him."

Their childhood had been filled with countless examples
how fussy Papa Joe had always been, even as a boy. He wash
his hands a hundred times a day, until the skin on them was li
paper. He refused to clean out the stalls on the family farm
Nyírábrány. He didn't like the push and pull, the dirt, of socc
handball, even hide-and-seek. He was bullied so badly in scho

he'd been put in a class with the girls. The only time he got dirty was when he was drawing, with pencil, charcoal, chalk, whatever he could use to make a mark, on whatever surface was available, it didn't matter if it was an old newspaper, a book fished out of the trash, a wall. Later, he always had his camera, and talked incessantly about whatever he was reading — histories of Dada or surrealism, treatises on photography, pamphlets on political movements that were abhorred in the family, Marxist aesthetics, Lettrisme, situationism. He was the only one of the brothers who'd loved communism — but not the communism of the Soviets, he always made that clear — and had been sorry to leave it behind.

■

A day later, they found the will, stuffed into the green case that held the Krasnogorsk-2. It was the last place they looked, András flipping the buckles and prying it open. The whole thing was a single paragraph, written in Hungarian, in that ornate cursive Papa Joe had perfected in grade two. "I leave all of my worldly possessions to my nephew and godson, Joseph Papp," it began. András and János glared at Henrik, wishing for one second they'd had the foresight to give Papa Joe what he'd asked of all of them: a god-child named after him. Henrik was the only one who'd agreed, feeling most acutely the debt they owed Papa Joe, maybe because he'd been the youngest, crawling to Papa Joe at night with his terrors, his oldest brother always there to put his arms around him when he asked where their mother was, what had happened to her, and, later, when they were still in Hungary, it was Papa Joe who'd given him money, bought him clothes, arranged for him to go to university, only to be then betrayed by Henrik when they forced him to leave the country. András continued reading: "May the Krasnogorsk-2 bring him the pleasure it brought me." The three men looked at each other and rolled their eyes, then went back to the last sentence. "It is my godson who is best placed to prevent any unwanted attention, or trouble, as a result of my pursuits."

Henrik grabbed the paper. "He left everything to Joey?"

"He was Papa Joe's one and only godson," said András, wi enough bitterness that both Henrik and János could taste it.

"He never trusted us," said András. "Not since we forced hi to leave Hungary."

Henrik looked at both of them. "You are not to show this Joey. The last thing he needs is to inherit any of Papa Joe's . 'unwanted attention.'"

János shrugged, looked at András, who frowned but nodd "He's your son. And Papa Joe is dead; I'm sure he couldn't care le about any of this now."

∎

The women of the family agreed. They sat around in Henrik a Irén's kitchen, picking through the secret Papa Joe had left the

Irén remembered how Papa Joe had always avoided kiss "He'd always lean back, turning his head side to side, like couldn't stand us."

"Well, I don't know about that," said Henrik. He looked arou the room. Everyone was waiting, and for a second he thoug that if he inhaled deeply he could suck back the words h spoken. "I got a call once," he began. He stopped, tugged each of his shirtsleeves. "It was Rudy DeLoi, down at The Gold Horn. He'd caught Papa Joe filming the strippers through t back exit."

"Bullshit," said András. "Papa Joe wouldn't have gone near th place."

"It only happened one time," said Henrik. "Four or five yea after we got here."

"How come we never heard about it?" said János.

"I promised him I wouldn't tell," said Henrik. "I don't knc why Papa Joe told Rudy to call me instead of you," he continu "Maybe because I'm the baby." He shrugged. "I was so asham Rudy was livid. Papa Joe just kept mumbling about 'blue lig how the strippers needed to 'see themselves.' I had to apologize for him. After we left, he begged me not to tell anyone. When I hesitated he started shouting that it was all our fault. He couldn't meet anyone here, he said. I think he meant women." Henrik tugged on his sleeves again. "I guess he figured out a way."

János whistled. "Wow. Our own brother."

"He was alone," said Henrik. "But I don't think I realized how alone until that night." He looked at his brothers. "What? We had wives, children. He never had anything!"

"That was his choice," said András. "We didn't ask him to be weird."

"You wouldn't even let him be a godfather to your kids! After everything he did for us." Henrik reached for his sleeves again, stopped, sat on his hands.

"He was always hiding something from us," shrugged János. "You refused to see it, Henrik. You loved him too much. Or maybe you mixed up your sense of obligation with love."

∎

In the weeks that followed, the woman danced in Henrik's mind. He wondered if Papa Joe had asked her to pretend she was moving in slow motion or if he'd actually filmed it that way. Who was she? Why had she let Papa Joe film her? How long ago? Papa Joe had owned the camera for several years before he and András and János had forced him into that horse trailer bound for Austria. Henrik smiled thinking of the stories they'd made up, telling the children of their escape, dressed in horse costumes, two brothers per horse, trying to keep on their feet as the truck bounced through the ruts and potholes of western Hungary. The truth is they'd held him down kicking and screaming. It was, he reflected, a kidnapping. But János and András had decided there was no life for any of them there, and they were the type of men who believed that the truths they arrived at were really objectively true.

Henrik traced Papa Joe's long decay, from the pictures shortly

before his death, pants belted up under his armpits — ov
three hundred pounds from a diet of *zsíros kenyér*, beer, chick
cracklings, onions spooned over with salt — back in time
when he was thin, smiling, at the height of whatever promi
life held. He was not an ugly man back then, though still oc
head too big for his narrow shoulders, standing in a tailor
suit in an orchard, tripod in hand, while everyone else was
shorts and T-shirts. He wore the shy smile of a victim, his ey
filled with disappointment.

After a while, Henrik came back around to watching t
videos again, alone this time, going through them one by o
in the hope of figuring out who the women were, what thre
they posed. The women turned slowly in the flickering lig
as if unaware that he was watching them, their movemer
falling between the beats of the ticking projector. Every day th
passed since the discovery of the will was another day in whi
Henrik regretted the funeral announcement in the paper, t
black and white picture of Papa Joe, the news spreading furth
and further.

He would visit his son, Joey, looking for signs that he kne
But the truth was, he and Joey had always had trouble commu
cating. There was the occasional phone call, visits once a mon
on Christmas and Easter and birthdays, but the conversatic
was always thin, no real content, empty of whatever might
happening in his son's world. Joey's younger brother Frank w
more compatible with Henrik. He was arrogant, a loudmou
always advertising himself in one way or another.

Henrik looked around Joey's apartment. There was an expe
sive racing bike mounted on the wall, a chin-up bar in the do
frame to the kitchen. The floor was clean; the furniture minim
angular; the books not dissimilar from what Papa Joe might ha
read. There was an old upright piano. No television. No stere

Joey was taller than Henrik, over six feet, sinewy from fan
ical workouts, thousands of miles on the bike, triathlons. Unli
Frank, he was unmarried, no kids, his relationships infreque

and brief and the women less and less suitable every year. He'd grown quiet in the years since he was an open, trusting child, having turned into an observer, always at the edges of groups, never giving away his politics, and Henrik sensed in him the sad fatalism of someone who believed that none of it — no string of logic, no airtight refutation, no list of facts — mattered in the long run anyway.

Henrik settled into a chair, rubbing his hands along his thighs. "Well, we've discovered some . . . strange things at Papa Joe's house." When Joey said nothing, Henrik continued. "There are some videos." He paused, then dove in. "Naked women."

Joey nodded. "What are you going to do with them?"

It was not the question Henrik had expected. "I don't know. I've watched them — a few only — and they're completely anonymous. That's what worries me. I don't know who these people are. They could appear any time. Lawsuits, police, anything. Did Papa Joe ever hint at this stuff?" But before Joey could answer, Henrik cut him off. "I'm sorry. This is not your problem. It's not fair of me to ask."

Joey jerked himself from the wall, and walked a few steps closer to his father. "Why did you saddle me with Papa Joe? You knew I hated being with him."

Henrik hadn't been expecting this either. He picked the first answer that came to him. "Papa Joe wanted to be your godfather when you were born. He asked me personally. After what he did when we were kids, he really looked out for us, and how we forced him to come out here, I couldn't say no."

Joey nodded. "So I got saddled with your guilt?"

"He treated you better than anyone. You got all the presents. Everything." For some reason, Henrik remembered all the presents Papa Joe had lavished on Joey, long after he'd forgotten whatever presents he himself had received during those years. Joey at eleven being given whole sets of rare stamps. Joey at twelve being given a new bicycle. Joey at thirteen getting a genuine bow and arrow set. Papa Joe was there every Easter,

Christmas, birthday and name-day, and there at other tim
as well, swooping in at intervals that seemed to grow mo
and more frequent with the years, as if the rate of giving mig
compensate for the diminishing of his godson's affectic ,
handing over boxes large and small with this sad, pleadi
smile, begging to be loved, or even liked. But it had never be
enough, and though Joey certainly hadn't seemed to mind tho
gifts back then — staring at the stamps every day, riding t
bike, shooting arrows into the targets Henrik drew — it becar
too much, too obvious and desperate, and Joey had eventua
started stacking the gifts in the garage, untouched, though Pa
Joe kept bringing them.

"I didn't want to be his favorite! The last few years, I'd go ov
for dinner, and he'd sit and explain to me why he had to wa
his hands thirty times a day. Infinitesimal detail. He would
let me use his toilet because he said that when anyone else us
it, even just to piss, he had to spend hours cleaning it. We'd
to a restaurant and he'd order two entrees. Everyone wou
be staring at us. It was like nothing was enough for him. I
always needed more. More newspapers, more books, mo
photographs, more food, more booze. Not one single other k ,
not even Frank, had to go through that. It was always me." Jo
stared at him with an intensity far beyond the words he w
using, as if he were under some gag order and the words co
for something else, another story entirely, that Henrik shou
have been able to decipher, though he was smart enough
know it was a ruse. There was really nothing to decipher. Jo
just wanted to make it look as if there was, to frustrate his fath
with his inability to crack the code. He's doing it on purpo ,
Henrik thought, being elusive, using Papa Joe's death to g
under my skin, to punish me.

"I know, I know," said Henrik, angry now despite himself.

"He would tell me about his tests in politics in *gimnázium* ba
in Hungary. The whole oral exam. Blow by blow. Must have tc
me a thousand times. Proudest moment of his life. I could repe

it word for word. How he defied the teacher. Told him what they called communism in Hungary was anything but. They'd wrapped the whole country in lies and propaganda. He really believed all that stuff — reawakening people to reality, helping them grasp their freedom, the systems that invade our brains and make us see things all wrong. He'd been working for true communism in Hungary, he said. But you guys forced him to leave. He never got over it. And he made sure I understood that — repeatedly."

"There were a lot of things he never got over," said Henrik. He looked at Joey, expecting him to understand, but his son was lost in private grievances — all of them next to nothing compared to what Papa Joe had gone through. But unlike his politics, Papa Joe had kept quiet about these things. So neither Joey nor Frank, nor any of their cousins, had heard of how Papa Joe had read to his brothers the letters their father sent from the front in 1943. Their mother sat off in another room, wanting and not wanting to hear the things those letters described, just far enough to make out the occasional word, piecing it together anyway. When the last letter arrived, from Svoboda, Henrik remembered how Papa Joe's hands shook as he read it — descriptions of Soviet artillery, the sheer numbers of the oncoming army, the bravery of the badly outnumbered and under-equipped Hungarian and Italian soldiers. Papa Joe had looked up at the end of the letter: "You may not hear from me for a while, but believe that I have survived. I will not die in this war. I will come back to all of you. Your loving father, József." Henrik, five years old at the time, had believed it, but he knew better now. Those were not the words that ended the letter. Papa Joe had made them all up. He was the only one who ever knew what had really been written there. Not once had he told them what it was. He'd been twelve.

A year later, their mother sent them to Budapest for safety. An aunt took them in. They lived in the cellar of her apartment building while the bombers rained explosives overhead. Afterwards, in April of 1945, when they went back to the farm,

they found a charred building. Papa Joe told his three young
brothers to wait, and he'd gone inside. They stood there an ho
scraping at the dirt with their shoes. When Papa Joe came o
his clothes were black, his cheeks streaked with mud. Only l
eyes were clean, as if he'd taken a rag and washed them. Witho
a word he gathered them up and they walked ten miles tc
family friend, who stood at the door astonished, the questio
dying on her lips with one look from Papa Joe, and then sh
smiled, opened her door fully, and taken them in. Judit Né
never asked a thing, never spoke about what had gone on
the farm, what happened to their mother, though in the yea
to come reports of what the Red Army had done in the villag
and cities they conquered, especially to women, would arri
as quickly remembered as shaken from the mind. During t
next few weeks of that spring Papa Joe paid the farm a numt
of visits, forbidding his brothers to come along, gone for t
better part of a day, dragging back what he could salvage in c
trunks and suitcases, saying he'd put chalk on his hands to g
a better grip, to ward off blisters, though the straps cut lines
them anyway. He was preparing for their return to Budapest.

"I snuck after him once," Henrik said, his eyes so wide, as
he was gazing into himself. "Followed him right to the far
Watched him drawing pictures of our mother on the walls wi
chalk. He never saw me."

When Henrik finally focused on the world in front of hi
again, he found Joey staring at him. "That's not what I aske
he said.

Henrik shrugged, no longer aware of what the questic
had been.

"What if I told you I knew what Papa Joe was doing with tho
women? What if I told you I made a promise never to tell anyon
Henrik sighed. He would have said his son was angry. I
would have said he didn't believe it. He would have grown ang
himself. "I'd want you to tell me," he lied. "I'd want to help."

Joey shook his head. "What difference would it make? Y

never listen to me — not now, not then. And now it's too late."

"Too late for what?"

"To stop Papa Joe."

∎

Later that night, Irén asked Henrik why he thought Joey was lying about keeping Papa Joe's secret.

"Because he's so angry with me. I can hear it in his words. He's just saying it to piss me off."

"I remember the look that would come over Joey's face whenever Papa Joe came to take him to the circus or the amusement park," Irén said. "It was the same look as when he had to set the table or mow the lawn. He hated it."

Henrik nodded, remembering Joey's face as he walked off with his uncle, glancing over his shoulder, begging to be given back all those wasted Sundays. It was like going to school six days a week when everyone else only had to go five.

At night, Henrik went back to the films, holding individual frames up to the light, trying to remember if he'd seen this or that woman's face before — in a supermarket, the local schools, church — but they were all a wash. Papa Joe had made sure to put enough make-up on them, and to adjust his filter so that they seemed to have left their identities behind, drifting free of who they'd been. Henrik counted the days since the funeral, marked them off on the calendar, every day a little more relieved that no one had called, that the police hadn't shown up at the door, that a friend or neighbor hadn't asked if it was true about his brother being a pornographer.

Three weeks after they'd laid Papa Joe to rest, Lindy Collins knocked on his door. She was standing on the stoop. Her face looked like it had been taken apart and reassembled. The nose had the kind of zig-zag to it you saw on retired hockey players. There was a scar along her hairline, like someone had wrapped a tiny chain around her head, and a longer one, including suture marks, down her left jaw. Her hands were shaking, and

she kept untucking nonexistent hair from the back of her coll
"Mr. Papp," she said. It was not a question. She had a bag in h
hand that jingled with change. "I'm wondering if you'd like
buy a ticket to the Pentecostal Church Annual Raffle. The winn
gets a new Pontiac."

"Uh, no —" He didn't know how to refuse. He was thinking
mentioning that he was Catholic, and didn't like the thoug
of giving money to Pentecostals, all those jabbering, spasmii
speaking-in-tongues lunatics.

"I used to teach music class to your boys in elementary scho
she said. The admission made her even more nervous, and s
jumped, literally, when someone sounded a car horn, at leng
in Henrik's driveway. Henrik peered at the windshield, b
couldn't make out who was inside. "Is it true?" she asked.
Papa Joe really dead?"

"Papa Joe?" Henrik looked at her. "Yes, he died. He . . ."

"The films." She interrupted him. "What about the film
Henrik nodded as the car horn sounded again, twice this tir
held longer on the second than the first. Lindy looked behii
her. Henrik thought she was going to burst into tears. "Oh, ca
you wait? Just this once? Can't I have this time?" Henrik realiz
she was not speaking to him. "Papa Joe promised me he'd nev
show them to anyone," she said.

Henrik shook his head. "No, of course not. You can have yo
film back if you'd like."

She started picking the nonexistent hair out of her coll
again. "No, no," she said. "If he found out about it . . . no. Son
times I'm happy to know that . . . that it's out there," she sa
"That I was like that once. Papa Joe said that it would make r
feel free. Oh, he offered me money, but that's not why I did i

"Free?" Henrik didn't understand. "He filmed you naked."

"It was the first time in my life I ever got drunk," she whisper
"I filmed myself. Papa Joe just held the camera. And that swe
boy, he came in with that backpack full of lights, he helped s
them up, he promised he'd look away, and he did. I was nervo

because I recognized him from my class. Oh, he was older then! But he kept his word. He didn't look."

"Boy? What boy?"

She said something to that, but the horn sounded again, and it went on and on and on for what seemed minutes, and Henrik never heard what it was. Then there was a man's voice, hollering at Lindy to hurry the fuck up, he didn't have all day, and Lindy's eyes squeezed shut with tears. It was the face of a dog that didn't want to get hit again.

"Joey was there?" Henrik asked. "Are you sure it was him?"

"Please," she said. "Buy a raffle ticket? Five dollars for one. Ten for three. I'll get the money back to you." Henrik stared at her, reaching uncertainly into his pocket. "Please hurry." He gave Lindy the first bill he pulled out, a ten. She handed him three tickets with his name and address already written on them, then turned without a word and hobbled down the steps, faster than her sixty-five-year-old legs would go, off-balance and rickety, and whatever questions Henrik still had vanished as the car pulled out of the driveway and he saw the driver, at least sixty-five himself, hair shaved to the scalp, arm thick and tattooed and dangling a cigarette out the window, his gaze as final as death.

During the night that followed, Henrik tried to find her film, but if it was there, then the woman dancing across the screen was not the Lindy he'd seen that afternoon. It was someone else, a woman who, in stepping in front of the Krasnogorsk-2, had stepped out of herself, shedding name and background and history as easily as her clothes. As he switched reels, ever more frantically, Henrik imagined Papa Joe behind the tripod, and Joey — how old had he been when these films were made? — turned with his face to the wall, like some naughty child forced to stand in the corner. That's what Henrik was really looking for: no flicker in Papa Joe's eyes toward someone off camera, no shadow wavering along the edges of the frame, no indication that anyone else, especially Joey, had been in the room with the dancers. At two in the morning Henrik ripped the reel off

the machine and threw it against the wall, picked it up ai
threw it against the wall again, kicking it where it fell, the fil
unspooling, wrapping around his ankles, the legs of a table, un
it was a celluloid tangle in the middle of the floor.

Henrik sat and put his head in his hands.

■

By morning he'd managed to wind the film back around t
spool, though it was creased and folded and torn.

Then he got in the car and drove over to Joey's.

He caught his son getting on his bike in the condominiu
parking lot, ready to pedal a hundred miles. His body was a sti
of muscle in the tight jersey and shorts.

"I found out," said Henrik simply. He'd stopped in front
Joey, not even parking, one foot inside the car, the other on t
tarmac, engine still running. "I knew they'd turn up eventua
That there'd be trouble. But not this," he said.

Joey didn't get off the bike. He looked at the ground. "Y(
never noticed anything," he said. "You felt bad for Papa Joe. Y(
let it happen."

"How old.. ? How old were you?"

Joey looked up. "Eleven. Twelve. Thirteen."

"You never told me."

"I promised." Joey's cycling shoes made a clicking and scrapi
on the pavement. "He gave me presents." Joey shrugged. "I did
want trouble."

"You wouldn't have gotten in trouble!" said Henrik, comi
around the car now to stand directly in front of his son. "Y(
think I would have been mad at you for telling on Papa Joe?!" B
the look Joey gave him made Henrik step back.

"I did tell you! Every Sunday I told you. But you never notic(
You ignored it!"

"Notice what? All we knew was that you found Papa Joe borin "
"I tried so hard to tell you without breaking my promise. B
you didn't want to know! It was like the more I complained t

more you turned away." Joey shook his head.

"Did you think . . . were you scared that we'd punish you if we found out?"

"Do you know the kinds of places we went?" Joey hissed. "The homes? What those women looked like under all that powder? He picked the most injured ones he could find." Joey seemed to be gazing at something terrible in front of him, but there was only Henrik. "I don't know how he got to them — I think they came to the lab where he worked — but they were damaged, in trouble. Prostitutes, addicts, beat up housewives. They were all scared. Drunk when we arrived, or high, falling over themselves and him. I think they just liked their power over Papa Joe, you know? This fat sheepish man with the movie camera and fifty dollars in his hand. They teased him. But then it became something else. They got lost in it."

Henrik nodded. There had always been something sexless about Papa Joe. Irén had once joked about how he'd looked in his bathing suit. "He couldn't have sex if he wanted," she'd said. "It would be like trying to fuck a bucket with a toothpick."

"He made them laugh," continued Joe. "There was all this stuff about his photography — his art, his politics. All that crap about freedom, stepping outside the world you know. He acted like carrying that camera was some doorway to heaven or something. I don't think they understood a word he was saying." Joe shifted his feet, the gravel scratching along the pavement.

"You should have told us."

Joe shook his head. "They were terrified that the films would be seen by someone else. But they were just as scared when Papa Joe offered to destroy them. He knew they couldn't choose. He promised they'd be kept safe. But that wasn't enough for some of them. They made me promise, too. They said that if I told anyone they could get hurt, badly hurt. They said if anyone found out they'd know it was me, and Papa Joe would bring me back. They said they knew who I was. Papa Joe always told them I was 'a good boy,' that they could trust me."

"He never told me anything about it," said Henrik, yelling n(
despite himself.

"I never peeked," Joey said. "I stood facing the wall, or sat
another room. But Papa Joe always did. He watched them — a
they were too far gone to care." Joey hit the handlebars of his bi
lightly with his fist. "I'd think of you and how you'd made n
go with Papa Joe even after I told you I didn't want to and wh
a creep he was, and then how maybe one day you'd be the o
to get hurt, long after, when years had gone by, and there w
nothing you could do about it. That's when I decided I'd nev
tell you. That I'd wait. It was better that way, being angry, ben
than being afraid."

Henrik reached out with a hand to say something, but 1
sound came out of him.

"But I don't feel that way anymore," said Joey. "I just feel soı
for them — the women and Papa Joe both. And maybe for yo
None of you ever got what you wanted."

Henrik nodded, remembering Lindy's face, and the face of t
driver glaring at him from the car. What would that man ha
done if he'd known about the videos? "It still scares me, ho
much those women made me promise." Joey shook his head
remembering, and Henrik stood there, thinking of the wome
with their bad teeth and whiskey breath and drug addled nerv
spitting at his son to swear, swear, swear he would never t
anyone or so help him God. He was still lost in it when Joey g
on his bike and pedaled out to the road, leaving him to wonder
the fear the boy must have felt then, not only his own but thei
the women frightened to death of the life the Krasnogorsk-2 h
momentarily taken them from, what Henrik himself had f
that day he'd followed Papa Joe to the farm and seen everywhe
the images his brother had chalked across the blackened wa
of what had been their home. The same woman, over and ov
again, in poses Henrik also remembered — hanging laund

in front of the stove, kneading bread on the kitchen table, stretching as she emerged from her bedroom in the morning. They were all there, in luminous white, and if you followed them fast enough, from one image to the next, you could see her once more, dancing across the room.

Black Hearted Villain

I n September of 2006 I was approached by *Free Jazz Europe*
write an article on the Black Hearted Villains. In the end, th
never published it — they never even paid me a kill fee — and
I'd known what they were really after I would have refused.
The senior editor, Helmut Fuchs, had read the book of stori
I'd published the previous spring and decided I had the rig
sensibility. "Listen, these musicians played together betwe
1960 and 1995 and they saw it all: repression, censorship, po
ical persecution, capitalism — everything. All your themes a
there. How could you not want to write about them? They're li
something out of one of your novels."
I don't write novels. But I didn't bother telling Fuchs th
Instead, I asked him to send some material, and a week later
envelope arrived, along with return airfare to Budapest, whi
like most Eastern European cities, makes its melancholy be
tiful in the fall, when the soot-encrusted buildings, many st
damaged from war and revolution, and decrepit factories
and down the islands of the Danube are obscured by the r
and gold of leaves, and you get the sense that the ruins test
less to history, to what fascism and communism did, than
what failed to emerge, some dream whose corroded outline
all that remains. The envelope contained clippings from vario
magazines, pamphlets and newspapers from the 1960s to t
1990s, about Ödön Ecseri, the founder of the octet, though

all its thoroughness the package never clarified when the band first got together, under what circumstances, or how they kept going for thirty-five years. It deepened the mystery, with its Cold War feel, of a band that advertised its concerts in whispers, and whose music, it was said, helped you escape for a few hours from a place where the sounds of state-controlled radio were like a wall, the seating in authorized concert halls like corridors of barbed wire — a place where whistling your favorite tune on a bus or tram was as risky as talking about the stories you read, late at night, from books smuggled in from Vienna, Paris, London. As one anonymous reviewer said, in an underground broadside whose title *Rejtett* translates as "Hidden," "You spilled from the concert onto the street and it was easy for a moment to believe you were free. Even with the drab architecture along the walk home you carried that feeling. It persisted."

The concerts took place in Budapest's out-of-the-way parks, abandoned factories, warehouses, and lasted as long as it took the police to show up. Even now, with the mass of Soviet-era archival material at my disposal, I can't say whether the first show took place in February 1962 in the dim light of Flórián tér at the end of the now disappeared tramline 43É, April of that same year in an abandoned drydock on Hajógyári Island, or January of 1963 in one of the sealed-off tunnels under Buda Castle. Those who were later interviewed by journalists, musicologists, historians disagree on the date and place but not Ecseri's music, which was spontaneous, wholly improvised, a whirling chaos with him at the center holding a conductor's baton that the musicians both did and did not respond to. "Black Hearted Villain" was the only song they ever played, and it was never the same, though the fans often devised subtitles for particular versions, some of which came to be listed on the Villains' bootlegged recordings and CDs.

I telephoned Fuchs and agreed to write the piece.

∎

I stayed at the Novotel on the Buda side. Every morning]
stroll down to the Danube and look out over a city absolut(
transformed since Ecseri's death in 1995 — new billboar(,
buildings scraped clean and renovated of forty years of settl
grime, Mercedes gliding by the hundreds along the *rakpart*, an(
wondered if Ecseri would have increased or lessened his violen
as a result of what he saw happening, though in some part of r
I felt I already knew the answer.

One of his saxophonists, Pál László, told me over shots
pálinka at the Hawkins Klub that Esceri's rehearsals we
"infamous among Budapest's jazz community" for being li
"fascist military drills." Ecseri would march in to whatever cell
or empty apartment they were using that week with a folder
sheet music for each musician. "It was always the same pie ,
'Black Hearted Villain,'" László sighed, and each time Esce
would set up a tape recorder, arrange the band into the or
configuration he allowed at rehearsal, and raise his baton a]
have them play what was in front of them note for note, over a1
over, sometimes upward of three hours. If anyone stepped c
of line, or played badly, the band had to start again, the play
would get yelled at, and if they yelled back Esceri would y(
louder or hit him, sometimes with a kick, sometimes a fist, a1
once or twice with an object, like the time in 1992 he broug
down a UFIP cymbal — the rotocasted kind, the *solid bell bron*
kind — on László's head. Parting his hair, he showed me
jagged scar running the length of his head. "Thirty stitches,"
said, laughing.

László was knocked unconscious for five minutes. On waki
he was so disoriented he thought the rehearsal was still goi
on and picked up his saxophone and began to play. The resulti
work, recorded by Ecseri's tape player, was soon making
rounds as a bootleg through the jazz community and causin{
sensation. It was the most amazing saxophone work László h
ever performed — tonally chaotic, harmonically disintegrat(,
melodically reversed — so totally *not jazz* that it was exac'

the sort of thing Ecseri had been exciting audiences with for three decades. It was also the only thing that saved Ecseri from going to trial, for László (once he got out of the hospital) was too intrigued by the recording to bother going to the police. He just wanted to get back to that solo as fast as possible and see where else he could take it.

Which makes the remainder of László's story so troubling. After Ecseri's death in 1995 he was hired by Milton Ives, the New York vibraphonist. But László's stint in Manhattan was marked by an increasing lassitude on the saxophonist's part, and there's concert footage of him standing on stage as if the saxophone is getting harder and harder to lift, the sounds coming out of it so thin you can barely hear them above the shuffle and clinking and chatter of the audience. There's this look on László's face as if all he wants to do is slip into some slippers, settle into one of the easy chairs, and light a fat cigar. By the time he returned to Hungary in 2000 he was all but done, uninterested in playing a single note, but replaying those old solos from the early 1990s anyway, making ends meet with that and the bits and pieces of royalty money that came his way. "I don't know," said László, looking at me guiltily, "without Ecseri I just didn't have the drive."

"Was that really it?" I asked. "Maybe you just needed a rest?"

"Look at me," said László. "Do I seem like someone who needs more rest?"

■

When free jazz was born, in the early and mid 1960s, it was associated with racial dissent and radicalism. Most of the big players — Archie Shepp, Albert Ayler, Ornette Coleman, John Coltrane — were in one way or another making music in the shadow of what can only be called apartheid: the Civil Rights movement, the bombing of the Sixteenth Street Baptist Church in Montgomery, Alabama, where four children died, the rise of Malcolm X, Black Nationalism and the Black Arts movement,

and thousands of other incidents involving disenfranchiseme ,
segregation, barbed wire, the Ku Klux Klan, shotguns, lynchi ,
disappearances. While not racially motivated, Ecseri w
dealing with a society marked by similar horrors, the torture
political prisoners, midnight disappearances, mass executio ,
a condition of daily fear. It was this connection, I think, th
Helmut Fuchs wanted me to emphasize in my article.

Ecseri had friends in New York sending him copies of t
important records of the time — Coleman's *Free Jazz*, Coltran
Ascension, Ayler's *Spiritual Unity* — smuggled into the country,
no small risk, inside the lining of overcoats, the false bottoi
of boxes, cut away sections of illustrated communist manua .
They were never sent to Ecseri, but to a series of pseudonyr
the composer adopted, along with addresses belonging
prominent state-approved artists, posting members of his bai
outside their homes to sneak up and steal the mail before anyo
checked it. More than once they were arrested in the attem ,
but they were loyal to Ecseri (a loyalty I couldn't get any of the ,
not one of the people I interviewed, to renounce), and never
on that they were doing anything other than stealing, and wh
the records were discovered and played for them they pretend
to be outraged at what came from the speakers. "Who'd want
listen to this shit?" they said, and for once their interrogato
had to agree.

But enough records got through. The Ecseri Archive, hous
in the Jazz Museum of Budapest on Városmajor Street, holds
of Ecseri's records, hundreds of vinyl and digital discs. Ther
marginalia scribbled along sleeves and liner notes and bac
of albums as if the ideas inspired by the music had to be not
as quickly as possible. It's all Ecseri's handwriting, though t
ideas are less musical than biographical, all commentary (
the political scene: "Let them play once in a while, then lo
them up"; "Here's music battering against walls"; "Silencing t
scream that would like to shatter the system." After four da
in the archive my notebook was filled with these fragmer

and one-liners, and for another four days I sat at the Fakanál Restaurant trying to sort out their intent, until the ambiguity of Ecseri's language — or what I thought was its ambiguity — made me push them away in disgust.

■

Many of the concerts they played were benefits for jailed or disappeared musicians, in some cases musicians who'd been part of the octet. It was assumed that Ecseri always nominated someone from the band to take up a collection from the audience, though both László and the other Black Hearted Villains I interviewed said he'd always left it to them who they were going to support and who would do the collecting. They never managed to free a single musician, though sometimes the money went to buying food, pens and paper, clothing that was smuggled into places where they were being kept, and perhaps the cacophony of those concerts, their dark percussion of notes, were an attempt to create a sound that would break down walls, rip open locks, undermine the foundation of every political prison. Because unlike the repetitive and fearful rehearsals described by the musicians, the concerts were the exact opposite — no two were ever the same — and the musicians improvised wildly on Ecseri's tune. There were three-hour versions of "Black Hearted Villain" — a tune that in rehearsals was exactly five minutes twelve seconds long — excursions into the most pleasingly dissonant music, experiments with instruments the audience had never heard of (HAPI drums, Aquaggaswacks, bikelophones, sequential resonation machines, tamburitzas, uncellos, violimbas). There was an ecstasy there, everyone said, a kind of heightened release, as if for a moment Ecseri and his musicians had declared a no-man's land, a non-political zone, in the midst of the Eastern Bloc. And all the while Ecseri stood in that wheeling chaos, his back to the audience and musicians both, so totally absorbed in swinging his baton back and forth it was like he was trying to scratch something indelible on the air,

a sacred letter that would keep the music forever unleashed. N
once, in all the history of their performances, did anyone in t
band experience either verbal or physical assault from Ecs(
while they were on stage. Most of them never even receiv
a glance.

This was the mystery that Helmut Fuchs and the editors
Free Jazz Europe wanted me to address: How a man so mania(
and authoritarian in rehearsal could become so benevole
eccentric, magical in performance. But of course they'd solv
it — or thought they had — even before they invited me
write the piece. A week before my deadline I got an email fro
Fuchs that asked: "Don't you think that it's almost as if Ecs(
was reenacting in miniature the situation of the creative art
under totalitarianism — the more tightly he screwed down l
rehearsals, the more he abused and constrained his musicia
the more ecstatically they exploded on stage?"

More than one musician agreed with Fuchs. Antal Bognár
clarinetist who played in the octet from 1965 to 1968 — and w]
had his one and only clarinet smashed across Ecseri's knee o
Christmas when instead of coming to rehearsal he decided
accompany his family to choir practice — remembers how he f
that day in front of the other musicians, his ears hot with wh
Ecseri was yelling at him about "discipline" and "accountabili
and how it would be "years and years" before he could affo
to buy another clarinet, if ever. "It took me a long time, a lot
meditation," Bognár told me, "to understand why Ecseri h;
been so upset. You see, he needed us to be there, to go throu
the rehearsals. It was necessary for what would happen lar
on stage." Bognár went quiet and sipped his coffee across fro
me at the Angelika. Outside it rained. "He was testing us. O
conviction. But I was too weak. Not brave enough to withsta
it, not smart enough to see what he was doing. And I missed r
chance to be part of history."

At night I'd look at my notes and photocopies once more. The
was Ecseri at six years old fighting with a piano teacher over h(

he should play, delighting in always sitting down to the keys in exactly the same wrong way, playing always in the manner she hated, until the teacher finally hit him, and he hit back. There was Ecseri at nine being kicked out of the state-sponsored scouts — the Úttörőmozgalom — for organizing "cruel games" whose purpose was to "defy and deride the principles of the Socialist Revolution the children were being taught." There was Ecseri at sixteen being fired from the Hungarian National Youth Orchestra for "taking commitment to the Socialist Repertoire so far that it has become parody, deriding what the orchestra is committed to." All his life he defied authority, often by amplifying its rules to the point of absurdity.

■

Despite the written materials on Ecseri, he never wrote a thing himself other than the marginalia and rehearsal score for "Black Hearted Villain," a piece so indebted to swing-era phrasing and syncopation that it's boring even for a non-musician. But the photographs I managed to collect — some from the archives, one or two from underground newspapers, the vast majority from those who'd been part of the octet — seemed to glow in my hands. There's something to Ecseri's face, even in the earliest picture — he is six months old, swaddled in blankets, held between his mother and father outside Szeged Cathedral after his baptism, surrounded by bare trees, dirty snow stuck with garbage and leaves, a sky the color of paste — that suggests, at least to my mind, that Ecseri was not really concerned with communism in particular. It seems as if he was born already in revolt against something he was never able to name, and for which Soviet occupation was only a convenient pretext. Pictures from later in life have that same glowing quality, though it's less visual than tactile, the sensation of holding something that is one minute intensely hot, one minute intensely cold, though of course the photos are neither. They are only pictures of a man wrapped in the intensity of some loneliness whose ulti-

mate expression — or so I thought at first — was him standi
on stage while musicians screamed around him, his bat
scratching out a secret alphabet.

Along with the pictures were the reports of what he'd done
the various musicians who'd played with him over the years, a
during the nights I worked on the article I'd try to square the
with the eyewitness testimony and reviews of the concerts. I
fired Péter Rónai for not following the charts during rehears
He poked Erika Szász in the face, almost taking out an eyeb
for revealing where one of their concerts was to be held. The
were numerous other reports of him shouting abuse, pub
humiliations, beatings, all aimed at musicians who didn't t
the line, who refused to accept his absolute authority, who did
grasp, as László and Ágnes and many others did, that "he und
stood freedom as a dialectical process, that the music of tho
wild nights, those secret concerts, required absolute dedicatic
and conviction."

"So it was all about earning your right to play free jazz?"

"Look, I'm not saying he was a saint," said Ágnes, "but the
were other free jazz combos around, and not one of the
succeeded in doing what we did, in keeping out of jail for th
long. Ecseri saved a lot of us, not just in terms of giving us wo
and organizing things so we avoided the police, but he saved
spiritually, you know? By giving us a chance to play that mus
She looked at me and then shook her head. "I know, I know, i
hard to understand the mind of a genius." She paused. "This
going to be hard for you to believe, but I was saved from arr
by those rehearsals." I stopped writing. "October 12, 1971. Th
came for me. I was with Ecseri. They never came again." A
she listed off dozens of other dates involving the secret poli
and other musicians and impresarios involved with the Bla
Hearted Villains, all of which resulted in their evading arre
"It could be coincidence," she shrugged. "Sure. But the point I
trying to make is that he created a place for us to be — in mc
ways than one."

■

In the last week before submitting my article I pinned up photographs of Ecseri along the hallway to my study, so that every day walking in there I'd have to stare him down. At the very end of the hallway was the biggest picture of all, taken at Ecseri's funeral in 1995. There was a crowd upwards of two thousand people, unheard of for an avant-garde musician in the West, but not so unlikely in places like Hungary, where the intersection of politics and art often turn artists into folk heroes. There they were, those who'd made it through, celebrating a man who'd brought joy to very many and a black misery to relatively few. The tasteless stone bust of Ecseri on the tombstone (a nice Eastern European touch) stared straight ahead, somehow less withdrawn than in the pictures of his living face, as if the sculptor had softened the eyes, made them inviting, as if the stone had more to do with Ecseri's place, now, in communal history than in life.

But it was the life I was interested in. And those pictures from the last years, when there was obviously something wrong with Ecseri's health — his yellowed skin, teeth always slightly protruding, a sickly twist to his shoulders, hair thinning in patches — what I see in his face is still that unappeasable drive, whatever he was after, that would keep him frantically working right to the moment of his collapse on November 3, 1995. He never regained consciousness and died two days later in the intensive care unit of Szent János Hospital in Budapest. Despite the end of communism he kept on making music, in exactly the manner as before, if anything with a greater urgency, as if the new freedom had brought with it new dangers — the promoters, the sale of bootlegs, the advertising, the money from tickets. "I think he saw in capitalism a danger as great as that of communism," said Ágnes. "He was afraid of what it would do to his music, to us. Look at what happened to Pál László," she continued. "Once he went out there. The good gigs. The good pay.

Nice food and hotels." She shook her head. "I'm sure he'd gi
it all up to be back with Ecseri now and playing as he once dic
    The list of injuries to band members during Ecseri's "ca -
talist years," 1989-1995, seems to agree with Ágnes' interpre -
tion. Apart from the head injury to László, there were brok
fingers (Mariska Horváth), black eyes (Norbi Cserei, Zotya Galt ,
Miklós Frey), destroyed reputations (too many to list her ,
psychological and verbal abuse (on a daily basis), as if whatev
pursued Ecseri was coming closer, his kingdom falling apart.
fact, his collapse occurred in the midst of an extended harang
directed at Márton Blaskó, whom Ecseri called "an asshole" f '
thinking he deserved a spot with the Black Hearted Villains, th
he wouldn't have been able to keep time even "with a metronon
stuffed up [his] ass," that his mother must "stay awake at nig
wondering why she'd not opted for an abortion." Blaskó wou
go on to considerable fame in post-communist Hungary, then
the free jazz community in Europe, recording as bandleader ;
album for ECM in 1999. But at the time he was fifteen years o ,
and the composer had him by the hair, and Ecseri stopped in t
midst of screaming into the boy's face and fell over.

■

It's unlikely I'll ever be asked by *Free Jazz Europe* to write anoth
article. I still have the letter Fuchs faxed after receiving r '
draft, and once in a while I'll take it out and wonder what effe
it might have had, if any, on Ecseri's now saintly reputation.
it was, Fuchs accused me of trying to drag the composer's nar
through the mud, of looking for the "most sensational" spin
put on the story, and that far from exposing Ecseri as someo '
"diminishing human freedom" I was really just "projecti
[my] own guilt onto him." Fuchs' greatest disappointment,
said, was that he'd expected professionalism, that I had be
"pretending to be a journalist when [I] was just a fiction writ ,
and a lousy one at that." I was just looking for a twist in the sto ,
an ending that would make me outsmart the readers, and i

couldn't find one I'd make it up, even if it meant reversing the truth, turning white to black. "Free jazz — and that's Ecseri's jazz — is not like your short stories, it's not about control. It's about release, about letting people be who they are. That's what Ecseri gave his musicians in concert, and what you aren't giving him in your writing." Fuchs had half a mind to demand that I return the money they'd spent on hotels and per diems and plane tickets.

I received the fax at three in the morning. Fuchs was so angry he'd forgotten about the time difference between Europe and Canada. I remember walking out onto my balcony after reading it through two or three times. It was dark out except for the moon and a few streetlamps shining through what remained of October's leaves. And I shivered, wondering if Fuchs wasn't right after all, that I'd tampered with Ecseri's legacy in order to arrive at the ending that appealed to me. But all I could see that night were the faces of the musicians Ecseri had brutalized and exploited — musicians, it seemed to me, he'd permitted to taste freedom in those rhapsodic concerts just so he could then further tighten the screws on them in rehearsals. At times, during those months, I wondered if he didn't know more about capitalism during the 1960s, '70s and '80s than he'd let on, though I don't think he cared for one second about communism or capitalism or even politics. The truth is, it had only ever been about his own pleasure. But of course this wasn't something Fuchs or any of the fans of Ecseri wanted to hear, and maybe not even the historians who are even now verifying the Black Hearted Villains' contribution to political resistance, since it's too troublesome, too unending a task to reconcile politics and personality, how they aren't congruent, how one so often bears only an accidental relation to the other, as if what we crave, what we plan for, what we do, can lend itself to entirely unexpected consequence, heroic or villainous, and try as we might to reconcile them they just stand there, taunting us with their contradictions. There was no way for me to go through that, to write anything definitive about Ecseri, and still do justice to those men and women, few in comparison to those he'd helped, who'd been injur or ruined in his service. Their faces and names were alrea being forgotten — the ones who hadn't managed to stick wi it, who'd been fired from the band, arrested and imprisoned f picking up his records, playing with the Villains, advertising h concerts — lost in the ecstasy of commemorating the music a performances and resistance. And in any history of that band, in that ecstasy, the sacrifice that made it happen was not Ecser but theirs, and their disappearance from that history was wor than any death, because to write it I would have had to expla them away, justify what they went through, downplay their pa And isn't that what Lenin did when he said that you could make an omelet without breaking a few eggs, that the glori of the cause demanded a few negligible sacrifices? It was, the end, what I disagreed with: clearing away the ambiguity that the glory could shine forth. And this is what made Fuc so angry.

For what Ecseri had loved, it seemed to me, was not tl music they played in concert — it was nothing to him, just pa of his coercion — but the music of the rehearsals, forcing t musicians to play the same bad tune over and over again, t fear on their faces when they got it wrong, the total obedien demanded of them, the terrible consequences he was so qui to take pleasure in. He could hear it in their playing, that was h music, and I could hear it still, transcribed note for note in r own merciless score, the record of it all, as if in the end it w my music as well.

Acknowledgment

Many of these stories appeared in earlier versions in literary journa
I can't say enough about how important these places are for keepi
me writing and in touch with what's current in the world of liter;
publishing. Their editors, especially those who've published multi
stories, have my eternal gratitude.

"The Hobo and the Archivist" was published in *Southern Review*.
"Ray Electric" was published, in two parts, in *Fiddlehead*.
"Four by Kline Caro" was published in *Agni*.
"Lester's Exit" was published in *The Chattahoochee Review*.
"The Glory Days of Donkey Kong" was published in *Big Muddy*.
"The Rise and Rise and Rise of Thomas Sargis" was published in *The
Literary Review*.
"The New Improved Oscar Teleki" was published in *Upstreet*.
"Spires" was published in *The New Quarterly*.
"Crosswords" was published, as "No. 10," in *Canadian Notes and
Queries*, and republished in *Best Canadian Stories 2017*.
"Ghost Geographies" was published in *Agni*.
"Krasnagorsk-2" was published in *The New Quarterly* and won gold f
fiction at the 2014 National Magazine Awards.
"Black Hearted Villains" was published, as "All The Black Hearted
Villains," in *Agni*.

I'd like to thank Rolf and Vlad and Melissa, for giving me a home
New Star.

Most importantly, I'd like to thank my four kids — Benjamin, Hen
Molly, and Lucy — who give me a reason to keep going.